A NOVEL

BILL NEMMERS

**CALUMET
EDITIONS**
Minneapolis

**CALUMET
EDITIONS**

Minneapolis

SECOND EDITION December 2022
CRUDE Copyright © 2016 by William Nemmers.
All rights reserved.

This is a work of fiction. Names, characters, places and incidents
either are the product of the author's imagination or are used ficti-
tiously. Any resemblance to actual persons living or dead, events, or
locales are entirely coincidental.

10 9 8 7 6 5 4 3 2

ISBN: 978-1-960250-36-0

About the Author

Bill Nemmers was born in Iowa. After college and two years in the US Army, he worked as an Architect in Boston. He then ran an Architectural Design and Planning business in Maine for three decades but now lives in St. Paul, Minnesota, where he is at work on a novel about the Cold War, and a nonfiction book about Prince Henry (the Navigator) of Portugal and his influence on 15th & 16th century Cosmology and Architecture.

Acknowledgements

I would like to thank my writing coach, Ian Graham Leask, who pushed me hard to produce a quality product, and Rick Polad for his copyediting. Marge Barrett knows she is responsible for igniting the initial fire, and Lee Orcutt, Jacquie Trudeau, Al Rieper, & Wendy Henry continuously poured oil on it. Thanks, guys.

A NOVEL

BILL NEMMERS

Crude, Unrefined

Prologue

"Ya gotta write the fricken note," she says to him. "Ya can't do your suicide without it."

"Helen was goin' to write the note." He puts the pen down. "But the Lord's taken her now and I... I don't know..." He dabs at his eyes with a tissue.

"Don't overthink this, Frank. Just do it."

"But I don't know her words. What would she want me to write?"

"I don't care." She turns and points to his wife's limp body slouching in her wheelchair, with her mouth agape and her eyes closed. "And right now she's not about to tell you, is she?"

"No, but—"

"You want to be with her now, right? That's a sweet thought. Just write that."

"Promise you'll take good care of Ruby?"

She stands up and slaps her hand hard on the table next to him. He starts and then drops his pen. It skitters across the table.

"Sorry for that." She retrieves the pen for him. "But I'm on a tight schedule here. I need you to focus on the note. Don't worry about your dog. I'll take care of her."

She walks across the yellow asbestos tile squares of his kitchen floor toward his side door. "I'm gonna wheel her out and put her in the Buick. Then I'll come back and get you."

"What should I do?"

"All you gotta do, Frank, before I get back, is just write the fricken note!"

Chapter 1

Wednesday, August 22, 2013
Near Rugby, Pierce County, ND – 2:00 p.m.

Leon Rolfes slouches in an ancient leather recliner in the small sunroom his father, in the 1950s, tacked up-side this farmhouse so as to watch his son play in his sandbox. Today Leon watches his sister, Louise, work in her massive garden. He watches a hot August sun pull the last bits of moisture from his wheat field spread out behind her. He sits, he watches, and he waits for the apocalypse. He knows it's coming, and his sunroom's window will allow him to see it clearly when it does.

Though he doesn't much live in this house anymore, it's still his house, still his window, and still his chair. The fields, the dust, the memories—still his too. His widowed sister, Louise, keeps the house now. She watches his wheat and alfalfa so he can watch larger-scale phenomena from his office, two hours south in Bismarck. He's older than her by a couple of years but she's had the harder life—lost her husband to 'Nam, her son to Jack Daniels, and eventually, her farm to the bank. It's turned her grim, mean, and surly. She certainly seems much older than she now is.

He hears her yell in anger and sees her throw her shovel several feet where it smashes into the squash plants. "Git," he hears her scream. "Goddamned rabbit." The thrown shovel does more damage than the villain, but she seems satisfied with the result. The rabbit vanishes. Louise's thin, sinewy body is slippery-wet from the heat. She walks over, retrieves the spade, and looks out to the east over the fields. Both Leon and Louise are waiting. Both know the harvesting machines will come. They'll slash through the fields, collect the kernels, grind the stalks, and blow the powdered detritus back onto the ground. "Thank the Lord," she often says. "He puts the snow out there just to hide the mess."

Leon will mourn the loss of his healthy grain, but then celebrate the beauty of its harvest. He understands this cruel yearly joke; the wheat must die so the prairie can survive. Something must be lost for something to be gained.

Rolfes is a North Dakota farmer like his father and his grandfather. He is a product of this prairie as surely as is his wheat. But Rolfes works another trade, one which allows him to view this prairie with a wider perspective than his sunroom allows. And from that elevated platform, he knows much bigger machines are coming. Ugly behemoths are parked out there in the haze, and they will soon attack. They also are designed to savage things, though their target is his state itself… its commerce and its citizens—and its oil. They too will spit out debris, litter the landscape with garbage, and truck away the golden harvest. And sadly, even in a hundred winters, not enough snow can fall to obscure the damage caused by those machines.

Leon is the Speaker of the North Dakota House of Representatives. He's been speaker for sixteen years and was a junior member of that body for a decade before that. Everything to be gained or lost by the state of North Dakota must pass his desk, must seek his approval. And yesterday, in his capacity as speaker, he watched as the operator of one of those ugly machines, parked just beyond his ability to see it, switched on its ignition and gunned its engine. It was a test of sorts, and a certain threat to him and his beloved prairie. While attending a top-secret meeting in the governor's office he'd listened as Prometheus Inc., a Houston-based development firm, introduced their proposal to soil his North Dakota prairie with an ugly oil refinery. They apprised him of their fast-track schedule, saying that the preliminary application would be submitted to the state Environmental Protection office immediately. They will expect Leon to roll up his sleeves and help push their oily machine through North Dakota's complex and unreasonable bureaucratic maze.

He'd been forewarned. Prometheus, though a second-tier Greek god, as a corporation drives a top-tier, well-oiled machine. The corporation needs Rolfes and his fellow lawmakers to be terrified of its certain arrival, and to be resigned to the fact that nothing he, or they, might do will stop it. As some sort of cruel incentive, these legislators were told that if the good people of North Dakota wanted to ease the pain of being ground up and spit out as detritus, they could throw bushels of official North Dakota money at the machine crawling by in its cloud of dust and debris.

Several of his associates attended this meeting and were intimidated by the sound of all those gears meshing. They immediately stepped back, bowed down, and worshipped Prometheus and its machine. Leon, scared to death he'd be run over, did take his step back. And then he ran. And he didn't stop running until he entered this farmhouse, two hours north-northeast of Bismarck, near the small town of Rugby.

He's able to think clearer thoughts up here, where he can't hear the gnashing and grinding. He needs to organize his response to Prometheus' proposal. He'll suck in some inspiration from the very prairie that sustains him. He'll also seek council from Larry and Nathan, his two best friends and soul-mates since grade school. They are smart and powerful men. They know many things, especially concerning machines like those Prometheus will soon be driving onto his prairie. They will know how to stop such machines, or at least how to engineer the defenses needed to frustrate or dissuade them.

He hears the side door slam and Louise's footsteps approach his chair. He keeps his eyes on his wheat.

"I've got the machines scheduled for the first week in September," she says. "That's later than I wanted, but I'm nowhere near the top of Jacob's list. I just have to wait my damned turn."

Leon seems not to hear her. He sits motionless and looks out his window.

"D'ja hear what I said, Leon? 'Bout the damn machines?" She points a stubby, gnarled finger at the drifting dust on the horizon. "Your eyes are goin', brother. Don't see 'em yet, do ya? I'd best get back to work."

"Sorry, Louise, I hear you. Thanks. My mind's taken with other machines."

Louise doesn't understand that. Or maybe she doesn't want to make the effort to decipher her brother's code. He often talks in parables that make no sense to her. She shakes her head and grabs the .22 from the gun cabinet in the corner.

Leon hears the side door slam again. He smiles. "Damn rabbits are in trouble now."

Now, he also sees it—that rusty rooster-tail of road dust Louise just alerted him to. He estimates it's about three miles out. The orangish plume hangs low in the air, enlivened by the afternoon sun. It could almost be a cloud. He watches it slowly drift southward. Not much motion, but enough to ensure Leon that the static prairie on the other side of his glass wall is not a painting.

Dust works better than a doorbell, he thinks. Eventually, a red truck materializes under the dust plume. That means Nathan's driving. That will also mean Larry's bringing the Grain Belt. His cooler in the back seat will be stuffed with fuel enough for a reasonable discussion.

Leon rises, goes to the far wall, and slips a Beethoven CD into the machine. Nathan claims he's never conducted serious business unless Ludwig is in the room, keeping frivolity from infecting profound conversation about serious business. Certainly, Leon thinks, this machine problem qualifies as serious business.

Blam!

He looks out the window and sees Louise angrily waving the .22. He sees the rabbit bouncing zig-zag across the lawn and thinks the squash will be feeling safe for the time being.

Chapter 2

Twenty-five or so miles northwest of Leon's farm, as the crow flies, another rooster-tail twirls up from another car. It's a probe sent out by the very machine provoking Leon's concern. The machine's advance man is way out of his element. Back in New York, he might impress his friends, and especially his enemies, by leaping over tall buildings in a single bound, or bending steel in his bare hands. But out here on the endless North Dakota prairie, John David Crowe, J.D. for short, sees no buildings to leap over, no steel to bend, and no people to impress. He is alone, hot, irritated, and tense. He senses his power sap, his advantage shrivel, and his fun-quotient evaporate.

He's lost any sense of motion, even though he's eased the speed-ometer on the Escalade over eighty. He senses nothing zipping past his window, no weeds waving at him, and nothing putting ripples on the surface of the ocean of dead wheat. No dust devils are twirling, no blackbirds are flitting, and no puffy clouds are floating in the pale blue sky. Nothing is moving between his dashboard and the hazy horizon. And the dark-gray scar of County Road 46 vanishing to a dim point on that horizon—that's not moving either. *Nothing in this damn landscape is moving,* he thinks.

But it doesn't stay the same either. Though unmoving, flat, and monotonous, the prairie's most arresting feature is its serendipity. The fields are irregular, crops are intermixed, circular hay bales are strewn about randomly as if they'd been dropped from an airplane, and no fence lines separate one field or farm from the next. Trees, single and in groups, are plopped like big weeds here and there and, periodically, swamp water fills a shallow hollow in the middle of a planted field. John David sees no evidence of any obvious attention to prairie design out there, either by the Creator or the farmer. He sees no houses, barns, or even tractors that might suggest that humans have a place in this strange landscape.

The high-pitched whining from the Escalade's AC fan ruins his concentration and mesmerizes him. He misses seeing a couple hundred feet of the gravel road. Maybe it was a mile. *How could he tell?* He slaps the side of his face with his open left hand to start the blood reflowing. A headache starts pounding. He slows and stops in the dead center of the damned road and calls his boss in New York for a bit of encouragement, or maybe sympathy.

Francelli laughs at him. "Oh, for Christ's sake, Crowe. What ya want me to do? Hold your goddamn hand? Bring ya a lemonade? You focus on your task. Let me focus on mine."

He should have pushed Francelli. "I'll get you for this, Enrico. You owe me, big time." Crowe pounds the steering wheel and wishes he'd actually summoned the courage to blast his boss for causing him such discomfort. Enrico Francelli, the 'F' in the hedge fund firm of HF&G LLC, and his partners, buy and sell businesses all over the planet every day. They do this to make money. That might seem obvious, as any business should make money. But for Francelli, making money *is* his business. Often he isn't aware of the product a company manufactures, or the location of its real estate, or the dedication of its employees... if indeed there are employees. It's the computers and the numbers. They tell him which companies to buy and which to sell. Francelli only does what his machines tell him to do: sell this, buy that, squeeze the cash out, halve the labor pool, extinguish the inventory, and then quietly slip the now eviscerated business onto the market. Advertise it as an efficient machine and then sell it to another faceless investor.

Were his machines' directives righteous or moral? Who knows? Who cares? What's important to Francelli is the money... and only the money. Francelli then, quasi-legally, maneuvers the bushels of money he makes on the transactions into his own one-room private bank in the Caymans, or somewhere else hidden in the clouds. Francelli's desk physically stays in New York, but his business hovers in the clouds. It operates in the vapor-sphere, an ethereal entity, untouched by human hands, and unreachable by regulators.

In this case, Crowe's job is to fix a glitch in the process... a pothole encountered on the way to the money. It's not an uncommon problem. A gear in one of Francelli's machines, a firm named Prometheus Inc., became jammed. Therefore, he sends J.D. Crowe to North Dakota to bludgeon the idiots responsible, repair the damage, and restart Prometheus' engine. The problem surfaced during a review in anticipation of submitting the package to NDOEP, the North Dakota Office of Environmental Protection.

A certain document, needed to substantiate Prometheus' right to use the land, had become compromised. The ownership of that land had been assumed since the start of the project, so no one paid attention, and the problem went undetected. But now, as Prometheus prepared the documents for submittal, they found a key piece of information missing, or at least so legally ambiguous it ceased to be factual. The OTPA, Option to Purchase Agreement, for one of the three parcels required for the project could not be substantiated. And, to further complicate things, the supposed owner of record for that property could not be substantiated either. The Houston subcontractor pushed the problem up to Prometheus, and they pushed the problem up to Herbold, Francelli & Gheary. HF&G then sent Crowe, armed with his bludgeon, to meet with Robinson from Prometheus, Shultz from the Houston PR Group, and Timmins, a local attorney representing the property's supposed owner. NDOEP is hosting the meeting at their office in Bismarck. Crowe's charge is to bludgeon these fools until the glitch vanishes, then push the button and restart Francelli's machine.

According to the submittal, an entity entitled Prairie Reclamation Trust Inc., PRTI, holds title to the land. PRTI acquired the properties by deed when the elderly farmers who'd previously owned them died. Two of the farmers had indeed died, and the property did legally revert to PRTI. However, the owners of the third parcel, Frank and Helen Gupchal, refused to die before the filing deadline, so PRTI couldn't yet own their land and therefore had no right to guarantee that land to Prometheus. To further complicate matters, Prairie Reclamation Trust Inc. seems to be a mirage firm with no apparent address, phone, or website. The only evidence the firm is real is that its alcoholic lawyer, Tommy Timmins, says it is. In the modern world of the Real Estate Trust (RET), mirage RETs are not uncommon animals; many weave over the landscape. They're hard to pin down, though most of them show tethers to some physical entity when their outer layers are peeled away. PRTI appears to be a very stealthy example of the genus.

Once the problem is understood, the easy solution suggests itself. A separate OTPA must be negotiated directly with the elderly Gupchals for their parcel, thereby bypassing PRTI's RET. That would allow the deal to proceed with or without the Gupchals' death. Implementing this solution requires someone to physically put their signatures on a proper OTPA form. And because the Gupchals have no fax or computer access, someone must drive way north to their farm to do the deed. Crowe, the crisis manager with the heaviest bludgeon in this group, assumed the responsibility of making the drive and removing the glitch. PRTI's lawyer, Timmins, most likely caused the glitch in the first place. He drank continuously, contributed little, dozed often, and was in no shape to make the trip himself. However, he did say he would call the Gupchals and alert them to expect Mr. Crowe in three hours and to prepare themselves to be bludgeoned.

***

The Escalade's GPS unit buzzes, flashes, and then orally warns Crowe of a right-hand turn one mile ahead. He squints, looking for some sign of an intersection, yet sees nothing but endless intertwined fields of wheat, soybeans, alfalfa, and corn. The dusty haze obscures both shape and distance, and Crowe's tired eyes play a trick on him. Several closely bunched buffalo appear in the field to the right. He rubs his eyes, refocuses, then realizes the forms are distant farm buildings surrounded by windbreak trees. He wills that image to be the Gupchal farm. Soon his GPS speaks to him again, and the driveway it promises appears out of the patchwork mass of fields on the right, accompanied by an irreverent line of thin, creosoted power poles. The corner is marked by a standard aluminum mailbox teetering atop a wood post and leaning a few inches east in respect to the prevailing wind. Fading, black, stick-on letters spell only part of the name—G PC AL—but that's enough. An address number, a red flag on a movable arm, and a silver–colored, official-looking medallion argue for attention, but without much order, on the side of the box.

Crowe hardly notices any of this. His eyes focus on the commanding presence of a blackbird that is standing atop that mailbox like a centurion. It's a shiny, black, mean-spirited, menacing-looking creature, and its eyes follow him as he makes the turn onto the Gupchals' drive. As the mailbox recedes in his passenger side mirror, he notices the centurion has left its post. He has a thought—*perhaps it's flying ahead to alert Gupchal of my impending arrival.* He's seen that happen in a video game.

***

That blackbird may not have the duty of overseeing J.D.'s arrival at the Gupchal farm, but other eyes do. They watch the Escalade make that turn and start the long approach to the house. She'd not wanted to place herself so close to the action, but she needs to be sure things happen just like they are supposed to. She views Crowe's progress through the high-powered scope mounted on the CheyTac Intervention .408 LRRS rifle. Her friend Travis allows her to use it. She's been preparing the scene and waiting ever since Timmins, the drunk, called her with Crowe's ETA. She's had plenty of time to sanitize the place... scrub it down. All she has to do now is make sure Crowe gets the proper message and does his job. And here he comes now. He's right on schedule.

***

The thermometer on his dash display clicks up a notch to 105 degrees. Crowe slows and enters the yard cautiously, aware of his intrusion into this strange still-life. The place reminds him of an Andrew Wyeth painting—trees, grasses, people cemented to the ground and forbidden by the artist to move. He parks at the front of the house near a set of weather-beaten, wooden steps that access the generous porch. No one comes outside to welcome him. A sane man would surely be indoors cuddling next to his air conditioner. That thought gives J.D. some comfort. Perhaps it means Gupchal is a sane man, and thus willing to help him. He wants out of the heat, and wonders if—he desperately hopes that—Gupchal has air-conditioned the old house. But when he steps out of his Escalade the absolute quiet assaults him. He does not hear the telltale whine of an AC condensing unit. "Damn!" he mutters. "I really don't need this." He breathes in a burnt smell from the sun-roasted stubble in the adjacent hayfield. It hangs in the muggy air like the odor of overworked brakes on a semi.

***

She can't quench the brief shiver as her body reacts to the sight of J.D. Crowe exiting the black car, wiping his sleeve across his forehead, and foolishly looking around as if checking to see if he is alone. One would think by now he should know that he will never be allowed to be alone. She's thankful for the muggy heat. It will dull Crowe's senses and keep his subconscious from reminding him of the real dangers that might be lurking... of even suggesting to him that a high-powered rifle is aimed at a spot halfway between his baby-blue eyeballs.

"Welcome to the play, Crowe," she says. "Too bad you missed the prologue." She's spent the last few hours arranging the stage set *and preparing the other actors. She whispers, "Get ready, J.D. Here it comes. Lights! Camera! Action!"*

***

He feels the heavy stillness, even more oppressive than the heat, drags himself up the steps to the front door, and forcefully jams the yellowed bell-button. J.D. hears the traditional *ding-dong* of the doorbell followed by the frantic yelping of a dog from deep inside the house. After a second try fails to summon Gupchal, he peeks in the windows that give onto the porch to the left of the door. He sees only black glass and, in it, the reflection of his own distorted face.

He looks behind him into the yard. No chickens. No cat. Not even a squirrel or a blackbird moving in the spruce windbreak. Frustrated, he turns back and smashes his fist against the wood of the door. "Damn you, Gupchal. Open this door." He can't just abandon the place and go home. Enrico sent him out here to complete the option, and he knows Enrico *must* be satisfied.

Anger quickly overtakes bewilderment. If this jerk's chickened out and blown off the interview, especially after he's spent three hours driving up from Bismarck, somebody will pay dearly for his displeasure. His throat tightens and he tries the knob. It turns. He hesitates. For the first time he considers the possibilities for misfortune within. Nevertheless, he slowly opens the door. Other than the muffled yapping of the dog, he hears nothing. Crowe carefully sticks his head into the opening.

He steps across the threshold. The wet heat inside almost overpowers him.

***

She switches off the red laser, puts down the rifle, and picks up her iPhone. She will follow him around the house using the several mini-audio recorders she's installed. The jerk will not be expecting to be watched. He doesn't realize what game he's playing. His mind, dulled by heat and the strangeness of the situation, will not be thinking creative thoughts. And, she remembers, he was always fairly numb... even at full alert. She smiles. He is unsuspecting of how close he is to being just another dead man on a lonesome North Dakota farm.

***

"Damn it Gupchal, where the hell are you?" Crowe instinctively looks at his watch, but the moist air inside the house fogs his sunglasses and he cannot read the dial. He wipes them off on a Kleenex and confirms that it's almost two-thirty. He makes it a point to be punctual. Billions of dollars could sometimes—especially with the Chinese—depend on one being seated in his chair when the client's clock strikes the appointed hour.

John David advances into the front room. The lonesome sound of his own shoes pounding on the pine boards resounds in his ears and energizes the dog. Its barking turns manic and is now accompanied by frantic scraping and pounding on the closed door in front of him. Crowe notes the deadbolt. It's been set! Someone deliberately locked that fiend in the basement. The thought terrifies him, trips a switch somewhere near his stomach, and starts things to churning. He's not a dog person. The thing sounds like a Rottweiler on steroids. Someone with more guts than he has will have to open that door. And his instinct tells him the Gupchals can't possibly be locked down there with that crazed dog, at least not if they're still alive.

He glances around and takes a quick survey of the place. It resembles a movie set from the 1950s. The furniture is ancient and well used but scrubbed clean and placed exactly as the director ordered. He sees the dining room table with a beige, lace tablecloth and a vase of semi-withered flowers, a coffee maker, and a toaster set on a Formica countertop whose surface has been scrubbed down through the flower pattern. It reminds Crowe of the set the Coen brothers built for *Fargo*. That movie had made an impression. Before today, it's been the only exposure he's had to even the *concept* of North Dakota.

After a quick look around the first floor, he cautiously ascends the stairs and confirms the lack of any life on the second floor. Finding nothing, he returns to the kitchen, takes a deep breath, and concentrates on finding some finer-scale evidence. He notes a sheet of white paper placed dead center of the round kitchen table. He bends over for a look. He sees the words written in black magic marker: "Helen and I thank you God, we're going home."

He has no idea what the words mean, but he senses an evil spirit creeping around. He hasn't thought about that word—evil—since maybe kindergarten, but he senses a dank vapor seeping from the page. He escapes to the heat outside and closes the door. It seems quieter outside on the porch, perhaps even cooler. He tries to think. He leans against the siding, closes his eyes, and takes a deep breath. The dog has quit barking, but now the silence screams at him. He yells back at the scorched fir trees, "Where the hell are you?" His words evaporate in the stifling heat, returning no response, no hint even of an echo.

***

She returns to the rifle scope and sees beads of sweat dot J.D.'s forehead. She imagines looking behind his forehead, into his brain. She senses his confusion and sees his anger. She smiles, and enjoys watching the sun roast his pallid skin and boil his brain fluid. "Okay, John," she says. "It is time to do your job. I haven't got all day. Take a look into the other buildings."

***

Crowe feels he needs to smash something. He kicks a small wooden chair. He watches it skitter across the porch, bounce down the steps, and land in a dirty shrub beside the entry walk. He notes the barn across the yard and the beat-up wooden garage some twenty feet to the right of it. He has no choice. He must check the buildings just to be sure. He walks down the side steps, crosses to the barn, and tries the smaller door centered between two commercial-sized garage doors.

He pushes the door into a dark void, then feels around on the wall for the light switch and flicks it on. Though he's never been in a barn in his life, this thing looks pretty much textbook for one. It's dank and smells oily. An ancient, spiderweb-encased pickup and a green John Deere tractor sleep in the dim light and shadows. Evil-looking, menacing machines with humongous wheels, multiple sharp but rusted edges, and operator cockpits high atop them, occupy the remainder of the space. Crowe recognizes these machines. He'd once seen such monsters in an apocalypse movie, chasing one another through burning debris fields.

He turns off the light, closes the door, and crosses the yard to the wood-framed, one-car garage. He opens the side door, but it travels inward only a few inches before it jams against something. He snakes his arm through the narrow opening and feels around for a switch. The light doesn't work but the door opener does. Pushing it initiates a rhythmic clanking noise and the door begins to rise.

***

She watches Crowe stumble backward from the side door and stagger around to the front of the garage. She sees his starchy white face contort in pain and astonishment as the curtain rises to reveal the stage she's set for him. The front of the immaculate, white Buick stares at him, as do the strangely distorted countenances of Frank and Helen Gupchal, sitting deathly still in the front seat, absolutely unmoved by his sudden arrival.

"Not feelin' much like Superman now, huh?" she says.

She watches John David Crowe corral enough courage to creep up a bit closer, perhaps in an attempt to verify this morbid tableau as an illusion, or some macabre manifestation of the excessive heat. She'd secured them both with their seat belts, though both their heads cant to the side and both mouths hang open. There's no doubt that he sees, and probably smells, death. He's had no experience with unexpected death this close to his expensive suit before. She watches him quake with spasm, then splatter what's left of his break-

fast toward the garage door opening. Some of it even makes it as far as the shiny grille of the white Buick.

She almost laughs. "What a pussy," she says. She thinks about putting him out of his misery. All it would take is one round slipped in right above the dark glasses. She pulls the trigger. "Bang," she says. The rifle isn't loaded, but the thought of the imaginary bullet slicing through his forehead makes her smile. She's grown way past the need to physically kill him, though the thought still has merit. Crowe has work to do and she must make sure he does it properly. "I'll save that bullet for your boss, Francelli. You go on, Crowe, you sorry piece of shit. You gotta do Francelli's work for him."

***

After a few moments, or maybe hours, of indecision—Crowe finds it difficult to get a reasonable handle on time—it occurs to him that humans are not designed to think at 105 degrees fahrenheit. He retreats to his car, fires up the AC, and waits for some cooler air to force rational thoughts into his hot head. "Christ! Dumped into this wasteland with two dead farmers in a Buick and a hyena in the basement." He keeps jamming the button on the AC, but his efforts cannot push the number below eighty degrees. "Shit!" He thinks the fact that he feels anger now, more than physical discomfort, is a good sign. Anger will stimulate his gray matter. But he sorely needs direction. He will call Francelli and let *him* absorb some of this bizarre scene; make *him* feel some of the discomfort; have *him* confirm the right path.

***

She watches J.D. use his phone and reads his body language. "What a pussy," she says again. "He's calling Francelli to complain."

She knows Francelli intimately, and knows exactly what Francelli will say. And Crowe, if he wasn't so stupid, should have known it even without calling. He is, after all, the one paid to be the assassin. She puts on her Francelli voice. "Two things you do, Crowe. Fax a copy of the OTPA to Anderson at Prometheus by close of business today, and then make sure no evidence remains that HF&G came within two hundred miles of that farm."

***

That's pretty much word for word what Enrico tells him, and with that same supercilious tone.

"Enrico, if these folks are now dead, do I even have to get an OTPA signed? Doesn't the land transfer automatically?"

"Get that OTPA now, J.D. We need to move immediately. That title will be tied up in court forever. We need this resolved in a couple of days. Just get it done."

"But how the hell am I…" The line goes dead. Enrico has moved on. He's left him to stew in this pot alone with all these smelly vegetables.

"Shit!" Crowe says.

But he quickly realizes that Enrico cut through all the superfluous stuff for him and illuminated his path to the answer. He has a simple job to do and he's brought the equipment to do it. He can't let the 105 degrees, the howling dog, or two dead people in a white Buick deter him from doing that job. "Just two small things," he says to himself. Everything seems clear in his head now. "I think I can do this, Enrico."

***

She monitors Crowe as he does chore number one, using one of the several pieces of compact equipment in his briefcase to scan both Mr. and Mrs. Gupchals' signatures from the insurance form she'd left on the desk where even he would easily find it. Then he transfers the signatures to the OTPA form, prints it out, and faxes it to Prometheus. She then watches Crowe meekly perform the second task and laughs as J.D. attempts to cover his tracks by erasing a few fingerprints. The fool acts like he's never cleaned anything in his entire life. And he had really bungled the clean-up job in front of the garage.

She understands she will have to correct his mistakes after he leaves. She should send a bill to Francelli. She should probably also alert Francelli that she is aware Crowe forged that document, submitted that document to a state authority, and perhaps did not report two dead bodies in a white Buick to the sheriff. And she could advise him that Crowe's neat maneuver with the scanner solved only the short-term problem. She's fixed it so Prometheus would never be able to establish ownership of this property. And without controlling the site, the refinery review process, and indeed the whole stupid project, would, in a couple of months, smash full-speed into the wall she'd erected in its path. "This is but the beginning, my love. Only Act Number One! Sit back and enjoy it, Enrico. It's the last thing you'll enjoy for a long, long time!"

When five years ago she'd started this convoluted scheme to financially ruin Francelli, she'd assumed since Gupchal and his wife were both over ninety, they would certainly be dead by the time they needed to be off their land. But the two of them had been kept alive by an overly compassionate neighbor and a big-brother-type county service agency. Their non-dead state had put her in the position of forcing their demise so the land transfer could be completed and Francelli's refinery could be moved to the next approval level. More obstructions awaited the project at that plateau, since she'd designed the collapse as a three-act play. For maximum impact, all three acts must play out.

Helen and Frank realized their responsibility. They must be deceased before the land could transfer. They'd discussed it previously and felt their continued existence was quite meaningless with their end so near. Helen and Frank knew it was the honorable way to leave. They did not want to be stashed in a hospital hooked up to machines. The three of them agreed Helen and Frank would die on their farm. They did not want to slowly roast to death in Texas like several of their friends.

She'd helped them both prepare for the event... helped clean the house and set everything perfectly. But then, in all the excitement, Helen had suffered a stroke or heart attack or something early this morning. When she died, Frank lost focus. He was inconsolable, moaning and crying, unable to concentrate on completing the pact. He didn't want Helen to be alone wherever she was now, but he couldn't figure out how everything would have to play out. He wanted to join his wife but didn't know how. His wife's mind was the one that worked, so she'd made all the decisions. She'd done all the planning.

And so, after Frank wrote the message at the kitchen table, she'd maneuvered the two of them into their car, strapped them in, turned the ignition, waved them goodbye, and then closed the overhead door. She recognized the potential for evil inherent in the Gupchals' deaths when juxtaposed with the metaphysical refinery project Francelli's firm was now proposing for that very land the Gupchals had just deserted. How could she not tether those two absurdities for the good of her morality play? She calls Timmins. He's the guy who'll start the process... if he ever sobers up.

After watching J.D. drive away, she makes ready to leave, but walks one more time through the rooms to make sure she's taken care of everything. Her footsteps trigger the muffled barking from the basement again. "Damn! Forgot about that dog." She finds the water and food bowls, fills them, and brings them to the basement door. She opens the door quietly and places each bowl on the top step. The dog limps halfway up the stairs, stops, glances briefly at her, then advances and starts in on the water. She shuts and locks the door. "You better stay in the basement, Dog. It's cooler down there, and I don't want you messing up my cleaning work."

She leaves by the side door and walks out behind the barn. She removes the black tarp she'd pulled over her ATV and pushes it out into the hay field. Then she goes back and erases any trace of tire tracks in the dirt around the barn. She checks the garage one more time to confirm that both the Gupchals and their Buick have finished breathing.

She walks to the ATV and takes off toward the east, following the same grassed-over farm trails she came in on. She would make no tracks in the ground, no dust plumes in the sky. Travis will be waiting for her in his pickup. But he's ten miles away and she has a rough ride before she'll see him.

She stops the ATV briefly and texts Travis. "I'm leaving the farm. You'd better be keeping the beer cold."

Chapter 3

Steffie Cobb uses the TV to push her into sleep. Sometimes that works. Sometimes it doesn't. Usually it's Letterman, but during football season ESPN performs the task. With the NFL preseason underway, the Sports Center guys are doing their best to lull her into unconsciousness... but it's not working tonight.

It's her son, David. As usual, he's the problem. Or rather, he's usually the one testing her mothering skills, which she readily admits are less than awesome. He's a sophomore at Bismarck North High School and he is smart, athletic, and popular. He's an ideal son in every aspect, but he has one big problem. His younger brother Jake, now a freshman, out-performs him at everything without trying or even realizing it. The current problem concerns football. David worked very hard on the junior varsity team last year and believes he has a good chance to make varsity this season. However, younger brother Jake, the freshman, seems to have procured a starting wide-receiver slot after only two days of practice. The boys had another silent supper. Steffie has no clue how to solve this thing and her husband, snoring softly beside her, exacerbates the problem by taking great pleasure in Jake's prowess while dismissing David's hard work. He sees Jake as the kid he never was and so is excited by his potential. He doesn't seem to see David, who is pretty much a clone of himself, at all. Even worse, he maintains that feelings, like David's jealousy, are the mother's responsibility to sort out. This is driving her bats and is preventing her from getting much needed sleep.

At seven minutes before eleven, her cell buzzes softly and skitters about on the nightstand. She leans over, grabs the thing, and tilts it to read the caller's name—Sheriff Gaffey. She doesn't want to wake Matt who, oblivious to the distractions of the lit table lamp and the yakking heads on Sports Center, fell asleep as soon as his head hit the pillow. She leaves the bed, unplugs the phone, walks into the hall, closes the door behind her, and only then answers the call.

"Sheriff, isn't it past your bedtime?"

"It most certainly is, Steffie," he says. "Sorry to be calling so late. I really need to talk."

"I'm headed down to the kitchen so I don't wake Matt. What's got you rattled, John? I hear frustration in your voice."

"I need your help. I've found a double suicide up here this evening and it's giving me fits. I'm hoping I can get you to drive up here in the morning and help me figure it out."

"Well, Sheriff, I don't—"

"Please, Steffie. I'll consider you a consultant… pay you for time and transportation."

"Of course I'll come up. I owe you big time. Got to pay down my debt somehow. And you won't owe me anything. My paper's paying me to find stories. I'm assuming there's a story in this for me, right?"

"That's true, certainly. But I can't figure what kind of story's hiding out there. Things don't look right for suicide. So, I thought, since Steffie's the expert on farmer suicides, maybe she should review the site before we mess the thing up too much. Maybe you can figure this out for a stupid old man… find me a clue or two."

"Okay. I'll feed my crew here, send them off to work and football practice, hop into my Honda, drive like crazy, and, assuming no

cop pulls me over for speeding, be there in two and a half hours...
say 9:45, plus or minus."

"Thanks, Steffie. I really appreciate this. I'll provide coffee and
donuts."

"You're darn right you will. Now, what's your story about?"

"A neighbor found this ancient retired couple, both of them
around ninety-five, in their garage, stone dead, apparently asphyx-
iated in their Buick. Everything points to suicide, Steffie, even the
short handwritten note. But the site's just unnaturally tidy. That's
assuming one can think of any suicide as natural. There's something
goofy going on up here. I need your expertise, and I need it fast, and
I'd like to get some sleep sometime soon. Maybe I'm just a silly old
man to question the thing, but I need an expert's opinion. Maybe
you can poke around the site and talk to the neighbor... make some
sense of this thing, Steffie. Ease my doubts."

"Or maybe confirm them?"

"I just want to be able to sleep. This thing is gnawing at me. I'm
thinking even the pills won't work tonight."

"Email me anything you can. I'll go over it in the morning
when my mind is working. That'll get me up to speed before I barge
through your door."

Chapter 4

Steffie Cobb is both a very respected reporter for the *Bismarck Plainsman* and a farm girl born in Pierce County, up near Rugby. She knows North Dakota's farmers and understands their death rituals. Last year, sensing that inordinate numbers of them were dying on an accelerated schedule, she'd written a series of articles for the *Plainsman* documenting an increase in the number of elderly farmer suicides occurring in the lonely rank of upper tier counties. Her series won an investigative journalism prize at the regional awards last May in Minneapolis. She'd documented the harsh conditions and the psychological pressures that confronted many elderly, isolated farmers as they headed into another cold, desolate, boring winter with no guarantee they'd pop out on the other side. Climatic and social pressures bombarded their psyches and exposed their fatalistic tendencies. Some folks made the reasoned choice of a quiet death on their own terms rather than fight another winter—either the brutal one promised by North Dakota or the boring loneliness of the Arizona desert, where some of the wealthier and more energetic natives fled. But, though they had escaped the cold, they unfortunately removed themselves from the comforting aspects of friends and family. Steffie used Sheriff Gaffey's knowledge and understanding to help form her argument for the suicide series. She now believes it's her privilege and duty to repay him.

Steffie also sees the sheriff's immediate problem as an extension or continuation of her previous work. She'd undertaken that series as something of a personal cleansing mechanism, an attempt to assuage the guilt for allowing her own parents to, in effect, design their own exit strategy, and perhaps also an attempt to understand her own struggle with North Dakota boredom. Her folks had retired to Tucson. Certainly that classifies as a type of suicide. Arizona sapped their strength and, after three years, killed them just as dead as North Dakota would have. Legally, and perhaps technically, their deaths weren't suicides. But their will to live evaporated very quickly in the desert heat. They stayed inside their sun-baked room in the desert with both the TV and the AC blasting at them, and they waited patiently for dry, hot, and lonesome Tucson to act the grim reaper.

***

The drive up north happens without Steffie being much aware of it. All of a sudden she clears the slight rise east of town and Bottineau appears in the shallow valley. Very light traffic during the drive allows her mind to concentrate on the problem with her son, David, though with all the thoughts running through her head, not much solution filters out. She sees Jake, both physically and personality-wise, as taking after her, while David seems a physical and emotional clone of his dad. She thinks herself guilty of favoring David as the one needing to be cuddled. She never thinks Jake needs her attention. He's comfortable plowing the fields on his own, although, unless she constantly applies a strong leash, he'll surely find trouble. She has no idea how her mother, who raised eight kids, found the way to do it without killing a few of them, or going mad.

Steffie pulls into the gravel lot at the sheriff's office at 9:50. There's reasonable time for coffee and donuts.

Gaffey's been watching for her arrival and opens the outer door as she approaches. "Mornin' to ya, Steffie. This old man's certainly happy to see you." He gives her a hug, a very serious bit of social interaction for him. "Thanks for coming up. I wanted to call you earlier yesterday but kept putting it off. Finally, ol' lady reason kicked in and convinced me she'd not let me sleep till I did it."

"I owe you big time, Sheriff. I'm glad to get this chance to help. Let's get to work."

"Come back to the conference room. I've got notes and photos tacked to the wall and your coffee and donuts on the table. And there's someone you have to meet." He opens the door and, as she walks into the room, a golden Lab limps over to her and licks her hand.

"Say hello to Ruby, Steffie."

She puts her briefcase on the table, sits down on a straight chair, and lets Ruby drop her head into her lap. "What a pretty girl you are, Ruby! What happened to your leg?"

"Neighbor tells me the leg's never worked right since a run-in with a pickup several years ago."

"Not quite the attack dog I'd expect to see hanging with the law, Sheriff. She's a bit lame and laid back for police work, don't ya think?"

"Ruby's not my dog. She belonged to the suicide couple. She kind of followed me home yesterday. I couldn't leave her up there in that empty house all by herself now, could I?"

"No, but I might be able to use her dog talents. Maybe I could take her up there with me. With both our noses poking around we're sure to find something. Right?"

"I'll let you two poke around by yourselves for a while. I don't want to be a distraction, though I'll send Deputy Turnquist up in a couple of hours. He'll be able to fit your observations into the case as we understand it."

***

Steffie had grown up on a farm just northwest of Rugby, thus she understands the symbiotic relationship between farmers and their landscape. It's an uncomfortable alliance, as Mother Nature has seen her natural prairie grasses replaced by invasive plants like corn and wheat. Steffie recognizes the visual evidence of this confrontation. She can see which farmers work in concert with Mother Nature, which have made her the enemy, and which have given up even taking sides.

She notices the tilting mailbox with the fading letters and the missing two vowels. She slows, turns off the county road, and then heads up the long driveway toward the farmhouse. She puts all her sensors on alert, drives slowly, observes the background, and jams as much miscellaneous information into her memory as she can. She wants to isolate the anomalies occurring in the uniform-appearing background and try to see the subtle things that might support a potential for suicide. She allows elements of the landscape to sink in.

Time moves slowly out here. It masks changes to the landscape, sometimes rendering them invisible. She tries to put herself between the actions of the Gupchals and the land's reaction to their efforts. She needs to determine the strength of the symbiotic relationship between these now dead farmers and their land. She notes the ratio of cultivated fields to resting ones, the intruding scraggly trees and brush in a drainage swale, and the short section of new fence with steel posts unprofessionally stitched into a section of ancient wooden ones.

She knows right away the Gupchals are retired and haven't worked the farm themselves for years. They must lease the fields to someone who obviously cares only about the areas leased and nothing else. The drainage channels, fence lines, farm roads, and outbuildings all need maintenance. Several pieces of equipment lie rusting where they've expired. There seems little sense of the future governing activities on this farm, which exhibits no pretense of maintaining its value. The Gupchals did not care; or, more likely, they could not marshal the energy to care for their farm any more. Steffie's reading of this farm tells her its owners might very well have been candidates for suicide.

"This place is depressing," she says to Ruby. "The more I study this damned prairie, the more lonesome I feel. I need to get myself away. Ya think it's time to move to the city?"

Ruby jumps to attention and jams her nose against the front window.

"Here we are, girl. Recognize the old homestead?"

Steffie drives across the gravel yard and parks by the side stairs. She takes the leash from the back seat and, with difficulty, attaches it to the squirming dog's collar. "Patience, old girl! Sorry, but I can't let you run off on me."

When Steffie opens her driver's side door, Ruby tries to force herself through it first, but Steffie doesn't release her hold. Order is quickly restored.

"Nice try, Ruby! Thought you'd catch me off guard, huh? You gotta learn I'm the boss here." She tugs lightly on the leash to emphasize the point.

Steffie may be the boss, but Ruby is guiding this investigation, and she drags Steffie up the steps to the front porch, pushes her nose into the mesh of the screen door, and growls softly.

"Good, dog! Want to search the house first? Me too! We'll work the grounds later."

After a struggle with the leash and the key, she finally gets the door open, and they stumble inside. Ruby's claws slip and slide on the tile in the entry area as she strains to free herself. With a bit of difficulty, Steffie lets her go. "You poke around. I need a few minutes to adjust my sensors to this place and get a feel for how your owners lived. Go! Find me some evidence."

Free of her tether, Ruby wanders off through the dining room and into the sun porch. She doesn't do much sniffing and doesn't appear interested in investigating.

Steffie finds the house just as the sheriff described. It looks cleaned to death. Maybe that's why Ruby's having trouble getting interested. "What's wrong, Ruby? You can't find anything to smell?" The whole place is scrubbed down hard, sanitized, with everything put back in place just so. Dishes are secure in the cupboards, counters clear, the floor immaculate, the wastebasket under the sink empty, and a sharpened pencil inserted into the little pouch on the notepad next to the phone. It's the same condition in the other rooms with everything stowed away, all the surfaces polished, no speck of dust anywhere. And, according to Ruby, no smells to smell either.

She remembers from the file that a neighbor told Gaffey that the Gupchals were planning a short trip and she wonders if this might be a normal pre-trip ritual. Perhaps suicide *was* the trip they'd been planning. This old couple apparently spent their last hours on earth ordering all their possessions as if they expected never to come back. She's thinking this might be reasonable behavior before a planned trip *or* a planned suicide. But such manic cleansing seems like overkill. She thinks, *what ninety-five-year-old couple would do that?*

She thinks that perhaps Helen, ninety-five and wheelchair bound, had someone help her with the cleaning. She looks for answers in her copy of Gaffey's interview with the neighbor, Verna Blakely. Finding none, she phones that neighbor.

"Good morning, Mrs. Blakely. My name is Steffie Cobb, and I'm over at the Gupchals' house now. I'm working with Sheriff Gaffey. He told me you knew them as well as anyone, and I have a question or two for you about the way they lived. Can you help me?"

"Certainly, Miss Cobb. They said they'd be leaving on a trip and would bring Ruby over to stay with us. But they never came by, and they didn't answer their phone. So my husband went over and he found them." Her voice disintegrates and she begins to cry.

"Sorry, Mrs. Blakely, but I have to ask you a couple of questions about her cleaning regimen. How would you rank her on the cleaning performance scale from slob to obsessive?"

"What a strange question," Verna says. "She kept the house clean enough. Average, I'd imagine. Though, with her wheelchair and all, I think Frank did a lot of her housework the last several months. He maybe vacuumed and dusted every few weeks but not so good as to move the furniture to get behind. He wasn't much of a cleaner."

Steffie senses a bit of social contempt in Verna's voice, aimed at someone less professional.

"Why do you ask?"

Steffie describes the immaculate movie-set condition, the proverbial 'putting on clean underwear to die' sort of clean.

"Well, Miss Cobb, to tell the truth, I can see many other women doing that before I'd think about Helen. Not speakin' ill, or sayin' she's lazy, but a professional job's not something she'd do. Then again, I wouldn't think suicide's something she'd do either. It's all so confusing."

"Did someone help her with housework?"

"No, not out here. We're miles from town. But the County Extension Service visited her regularly. Ms. Cobb, that house has never looked like you're describing. Never!"

"I appreciate your help, Mrs. Blakely. If I run across something else I don't understand, can I call you again?"

"By all means, Miss Cobb. I'm glad to help any way I can."

"Thank you. You've been a big help."

Steffie stows her phone and walks into the sunroom. Ruby follows dutifully. They stand quietly and take everything in. Magazines are neatly stacked on the end table. An ancient computer takes up an inordinate amount of space on a desktop, with the mouse positioned exactly in the middle of the mouse pad. "I wonder what they did on the computer?" She checks to see if the thing is plugged in, then pushes the power button. Nothing happens. She checks connections and tries again. "Looks like this is dead, Ruby," she says. "Don't suppose you know if it works? Or why the mouse might be perfectly placed if the machine isn't used? What's the point?" She makes a note to ask the sheriff if he'd been able to access the memory.

A bronze holder contains loose bills and letters, and next to that, what appears to be a roll of rubber-banded mail. Chair pillows and bolster covers rest in their correct positions, the footstools directly symmetrical with their respective chairs, and the TV remote positioned dead center on top of the TV. A severely disinterested Ruby doesn't even give the room a circuit, though her eyes do follow Steffie as she pokes about.

Steffie sees few mementos from the long life this couple must have spent here. There is no pithy saying hanging on the kitchen wall, no shelf of knickknacks, no ceramic angels on the end table, and only two small photographs on the living room mantel—an elderly couple in 1950s dress, probably a set of parents, and a head shot of two happy young women dressed for a party. No photos of children or grandchildren are displayed, no religious wall hangings, no crucifix, no 'God Bless This House' plaque. Might the dearth of memorabilia increase the suicide index of the household? Or, might it mean nothing?

"What's the matter here, Ruby? Even after a dozen strangers have walked all over the place, you don't feel the need to sniff?" She walks over to the large windows and looks at the still-life outside.

After a while she walks back to the desk, studies it for a bit, then picks up the rubber-banded stack of unopened mail. She finds several ads, two apparent bills, and a couple of solicitation letters, all wrapped in a *Better Homes and Gardens* magazine and a small farm-service newsletter. She notes the dates stamped on the letters—a few days before the deaths occurred. *It's a very recent stack! If this mail came in before the Gupchals died, why is it still rubber-banded? If it came after, then that would have been yesterday and then who brought it in from the mailbox? Does unopened mail argue for or against suicide?* She'll have to think on this for a bit. It doesn't feel rational.

"Okay, Ruby, you make sure I check the mailbox on our way out." Steffie is bored. Normally, the questions such abject normalcy provoked would put her on alert. But that isn't working here. The site's telling her the precise presentation of the scene must be too elaborate for a suicide. On the other hand, she isn't seeing the sense of disruption associated with a typical murder. Like the sheriff said—'things seem spooky.'

"Let's take a tour around the yard. Show me something I can't see... something all the humans poking around here yesterday missed." They exit the kitchen and head down the stairs. A makeshift wheelchair ramp, built over the stairs between the handrails, narrows the access so that Steffie and Ruby must descend them single file.

Steffie wants first to look at the death scene in the garage, but Ruby follows her own agenda. She sniffs around the porch at the front of the house, picks up something interesting, and lets it lead her toward the barn. Ruby goes directly to a door, sticks her nose into the weather-stripping at the bottom edge, and then stands motionless with her nose smashed into the gravel in front of the door.

"What is it girl? What do you smell?"

Ruby apparently doesn't have an answer. She looks up at Steffie, then is off around the right side of the barn toward the garage. She sniffs at the side door and then trots around to the front where, apparently, she finds something else worth her interest in the gravel just off the concrete slab in front of the overhead door. She paws vigorously, builds up a small mound, exposes a shallow hole, sticks her nose into that hole, and then, like the birddog she is, steps back and points at the hole with her nose.

"You find something, girl?" Ruby doesn't answer, so Steffie has to get down on her knees, bend over, and sniff the hole for herself. Ruby sticks her nose in too; it is, after all, her hole. "Ruby, you gotta let me smell this." She catches a hint of a pungent odor. Or maybe it's only Ruby she smells. Understanding that Ruby's nose has hers outclassed, she gives up trying to confirm the presence of a smell, especially since Ruby is tugging at her, the nose wanting to move on to other things. Steffie, however, has equipment other than a nose. She has a ball-point pen. She carefully pushes enough gravel stones out of the way to reveal bits of what look to her like human vomit. Small mushy lumps, maybe green pepper and sausage, are hiding in between the stones. "What have we here, Ruby? Looks like somebody's Denver omelet, huh? And it hasn't even started to decompose yet. This is recent!" She takes several photos of it, thinking it's what the sheriff would do and she calls Sheriff Gaffey.

"I am not at all sure about these deaths as suicides," she tells him. "I'm not sure of anything except for one thing. I'm thinking this scene has all the marks of some intense female attention. Everything's so tidy, so exactly placed. I've spent an hour poking around here, and no man I'm aware of would be nearly so thorough covering up a mess. Someone who knew how to clean did this cleaning. And most likely that someone was a woman, and some woman much more a housekeeper than Helen Gupchal ever dreamed of being, even when she wasn't in a wheelchair. What do you think?"

"I think that's interesting, Steffie. But I need something far more definitive."

"Okay, I'll give you definitive. I think your meek police dog did find something. Ruby, she's a female mind you, found us a clue. She found something sniffable in the gravel in front of the garage door and dug herself a little hole to mark the spot."

"Something sniffable? I think my forensic team needs something more precise, Steffie."

"I supervised her work, Sheriff. I got down and looked into her hole and confirmed she found something. It's rather fresh human vomit from the looks of it, in the stones just off the concrete garage slab. Should I dig some up and bring it in to you?"

"No, Steffie! Just leave it be. Deputy Turnquist should be showing up soon to check on what you're doing. He's got the proper equipment to secure a sample. You don't touch anything. We can't have the chain of evidence broken. And if you find anything else, just note it and tell Turnquist. Let him do his work. Okay?"

"Got it, Sheriff. I'll wait for your deputy. I've got several questions for him."

Ruby wanders over to the spruce tree windbreak, then along those trees to the back of the barn. She sniffs a black tarp crumpled behind a frame that once supported a propane cylinder. She grabs the tarp with her teeth and tries to dislodge it. Steffie pulls out the tarp, wondering if she'll find another body. Nothing—just an old tarp. After a few minutes both of them lose interest and head back to the front of the house. Ruby stands rigid with a look that says, "Okay, I'm finished here, now what?"

"Damn!" Steffie says. "What am I missing? I don't feel I can go home yet. I haven't found anything." She remembers Gaffey told her that sometimes life just doesn't make a lot of sense. Sometimes you just have to live with what you got.

Steffie thinks that's probably the difference between a reporter and a sheriff. She wants the pieces to line up, to tell a story. He only takes what he finds, types up the report, and calls it a day.

She's almost ready to accept the 'call it a day' path when Ruby's sudden bark alerts her to the deputy's cruiser coming up the driveway.

An hour later, after she'd watched Deputy Turnquist complete his work, she leaves the farm and heads home. A half hour after that, she realizes she's already made one big decision. She completely forgot about bringing the dog back to the sheriff. She looks over at Ruby curled up on her passenger seat and smiles. She'll have to throw an extra burger on the grill tonight.

Chapter 5

Thursday, August 23, 2013
The same morning in New York City – 7:02 a.m.

J.D. Crowe opens the French doors to his balcony, breathes in a lungful of New York City air, and looks out over Central Park. The early sun sparkles off the reservoir, and the path parallel to the shoreline glitters with varicolored joggers and walkers. J.D. contrasts this with the bleak Dakota landscape that assaulted him yesterday. "Now tell me," he speaks to whatever deity may be listening, "isn't this beautiful?" A couple of pigeons alight on his rail a few feet from him, nod in agreement, and invite him to come out and play. He considers it. "Be glad you guys are here and not in North Dakota!"

His friends coo appreciatively. Eleven floors below, Fifth Avenue is a colorful blur of pedestrians, cyclists, cars, and buses. "Can you guys appreciate the beauty of this noise? Look out there. Real trees and other greenery. And look at those things actually moving—people walking, dogs running, even your bird buddies swooping about." The comparison with the stark brutality of yesterday's science fiction landscape impresses him—the whitish pigeons versus ink-black crows. Inspired and refreshed by his usual landscape, he returns inside to prepare himself for another day toiling in Francelli's glass tower.

***

At ten minutes before eight he walks through the mahogany-framed doorway into Francelli's kingdom and extends the envelope enclosing his freshly minted original of the signed OTPA form toward Francelli's secretary. "Morning, Angelina. You're looking lovely on this fine day. Would you be so kind as to give this to Enrico when he comes in? He's expecting it."

"And you're looking very lovely yourself this morning, Mr. Crowe," she says with a smile. "You can go right in and give it to him in person. We've been *waiting* for you."

That staggers him. First thing that hits him is what's with the 'we' word? Does that mean she came in this morning *with* Francelli? And that can only mean one thing. Second thing is that Francelli seldom graces the crew with his presence this early. J.D.'s cocky and frisky parts evaporate and are replaced by anxiety. He knocks twice, opens Francelli's door, and shuffles through the thick carpeting.

Enrico looks up and actually smiles at him. "Hey, J.D. Welcome back."

Crowe feels his tension ease and his breathing return to normal. "Thanks, Enrico. Here's the option. I sent a copy to Prometheus from the house yesterday. They should be able to complete the submission in a few days. That new scanning and printing equipment worked out slicker than shit."

"Speaking of shit, John, I've an email here I think you'll find interesting. Come around and read it off my machine."

Whoa, thinks Crowe. *This can't be good news.* After the short hike around the desk he looks at the screen and reads the message, sent by an outfit called prairiefarmer@prairieway.org. The text is minimal: Helen and I thank you God, we're going home.

"What the hell!" John David Crowe feels his knees go weak. He grasps the finely-turned edge-molding of the huge desk for support.

"This gibberish mean something to you?"

"Enrico, I…"

"Looks like you've seen a ghost. What's going on?"

"Those words! I know those words. That's the suicide note old man Gupchal left on his kitchen table. Who possibly could see those words on that note and also know your email address?"

"Besides you, you mean?" Enrico gives him a strange look. "That's a great question, John. Someone's connected Prometheus' refinery to my office, and he's letting me know it."

"How could that possibly happen, boss? Nobody but the people in my meeting yesterday knew HF&G had any connection to that house. And I can't believe any of those guys know your name, let alone your private email address."

"I assumed that option problem was a normal snafu," said Enrico. "So I attacked it as a normal snafu. It's my fault. That assumption is now garbage. This email means someone knows precisely what I'm doing. This thing is personal. It's a very clever attempt to rattle me, to throw a crowbar into my machine."

"But there wasn't a damn soul within fifty miles of that godforsaken place. How—"

"Someone's hacked our system, found out where Prometheus is putting that refinery, and knows I'm connected to it. God only knows how he did it, but he also knows the intricate details of those suicides you saw yesterday."

"Enrico, whoever sent that e-mail has to be tied to that meeting yesterday at NDOEP's office. It's the only possible connection. We've been our normal sneaky selves, so no one else in the whole state of North Dakota even knows our name, or of our interest in that farm."

Francelli pounds on his desk. Things skitter and jump about on the glass surface. "We've got a security breakdown right here. I'll get Pick on it, pronto."

"Angelina!" Francelli shouts out through the open door. It's an immediate summons, faster than the intercom. "Get your ass in here!"

"I'll take a look at the attendees of that meeting, then see if—"

"Didn't I just tell you, John. It's not them! Those guys are amateurs." Enrico looks at the screen again. "This email is a personal attack. It has a New York City stink about it. The answer is here—probably within six blocks of this office."

"Angelina!" He slams his palm on the desktop. "Where are you?"

Angelina stumbles through the door looking scared and stands at attention just inside it. "What's the matter, Enrico?" she asks, timidly.

"In ten minutes…" he looks at his watch, then points to the floor at her feet. "…I want to see Martin Pick standing right there where you are standing. I don't care if he's in Hong Kong!" He stabs his finger again. "Ten minutes!"

Angelina doesn't move. Her body quakes with fear and anger.

He shoos her away with a flick of his hand. "Scoot!" he says. "Just find Pick for me, damn it."

"And you, John. I think you need a brandy. We'll have to turn this thing around quicker than we planned. Let some fricken Saudi or Chinese worry about those dead farmers. We dump this piece of shit fast. Comprendo?"

"Don't see why we can't, Enrico. That development fund in Dubai is chomping at the bit. They're ready to take it off our hands. We just say the word."

"Yeah, but just to be safe, I'm thinking we'd better fly out there, turn on the spigot, and spread some money and muscle around before this suicide stuff gains any traction, or some fool does something inflammatory on the Internet. We've got to push it hard. Once the state's taken their first peek at it—BOOM!" He pounds his fist on his desktop and points to J.D. "Then we dump it."

"You're right, Enrico. Money always trumps emotion. It couldn't hurt to hit the governor again, and maybe a few key legislative leaders, before this 'prairie farmer' guy has a chance to do his negative work. We can't leave anything to chance."

"This really bothers me, John. Some jerk knows what I'm doing. I see two separate games going on here—Prometheus playing 'let's build a refinery' in Dakota and 'prairie farmer' playing 'screw the hedge-fund guy' here in the city. We'll counter-attack in both venues. I'll get Pick on it. You have the gnomes downstairs track that email address. It's probably expertly cloaked, but give it a shot."

"You're right, Enrico. I can't believe this hacker's from Dakota! He's much too sophisticated. I can tell you first hand... those yokels haven't figured out air-conditioning yet. I'm not confident they even know what email is."

"You may be right, John."

Enrico activates his shield wall. Crowe recognizes the external signs—the blank stare, shoes jumping to the desktop, and the lack of air in the room for Crowe to breathe. Enrico's mind has left its body-shell and is rummaging through his cloud storage for the clues necessary to solve his 'prairie farmer' problem. For all practical purposes, Crowe is alone in the room. So Crowe leaves Enrico's office before his pyrotechnic phase begins.

Even after the security leaks just presented to him, Crowe feels pretty confident. North Dakota is—at least he's pretty sure it is—still back in the dark ages, populated by a tribe of Neanderthals from a millennium past, and nowhere nearly as advanced as the financial wizards in Dubai and Shijiazhuang who are likely the next owners of this refinery project. A thin sliver of unease toys in the back recesses of his mind and makes him pause for a second. But since he can't give the specter any form, it quickly goes away. He nods to Angelina as she frantically punches numbers on her phone, and takes a piece of chocolate candy from the bowl on her desk. "Let me know when Pick shows up. I need to be in on that." He lets the door close behind him and heads for his desk.

On the way back to his office, J.D. starts thinking intricate thoughts. Enrico is not only in trouble with 'prairie farmer,' but he's also got Angelina furious with him. He feels something—perhaps it's sorrow, or it could be lust—for Angelina. Enrico treats all his women like shit. Maybe this time, however, Angelina will see the light. Could be now's the time to put his move on. A kind word, some flowers, a shoulder to cry on? That formula has worked for him before. He might find her in need of comforting. He might take care of that need, then slip her into his bed while Francelli's still stomping and raging.

On the other hand, Enrico is probably right that both the email and Angelina are meant for his eyes only. At any rate, J.D. knows he badly needs that brandy.

Chapter 6

Steffie Cobb leans against one of the dozens of American elm trees lining both sides of the Capitol Mall. Her jeans, heavy blue sweater, and matching stocking cap allow her to blend in with the several hundred other people now converging on the Capitol grounds this nice brisk morning. She thinks herself to be quite invisible. She's here to meet Jane Blackburn, the supposed organizer of this event. Jane is now interviewing with other reporters at the secure area next to their satellite trucks. Steffie has questions those other reporters don't know to ask, and must not hear answered. Her questions about this demonstration are not about motivation, but about timing, speed, and financing. She knows Jane is not capable of pulling this off by herself and wonders who's wielding the power and the money behind this effort. She watches Ruby harass a couple of gray squirrels.

The massive concrete and stone tower of the North Dakota State Capitol Building pokes into the sky in front of her. It's now lit by the morning sun and it looks impressive… perhaps suggesting a powerful imperial property. On the other side of the elms, the expansive and still very green Capitol Mall isn't nearly as impressive. Nothing imperial-suggesting is going on out there. It supports no exotic planting, and has only one lonely statue at the far end. The focus of this controlled vista is the facade of the hardware store across the street behind that statue. That's not impressive. One of her reporter friends calls this grassed field the *State Pasture*. He says it forces visitors to appreciate the concept of open space, even though most of these prairie dwellers have no understanding of any type of space *other* than open.

Steffie knows this well-engineered demonstration could not have been organized this quickly, especially in North Dakota during harvest time. Everyone is concentrating on the harvest now. It sucks up all the energy. She knows any non-agricultural story must overpower the noise of the combines to get her attention. And, this September, additional noise interferes—the shouting and screaming required by the election season. Yet, this gathering she's now monitoring has generated enough noise to attract TV trucks, outfitted with rotatable rooftop disks, from Minneapolis, Yankton, and Cheyenne. She is duly impressed.

And here comes still more noise in the form of Channel 7's cute blue helicopter. It zooms in above her, overpowers all the other sounds, and forcefully grabs her attention. *Wow!* she thinks. *That helicopter showing up, even as the crowd is still gathering, means this party was put together by some gorilla with a lot of clout. And a lot of cash too.* The speed aspect bothers her. Similar to recent events in Iran, Yemen, and Egypt, this get-together on the mall must have organized itself quickly using email, Twitter, and Facebook. That seems odd, but then, if it happens in the third world it could happen here. She knows educated folks in New York and Washington entertain the fantasy that North Dakota is part of that third world.

A part of her subscribes to that fantasy also. At times, this place drives her bats. "Three more years, Ruby, then maybe we move to Minneapolis, or California." In three years, her boys will be away at college, and she envisions her tether loosening. She and Matt talked about moving to some civilized place after the boys left. Or rather, she talked and Matt snarled. It's not going to be easy, but she feels she has to go. There's no nice way of putting it—North Dakota sucks. Life's too short to spend any more time here than absolutely necessary.

Steffie doesn't care for many of the people out here either. Most, like Matt, are good folks. But they wear blinders like plow horses and care little about events outside their own well-manicured field of view. She tries to curb her bias, but it doesn't always work... like with Jane Blackburn, for example. Her organization, Prairie Preservation Foundation, organized this morning's demonstration. Steffie doesn't like Jane, and doesn't think many other people do either. A stern expression, like a mask, ensures her eyes never twinkle and the corners of her lips never tip up. Like Al Capp's cartoon character, Joe Btfsplk, she's anchored a private black cloud above her that prevents any of this nice sunshine from illuminating her facade. The organization she fronts, the Prairie Preservation Foundation, sucks support and enthusiasm from young idealists at the University's several campuses and now coordinates branches at schools from Iowa to Montana. Jane's volunteers demonstrate against sprawling commercial development, toxic fertilizing, factory-farm livestock operations, landscape-raping in the western oilfields, and other projects. And they're ready to run whenever she blows the chrome-plated whistle dangling from the pink lanyard flung around her slender neck.

Steffie now sees Jane crossing the State Pasture. She is walking with a young woman who is gesturing exuberantly. As they get close, the young woman breaks away and runs, rather clumsily, back toward the news trucks. Jane continues toward her position, and Ruby lumbers off looking for another squirrel to play with.

"Good to see you again, Jane. Nice day for a demonstration."

"Hello, Steffie. Sorry I'm late. Those TV guys kept me longer than I scheduled." Jane looks distractedly back at the TV guys, or maybe at the figure of the other woman she'd been talking with.

"You created this buzz very quickly. I see plates from Minnesota, South Dakota, even Montana. I'm impressed. But I'm puzzled by the short response time after the sheriff's announcement. Can you tell me how all this hoopla came together so quickly?"

"You're right, Steffie. It did move fast. I really didn't expect to jump on this murder story so quickly. But I can't throw such a great opportunity away. I could've waited a day or two, but those criminals from New York have already set their hooks into the governor." She looks back again, toward the TV people.

"Criminals from New York? Who do you mean?"

"They own the governor's attack-dog, Brian Bast. You know he's our *acting* governor? And they're plowing ahead full bore and not caring who they run over. I felt I had to throw that murder log on the track. Once they gained momentum, I'd never be able to keep up with their freight train."

"Again, Jane, what criminals are you talking about?"

"I know how these big developers work, Steffie. I've no doubt Prometheus runs a very fine steam-roller operation. They can cut every corner, pay any bribe, manipulate their environmental studies, hide assets, and do hundreds of other marginally legal or arguably illegal things along with the best of them. But they do it cleanly and usually have their lawyers do the dirty work. However, I wouldn't put a timely murder past them if the pressure pushed them." Jane removes her backpack, zips it open, and looks through some papers.

"Perhaps those New York thugs act like it's the wild west. Maybe they use some frontier-type persuasion."

"This is *not* the wild west, Steffie. For God's sake. We're talking serious organized crime."

Steffie realizes her mistake; the lady doesn't understand levity. "But you ran with this murder thing even though, as you just implied, what happened probably isn't murder?"

"I implied nothing, Ms. Cobb. With the train leaving the station, I couldn't take the chance we could stop it once it got up a head of steam."

The lady has a problem with a metaphor, thinks Steffie—trains, steam rollers, lots of big ugly machines. "These criminals in New York, do they have names, or crimes?"

Jane pulls a paper from her backpack. "The bad guy here is a hedge fund called HF&G LLC. They're running a scam with that refinery thing. Most rational people will think it's criminal behavior."

"Where'd you get your information? Somebody tell you those New York guys murdered the Gupchals?"

"It was the sheriff up there told us. He said he couldn't rule murder out."

Steffie thinks it's time to move in, get confrontational. She pokes a finger at Jane.

"I attended Gaffey's news conference. And I didn't see you there. Gaffey talked only about suicide, not murder. Nothing environmental. Nothing about New York criminals either. In the real world, nothing Gaffey talked about would have tweaked your antenna. You'd hear nothing about it till you read my story in yesterday's paper. That would give you one afternoon to put this circus together. But you knew these things several days before Gaffey's news conference—several days before I or the sheriff knew. So the reporter in me wonders how you got the word before Gaffey did."

"I think you're jealous, Steffie. You have your sources and I have mine."

"Who told you this stuff? Somebody tipped you. Tell me who."

"I can't comment on that, Steffie."

"Even a wonder woman like you couldn't put this together in one day. You need lots of time and mega-money. Can you tell me where the mega-money is coming from?"

"No comment!"

"Maybe it's those 'criminals in New York' financing this show?"

"Don't be stupid."

"Okay, then tell me how to reach your New York criminals. I can ask them if maybe they gave you the money, or committed the murders."

"Ask me something else."

"You didn't do the murdering yourself, did you?"

"Steffie!" Jane pouts and turns away, looking back at the TV crew.

"If I had a source that deep into the enemy's camp, I wouldn't reveal it either—especially to a good reporter like me. Is that your source?" Steffie points back to the TV trucks. "Is it the woman you were arguing with back there? Should I go talk to her?"

"A good reporter like you should get to know me better." She flashes a smug smile. "You'll find I never reveal my secrets. And neither will Nancy."

The words startle Steffie. She thinks, *that woman actually smiled—smiled at me. That can't be a good sign.*

Jane strides away. Steffie lets her go. She has nothing left to ask her. She came to the mall today because Jane's press release arrived in her in-box yesterday afternoon, and with it came about four dozen questions, none of which were answered by Jane. "Must be losin' my touch, Ruby. Let's go see Leon. Maybe he has answers."

***

She looks up at Channel 7's Bluebird copter. She watches it zig and zag overhead, then move off toward the other end of the mall. The noise abates some and she looks toward the parking area. She sees Travis waving, giving her the thumbs-up. She had secured the helicopter coverage, and his job was to affix the big white letters to the roofs of the black Land Rovers. The whole purpose of this party is to send a message to Francelli. And so now it is done. The rest of this nonsense playing out on this fine fall day is but fluff and confusion.

Well, not exactly fluff. This demonstration is more like grit and dirt, or maybe a virus. Eventually it will foul the gears of Enrico's ugly machine and covertly grease the gears of Nathan's much more beautiful machine. And it didn't take much. Just that little note she had Timmins stick into Nathan's truck to get him going. He had reacted like she knew he would. He's done such a beautiful job. But predictable? Nathan is certainly predictable.

She watches the vulnerable and ignorant Jane Blackburn, walking with her partner, stumbling often on the uneven grass, completely unaware of how she had been manipulated. They seem to be arguing. She watches Jane shove Nancy, who then turns away and runs clumsily back to the street. Jane, acting the stoic professional, continues alone, annoyed and with purpose, toward the line of giant elms.

She then recognizes Steffie Cobb, that reporter for the Plains-man, the one who's buddy-buddy with Sheriff Gaffey. She's standing in the shade watching her dog chase squirrels. She's obviously wait-ing for Jane, now crossing the grass toward her. Then she connects the dots and recognizes the limping Labrador. Damn, that can't be a coincidence. Gaffey must have given Steffie the Gupchals' dog. She's watching from too far away to overhear the discussion but knows now she can't get closer and risk that dog's nose recognizing her smell. But she trusts Jane unequivocally. She'll feed Steffie nothing, absolutely nothing. "Lots of luck Steffie," she says, then starts the walk back to the street across the State Pasture. Her work here is finished.

She's very pleased with herself. She's succeeded in connecting the Buick deaths to Prometheus' machine, even doing it with a bit of high drama. And in so doing, she's inflicted her retribution on En-rico, advanced her father's dream of his own machine, and fatally compromised Jane's sanctimonious Prairie Preservation Founda-tion. Jane won't realize it for a while, but she'll eventually find she's lost all ability to influence conditions in the western oilfields.

Win, win, win. She's very pleased, especially regarding Enrico. It'll also take him a few days to get it. Eventually he'll understand this opera. She'd give anything to witness that, and to see his de-struction first hand, and to rub his face in it.

***

As it is designed to do, the conflicting mixture of tinny bullhorns and thwopping 'copter blades penetrates into the fourth-floor of-fices of the North Dakota House of Representatives and seriously annoys Leon Rolfes, the speaker of that chamber. The discordant noise interferes with his concentration. He tries to make sense of the Agriculture Department's new interactive chart that compares statistics concerning the current harvest. Having nothing else to do over at the Ag Department, other than to make his life miserable, they'd put the data into a new format this year. He has little appreciation for that sort of progress. It requires excessive amounts of his time and effort, and he has little of either to waste on such nonsense.

The drone of many people repeatedly chanting an indecipherable slogan grows louder. The din forces his attention away from his computer screen. It's too much, even for him, the 'ultimate concentrator,' according to Margie. He remembers a time when the sound of a bullhorn carried authority, maintained a certain heft, and guaranteed a listener's attention. The folks barking outside his window don't understand that. They've rented cheap, shrill horns designed to wail in a higher register. They solicit neither his respect, nor his attention, but they *do* annoy him. As a conscientious representative of those demonstrators, he's required to decode the confounding, unclear noise.

Harvest forecasting must wait. He takes his coffee and walks over to the window for a peek at the ruckus. There's a knock on the doorframe and Rolfes' secretary, Margie, crashes into his room.

"Leon, turn on channel... oh..." She sees him at the window. "You're watching it in *real time*! I think we're famous. Channel 7's showing beautiful live coverage of our mall."

"I don't know about beautiful, Margie, but it is loud. And why does some button-pusher at Channel 7 know about this ruckus before I do? Even before you do? Find out who's shouting and what they want."

Margie switches on his TV and finds coverage of the event. That allows indecipherable noise to pummel Leon in stereo. "Oh!" she says, apparently able to immediately interpret the cacophony. "Those folks are demonstrating against some oil refinery."

During his extended residency in the House, Leon has witnessed demonstrations in many places, so thinks he understands crowd dynamics. He wonders how so many refinery protesters could be found so fast in a place with no history of refineries. Some guy who knows his trade organized this show quickly. *I need to talk to that guy*, Leon thinks. "Get on the phone, Margie. Find out who's directing these people to stomp on my well-manicured lawn. I sense skill, money, and perhaps some serious information leaking. I'm the speaker, aren't I? I'm supposed to know everything. I only learned about a refinery a few weeks ago. And the developer swore us to secrecy until N-DOPE gave the word. I haven't heard any magic words yet, have you?" Leon pronounces his state's Office of Environmental Protection's cumbersome name irreverently as do all its detractors, and many of its friends.

"No, I haven't, Leon. And since I've not heard them, theoretically they haven't yet been uttered. So those people on your lawn shouldn't have heard the refinery word uttered either. However, since the whole world now knows all about it, Mr. Speaker, you are going to enlighten me, right?"

"Bah! You're thinking this noise acts as an official announcement, thereby freeing me from the vow of silence I promised Prometheus?"

"What's Prometheus?"

"It could be a what, or maybe it's a who."

She gives him the *look*.

"Okay. Prometheus is an ethereal corporation planning to build us an oil refinery. They're hiding behind a fancy-shmancy name. It's a superhero pilfered from Greek mythology. Apparently they believe a super-name will cause intelligent folks, like me, to worry less about the impact of smoggy smokestacks and smelly sludge pools. But I think we can already smell the stench. Can't we Margie?"

"I believe we can, sir. At least we can hear it."

"I'm told Prometheus filed its preliminary application on Monday, and I'll bet N-DOPE hasn't had time to even open their package yet. They move like snails over there, since they are being pummeled by applications from oilfield developers out west, and are way understaffed."

"You need to be careful about who hears you say N-DOPE," Margie says. "You know how sensitive they are about their name being abused."

"Ask me if I care. Everyone says it. Those people are idiots over there."

Rolfes watches a few dissidents unroll a banner with red lettering on a white background. When it's all stretched out flat on the grass, he reads the computer-generated, upper-case letters: KILL THE REFINERY; NOT OUR FARMERS.

"That sign is a professional product! And that means this is a non-spontaneous gathering. Something screwy, and maybe not honest, is happening out there."

"I understand the first part," says Margie. "Nobody in their right mind wants a refinery chortling away on their back forty, but what's the killing farmers part about?"

"I have no idea, Margie. But it's fancy, huh? And note the semicolon. In my long career I've found your run-of-the-mill rabble-rousers don't use semicolons. They aren't usually that sophisticated."

"But what do the words mean?"

"You're the expert, Margie. You tell me."

Several men using ropes, pre-cut to length, attach the sign to two elms and orient it toward his window so he's forced to look at it.

"Those are the same words the bullhorns are chanting, aren't they?"

"Maybe, but they still mean nothing to me." He makes a shooing motion. "Get me help!"

"I'm on it, Leon. It's gone viral, as they say. And I know everyone, from your favorite governor to your mother, will be calling you. Everyone will want your learned opinion."

The phone rings. Margie picks it up. "Yup, he's here, and waiting for enlightenment." She gives Leon a smug look. "He'll be glad to make room in his busy schedule for *you*."

She gives him the 'I know things you don't know yet' smile. When she sees he's duly impressed, she continues. "That was your reporter buddy, Steffie. She wants to get your take on the excitement out there. She's coming up. Okay?"

"Sure, Margie, that'll be good. Enlightenment's on the way! You've provided wisdom rather quickly. I owe you a beer."

"I don't need beer," she says. "How about flowers?"

***

Leon's not naive enough to think *he* is the reason the rabble is targeting his window. He knows the real rationale for the pyrotechnics. The focus of all this noise is Channel 7's bright blue helicopter, nervously hovering above the commotion. Leon feels a pang of jealousy, mixed with a bit of sadness. This messenger-machine captures what little action is happening down there and streams it in real time into his TV. Eventually this movie will get to a national morning news show.

"Soon everyone in the world will be gawking at my mall. They're bypassing *me*. Whoever organized the party is putting their message directly to environmentalist interests all over the world. I'm but a bystander... and on my own mall yet."

"Cool it, Leon. Calm down. I'm going downstairs to get the mail. You watch your grass."

"Bah." He looks up at the noisy thing hovering in the sky. It reminds him of another Greek deity he'd studied in college—Hermes, the messenger god, protector of merchants, thieves, and orators. "I can imagine Prometheus dueling with *that* guy. He'll have his hands full." Leon figures that now, since the opposition's got their god pushing an alternative message, Prometheus will be required to be very careful as he stomps over Leon's pristine prairie.

***

Same Day
New York City – 9:22 a.m.

Hermes records the activity on the mall and sells it to several regional news rooms. One of them then resells it to a national morning news show. That allows Enrico Francelli, sitting in his thirty-eighth-floor office in one of New York City's edgier towers, to watch the excitement on the flat-screen he's fitted into a mahogany cabinet in his mahogany-paneled wall. He appears as flummoxed by the message as is Speaker Leon Rolfes. And, propelled by anger rather than inquisitiveness, he is reacting to that nonsense on his screen much faster than Rolfes. In two minutes, he assembles the several younger partners under his tutelage. They watch the video of a small crowd and a big banner re-run itself in a forty-two-second loop.

Francelli points to the screen. "This public theater is what happens when we get careless and take things for granted. Crowe, you promised no opposition, a clueless governor, and a cartwheel-jumping Republican legislature. I don't see cartwheels here. I see fuckin' disaster. Aren't we supposed to be tiptoeing through the regulatory process silently in our cushy moccasins? So what the hell exploded here?"

J.D. Crowe tries to explain. "The governor guaranteed us there'd be no opposition. Said... I'm paraphrasing here... 'That landscape's so damn flat and boring, even God can't find any environment to damage.'"

"Well, that jerk's wrong, isn't he? And what's that fool's guarantee worth now? Bullshit, that's what. And that's what this entire fuckin' project is worth right about now—bullshit!" Francelli is overplaying this tirade for the educational benefit of his flock. Periodically, they need to taste the real world. "This here's lesson time, guys. Don't *ever* take *anything* for granted."

"But," says J.D., "Mr. Bast, the Governor's Chief of Staff, told me—"

"That idiot's a fuckin' bootlicker. Like any political toad, he'll tell you anything you want to hear. He lives in the fantasy world of state politics. He don't know squat, and he's a serial liar."

"Hey, Boss!" One of the young MBAs points at the TV. "Look at this! Damn! It just went off the screen. Wait till the loop comes back around. I saw three SUVs in the parking area. I can't believe I saw that! Just watch! Right about... here." He points at the lower left corner of the screen. Twenty seconds later, Francelli pauses the video so they all can see the three black SUVs parked side-by-side with large white letters fixed to their roofs. "See? Right here! The letters H, F, and G."

"Damn it, Enrico," says Crowe, "we're in some guy's crosshairs. He's signing that picture like a fucking painting. I get it! This whole play is a message aimed specifically toward this office. Those three cars are the only reason this whole circus got itself orchestrated. But nobody out there except the governor even knows our name. How'd this all leak out?"

"What'd I tell you before, Crowe? This stinks like New York. This attack is directed at me, even though it's happening out in the middle of nowhere. Okay, class," Enrico says, depreciating the value of his highly paid and credentialed underlings, "this isn't the end of the world. We have enough power to fix this. We have money and influence and we can be sneaky smooth. We'll quickly sell this hot potato. Won't we, Mr. Crowe?"

"Yes, sir," says Crowe. "I've got that broker in Dubai foaming."

"Manage his enthusiasm, J.D. We've a bit of dam-plugging to do first. I've an enemy crawling around in my basement, and you must find out who he is… and fast! Take Martin Pick from security and jet out there again. Talk to the police, talk to everyone. Find out what the hell is going on. Bludgeon people until you get this dead farmer thing pushed into some dark corner. Comprendo? Find who's stabbing me and silence the bastard. Then we can turn this turkey over to your friend in Dubai!"

J.D. acts like the Jets' quarterback after a sideline chewing-out. "I'm on it Boss!" He heads back to the field to call the next play.

Enrico calls after him. "While you're out there, have a frank discussion with that loser of a governor. I don't care if it gets bloody." He mutes the TV and shoos the rest of the group from his office. Sometimes a snafu allows him the chance to refocus his crew's antennae, to ensure they sharpen their swords and polish their bludgeons.

"And you, DeVrane, find out who at Prometheus let this happen and then fire his ass."

***

Wednesday, September 18, 2013
The Capitol Mall Bismarck – 8:25 a.m.

Channel 7 is broadcasting Hermes' message in real time to the people of North Dakota, to Leon in his office, and to thousands of smartphones and iPads, including several in the hands of folks milling about in the very crowd being monitored by the helicopter's camera. Nathan Goodbrother thinks this technology is marvelous.

"It's instant feedback, Larry," Nathan says to his friend. "A self-referential phenomenon. We're watching ourselves on our own cell phones. Lookie here!"

He shoves his phone under Larry's nose and points with his pinkie. "Notice these two outstanding citizens standing next to the Prairie Pioneers statue?"

"Everything's blurry, Nathan. Blurry people and a blurry statue. That supposed to be us?"

"That *is* us, Larry. Now, whatever you do, don't look up."

Larry immediately looks up at the helicopter.

Nathan swats him. "I just told you not to do that! You gotta be careful. The CIA and FBI are watching us from their satellites, and they have *sharper* cameras and machines that match individual faces with drivers' licenses. Mark my words, Larry, they'll be knocking on your door this afternoon, concerned you're trying to dismantle our economic system."

"This is North Dakota, Nathan. It's a small place. We don't need satellites or computers to connect with *our* people. They see anyone they need to on the street or on the grass outside their window. Hey, I should call Leon. I'll bet he can see us down here from his window. The hell with your sneaky satellites, Nathan. I'll show you the power of the naked eye." He walks around to the back of the statue, places himself in a direct line between it and his buddy Leon's office window, and then punches some buttons on his phone.

While Larry talks to Leon, Nathan leans against the Prairie Pioneer's massive bronze knee and relaxes. He's removed a bit from the frenzy of the chanters and sign wavers, many of whom he had arranged to be on this stage for this drama. He allows the enthusiasm of the crowd to invigorate him. He delights in the fact that it took so little effort to impassion hundreds of these sheep to react to a stimulus they know nothing about. He does, however, wonder who put that note about all this in his truck last week. And who got Sheriff Gaffey to link the Buick deaths with the Prometheus machine? *Someone is playing in my sandbox without my permission.* That thought frightens him. It sends a shiver down his spine.

***

'All the world's a stage, and all the men and women merely players.' Nathan's buddy, William Shakespeare wrote that. Nathan believes most people assume it means that everyone gets to dress in fancy clothes and pretend to be exotic characters. But there is another way, a darker way, to look at it. He believes Shakespeare either emphasized the wrong point in the analogy, or perhaps cloaked it in too much subtlety for the truth to jump out. The world is a stage; he got that right. But most men and women are *only* players. Nothing else. They're only as interesting as the script lets them be, and they can only do what the script directs them to do. Most men and women are essentially machines—agile and capable machines often, but still, they're only machines.

On the other hand, the people who matter, creative men like Bill Shakespeare and Nathan Goodbrother, write and produce the play, and oversee the design and direction so that the effect on the audience is exactly what they, as authors, want it to be.

Nathan figures he's put together at least as many plays as his buddy, Shakespeare. But whereas the Bard limited his work to the theater, Nathan takes him at his word and aims his productions at '*all the world*.' He thinks the English Bard might be pleased with how he's energized this enchanted crowd and manipulated these individual machines now demonstrating on the State Pasture. Nathan understands such very public theater can be a force for good, especially for his own personal good. Sadly, he believes it's underutilized in *all the world* outside his influence.

While Larry talks to Leon, Nathan calls up memories of another extraordinary production, one he'd produced several months before at the Target Center in Minneapolis. He smiles and congratulates himself again for the design of that masterwork. The memory still tingles his nerve endings. "Now that was one great performance." He yells this up to the Prairie Pioneer's twice life-size bronze ear. Then he closes his eyes and blocks out the sound of the tinny horns. He can almost hear Kharyn McDougall's husky voice reverberating about that cavernous theater, setting the mood for *his* recent theatrical masterpiece.

Chapter 7

Friday, May 17, 2013
Target Center, Minneapolis, MN – 10:26 p.m.

For his performance work in Minneapolis, Nathan did not use cheapjack noisemakers. He'd gone high-budget and taken advantage of Miss McDougall's techno-wizards and their ability to pump her voice through amplifiers strong enough to power a third world country, and four semi-trailers worth of loudspeakers. For over two hours they had blasted her voice into 26,000 raucous fans such that, sometime after the show ended, much of that energy still bounced around the place, tingling nerve ends and softening brain tissue. It vibrated at different wavelengths, triggering the firings of different neurons in the cortex of many emotionally spent concertgoers. A stew of ecstatic joy and black anger had still lingered in the minds of the enraptured few remaining on the auditorium floor.

Nathan had taken care to isolate himself from those raw exhibitions of emotion. He waited above it all, in the relative silence of a lushly appointed skybox, positioned high above the displays of exposed passion exhibited by McDougall's 'sweet, God-fearing, blue-collar patriots.' He patiently watched the steam leave the building and observed one group of women holding hands and quietly weeping. Not twenty feet away, a group of men worked themselves into a post-concert emotional lather that might require a physical release, once freed from the restraints imposed inside the building.

He stood quietly in this skybox rented by the Coalition of *Real* Patriots. CO*R*P—a self-serving, big-business-funded political organization, relentlessly pushing for lower taxes and reduced regulation—sponsored this event for the adherents of McDougall's syrupy, patriotic songs which she stuffed with vague references to pseudo-patriotic issues, like self-determination, family values, and cultural purity. CO*R*P hoped that dangling her husky, penetrating voice in front of them might obscure the self-serving aspect of CO*R*P's obvious agenda: to convince these losers to vote *against* their own interests, and *embrace* the business-friendly Republicans.

Most of Nathan's companions, isolated in their skybox, exhibited the outward signs of the wealth they'd accumulated. Most still wore their suit coats as protection from the overcompensating air conditioning necessary to keep the shrimp plump and wine cool up here at this altitude. Nathan, however, dressed himself casually in boots, jeans, and a chamois shirt. He kept his attention focused on the one other non-suited gentleman in the room, the dot-com billionaire Russell Cordoba. With the performance over, and only a few skybox patrons remaining, Nathan maneuvered across the plush carpet and zeroed in on his mark, now slouching his large, pudgy body across a leather couch, balancing a plate of shrimp on his gut, and resting his custom–tooled, leather boots on the arm of an adjacent chair. Cordoba concentrated on a super-sized flat-screen replaying the night's concert. That made him oblivious to other things happening in the room.

Nathan approached his target. "She puts out a powerful message for her people, doesn't she?"

Cordoba paid no attention to him. Nathan turned up his volume. "You enjoy the show, Mr. Cordoba?"

The languid blob popped another shrimp into his mouth. "Yup. Love to hear that little bird sing." But he did not remove his attention from the replay.

Nathan realized he'd have to do the heavy lifting required for this encounter. "Mr. Cordoba, I am pleased that you were moved by the content of tonight's program. However, there is a greater thrill than listening to someone—even someone with as striking a presence as Miss McDougall—and that is actually doing something to foster her spirit of independence in America. I'm wondering if you might be interested in taking your passion to the next level?"

That, at least, got a reaction. Cordoba turned toward him, nudged his cowboy hat an inch or two up his forehead, and made eye contact. "You leeches are all alike," he drawled. "You after some o' my money too?"

"I've got all the money I need, Mr. Cordoba. I'm offering you my help. You badly need it."

"I do? News to me. And you are…?"

"I'm offering you guidance and stability. I am your future."

"Heh, heh. I think my past's more accurate, partner. I'm—"

"I'm deadly serious, Mr. Cordoba. It's in your best interest to pay attention. Your future depends on hearing me out."

"I don't have time for this shit now. I'm busy. Call my office and set up an appoint—"

"By then it will be too late… too late to protect your recent land acquisition in North Dakota. It's vital you give me an hour of your time so I can save you from yourself. But I know you and Kharyn will be busy tonight, and I wouldn't think of upsetting your plans."

Cordoba swung his boots down and stood up, moving quickly for a six-foot-four, three-hundred-pound blob.

"Okay, buddy, you've poked me in a couple of wrong places. I don't know you, do I? How could you know about North Dakota, and how the hell'd you find out about Kharyn?" A bit of crimson shrimp sauce dribbles down his chin. He wipes it with a napkin. "You keep her out of this. Whatever *this* is."

"I don't want to interfere with you tonight," Nathan said. "But for your own good, we must talk. Your jet's not going to be ready 'til noon tomorrow. Some maintenance issue, I believe. And that leaves us tomorrow morning. I want us to meet tomorrow morning, 9:30, at the outside porch on the cantilevered sky bridge at the Guthrie Theater. You'll not be disappointed."

"Who told you about my jet's problem? I only found out an hour ago."

Nathan thrust a card at the surprised Cordoba. "You've been careless, Mr. Cordoba. I cannot afford to allow you to continue such careless behavior. Think of me as your guardian angel. I must watch over you, whether you want it or not. Obviously, it would be better for both of us if you wanted it." Nathan smiled. "I won't go away, Russell. Be there! Tomorrow morning, 9:30, upstairs at the Guthrie."

Cordoba took the card and looked at both sides hoping for some clue as to what was happening.

"Have a great evening, Russell. But be ready to do business tomorrow morning." Nathan turned and quickly exited the almost vacant skybox, leaving the stunned Cordoba still turning the business card over in his hand, thinking it might hold a clue. 'Nathan Goodbrother – shajespeare@yourfuture.org' is printed on one side, and '9:30 – at the far end of the Guthrie's cantilever' handwritten on the other.

Chapter 8

The long blue arm cantilevered off the fourth floor lobby of the dark-blue Guthrie Theater. It extended horizontally two hundred feet like the arm of a giant robot, and reached its fingertips out almost above the churning Mississippi. At the end of that robot's arm, in the up-turned palm of its huge hand, nestled an outrageous porch, accessed by a flight of several steps that tumbled down the robot's wrist. A bit of architectural bravado certainly, though such bravado does indeed befit a theater building. Suspended high above the noise of the Mississippi's rapids, a theater patron can feel a heightened sense of wonder, of drama, and to be honest, of fear. The French architect who designed this flamboyance hoped that experiencing this dramatic space would prepare one's psyche for the drama provided by the next course in the theater itself.

Russell Cordoba exited the narrow escalator into the deserted lounge where many visitors stood while summoning the courage to walk themselves out onto the long arm of the cantilever. He paused a moment, then took a few tentative steps out onto the arm, unable to completely staunch the feeling that, with his ample weight now applied to it, the entire thing might give way. He smiled at the act of manipulation this Goodbrother fellow had designed for him and anticipated an interesting confrontation. He walked quickly to the glass wall at the far end and opened the glass door.

He saw two men in the little garden. Goodbrother was sitting on a stone bench on the right, and another man was on the far side, leaning over the rail taking pictures of the Mississippi. He saw Goodbrother recognize him, wave, rise, and walk toward him. Russell acknowledged the wave. "Morning, Goodbrother," he said.

"Morning, Cordoba. I assume you had a pleasant night."

Russell glared at him. The casual use of his surname, together with this man's intimate knowledge of his relationship with Kharyn triggered an anger button, but he maintained his composure.

"I'm here, Nathan, though I've no idea who you are or what you're selling. This better be quick and you better live up to your hype, or I'm outta here."

"Thank you for meeting me." Nathan pointed to the garden. "Come, it's a nice day. Let's go down into the garden and have our little talk."

"I must warn you, I've a low threshold for fools, so tell me what's going on here quickly, or I'm friggin' gone."

"I appreciate that, Russell. Be assured, you're not wasting your time."

Once they entered the small garden, Nathan walked over to the guard rail and looked down at the churning, white water of the Mississippi, bounding over the rocks a hundred feet below. "Isn't this a spectacular view?"

"It's nice, Goodbrother. But I've no time for chitchat. Who are you? What's this all about?"

The tourist taking pictures over by the far rail quickly stood up, turned, and instantly realized he was stranded in the middle of a serious business conversation he wanted no part of.

"Sorry, gentlemen," he said. "I'll get out of your way. Don't mean to interrupt." He held up his phone. "Have to get photos for the wife. I promised her."

"Information, Nathan. Talk to me! Who are you? And what's this all about?"

"You and I, Russell… we look different, we dress different, we think different, but we've got much in common."

"I don't think so. I got money and you want my money. That's the only connection I'm seeing here."

"Both our fathers started out as dirt poor North Dakota farmers, and both of us sons, me on the east coast and you on the west, educated ourselves, then used that education to build our fortune. Then neither of us could remove ourselves from our Dakota homeland."

"Them's real pretty and poetic words, but it's superficial crap! And you know it. Lotta smoke is all you're blowin'."

"I got much more, Russell. I'm just getting started. In addition to all the ethereal stuff, you and I are both connected to the same piece of North Dakota real estate. And the fact that I know this and you don't means I have an advantage over you."

"What the hell are you talking about? I'm living on my daddy's ranch. You got no connection to that land."

"Don't go pullin' the hick dirt farmer on me. Two months ago, you purchased twenty thousand acres of sand and grass up near the border."

"How the hell'd you find out about that? I set up a double-blind real estate trust. Hid the damn thing offshore… hell, even I don't know where the papers are."

"But I do, Russell. They are in Luxembourg. And the trust is named NostraDamus LLC. Nice touch with the uppercase N and D, but it is way too cute. I used your *Z-Factor* program, and it easily cut through that sort of silliness."

"So you found out about that. Good for you. Doesn't mean just 'cause you know that, we gotta be buddies. You gonna threaten me?"

"That's not the sort of connection I mean. I own the mineral rights to the piece of land you bought from that senile Hollywood producer. I own the oil hiding under your twenty thousand acres of sand and weeds."

"That's… that's preposterous! I read every word of that deed myself, and there's no mention of the mineral rights being sold."

"Technically, you are correct. There is nothing about it on your deed. But in North Dakota, mineral rights are separate from the surface deed. I claimed the mineral rights under your land twenty-three years ago, and properly renewed the claim three years ago when my first claim expired. I have a stamped and notarized copy of the claim to show you. If it makes you feel any better, the man you bought it from didn't know I owned *his* mineral rights either."

"But my deed—"

"Deeds and mineral rights claims are registered in different offices, in different buildings in Bismarck. They exist in separate worlds. The courts are full of suits trying to put them back together, but like Humpty Dumpty, that ain't gonna happen."

Nathan walked over, sat down next to Russell, and put a hand on his shoulder.

"But you are one lucky guy, Russell, and you got lucky once again. I noticed you before the *others* did. My job this morning is to quickly educate you, so you can then make informed decisions."

"Bullshit, Nathan. I don't need no friggin' education."

Russell turned away then quickly pivoted back. "Who do you mean, *others*?"

"Begging your pardon, Russell, but you *do* need an education." Nathan walked over to the edge rail, stuck his head over and made a point of concentrating on the rapids roiling far below.

"You can quit looking down over that ledge, Nathan. I get your point—secret projects are inherently dangerous, and so are you. I should pay attention to what you're offering or, whoops, it's a long, quick fall down to those rocks. Well, friggin' whoop-de-do. You're not very subtle. I get the message."

"I need you to trust me. I'm not your adversary. I need you as a business partner. As surface rights owner and mineral rights owner, we need each other somewhat like a married couple, or two guys on a tandem bike. We are going to have to work together, to be cognizant of the vultures waiting for either of us to move separately, and thus be susceptible to an attack."

"Experts told the previous owner there's no oil under there. Nothin' but sand and rock. I can't even see an oil well within thirty miles of my land. So what good are your oil rights?"

"So far, Russell, everything you've said is correct. But your land *is* within the boundary of the so-called Bakken Formation. And that means that somewhere down there the oil *is* waiting. It is just too expensive to find and develop yet. But perhaps in twenty to fifty years, when some future exotic technology kicks in, and oil prices hit a hundred dollars a barrel, you'll see the well drillers show up."

Goodbrother removes some papers from his coat pocket, briefly reviews them, and hands them to Cordoba. "Here is a copy of my claim to the oil rights under your land. North Dakota land law is extremely convoluted… makes great work for lawyers. Many real estate folks don't know how the system works either. But I'm an expert, and I will agree to educate you. I must persuade you to ally your interests with mine. I will help you see the real value of your land, and I hope that by working together the value of that land can be maximized. I truly believe we can help each other." He extended more papers to Russell. "Here's an outline of my thinking. I want you to take this to your legal guys and have them study it."

Cordoba sat down on the stone bench and leafed through the papers.

"This is amazing, Goodbrother. Is this true? How do you know all this? How can I even think about this… what… venture, until I know who you are?"

"A good question. I've taken great pains to disguise my holdings in North Dakota and elsewhere so as not to arouse any potential opposition, business or political. Such security is absolutely necessary. The oil vultures are circling! I want you to understand how well I have disguised my holdings, Mr. Cordoba, because I believe our interests are most valuable if aligned. As of right now, I can see you, but you cannot see me. That makes you extremely vulnerable to any vulture swooping by." Nathan looked up to the sky, pretending vultures were hovering up there. "I know how to make *you* invisible too."

"It does appear that, on the surface, you've a better handle on security than I do. That's admirable and I'm intrigued. I've been offered many weird business proposals but, I've got to admit, this one is perhaps the strangest."

"I need your answer quickly, Russell. There's a clock ticking. Even as we speak, your enemies in New York and Dallas are moving their pieces around the North Dakota Monopoly board."

"Don't overplay it, Nathan. I'll agree to do my part, study and think about it. And I'll be prompt. I can make quick decisions—it's in my history. But you know that too, don't you?"

He ceremoniously looked over the rail so as to show he's not afraid of heights either, or of Nathan's threat. Then he smiled, picked up his hat, slapped it against his leg, and fit it to his head with a bit of ceremony.

"G'day, sir. Talk to you soon." Cordoba headed up the steps and through the door to the enclosed area. He took out his phone. He understood the seriousness of the situation. He had to get the lawyers involved immediately.

***

Trevor leaned over the rail and took several pictures of the Mississippi bounding over the rocks below him. He heard two voices from the patio behind him, discussing serious business. He turned and realized he would be expected to leave them alone. He quickly headed toward the exit and gestured apologetically as he passed Nathan on the way. "Sorry, gentlemen," he said. "I'll get out of your way, Don't mean to interrupt." He held up his phone. "Have to get photos for the wife. I promised her." He hurried to the stairs, misjudged the first step, and stumbled briefly but caught himself with a hand grabbing the edge of the planter. He then hurried up the stairs through the door into the dark blue arm of the cantilever.

Once inside, he took a seat in the lounge where, without being noticed, he could monitor the traffic to and from the cantilever. After several minutes, he watched Mr. Cordoba exit and then a few minutes later Mr. Goodbrother walked by. Ten minutes after the down elevator swallowed Goodbrother, and thinking the coast now clear, Trevor rose, walked back out of the arm, through the glass door, and down the steps into the garden. He retrieved his phone from the planter where he'd carefully dropped it as he was stumbling. He stopped the recording, then emailed a copy to Kathleen. She'd told him about Nathan, about his theatrical productions, and about his devious ways. He'd been in the sky box last night, overheard Nathan's discussion with Russell, and smiled. I'm a pro, he thought. For a macho Special Forces type guy, I'm a pretty good actor, and can be as devious as the best of them.

Chapter 9

Leon re-reads Steffie's story in the *Plainsman* about Sheriff Gaffey's news conference, thinking he must have missed something big the first time. He's known Sheriff Gaffey for twenty years and knows he wouldn't be so casual as to allow his words to be misunderstood by reporters. Sheriff Gaffey fed this fresh meat to the media wolves knowing the subtlety escaped none of them. He hoped the explosion would generate several dozen clues he might use to solve this mystery. The story says Gaffey assembled several reporters and told them that, based on the state crime lab's test results, he could not legally establish the cause of the two deaths as suicides. Such ambivalence had fooled none of the reporters. They assumed he'd intentionally put murder on the table. Reporters certainly know the word *murder* sells a hell of a lot more papers than do the words *death from unknown means*.

To reinforce the mystery and horror quotient of these deaths, Sheriff Gaffey then told them he'd found that Gupchal's farmland was included in a proposal for an oil refinery about to be reviewed by the state environmental office. Gaffey had told them he could not so easily consider the timing of the deaths and the proposal filing as a coincidence. He was forced to assume the two events belonged to the same story. He strongly suggested that good reporters must do their job and should dig around and find the good sheriff some clues. He certainly had challenged the reporters, but Leon sees no reason for an environmental hothead to rush helicopters, bullhorns, and chanting bozos out to his lawn to disrupt his work.

Rolfes looks out at the crowd. It had grown larger and more energized. He is confused and angry—confused by how the sheriff could find out about that refinery when only the governor and a few others knew of its stealthy approach, and angry that Prometheus neglected to tell him, *the speaker who should know all*, that they'd intended to plop their oily machine down in *his* house district!

"Damn!" he says, then slams the window closed. "Damn sneaky bastards, didn't even tell me they're building it in my backyard!"

Margie hears angry words and rushes in to see what her boss' problem is.

"Prometheus is going to pay, Margie. What gall! Trying to sneak that thing past me. Now this murder thing is dumped in, also in my district! You mix oil and blood and interesting things happen. No wonder these folks are excited. It's got *me* excited. Get me Sheriff Gaffey up in Bottineau. He's got some explaining to do."

"Will do, Leon. But now, just as I predicted, *your* governor, on line one."

"Good. He needs an earful too. If he knew they were putting it up in Bottineau and he didn't tell me, I'll smack the bastard."

Leon doesn't much like *his* governor, and Margie likes him even less. Christopher Sandstrup is a cold, insolent man who doesn't really like people. A Bismarck lawyer with no previous political experience, he'd won a three-way race because a popular independent candidate sucked too many votes from the weak Democrat. Even after almost four years in office, Leon doesn't know the man well because he's an outsider, not a longstanding member of the 'honorable fraternity of elected officials' as an old buddy of his once put it. Sandstrup has few ideas, no vision, little passion to serve, and no gumption. He makes few speeches, kisses few babies, and rarely meets with people. He does have the religious right behind him, and that support resulted in the win four years ago. But he is not running for reelection, apparently assuming a second term would not much increase the monetary value of the word 'Governor' on his resumé. Because of his inexperience and lack of interest, Leon and many others think him a puppet of his Chief of Staff, a Svengali-ish character named Brian Bast. Bast also has soured on the boring Sandstrup. His wagon is now tied to the new GOP gubernatorial candidate, one slightly more lively Arthur Conlin. Leon sighs and punches line one.

"Good morning, Governor."

"If I find out you had anything to do with leaking the refinery story to the press—"

"Stop right there, Governor. You're about to step over the line."

"Brian told me you're skeptical about the viability of the refin-ery, and you could be the one putting bad words on the street, just to sabotage—"

"Bast is an idiot. And you've got a much bigger problem than vi-ability. I'm gonna ask you a question, Governor. And I want a clean answer, or you ain't never gonna get your damned refinery."

"Wait, Mr. Speaker. I'm sorry. Didn't mean... what problem?"

"Where is Prometheus planning on building their refinery? Where, Governor?"

"I don't know, Leon. Brian didn't tell me. Out near Williston, I assume."

"Wrong. It's planned for my district. And that coward Bast did not think it necessary to tell me. He is in big trouble. And he didn't tell you either? Which one of you two is the real governor? I've got some choice words for him. You two can kiss your goddamned re-finery project goodbye!"

"Mr. Speaker, you're on the wrong road. The refinery is a great investment for us. I don't want to scare Prometheus, have 'em run off to Wyoming or Montana. Do you?"

"Are you listening to me, Governor? I'm telling you as plain as I can. Your refinery is dead. It ain't gonna happen. Have Bast call me, so I can yell at him too. You guys are never gonna swing open our vault doors and empty out our bank, just so's they can take our hard-earned money and run it over to Dubai."

Leon slams the phone down. Before he can find his antacid pills, Margie shouts to him, "Your mother's on line two, Leon. Right on time, huh? Two for two!"

"You're awesome, Margie. Even clairvoyant. Bring me coffee. I need caffeine to keep up with Mom."

Leon lives with his eighty-four-year-old mother. She does not live with him. She owns the house. She cleans, cooks their meals, does his laundry, sorts his mail, and hovers over him pretty much like a mom is supposed to treat a son. Leon's been married twice, though neither worked out for reasons he doesn't much think about any more. Just bad choices… both of them. He'd dated Marybeth during his last years at North Dakota State and they had married quickly after graduation. Apparently she never considered that a farm boy might want to go back to the farm after experiencing college in the big city. She hated being in the country surrounded by nothing but corn and cows and didn't stay long before she escaped to Minneapolis.

Theresa came later, after he'd been elected to the legislature. She worked for a fellow House member down the hall, and they had great times partying together. But she kept the partying up even after the wedding, and soon people began to talk. She also fled to Minneapolis. That happened just after his dad died. His mom moved to Bismarck where her family had roots, bought a house down the block from her sister, and offered him a room for when he was in town playing legislator.

Officially, he still lives in Rugby. It's *his* district. His house is there, and he spends many weekends and free time up there talking with his constituents. Rugby is his real home. But, since he's now *Mr. Speaker*, he spends more time in Bismarck and more time at his mom's bungalow, a twelve-minute walk from his office. He sometimes walks home for lunch and often brings a constituent, or fellow member, or any number of his friends. His mom loves that. It gives her something to do.

He appreciates her analysis of the high-intensity discussions fueled by her food. He has a reasonable ability to appreciate innuendo and insinuation, to decipher coded messages, and to read faces and postures for clues of a disingenuous response. But his mother operates at another level. Her mind includes a highly developed data mining software package. She's especially effective since many of his guests make the mistake of thinking she's at the table only to satisfy a maternal duty, or to assure civility, or to receive appropriate compliments on the food. But she misses nothing, remembers everything, and after the guests leave, the two of them sit with a brandy and she tells him who lied, who knew more than he let on, or who should make him wary.

Though he never treats these lunches as public business, the meals at mom's house are political events. Policy and procedural issues might be outlined, coalitions assembled, strategies confirmed, and certainly information exchanged between forkfuls of mom's roast or pie. A satisfied guest might let his guard down and relax a bit. Sometimes that was enough to unintentionally allow some truth to slip out as the scalloped corn went in. And, in order to take the best advantage of his mother's sensory equipment, they both know he must keep her in the loop. So he talks to her often, feeds her background, and fills her vaults with information she can put to use during future mealtime discussions.

"Hello, Mom."

"Leon, I saw in the TV..." His mom puts the TV into the same media box as the newspaper and uses the same words when describing both. She sees things *in* the TV, not *on* it. "...where those awful Prometheus folks killed the poor couple up near Bottineau in order to steal their farm. Even if they're hiding in New York, can't they be arrested?"

"Whoa! Don't jump so fast, Mom. Hold on just a second."

He cups his hand over the phone. Margie puts a fresh cup of coffee on his desk.

"Margie, this is going to be one interesting day. Do me a favor and call Andy Gustofson at the University. He and I are going to link our computers so he can walk me through his harvest projection software. See if he can do it tomorrow instead. I'm afraid I won't be able to find time for real business today."

"Will do. Oh, and when you are through with your mom, your friend Larry Oosterhaus is on line three. I got that one wrong… thought Nathan would have called you first."

Leon shoos her away. "Tell Larry it'll be just a minute."

"I gotta be quick here, Mom, I've got calls waiting. A couple words of warning. The media and the crowd are yelling 'murder' but remember, all Sheriff Gaffey said was that he's not ruling it suicide *at this time*. There's a bit of a gap between that and murder."

"Oh, I understand that," his mom says, as if she thought he'd, once again, underestimated her common sense. "But I also know Gaffey did that for a good reason, and that reason has murder right there in the subtext, screaming to get out. And it's my opinion that he's right. Murder is in there somewhere, and that means you have to be careful, dear. If someone murdered once—"

"Don't get too far out in front of the dogs on this, Mom, or you'll be stranded when they turn and look elsewhere. But I hear you. I'll watch myself. I'm not going to say anything stupid. I gotta go, Mom. Talk to you later."

"Be careful, dear."

"Oh, and I'm not going to make it home for lunch today." He squeezes this bad news in just before he hangs up, to prevent time for her to sneak a little dab of guilt into him. "I think this refinery party's going to keep me busy here. I got phone calls stacking up already."

Leon punches the button for line three. "Hi Larry, you still there? What's up?"

"Look out your window, Leon." Larry yells this into his ear. Crowd noise and party sounds argue with Larry's words and negatively affect the sound quality. "You hear me, Leon? Quite a party out here, huh?"

"I hear you, and I've already noticed the party… lots of people and lots of noise. I even saw it on that new flat-screen you had installed in here. Thanks again for that, by the way. Means I can watch the action from my chair. Whoop-de-do!"

"Doesn't sound like you've acquired your party mood, yet."

"This party's cut your government's efficiency down to single digits, Larry. You should be worried about that."

"There are a couple of very important people hanging with this crowd, Leon. I'll bet you didn't happen to notice them when you scanned the mall with your binoculars, did you? Too busy trying to keep that efficiency rating up?"

"What the hell's that supposed to mean? And my binoculars are in my truck. I've got this view memorized... I don't need optical enhancement."

Larry didn't take his answer seriously. "We're enjoying ourselves out here amidst your constituents, good buddy. I'm going to hand you over to Nathan. He wants to say hi."

The three of them, Nathan Goodbrother, Larry Oosterhaus, and Leon, have hung out together since before grade school in the northern farming town of Rugby. And these three best friends still consider themselves musketeers, as they did as youngsters. 'One for all and all for one.' That sort of thing. Leon is a little put out that he hasn't been invited to hang out with them on the mall. He gets up and looks out the window again.

After some rustling sounds, Nathan's voice comes through. "Are you looking out the window, Leon?"

"What's with the two of you? What do you care if I'm looking out the damned window? I'm hiding in my closet now and I can still hear the noise, even with the door closed."

"Time to get out of your closet, Leon. Look out the window. Over here, next to the Prairie Pioneer statue. Tell me what you see."

Leon directs his gaze to the proper spot at the far end of the mall, and is rewarded by the sight of his two buddies, waving their hats quite energetically to get his attention. "Are you nuts, Nathan? What the hell are you two idiots doing hangin' with all those rabble rousers?"

"We're partaking in an extemporaneous civic event," says Nathan.

"Extemporaneous, my ass!" Leon laughs. Nathan can always make him laugh. He's perhaps the funniest guy he knows. "More planning went into the rally this morning than you two jerks have done all week. I also sense the involvement of beer, even from way up here, even though it is still quite early in the morning. Why don't you two do something useful? Come up here and tell me what the hell's going on down there. And it'd be best for you if you're thoughtful enough to bring me some of that beer. Might be a long day. You two get your asses up here, right now."

"We'll be up shortly, Leon. Got to troll for some information first."

"Well, then, please do. Find out what this ruckus is about. Then maybe you'll tell me how all this got going so fast. This party caught Margie off guard. Somebody has to pay for *that*. Don't ya think?"

"We'll get the skinny for ya."

"Someone did a very smooth job here, Nathan, but I'm confident extemporaneous is the wrong word. Enjoy yourselves. But, since somebody has to be serious around here, I'm gonna get back to work."

***

"He invited us up." Nathan says. "Imagine that. We must've caught him off guard."

Larry laughs. "If I remember correctly, last time I was up there he told me not to come back."

"And that after you brought him the TV, right? So, this time Larry, you behave yourself, huh? Don't spit on the floor—hayseed shit like that."

Chapter 10

"Line two, Mr. Speaker. Yet another of *your* friends, Brian Bast."

He sees her smug face smiling at him through the open door. He shakes his fist at it, then glances at his watch. Only twelve minutes since he hung up on the governor and already his attack dog is off the leash. He punches line two.

"Good Morning, Brian. What's on your—"

"Just talked to the governor, Leon."

Bast, as usual, starts right in with business. He pays no attention to either the standards of polite telephone etiquette or the elevated stature of the Speaker's office. *The jerk doesn't care if I'm having a good morning*, Leon thinks and considers hanging up on him.

"He told me you needed convincing. You gotta understand the need for moving fast on Prometheus' incentive package. How much convincing I gotta do? Should be a slam dunk."

"I got bigger issues here, Brian. Your boss tell you why I'm breathin' fire down here?"

"He said you had trouble jumping on board... told me I gotta twist an arm or two."

"I got several big questions, and the biggest one is why you didn't tell me back at our first meeting with Prometheus that the refinery is planned for my district. You tryin' to sneak that little detail past me? Think I'm some kind of idiot?"

"Who cares where the thing is built? A great deal is a great deal. Who wouldn't like the great jobs? It's a gift to you, Leon. What's to feel bad about? You should be dancin' in the street."

"I'm not letting you off that easy, Bast. You tried to pull a fast one and I don't appreciate it. Not one little bit."

"I think I'd better come over and talk... give you the real story."

"You do that, and you better be contrite. And you better answer me some big questions."

"I don't see questions, Leon. Only one great jobs machine bein' dropped into our lap."

"First, you're dropping it in *my* lap, Brian. And I don't like the mess that might be causin'. And there are other questions you need to answer for me. Question number one for you is—if there's any hint those Prometheus guys used some frontier persuasion on that old couple, does this whole thing get blown out of the water? I, for one, am not going up into the air with it."

"Jesus Christ, Leon. Calm down, will ya? Nobody's trying to tie those poor folks' suicides to the refinery project. Don't let a few environmental wackos hyperventilating in the park distract you. All you gotta think about is *jobs*. Lordy, talk about a jobs bill. This project is a gold mine."

"I'll agree that lots of jobs are at stake, Brian. I'm aware our people must be gainfully employed, but before I follow along behind some money guy from Texas or New York, you answer me question number two—how many unemployed refinery designers and technicians do you suppose actually live up here in Bismarck and are looking for work?"

"Come on Leon, you're starting to sound like those whiney folks outside our windows."

"Or pipeline installers, Brian? Or cracking equipment operators? You might find some of those guys temporarily out of work in Texas, Louisiana, Alberta… maybe even Iraq, but not in North Dakota. You show me how some anonymous hedge fund in New York, spending money from a cloaked investor in China, using a development team from Louisiana, and labor from wherever out-of-work oil guys can be found these days, is gonna have any positive impact on the labor situation here in North Dakota, especially as we already have the lowest unemployment rate in the country—close to zero according to that nifty diagram in yesterday's *Plainsman*."

"You're on the wrong track Leon. You're losing contact with your conservative Republican roots. Concentrate on job creation. That's all you have to worry about. Jobs, jobs, jobs. It's what people want to hear, right?" Bast is so into his 'Jobs for North Dakota' act, he sees nothing else on the table. But Leon knows his problem, and knows he must choose his weapons carefully.

"We've got to talk in person, Mr. Speaker. You must be aware of the unintended consequences of dragging your feet and consider the benefits of swift action."

"That sounds like I should now ask question number three. You're not gonna step over that line from persuade to threaten, are you? Or have one of your goons slip a monetary inducement under my back porch door?"

"Goons? I don't know goons. You're my speaker, Leon. No one can threaten you. But you realize, don't you, that the people of North Dakota are depending on you. We gotta talk."

"You know me Brian. I like to talk. But when you come over, no more trying to sneak an elephant past me in the dark. You bring me solid answers to the questions I've raised."

"I'll be at your office, 10:00 a.m. tomorrow, and I'm gonna bring along someone from HF&G, Prometheus' money guys from New York, and by God he'll give you plenty to think about." Bast rang off quickly. He never did have time for chit-chat. Rolfes puts his phone down slowly. He'll have to be careful. He senses the hint of a threat in Bast's words. But then, there are always threats in Bast's words. He distributes threats like candy. "And you didn't say goodbye, you impolite slob!"

I must get information quickly, Leon thinks. *And I know just who can give it to me.*

Right on cue, Margie shouts, "Steffie just called. She's on her way up."

***

Steffie Cobb understands the ritual. She chats with Margie until Leon is off the phone with Bast, then takes a cup of coffee with her into Leon's office.

"How's my favorite reporter doin' this morning?"

"It's the best time of the year, Leon. Fields ready for harvest, boys back in school, air's not boiling, ground's not frozen. I'm doin' all right."

Leon smiles.

"What's so funny?" she asks. "You don't like my outfit or something?"

"No, no. I just got off the phone with the representative of the dark side. I would much rather talk with you than Brian Bast. You wouldn't want to teach him conversational ethics or an 'acting-po-lite-like-a-human' course, would you? It'd make my life much more pleasant."

"Bast's a barbarian. He's beyond being pressured, even by my considerable arsenal of persuasive tools."

Leon walks his coffee over to the couch and sits next to Steffie.

"How're Matthew and the boys, doin'?" Leon thinks this is the way a conversation should start. But, unlike with Brian Bast, politics is only one of several balls Leon is juggling. He also keeps an eye out for high school basketball talent for his friend, the coach at ND State, and thinks Steffie's younger one will be able to handle college ball. He knows it's important to ask after her boys. And he knows she appreciates it.

Steffie smiles. "Everything's running smoothly back at the ranch, 'cept for the fact that I'm so busy I have hardly seen my boys in a week. That's not good. Nice of you to ask, though I can tell you're more interested in the activity out there." She nods her head toward the window.

"I am that," he says. "Figure you'll be the one to bring me up to speed. You're covering the 'bodies in the Buick' story, right?"

"Yes, I am. And since you've read my stories, you know what I know."

"Awww, don't give me that, Steffie. We both know there's more juicy stuff in your notes and even more inside your head. I want *that* stuff. And I need it before I make a fool of myself in front of some other reporter's microphone. I won't reveal any sources, you know that. This little talk never happened."

"You actually talk to other reporters? Without my permission?"

"Cut it out."

"I understand your position, Mr. Speaker. I'll do my duty, and I'll tell you what I know. I won't tell you everything I know because I'm not ready for that yet. Fair?"

Leon, like Steffie, grew up on the northern tier—the row of counties bordering Canada—and now he, like her, spends most all his time away from that lonely frontier land. He knows she still carries a chunk of the northern tier around with her. He does too. And so do his two buddies, Nathan, and especially Larry, who actually spends most of his time on his cattle ranch when he isn't flying around the world peddling his livestock.

"I think I know more than anyone in the state about the Gupchal suicide story," Steffie continues. "But until Gaffey's news conference I knew nothing about that accompanying refinery project story. Not even a whisper fluttering in the wind. The sheriff forced me to link the two stories, but the mechanics of that linking remain mysterious. For the time being I'm keeping the two files separate, allowing each story to develop its own dynamic and hopefully the real story will soon emerge. My *White Buick Death* file is still pretty thin, but my *Evil Refinery Machine* file is naked empty. I have to mine your files, Leon. I'll trade you Buick murder stuff for Prometheus refinery stuff."

"Sounds fair to me, long as you go first."

"Okay. But understand, I've promised Gaffey I'd keep this off the street."

"Don't worry Steffie. I'll be good. Just so you know though, Nathan and Larry are going to show up shortly, and after they do, I don't expect you to tell me anything I have to keep confidential. So you'd best give me the juicy stuff first."

"Good! Oh, and I did see your two buddies down there, with Neubauer and Jankovich, and a few others. Kind of an unusual crowd for such reputable business folk to be hanging with, don't you think?"

"They're big boys." He grins. "Told them they could hang with whoever they want. So what have you got for me?"

"Okay, here's the sheriff's problem—there is *no* evidence. There's no evidence either way, for murder or suicide. Murderers are sometimes careful folks who try to erase potential evidence, but suicide-committers don't do that. One would normally expect to find *some* evidence hanging around."

"Didn't I read about a note?"

"Yeah. Sheriff found it neatly arranged on Gupchal's kitchen table. Whoever put the thing there presented it so's 'we dumb hicks up here wouldn't miss the damn thing,' according to Sheriff Gaffey. The writing and signature appear to be Gupchal's. The message is a bit cryptic for an elderly farmer, but the preliminary reading from the state crime lab has Gupchal writing it. Gaffey sent the original to the FBI for another opinion and that'll take some time, but it's probably Gupchal's writing. But the bigger question is, why would Gupchal arrange it so precisely in the center of the table for the sheriff to find? That seems odd for a ninety-five-year-old guy committing suicide.

"Gaffey said everywhere he looked it appeared somebody'd placed things like on a stage set. I saw what he saw, and I concur. And there are other things that don't make sense."

"Like what?"

"The neighbor who found the bodies also found their dog locked in the basement. She's a mature dog who'd had the run of that house for years, apparently even slept on the foot of their bed. Why lock her in the basement? That's not the act of someone who loved their dog. It's not even the act of anyone who ever *had* a dog. Although it *might* be the act of someone who didn't want to be bothered by an angry dog while they wandered around the house killing her people and cleaning up their mess."

"Sounds like a reasonable deduction."

"Like scrubbing the house down. There's not a fingerprint any-where, not on the second floor, not on the front door knob, not even on the basement door where one certainly must have been if some-body, especially the Gupchals, locked the dog down there. Gaffey thought no one in the history of suicides completely wiped down all the fingerprints like that before he took his final step."

"I do see the sheriff's problem."

Steffie nodded. "Then there's the gas can. Gaffey found an emp-ty can in the garage smelling of gas, but both the can's bottom and the concrete under it were still moist. That seemed unusual, so he poked around a bit and found a spot behind the shed where even his human nose could smell gasoline-saturated soil. He figured sever-al gallons had been dumped. Gaffey wondered what person, bent on taking his own life, cares whether or not the damn car runs for ten minutes or two hours after his own life is over. Or if he does care, why dump the excess gas way behind the shed and not just on the gravel in front of the door? Thoughts about tidying-up don't usually pop into one's head while committing suicide. The whole thing seems staged. Gaffey thinks some control freak had to be sure the tank emptied before he left the site. Wanted to leave nothing to chance. And the gas can was wiped clean of prints too. Who would clean up a suicide scene like that?"

"Certainly not two farmers in their mid-nineties," says Leon. "It's far too much work, for one thing. The effort alone would kill 'em."

***

Margie knocks and ushers Nathan and Larry into Leon's office.

"Mornin', guys," says Leon. "You both know Steffie Cobb, from the *Plainsman*. She's been telling me the interesting story behind the ruckus outside my window."

"Hi, Steffie," the guys say in unison.

"When she's done, you two clowns are going to tell both of us all you know about this circus."

Steffie smiles. "You know, of course, I can't tell you everything I know. Sheriff tells me I gotta keep some secrets."

"Me too, Steffie," says Nathan. "I know stuff I wouldn't tell my own mother."

"Stay in real time here, Nathan," says Leon. "I know you well and understand you're making an apocryphal statement, but Steffie has a right to know that your mother actually died a dozen years ago. We all understand artistic license, but right now I want only real information from you two goons."

Steffie sits on the couch and relates her redacted version of the sheriff's press conference. The *three musketeers* sit around the smaller of Leon's two mahogany conference tables and listen.

"Ten o'clock Tuesday morning," she says. "That's when everything exploded. The local sheriff—you both know John Gaffey—held his news conference. He announced he'd officially changed the cause of the Gupchals' demise from suicide to unknown causes. That opened a huge door. We reporter types in the room assumed he'd put murder on the table."

"Wow!" Larry says.

"And not just put down delicately, but slammed down with some force. Things at that farmhouse were so strange he's having trouble making them work with suicide. But we all read between the lines and took his words to mean *I'm now treating this as a murder investigation*. You'll notice everyone from Channel 7 to my paper called it murder, even though Gaffey never mentioned the word. The simple truth is, the 'M' word sells papers."

"And certainly stirs up more people," adds Nathan. "And how does this tie in with the refinery thing, Steffie? There's no evidence the refinery developers had anything to do with the deaths, is there?"

"No. However, once Gaffey realized the refinery had targeted Gupchal's farmland, that possibility jumped at him. He thought it improbable, and therefore suspicious, that the deaths—let's call them murders... hell, everyone else is—occurred just as Prometheus submitted that very piece of land as a part of the single most controversial proposal that N-DOPE will ever have to review."

"Wow," says Nathan. "Isn't that one unbelievable circumstance? If it's just a coincidence, it's damn tough luck for Prometheus. It'll act to bog down their approval hearings and probably cost them a bundle."

"And if it's not a coincidence, it may mean someone other than the Gupchals staged this event. But there's no evidence yet that a 'particular' someone did it, or whether the staging was meant to cover a murder or look like a suicide, or maybe neither. It can be read many different ways. It's got the sheriff confused. And until he's not confused anymore, he's going to assume no one is innocent and everyone is potentially guilty."

"How did Gaffey learn the refinery was coming?" asked Leon. "That information is very tightly held. It's an extremely big secret. Even I didn't know where, and it's in my district. Seems strange that an isolated lawman, one unskilled in petroleum facilities development, would have access to such secret information, doesn't it?"

"Gaffey was asked the question, and he deftly avoided answering it."

"I'll bet he did," Nathan says. "Some hacker told him. An eye in Prometheus' office, or ear to their phone system. Nothing else makes sense. Could have been a confidant working at N-DOPE, maybe."

"I doubt John Gaffey is so sophisticated as to have moles planted in state offices," Leon says. "Someone told him a secret, with the express purpose of implicating Prometheus in the Gupchals' deaths. Now Prometheus cannot be cleared of wrongdoing until the cloud of murder hanging over their project is lifted. That'll suck the value right out of that refinery and make it a riskier investment."

"But that also means," says Nathan, "that the someone who leaked to Gaffey cannot be a Prometheus insider. Who would be so stupid as to sabotage their own deal?"

"Steffie," says Leon, "before we go any further with this, I'll give you some background. Several weeks ago Prometheus had a top-secret meeting with the governor and leadership. We were told they were shoving their refinery down our throats and we had better learn how to swallow fast."

"They scared the hell out of Leon," says Larry.

"So," Leon continues, "we three got together up at my farm in Rugby to figure out how we natives should react. There are things we discussed up there that we have to talk over with you now. We've got to act fast, or I'm thinking I'll be finding dead bodies and slick oil spilled all over my district before this is over."

"Yeah," says Larry. "And how do we avoid having it be *our* blood and *our* oil being spilled?"

"You are going to have to be the goddess in this story, Steffie... the one who attacks the Prometheus and Hermes gods, and whoever else flies in to help them," says Leon. "Expose the bastards before they savage our state."

Larry finishes Nathan's thought. "And that goes for the god who's financing the project also. We don't know who that is yet. And you, goddess, have to expose them all."

"I was not prepared for this little surprise, guys. I don't know what to say."

"You don't have any option, Steffie," says Nathan. "If I had big money in this refinery, I'd be mad as hell and start swinging at some-body. They will not take this lying down, not bloodthirsty money guys like them. If I were you, Steffie, I'd expect some pyrotechnics. Things are going to start exploding."

"I wouldn't worry about those guys." Leon counters. "Whoever they are, they have lawyers, and connections, and money, and they should be able to extract their machine from any quagmire it tum-bles into. I just don't know if us Rugby folks can fight them."

Leon points out the window. "So how did this noisy party get put together so fast, Steffie? Must be someone with a high-powered organization. Slogans, people, bullhorns, and that bloody sign."

"And don't forget the helicopter. Whoever got that copter must be connected to some power."

"Might want to use them in your reelection drive," Nathan says. "You realize it's less than two months away and you haven't started to organize anything yet?"

"He doesn't have to be organized," says Steffie. "Polls in his district show him with seventy-five percent of the vote, and there's no Democrat in the race, and hasn't been for a dozen years. Any pre-election-day organization would be a waste of Leon's money. Let his mom do it." Steffie is one of his mom's primary boosters.

"Leon's got till the end of next week to get his paperwork in," says Nathan. "He'll get it done. He always runs his form up to the tenth floor at the last minute."

"But, back to your question, Leon," says Steffie. "Jane Blackburn and Nancy VanderMeer at the *Prairie Preservation Foundation* seem to be the leaders of the partying. They have the experience and organization to pull something like this off. But, I personally think they used inside information. And there's part of me thinks Jane and Nancy are only pawns in this game."

"That's interesting," says Leon. "Any ideas about who the kings or bishops might be?"

"I don't know. The big thing here's the money. Response time's a factor of money, and Prairie Preservation is a normal, college-based organization, which means little money but lots of people-power. But someone shoveled hundred dollar bills onto this fire, and quickly. Couldn't have been much time for planning."

"You have to find the source for that money, goddess," Larry says.

"Will you quit calling me goddess, you idiots? One more time and I'll take out my Uzi."

"They'll behave, Steffie... they're in my office. Please continue."

"Then there's the weirdness aspect to this crowd. It's not the usual leftist, anti-development folks. That word 'murder' acted as a siren and brought in a part of the normally rightist, moral-values crowd, and maybe some fair-play and law-and-order guys. There are even quite a few local business community movers and shakers... not the usual jump-into-a-demonstration types, even on such a lovely fall morning as this."

She looks at Nathan. "Like you two good ol' boys, for instance. I didn't get a straight answer from your buddies Neubauer and Jankovich, so maybe you'll tell me. Why, pray tell, were you down there?"

"*My buddies...* " Nathan emphasizes this so Steffie will know she won't be catching him off guard, "...told me about the murder part after I got there. That surprised the pants off me. I went because I gotta know who's abusing my prairie, and how and why. That goes for my buddies too. It's our job to know about everything having anything to do with land use. I'll admit I have concerns with guys from Texas or Dubai who know a lot about making a quick buck, but care little about big machines stomping through my prairie. And they've got the nerve to do such stomping without my permission... not even a courtesy call."

"That's what really ticks him off, Steffie." Larry runs with his friend's thought. "Many of my rancher and cattlemen friends are concerned that pollution-laden oil equipment, sprouting out of the ground up north will spoil the nature of the prairie." He stretches his legs out and crosses his expensive cowboy boots so she can appreciate the hand-tooled leather. Only someone wearing boots like these can be trusted with the welfare of the ground they do their stomping on. "We don't mind development. We just can't let it get out of control... change the dynamics... ruin the prairie culture like they're doin' out 'round Williston. That's all out-of-state money too."

"Houston north!" says Nathan. "Half the license plates out there shout *Texas*!"

Steffie listens to Larry and Nathan continue each other's sentences, rather seamlessly, like they've practiced the spiel. "I saw you two concerned citizens talking with Charlie. He's another 'save the prairie for things that grow' kind of guy, isn't he?"

"Sure," says Nathan. "He's the reason I came. He called me last night and told me he'd buy me a beer if I came over to the mall. Charlie's paranoid somebody's going to dribble oil byproducts on his pristine prairie. Agribus is heavy into ethanol refining, with a big investment in cropland to supply them with raw product. They're concerned about the health of the prairie."

"Agribus requires healthy fields and happy farmers," says Larry. "That makes for a steady supply of grain for their ethanol plants. Agribus pays Charlie so he'll worry about his prairie!"

"You good ol' boys aren't just a tad bit jealous of those money and development guys, are you? Big agriculture fighting big oil, thinking they'll be sucking all the fat off the local economy? Maybe with a little persuasion big ag can frighten big oil and big money, scare 'em off our lonesome prairie and back to their marble canyons? Leave us out here to ravage the land on our own, thank you?"

"Nice try, Steffie." Nathan laughs, then says, "Do you know what you see when you plop a big city wheeler-dealer down in a North Dakota farmyard?"

Leon and Larry laugh and give each other high fives.

Steffie asks the obvious question. "Okay, boys, I'll bite. I can't be the only one here off the joke, can I?"

"Bullshit!" All three say this in unison.

After a hearty laugh, Steffie stands up, grabs her bag of tools, and makes ready to leave.

"Since the level of discourse here is fast deteriorating, I think I'll exit this here farmyard. You boys have a good time."

"Thank you, Steffie." Leon gets up and escorts her to the door. "Don't pay too much attention to my rowdy friends. They mean well."

Nathan jumps up quickly. "Oh, and speaking of friends, I want you to hear something before you go, Steffie. You've got to understand the bond between us three. It'll just take a minute." He pats Leon on the shoulder, walks over to a shelf on the far wall and picks up a small item. He brings a pocket tape recorder over to her and switches it on. An excited, scratchy voice speaks energetically, as a raucous crowd noise almost overpowers it.

"And Central grabs the rebound, gets it out to Hanson. He brings the ball onto their side of the floor. Only ten seconds left now folks. This looks like it could be over. Wait! Rolfes steals the ball! He's got Goodbrother breaking down the floor, and he hits him with a perfect pass. Goodbrother lays it up, and… it's good. It's good! And there's the buzzer. Rugby wins it! Rugby pulls it out. They're a charmed team, folks. Wow, what a perfect pass, just out of the reach of the Central hands! Wow! What an ending! Rugby wins the championship! Rugby wins the championship!"

Nathan clicks the tape off.

Steffie sees emotion, still evident on all three faces.

"That guy's right, Steffie," Larry says. "Leon throws the perfect pass. Nathan grabs it, one step, one dribble, then carefully lays it off the backboard and into the net, and with only two seconds left on the clock."

Nathan confirms. "And Larry is right behind me if a rebound's necessary, but it's not, and we both run to mid-court, Leon jumps into us, and we all three go down. Then the rest of the team piles on."

"You two don't miss a shot." Leon, as usual shifts the credit to his *twin towers*. "All night it's swish, swish, swish. There's magic in the room."

"We win the state championship. We upset heavily favored Bismarck Central. What a high!" Nathan says. "Some might argue that high still lingers, Steffie, especially when we three goons get together in a room."

"And Leon makes the whole thing work. He's our assist wizard. He always finds one of us big guys for an open shot. He pulls the defense with him, then fires a pass back against the flow. He's the master of the outlet pass, like the one to Nathan to seal the championship. Leon, the assist wizard." He raises an imaginary glass in tribute. "Always makes us two bozos look good."

Leon gives Steffie the *aw shucks, it weren't nothin'* look.

Nathan counters it. "We understand his contribution. We gave him the game ball for his efforts." He points to the ball on the shelf behind Steffie's head where he'd picked up the small recorder.

"Leon's the man!" shouts Larry. "The assist wizard."

Steffie checks to make sure she has all her stuff. "Thank you for sharing that, Nathan. You're right, it's hard to know what makes Leon tick if I don't consider you two goofballs right there with him. I knew all that basketball stuff before, you know. I'm a Rugby High girl. You guys got me by fifteen years or so, but your legend's still very much alive up there.

"And I notice you guys are talking about that night in the present tense. Do you realize that? The dynamic between you hasn't changed for forty years. You two both still see Leon as your assist wizard."

She exits the room, closes the door, and walks past Margie. "Those guys are livin' in a time warp," she says.

"Something other than time is warped in there, honey," says Margie. "That's for damn sure."

Chapter 11

After Steffie leaves, Leon notices the atmosphere in his office change. A chilled, deliberate vapor seeps in, one more appropriate for serious discussion. It replaces the close, warm atmosphere of affinity. He checks the windows to make sure they're tightly closed.

At the credenza, Larry pours splashes of bourbon into three glasses.

Nathan seats himself at the table and motions to Leon. "Come over here under the *dome of silence.*" Nathan actually reaches up with his hand and pretends to be pulling cables. He watches the invisible dome of silence descend from the trap door concealed in the ceiling.

Leon swats him.

"We've gotta talk serious business for a bit. Let's reconvene the meeting we had at your farm a few weeks ago."

Leon understands these two. They're never far away from serious business. They can perceive a business opportunity, or business threat, poking its head out from behind a rock in any landscape, especially the barren flatland prairie of northern North Dakota. Leon is sure these two have caught a scent of something wafting through the mall, and now he is about to be let in on it. "Okay, you guys. I understand. It's time to get serious. What's going on?"

"Things are happening fast, Leon... way too fast for the good of North Dakota. We've got to slow things down."

"Come on. I'm tired already. And I'm afraid to ask this, but just who do you mean by *we*, kemo sabe?"

"By we," Nathan laughs, "I mean the good people of North Dakota, as led by their representatives, elected and otherwise."

Leon glances toward the ornate ceiling. He senses that dome of silence slowly descending, pressurizing the atmosphere beneath it.

"First, we have this Prometheus refinery come screaming in at us from New York or somewhere, then this murder thing jumps out of a lonely farm—all this happening just as the harvest is due, and just as the election circus is, or should be, grabbing our attention. Things are being pressurized." He glances up toward the descending dome. "Stuff's threatening to implode. That's not good, Leon. We, and by *we* I do this time mean *you*, acting as the people's chief representative of this state, have got to take control here."

The dome of silence drops another foot. Leon feels it tingling the few hairs remaining up there on his own dome. "You forget, Nathan. I'm not the chief representative. That would be our wonderful governor."

Nathan pays no attention. "Prometheus and their investors are on the fast track. Get in and out in a hurry. That's how they make their fortune. And they care nada about collateral damage."

"It's like rape, Leon," says Larry. "Let's call it what it is—*state rape*."

Leon winces. "That's awful. Even for you, Larry."

"And it's gonna get worse. Larry and I were talking down on the green with a few of the guys and we feel that the Gupchal murder story can be used as an informational crowbar to foul the gears of Prometheus' machine before it plays chicken with North Dakota's economy."

"Foul! Foul!" Leon yells. "Too many metaphors in a single sentence."

"Concentrate, Leon. Prometheus' mad rush through N-DOPE approvals can be substantially slowed if we solidly link that murder story to that refinery proposal story."

"And so you two are now going to show me exactly how they're linked, right?"

"Oh, we can't do that, Leon. I can't imagine they are *actually* linked."

"What's that mean? Don't you see that humongous sign out there aimed at my window? It looks to me like that's what the hubbub is exactly about—it's the murder-refinery linkage."

"Oh, no, no, no!" says Nathan. "That's what the hubbub is about certainly, but the unsophisticated rabble out there doesn't get the real story here either."

"And," says Larry, "that's exactly what Prometheus wants all us stupid peasants up here in the boonies to think it's about."

"And that's the beauty of this," says Nathan. "We three muske-teers can use the appearance of a linkage to get that real story out, and that will kill Prometheus' refinery deal. But first, a little story."

"Aw come on, Nathan, I don't want a story."

"Yes, you do. Remember Larry's little joke about rape? For the purposes of illustration only, let's say that Larry here wants to have his way with a pretty, young, unsophisticated farm girl. One thing he will *not* do, as he steps into her foyer, is say, 'Hey, honey! I came over tonight to rape you, so let's get at it!' Besides being crude—and Larry's not a crude guy—it probably won't work."

Larry attempts a pout, as if he's been wronged. "Crude guys don't target high class girls, ones with foyers."

"No offense, Larry. Just an example."

"I understand, Nathan. And you're right. I'm way more suave and debonair."

"Exactly, Larry! And you're not even from New York."

"Can we get back to my question? Hell, I can't even remember what it was any more."

Nathan doesn't flinch. "The answer, Leon, is 'no.' Of course Larry wouldn't do that. Larry would take her out to dinner and maybe a show, buy her flowers and candy, hold her hand, open the doors, carry her across the puddles, and by the time they got back to her place with brandy and soft music…" Nathan smiles. He's actually proud of his crude metaphor. "Like he just told you, Larry's far more sophisticated than those Neanderthals at HF&G."

"Time out!" says Leon. "How do you guys know HF&G? That name's so secret even I didn't know it until Brian Bast let it slip out beneath his squirrelly mustache about an hour ago. If their name's such a big secret even I can't handle it, how come you two bozos know?"

"That's the kind of secret stuff real estate guys like me have to know, Leon. I have eyes. I have to know who's waving the stack of thousand dollar bills and enticing the speaker of my house to jump over the crevasse to the dark side."

"Cut it out, Nathan! I want no more of this rape and enticement garbage. Just tell me what the hell is happening to my state. Damn! This used to be such a sweet job. Maybe I won't run for reelection." He cranes his neck and looks dreamily up into the dome of silence. "I'm seeing a beach in the Bahamas, and a sweet girl in a yellow bikini calling my name."

"Run away to the Bahamas if you want to," says Larry. "But mark my words, *enticement and rape* are what those New York goons are planning for sweet, innocent, Miss North Dakota."

"It's not about Prometheus' stupid refinery," says Nathan. "It's about that shadowy bunch, HF&G, taking bags of money out of North Dakota. If HF&G has its way, the project gets quickly approved, and then just as quickly HF&G sells both the development company and the project to some Arabian Emir, or Texas oil billionaire for a bundle. They can make all sorts of promises that way and will never be around when implementation is a question. Somebody we never heard of buys Prometheus Inc.—now, thanks to HF&G, saddled with massive debt—and takes over.

"And the bigger problem is that I see no consensus that a large refinery project up by the border is a prudent thing to do. Long term it may be viable, but not now. And none of that prognosis has anything to do with things happening now in North Dakota or Canada. The Saudis will control the price of the world's oil for the next fifteen to twenty years, and global warming legislation will control the quantity being pumped. With such price and quantity controls, in fifteen years any refinery may be a worthless piece of junk. Who is going to risk any money on that now? Only those who can get in and get out in a hurry. Unfortunately, Leon, I think that's what HF&G is doing—they make their quick bucks and then sneak out the back door." Nathan throws both his hands up toward the ceiling, feigning despair, almost smashing his knuckles on the dome of silence. "Then gullible Miss North Dakota, to continue Larry's metaphor, gets screwed again."

"And I am afraid, Leon." Larry takes a pause to top off Leon's glass from the decanter—a bald attempt to emphasize that more courage will be required for his next step. "I am afraid that you're going to have to be the one here who stands up, yells *rape,* and alerts our poor damsel to her peril, before she's assaulted."

"Who else will do it?"

"As we speak, HF&G is promising huge wads of cash for a guarantee of quick N-DOPE approval. The speed of this gambit is the real problem. We unofficially, and you officially, have to take immediate steps to slow this thing down—not allow Mr. Hedge Fund access to the poor damsel's bedroom. Oh, I can see it now— the thin line of blood trickling from the bedroom across to that foyer…"

"Cut it out, Larry. I get the point. Don't give me the graphic video." Leon feels the dome's heating element starting to roast his scalp.

"Larry can get carried away sometimes," says Nathan. "But he's right. And I think this murder talk has the potential to slow things down. Maybe throw a bit of mud and suspicion on our suitor to make him appear less attractive. Peel back his mask to reveal his pimply, ugly side. That might allow our damsel time to call 911, maybe even a friend, some virtuous lad willing to man up and extricate her from—"

"I get it! I get it! You two are overplaying the rape metaphor just a tad. But I get your point. HF&G may have already delivered some flowers to His Honor, and his buddy, Bast. I've heard from both of them this morning and they're hot to trot. They even threatened me, promised dire things will happen if I don't partner up, and quickly."

"Don't take those threats lightly, Leon," says Larry. "HF&G can back them up. Just ask those poor farmers upstate in their Buick."

"You don't know that, Larry. Bast's a hot head, sure, and at times an idiot, but even he wouldn't stoop to murder."

"I believe you Leon, but I don't know this shadowy New York group. *They* just might do it. Or they might capitalize on it—allow it to stand as an example of their determination, even if they had nothing to do with it... which, by the way, even I don't think they did."

"I'll find out more tomorrow. Bast's coming over to educate me." Leon has this awful feeling that he's about to step off the cliff without his parachute. "What do you think? Should I punch him in the nose?"

"I don't know right now, *kemo sabe*."

"You two get out of here."

Nathan and Larry prepare to leave. Leon's received their message. He feels it simmering in the dome just above his head.

"I've a feeling all hell's going to break loose in the next couple days, Leon. So we'd better be thinking about how to tiptoe out of this mess without getting it all over our shoes."

"You've butchered one too many metaphors, Nathan. Get out."

Nathan and Larry turn and, like two Vaudevillian clowns, prance out of the room silently on their tiptoes as if they are leaving that poor damsel's bedroom, not wanting to wake the drunken husband sleeping on the couch. With one finger sealing their lips, they wave lamely to Margie as they sidle past her desk. Larry, very quietly, and very slowly, closes the outer door behind them.

Margie asks Leon, "Are you going to tell me what *that* was all about?"

Chapter 12

After his buddies leave, Leon peeks out the window and sees that professionally produced sign hanging from the trees, still aimed straight at him: KILL THE REFINERY; NOT OUR FARMERS. He has to admit the phrase has a certain flair—a concise political statement, aimed straight at the jugular.

Margie brings him coffee and some reports, puts them on his desk, and assumes the pose of his conscience and guru, her hands on her hips and the *look* in her eye.

"Even I, who understand those two gentlemen quite well, cannot begin to fathom what they are up to, prancing out of your office like that. What went on in here, Leon?"

"It's called theater, Margie. Nathan and Larry put on a little show for me and they're having trouble getting themselves out of character. They're suggesting I must do something, although they're not being specific as to what it is I have to do."

Margie stops in the middle of straightening his desktop and gives him the two-barreled version of the *look*.

"What? I suppose *you* want to tell me what to do too, huh? Jeese, everybody knows what I should do better than poor little ol' me." He drinks some coffee, runs both hands over his forehead, then looks up, checking to see if the dome is still there.

"You know, don't you Margie, that certain gods I have no control over wrote the rules that apply to political discourse?"

Margie steels herself for another of her boss' philosophical parables.

"Being a diligent sort, I've been able to memorize a few, over the years. There's Rule number seven—only twenty percent of voters are passionate about any one issue, and the rest don't care. Rule number twelve says in the primary you push the edges, in the general, push the center. And rule number twenty-two... voters don't care about programs and policies."

"Will this rant end soon? I've got work to do, you know."

Leon could go on. His rules have one thing in common; they tend to push interest and passion toward the extremes and leave a big void in the middle. That void gets little attention from the news coverage or the legislature.

"The people demonstrating down there are not your average Joes," he says. "They don't pay my salary or expect me to take sober, efficient, actions on their behalf. They're the ones balancing on the fringes."

Leon points to the window with one hand and the TV with the other. "Listen, Margie, we both can hear that fringe now. It happens every election cycle. We Republicans love the refinery idea. You know the drill—jobs, jobs, jobs. We have a national, self-interested constituency that rakes in lots of money from hedge fund guys, religious values organizations, the Chamber of Commerce, big oil companies, et cetera. The louder they yell, the more money the buffoons throw at them. Many Democrats are also in favor of a refinery. They want the union jobs it will bring. Then you got the rabid lobbyists on the left—the nature lovers, the 'save-our-prairie' folks, Indian rights interests, and environmental wackos. None of them want a refinery in their back yard.

"And think of my district up in Rugby. Remember, all this refinery and murder theater stuff is being staged in *my* district, Margie. How do those good people want me to react to all this hoopla?"

"Probably just like you are reacting, *Mister Speaker*."

Leon's antennae tingle whenever Margie uses his formal address in that tone. It indicates she spoke her words *ex cathedra* and that he had better pay attention.

"And, O' Swami who knows all, how am I reacting?"

"You are thinking all this hoopla is reflective of self-interest. On the one hand, you see big money and power interests, eager to make some easy money. On the other side, you see scared farmers watching the apocalypse tromping across their wheat fields from the east. They see you in the middle. You are speaking with the voice of reason."

"You're in Nathan's theater group too, huh?" Leon turns away from the window and heads back to his desk. "I'm not sure, Margie… although that apocalypse did run through my mind a few weeks ago."

"The apocalypse comes in different guises, Leon. For some it looks like gay marriage or higher taxes, and for others it's a dirty oil refinery."

Leon can hear another apocalypse rumbling in his stomach right now, and it sounds awful. It feels awful too. He opens a desk drawer and removes a couple antacid tablets. He can fix his stomach rather easily. His lovely state of North Dakota is a nastier problem, and he hasn't a clue as to what medicine *she* requires.

***

Same Day
HF&G's Office in New York, 10:30 a.m.

J.D. Crowe stands in front of his window and watches the city activity below him. He's looking for answers. He knows they must be out there, but they're not visible now. His phone buzzes.

"You've a call parked on line six, J.D. A Brian Bast. Says he's from Bismarck. Where's that, Germany?"

"Close, Angelina. It's far away, and no place you'll ever visit. This can only be bad news. I think I want Enrico in on this. I'll take the call in his office. Let him know I'm coming over, then tell Mr. Bast I'll be with him in two minutes. Thanks."

J.D. walks down to Enrico's glass cage with the great view of the city below and Lady Liberty in the distance. *No office in Bismarck has a view like this!*

"Thought I'd better have you listen in on this call, boss. It's from North Dakota—the governor's toad, Brian Bast. That slimy meatball would never call me unless something messy's hit his fan. Sorry, but I'm too much of a chicken to listen to this all by my lonesome. I'd like to assess your reaction before I go out there and bludgeon that Goddamned weasel."

"I agree, J.D. Let's hear what problem's bothering your slimy meatball." He punches a button, then nods toward his junior partner.

"Crowe here, Brian, with Mr. Francelli. I'm assuming this call means things are not all rosy out on the lonesome prairie?"

"I need help fast, Mr. Crowe. You want us to accelerate the state infrastructure and tax contributions. But I'm getting resistance from Speaker Rolfes—massive resistance. Both the governor and I yell at him and get nowhere! He's a one-step-at-a-time kind of guy, not a strategical thinker. He wants to evaluate options. Wants to study and research. What kind of shit is that?"

"So why are you calling me, Bast? D'ya think maybe I'll say a secret word and magically the sun comes out? Can't you dimwits tie your shoes without calling me? For Christ's sake, you've got to figure it out for yourself. I'm a busy guy. And I don't have a magic wand."

"I don't much believe in wands, Mr. Crowe. Speaker Rolfes is sitting in the middle of the road like a big rock. I need big machines, and some freakin' heavy-duty guys drivin' 'em. I need your big machines to push him out of the way."

"I don't need to hear this. What? You can't find any machines yourself?"

"I've set up a meeting with him tomorrow morning at ten. I think it would be in your best interest to fly out here and smack him. You can be back home by cocktail hour. Not a big investment."

"I beg your pardon, Mr. Bast, but that's a *huge* investment. You gonna pay my twenty-thousand-a-day fee?" Crowe winks at Francelli.

"Plus expenses," Enrico says. "And remember, my percentage comes out of that too."

"Christ's sake!" says Bast. "I'm working for *you* here, Mr. Crowe. Take it easy. I just want to move this Rolfes guy for *you*. I'm not the bad guy."

"Are you suggesting I'm a bad guy?"

"You're goddamned right. That's exactly what I'm saying. And I want a bad guy out here quick. Like tomorrow. And you gotta bring the explosives that can move the goddamned rock off my goddamned highway."

J.D. looks over to his boss. Enrico nods. "Okay, Bast. Set up that meeting. I'll hop out there and bring my bludgeon."

"Good!" Bast says, then disconnects the call.

"What a weasel," says Francelli. "Not even a thank you, or a goodbye. I don't feel good about the competence or dedication of the public servants we must deal with out there. Go see what you can do. Keep the charade up for another week or two. After that, I don't care what rocks Bast might find blocking his road."

"I'm thinking I might take Martin Pick with me. Let him talk to that sheriff. Flash a bit of artillery; do some shock and awe. It might make an impression."

"Good idea. Have Angelina call our crew in White Plains. They can get the jet ready. You can go out tonight; have dinner and a good sleep. Then tomorrow morning, you do some smashing. You push Bast's rock off his highway."

Chapter 13

Leon has seen the pretty pictures, the high-tech graphics, the computer generated charts and diagrams, the razzle and the dazzle. A few weeks ago, at Prometheus' initial presentation, he watched as even his governor and Brian Bast laughed at the clean-shaven, multiethnic workforce with their crisp, white uniforms and yellow hard hats, driving their spotless trucks and erecting glistening stainless steel tanks. He'd leaned over and told the Senate President, Deric Olson, that it "seems less an oil refinery than a theme park."

Deric had laughed. "Not a bad idea, is it, Leon? A big oily machine as a theme park. Great educational stuff! Teach us hicks 'bout the Industrial Revolution."

They'd laughed about it then. But Leon now thinks the comment accurate. They'd been told very little, and nothing substantive, about the refinery project in that secret meeting in that hot, semi-darkened room. Prometheus' inspirational videos with patriotism-infused soundtracks served up lots of fluff but only a tiny portion of meat. Leon recognized the darker message, the not-too-veiled threat: *you doofuses are going to accept our project immediately and throw great sums of money at us quickly, or we're going to Wyoming.*

Prometheus' hoopla-laden preliminary meeting reminded Leon of the preliminary activities at a basketball game, with cheerleaders bouncing around, pep bands playing, and players running preset drills to show off their cool uniforms and to impress the fans. It's supposed to get everyone worked up. But the team members know the real game doesn't begin, and the real opponent doesn't materialize until the whistle blows and the clock starts. He thinks that maybe all the noise he heard outside means the game's about to start. With the big clock now ticking down to zero, he'd better get his mind in this game.

Earlier this morning, Leon had made some quick, knee-jerk responses to Bast's remarks. But they were pre-game, show-off stuff and he'd nothing to substantiate them. He must get himself some hard facts for tomorrow's meeting. And Leon knows people who'll enlighten him, such as Sandy O'Donnell, the head of the State Development Office. Although one of Bast's cronies and a big, rah-rah business guy, he conscientiously works hard for the state and does a lot of good. Unlike Bast, he has a pleasant personality as befits a development guy, and he's been quite successful pulling in some business from Minnesota and Wisconsin. Leon gives him a call.

"Hey, Sandy, how are you doing? Speaker Rolfes here. I find myself in need of enlightenment. You got a few minutes to give me a crash course on this oil refinery project? Just the basic stuff... people involved, pluses and minuses, outlook for jobs?"

O'Donnell isn't a cabinet officer for nothing. He knows Leon's problem. "Those numskulls marching outside your window getting to you, huh?"

"They certainly are, and so is your boss, Brian Bast, tellin' me salvation is on the way. I want to be sure of what I'm doing here. Ya got twenty minutes to fill me in?"

"Sure, Leon. Come right over. I'll even spring for a cup of coffee."

***

After talking to Sandy for only ten minutes, Leon has collected two yellow-tablet pages of notes. Sandy tells him that the developers do indeed have this thing on a fast track, and they are fully intending to steamroll it through approvals as quickly as possible. Sandy, however, can't give him a reason for such speed. Leon senses even Sandy, a pro-business friend of the Chamber of Commerce, seems a bit taciturn and less a cheerleader for Prometheus' machine than he expected.

"The Canadians are ready to ramp up production because they think they've solved the technology problems of extracting Alberta's oil-sand deposits. They're pushing hard to construct their huge Keystone Pipeline down to Louisiana, where most of the current North American refining capacity is located. That way they can more easily export the stuff to the Chinese. And they're running a pipeline east where most of their internal need is located. There is nothing in all this for the US, let alone for North Dakota, that I can see."

"What's that pipeline got to do with HF&G's refinery?"

"Canadian oil is gooey, expensive to mine, dangerous, and worst of all it's difficult and expensive to pump. A refinery in northern North Dakota, built close to the Canadian border, and feeding into either of those existing pipelines would, so the story goes, have an unending source of supply. And the Canadians could pipe that sweeter product faster, all the way to their eastern provinces, and not have to spend the big money to pump it east or refine it.

"Sorry, Leon. I'm not being a good host. You want coffee, or beer, or something?"

"No, I'm fine. All I need is information. I have a meeting with an HF&G guy tomorrow, and I gotta build a foundation. I still don't get it. Why build a refinery?"

"Pipelines are short-term things, whereas refineries are forever. They need a refinery in case the Keystone project doesn't work and, even if it did, to generate some financial leverage on the Louisiana refiners to keep them honest. Know what I mean? So, behind the scenes, they're pushing hard for some developer to take that chance and build a refinery to apply that leverage. Alberta, most likely, will throw much of their own money at it. It'll ease their financial imbalance up there, especially if oil prices drop. It'd be a good deal for them, and might, if oil prices don't drop too far, be structured correctly so as to be a good deal for North Dakota too."

"But you're sayin' we gotta understand this subtle stuff if we're to ensure North Dakota gets a good deal?"

"Ah, Leon, that there's the tricky part. With everyone being so sneaky and running so fast in the dark, I'm not at all comfortable we, at the state level, can *ever* control the deal. And because Houston oilmen own most of North Dakota's expensive oil, we can't allow Alberta and Louisiana to push us where *they* want us to go. North Dakota must start thinking about our own long-term goals—ensure our *own* objectives, which protect *our* position in the market. And, Leon, none of that thinking is getting officially thought. Not that I know of, anyway."

"So you think Prometheus wants to ram their monster through before we start thinking about all the debris that might soon be littering our lawn?"

"Exactly! We're now ranked second, behind Texas, for barrels pumped. Most of the easily reachable stuff has already been divvied up. Much of the rest of it is eight to ten miles underground, and it's much trickier and more expensive to extract. But sooner or later, if or when higher prices can be stabilized, those deep deposits may become more viable. Whoever owns the refinery when that happens owns a money-making machine, nicely located, with minimum pipeline costs, and able to process the crude from those fields as well. It could be a good deal if the timing works out or an extremely big turkey if it doesn't. It's a huge gamble. The timetable is long term, and the big question for you guys in the legislature is who gets stuck with the turkey if the timing doesn't work?"

"You mean," said Leon, the full weight of the thing smashing him, "that the money guys pushing Prometheus are too smart to get left holding the slimy turkey. They'll find a way to make a buck on the thing before they ditch it. So Sandy, my question is… how must this hick lawmaker respond to this threat so as to ensure North Dakota's not the one that gets caught holding this crippled bird?"

"Exactly! And other uncomfortable sub-arguments are strung through this project. Both North Dakota and Canadian oil is expensive to extract. Both sources require high international oil prices to be profitable. Canada imports a gazillion barrels of cheap Saudi crude under long-term, fixed-price deals. That means they are hedged, and Dakota is not. If international prices fall, say below fifty dollars a barrel, the Dakota fields will be forced to shut down production before Alberta does.

"Like I said, the Canadians want to throw money at a northern refinery. And there's evidence that some investors are looking at grabbing that money. But it seems Prometheus beat everyone to it. Some think the first guy to submit a package wins, or at least has a huge leg up. However, he also takes the bigger gamble, and that first guy in also has the biggest chance to fail. And that failure will unwittingly illuminate the pathway for the second guy, who might have an easier time navigating the pitfalls to approval."

In one five-minute conversation, Leon learns the reasons for all the pressure he is being put under, and it doesn't have much to do with the interests of the good people of North Dakota. It's all about out-of-state carnivores fighting for a piece of ripe meat. The potential downside of this super-hyped project reinforces every argument Nathan and Larry made to him in their nutty 'state rape' discussion.

Leon next talks with Clayton Vollmar, at the Department of Labor, about jobs. Clay tells him a refinery would produce local jobs, but mainly for construction of the state infrastructure improvements needed—roads, drainage channels, and inspection facilities. However, the idea of *new* jobs is an illusion, since they'd be funded with state money that simply replaces funds authorized for existing state projects approved by the legislature. The big source of local jobs would be the temporary service sector and support for the transient construction workers, like motels, restaurants, auto service, and fuel supply. Vollmar, not much of a jolly guy, doesn't smile when Leon adds brothels to his list. Vollmar sees few long-term jobs benefiting the existing local population.

"I live up in Rugby, Clay. And as far as I can tell, there is no population up there to worry about; the few natives are already working two jobs."

And Vollmar tells him that once operational, the refinery will need several hundred technical workers from Louisiana and Texas, and some low-level maintenance and service jobs for illegal immigrants. But, except for truck drivers and heavy-equipment operators, there's not much of the good stuff for the folks of North Dakota. And even most of those jobs will be filled by out-of-state talent because every North Dakota truck driver is already busy driving a truck. And every new truck is owned by out-of-state interests and leased to other dark entities in Houston, which then sublease them to the local contractors. There's not much income for good old North Dakota in that money trail either. The situation would parallel the current situation in Williston, where many non-technical, service-sector jobs are filled mostly with newcomers from out of state. All the high-priced technical talent comes from out of state too, and these guys will move to the next boom area after North Dakota gets sucked dry or oil prices fall. He sees no long-term help for native North Dakotans.

By late in the afternoon Leon has talked with industry experts, state department heads, and other folks with differing perspectives on both sides of the issue. He's filled a couple dozen sheets on his yellow legal pad. He can now go home, sit out on his patio with coffee or a beer and review all this stuff. He must digest it before his battle with Bast and be ready for the next session with Nathan—because he knows that, back in his office, the echoes of that rape discussion still reverberate in the dome of silence.

***

Same Day
HF&G's Office in New York – 3:30 p.m.

By the middle of the afternoon, Enrico Francelli finds himself in a funk. He's having one of those days when absolutely nothing goes right. It started early with the news broadcast from Dakota showing those white H, F, and G letters aimed smack at him. And it went downhill from there. But Francelli knows how to remedy a funk, and at 3:30 he surrenders. He grabs Angelina, hails a cab, and escapes to his club. He slouches comfortably on an isolated couch in a dark corner of the back room, his head on a soft fluffy pillow, intent only on nibbling Angelina's ear. After a few scotches he feels his headache ease and his muscles relax. It's now possible that his problems can be more fully illuminated, as can the paths to their solutions. The easing of the weight of these several burdens suddenly jolts him. A fresh, perfumed air swirls in and replaces the smog. But enlightenment brings with it a horrible thought.

He slams his open palm on the coffee table. "Damn!" Ten dollars' worth of single malt scotch splashes onto the table top.

Angelina jumps and smacks her knee on the woodwork. "Ouch," she whimpers. "What'd you do that for?"

Feeling suddenly naked, she scans the room to assess the embarrassment potential. Two other couples hidden in other corners seem absorbed in their own worlds. She thinks maybe the damage is minimal.

Then Enrico slams the tabletop again. "Five fucking years!" More jumping from both the scotch and Angelina. A third slap and the pain bites into his fingers.

"That crazy bitch!"

The hidden couples now turn and stare at them. Angelina recoils and flushes red, and her face now matches her dress. "Enrico! What's gotten into you?"

"I need air," he says. "I need to cool off. You have another drink. I'll be back in a bit."

He grabs what remains of his scotch and stomps through the French doors and outside to the courtyard. He sits rigidly on the stone ledge that surrounds the gurgling fountain. Two starlings argue in a bush, and a couple of pigeons waddle up to help. He kicks at them.

"Could that vampire boil an anger for that long? Five fuckin' years?"

He quickly answers his own question. "Damn right!"

He kicks at another pigeon. "Take that, Kathleen!" If only it was as easy as kicking pigeons. Francelli and his partners kicked Kathleen out of HF&G after only four years. She'd been the reason, or at least one of the primary reasons, behind both of his divorces and several other family wrecks the firm sustained. She was incendiary. Everything she touched exploded. She did, however, know how to work a hedge deal. He couldn't fault that. And she'd made him semi-trailers full of money. But the price! Like Sherman through Georgia, she'd left a swath of charred devastation spread out behind her, affecting his firm, his client list, his bank account, and of course both his marriages. She had strange powers, somewhat like coke does. She could make him do illogical things. He wasn't able to help himself. He'd even threatened to kill Crowe for the act of introducing her to HF&G.

She had a powerfully attractive force field. "She *is* like coke," he says. "So sweet. But so toxic." He couldn't leave her alone. He had needed another hit. So five years ago he had attempted a reconciliation with her in Houston, and once again he allowed her to stick her fangs into his neck. That soap opera took six months to play out. It cost him two large clients, a major chunk of money, and his third wife almost shot him.

Kathleen insisted, "Forget New York and move to Houston with me, or I'll kill you." She'd promised to kill him, but then all women did that. Words are cheap. But he knew she was one of those few capable of carrying through with the threat, and that worried him some. It amazes him now how easy the choice to leave her was, even though she'd promised him that the separation had consequences, and that she controlled the levers working those consequences. He figured he would have to continuously watch his back and stare into his mirrors. But that was five years ago. He figured since no one was dead, the volcano had gone dormant.

He's mellowed a lot during these last five years. He's grown too old for her fireworks. He assumes after five years Kathleen's fire has died down as well. Life goes on, right? He has Angelina on the side now. She's much more comfortable, great eye-candy, always available, no threat to his family, no knives, shotguns, or carnivorous hedge fund deals. Life is good.

But now there's this message from Kathleen. It's telling him she's just thrown his life in the dumpster. That's what those letters on the SUV roofs out in Dakota are telling him. Who else but Kathleen would do that? But what might it mean? Damn. It might mean he'll have to check every goddamn computer in the whole firm. She certainly could fashion a furtive boomeranging hedge fund monster that, if she wanted to, would wipe out his bank account faster than you could say New York City. He'll have to double-check every piece of security and every deal and watch his mirrors... and certainly keep his Glock handy.

***

Same Day
Leon's Mom's House in Bismarck – 6:16 p.m.

During a high school basketball game, ten players and two refs are on the floor. A point guard, while running around like crazy trying to control a bouncing sphere, also has to keep track of all those other people on the court while instantaneously understanding which ones have their heads in the game and which are out of position, off balance, or mentally coasting in that valley of indecision between the peaks of action. Who is lost? Who can see what will happen next? Leon, the ultimate point guard, can do that. He understands the game in all four dimensions, and can instinctively absorb, and then break down, the distinct elements in this discordant activity. He anticipates—at times actually knows—what will happen next. Then he'll move so as to put himself in the right place to intercept a pass, to alter the timing of the action by stepping on the foot of the man guarding him when the ref's looking the other way, or to make a pass to one of his buddies streaking down the court who will be open a couple seconds later. He instinctively knows the best thing to do. The arena of North Dakota politics presents a similar challenge. He only has to concentrate, put himself into the game, and absorb the swirling information. Soon the searchlights he knows are up there will illuminate the clear path to the goal wide enough to drive a big fracking-sand dump-truck down it. And that will present him with a chance for a lay-up!

***

As usual, Leon and his mom eat their evening meal in front of the television and dissect every story they see on the news, chewing it over with the pot roast. The demonstration on the mall takes up most of the local news and more of the national coverage than he'd expected. Brian Bast steals much of the face time, as he knows how to do, poking fingers, throwing mud, knowing all. His mouth is a gift to any reporter. The dreary *Prairie Preservation* folks stick to their facts and charts and are quickly dismissed by both the reporters and, Leon surmises, the viewers. The governors, both existing and presumed future, and many other officials, screamers, and busybodies, parade past various microphones leaving juicy dollops of newsy bites.

Leon's mother owns the TV and, with it, the control of the remote. She expertly switches channels back and forth mining twice the content, although with a bit of repetition. The national coverage comes from a different time zone and a different theater with finer-suited players. It concerns itself with the big-picture, national implications of this local dust-up of the oil development versus environment argument. A Texan lawyer speaking for Prometheus assumes he alone sees a future paradise in North Dakota and trades high moral platitudes with a Laura somebody who represents goodness and light and everything green.

Leon absorbs all of this extraneous racket at a risk. If he doesn't take a time out, relax on the porch with a cup of coffee and a symphony, and watch the September night sneak into the backyard, his malevolent stomach will attack him. He hears the microwave timer ding. He retrieves his coffee mug... the big one with the Agribus Seeds logo, a gift from a lobbyist, like almost every other trinket hiding in the kitchen cabinets. He retires to the winterized screen porch his mother added to the back of her house. It overlooks an extensive flower garden she lovingly tends. He sees her out there now in the purpling twilight, fussing about needlessly, not unlike the starlings and ravens dancing on the lawn behind her. He turns on NDPR for some background music.

Leon has been adding notes to his legal pad. He understands the landscape of his notes as well as the landscape of the basketball court. Once he has everything organized the action will be clear. He'll know what will happen next, and he'll know what he has to do to counter some lie or encourage some action. He'll be ready to have Brian Bast served to him for breakfast in the morning.

Chapter 14

Thursday, September 19, 2013
Bismarck, ND – 7:32 a.m.

Leon walks from his mom's house to the Capitol Building under the turning maples. He's entertained by the screams and giggles of children on their way to school and the crows arguing in the colorful canopy above him. Normally such civilized sounds sooth him, revive his basic humanitarian instincts. But, this morning, discordant noise is attempting to overpower these gentle reminders of real life in a small town. He's walked this same route for twenty years, comforted by the same background music, but has never heard blasting horns, revving engines, and harsh words aimed at bicyclists before. Such sounds belong in Chicago or Minneapolis—not Bismarck. He doesn't recognize the people brushing past him, hurrying to work obviously more important than his. He steels himself for another day of protest on the mall. And this commotion informs him today's show will be bigger and noisier than yesterday's. Leon thinks about turning back, calling in sick, and working from his porch. He could let Margie wrestle with the rabble, and he could work without interruptions. He might make a dent in his to-do pile.

"Damn!" He remembers the ten-o'clock with Bast. He can't miss that and have Bast assume the position of winner by default.

That this demonstration on his lawn requires a second day surprises him. He'd assumed it would be a one-day circus. They had got the helicopter, CNN, and the big PR stuff taken care of. What's left to do? He realizes today's crowd differs from yesterday's. Jane what's-her-name's hard-core demonstrators are still here, now augmented by many college-age kids, wearing jeans and sweatshirts, and plugged into their electrical devices. But it seems the fun is over for the local folk, who have returned to their day jobs. He hears no bullhorns yet, but sees signs and hears chants competing with the single-minded, murdered-farmer themes from yesterday: 'protect our fragile earth,' and 'save our native culture.' He watches two college kids nailing a hand-printed cardboard sign to a tree trunk: "North Dakota is for us humans! Texas oilmen go home!"

All this hoopla impacts him and, by the time he walks up the Capitol steps, he's talked himself into thinking that the excitement might make some marvelously disagreeable background music for his meeting with Brian Bast—a bit of crowd noise as a home court advantage. It may be enough to rattle the sneaky bastard and perhaps throw him off his game.

Leon walks around his office and opens the windows. The temperature dives, and so the room is relatively cool and filled with noise from the mall when Margie ushers Bast through his door. A fancy young man in a several-thousand-dollar suit accompanies him. "This is Mr. J.D. Crowe," says Margie. "And you know Brian."

"That I do," says Leon. "Morning, Brian." Though he'd like to punch him, he remains polite, shakes his hand, and pats him on the shoulder. "And Mr. Crowe! Welcome to Bismarck. You two remember to check your firearms at Margie's desk?" He glances at Margie. She rolls her eyes.

Mr. Crowe seems lost, like he's in the wrong meeting. But Bast stays focused, doesn't even crack a smile, and immediately begins the expected sales pitch. "Mr. Crowe represents the consortium financing this refinery project. He's made a special trip out here from New York to assist you in overcoming the effects of that noise out there."

Leon notices Mr. Crowe isn't carrying an AK-47, though he intends to project the image of a dangerous man. He smooths his slick black hair with a black leather-gloved hand, then pats his slick little briefcase to suggest he's folded his rocket launcher inside. His job is to make sure that the cowering idiot who heads the North Dakota House of Representatives understands that his boss in New York is calling the shots and must be obeyed. Leon understands it as pre-game warmup stuff. Let's see if these two can run an effective offense after the whistle blows. "We've paid our heating bill, Mr. Crowe. You can remove your gloves now."

"You can stuff the folksy farmhand stuff," says Mr. Crowe. "This is a serious discussion, and I suggest that you show me some serious attention." He does not remove his gloves.

Leon gets up and makes a show of closing the windows. "Okay, Mr. Crowe. Is that better?"

"I'm a serious guy, Mr. Speaker. I did not come all the way out here to play silly games. I'm here to inform you that you're now on our team. Therefore, we demand you do what we tell you to do. Everything has changed now, Mr. Rolfes. Power has shifted. You now work for us, and I expect you to do what we tell you. And I'm telling you as plain as I can. You must push this project through approvals as fast as you can and throw as much money at it as your governor tells you to throw. Am I clear?"

"Oh, you're clear enough, Mr. Crowe. Clarity is not your problem. You've got a much bigger concern. I actually understand what you are saying, and I think it is rubbish. And if I hear much more of that, you're going to have to leave. Am I clear?"

"Just listen to him, Leon. Common courtesy." Bast is sweating. He keeps wiping his forehead with a cloth. "He's bringing jobs and tax revenue to us. A goddamn gift! Ya gotta sign on, Leon."

"Mr. Speaker." Crowe switches to a second persona, that of the learned counselor, the mighty developer from Wall Street. "We are both on the same side here. We want to provide new industry in these struggling economic times, create great jobs, and raise living standards in your state. That sounds like a dream program, doesn't it? It's right up your conservative pro-business alley. Surely you can see that the strangling regulations and time-wasting approvals you have in place here will not work. Those are procedures left over from more leisurely times and are threatening the march of progress. Don't be distracted by that rabble outside your window, Mr. Speaker. Real business interests in your state are behind this project one hundred percent. I'd bet most of those lefties out there in the park are imported. They don't know diddly-squat about North Dakota."

Leon almost asks him *and how do you know that, Sonny? Where in Dakota are you from?* But he holds his tongue. Margie would be pleased with his show of restraint. The pause also gives Crowe time to curl more rope around his own neck. Crowe makes the mistake of assuming it's just three good ol' boys jawin' in a back room. Technically that's true; they are all Republicans and, at one level, philosophically aligned. Crowe doesn't see pushing Leon's rock off his superhighway as a philosophical problem, merely a tactical one. He needs Rolfes to vacate the highway fast, then inaugurate some legislative speed.

As Bast and Crowe drone on, Leon recognizes the hints of desperation. A good point guard can always tell if his high-pressure defense is working. The opponent starts rushing passes, taking chances, concentrating on offense, and forgetting about defense. Bast considers word quantity a higher debating virtue than common sense or truth, so Leon lets them jabber on for a while. Although Crowe seems comfortable throwing bombs and insults, the beads of sweat above Bast's upper lip indicate he's become conscious of the inextricable fact that his argument is going nowhere. Bast has misread the landscape and finds himself lost. He can't see Rolfes following him through the swamp any more.

Crowe tries a third weapon. "What's it going to take, Leon? We have a reasonable budget for greasing skids. It's just one line-item in our overall budget. We must hire the best consultants, and we understand the best consultants are not cheap. We expect a high consulting fee is worth the time we save and trouble we avoid. We could use you as part of our team, Mr. Rolfes. Your expert understanding of the local situation is of great value to us, and I know it can be rewarding for you."

Leon feels a smidgen sorry for Crowe. If he is supposed to play enforcer, he should've actually packed his AK-47. "Mr. Crowe, I'm not stupid. I understand your coded talk of budgets, consultants, and rewards. I also understand that you mistakenly consider North Dakota as a third world dictatorship, in the same distressed economic situation as Venezuela, Nigeria, or Louisiana. You seem unaware that North Dakota has no unemployment to speak of. We are bathing in our own oil, and our harvest is pushing record levels. Folks here are quite happy with the status quo, thank you very much. Try another weapon."

Leon gets up and reopens a window. "Your 'jobs, jobs, jobs' argument carries no weight here. You two have brought bowling balls to my basketball game. Your team is twenty points behind at halftime, Mr. Bast. And your best shooter, here, is in foul trouble."

Leon recognizes many applicable metaphors, but he senses Margie would think he should stop about now. He takes a long sip of coffee. The clock on the shelf behind him ticks. Leon straightens up a few papers on his desk, as if looking for something.

"Mr. Speaker, you're not going to help us, are you?"

"Brian, I know you want that refinery. And it appears you're in a big hurry. That's okay with me. You may even have good reasons. But they're Mr. Crowe's reasons, and they've little to do with me, or Dakota, or even you. Mr. Crowe's arguments generate no pressure on me. North Dakota does not need this development. I am not saying you shouldn't build it, but it must be done correctly. Yesterday I told you I needed answers to three questions. Neither you, nor Mr. Crowe here, have even attempted to answer them… and I wonder why. I'm not opposed to a refinery. It may be a sweet idea. But neither of you have convinced me of the value of this project. You want me to buy into the *process* of approving the thing, not the *concept* of the thing itself. All you want is quick, and quick does nothing for me.

"And you, Mr. Crowe? I'm sorry, but you blew your coverage big time. Your primary job should have been to convince me that your buddies back in New York are squeaky clean with respect to that murder up there along the border, but you haven't touched that. I get the idea you're only interested in the money this deal makes for you. I, however, see two dead farmers staring at me from their white Buick. I think that's *your* problem, and all those folks shouting at us from the mall outside that window think it's your problem too. But you don't see that, do you? You want to move beyond their deaths and talk about profits."

Crowe flushes crimson. "Mr. Speaker, how can you even suggest that our firm could have something to do with those farmer's deaths? That's an insult!"

"Oh, I'm suggesting no such thing, Mr. Crowe. But I do want you to convince me that neither you, nor anyone under your direction, walked into that isolated farmhouse and used a bit of New York persuasion."

Crowe points a still-gloved finger at Leon. "You'd better pay attention, Mister Speaker, or you will be run over by our machine. The weight of the thing will grind you into prairie dirt."

Leon sits down comfortably in his chair. "Mr. Crowe, every time I give you the chance to convince me that you, yourself, did not go up to that farm and personally stuff those poor farmers into their Buick, you change the topic and don't answer my question. All the question needs is a simple *no* answer. You not saying that *no* is making me very nervous. You seem to think I should appreciate your goal as my own and help you make your money. Bullshit! Don't talk about your profit margin, Mr. Crowe. You guys run a hedge fund or money laundering scheme of some sort which, I understand, is *only* concerned with making money—*and only for you.* That's why you took that MBA from Yale or someplace, so's you can make piles of money while not concerning yourself about any folks who end up as collateral damage."

"You're wrong, Mr. Rolfes. I didn't kill anybody, and it's Harvard. You should know MBAs from Yale are worthless."

"Whatever, Mr. Crowe. Seems like you've got your priorities screwed up, and until you straighten them out for me, I'm afraid you're going to find your project out here dead in the water... or perhaps dead in the front seat of a Buick."

Leon smiles. He almost takes pity on the poor guy. The two of them stomp out of his office and, without even saying goodbye to Margie, slam the door shut behind them.

She sticks her head into his office. "You still alive in here?"

"Margie, it's only eleven, and I've already done a day's worth of heavy lifting. I need a steak, but I'll settle for coffee."

***

Same Day
The Speaker's Office – 12:06 p.m.

An hour and a half later, Leon returns to the speaker's suite from a scheduling meeting downstairs. He opens the door to a party. "Decorum's slipped a bit in here, hasn't it Margie? What's going on?"

Margie is entertaining several representatives, staff members, and a few hangers-on while the noontime news blasts from the TV. "We're having a picnic. There's pizza here. We're listening to Bast, his New York sidekick, and a representative of Prometheus warning us that bad things might happen to us good people in North Dakota if we, meaning you Mr. Speaker, disrupt their refinery thingy."

Leon can't wait for the repercussions from that stunt... another day probably shot, with the phone ringing off the hook. "Bah!" he says, and retreats to his office.

The crowd of legislators and assistants assembled in his outer office to watch the Prometheus news conference grows larger and more raucous. Leon gets up from his desk, walks over, and slams the door. He knows Margie enjoys this distraction. She's playing stewardess out there, dishing out donuts and coffee, happy as a clam. She's even enjoying his own building irritation. He knows she will open that door in a few minutes, check if he wants to join the party, and bring him his coffee.

She proves him right. She knocks and sticks her head into his office. "Would you like a cookie, Mr. Speaker, before they're all gone?"

He refuses to leave his desk, making a show of trying to work, thinking maybe he might be able to lead by example and shame some of these idiots into leaving him alone. But with Margie encouraging them, he isn't sure that'll work.

"Bah!" He grabs a cookie from Margie's box but doesn't leave his desk for her party.

On the TV, a combative Brian Bast, apparently learning nothing from his failure with Leon earlier in the day, blasts ahead with the same argument—jobs, jobs, jobs. He introduces the imported talent from New York. J.D. Crowe is there with Martin Pick, a fiftyish, ex-special forces type with muscles bursting through his suit. Pick stands fixed at parade rest behind Bast, while Bast stands behind a small bush of microphones in front of a white screen splattered with official Prometheus logos. He sounds like an NBA coach addressing the media after a tough loss.

"Folks, we are very disappointed that the economic future of North Dakota is being hijacked by the low-class rabble-rousers-for-hire screaming over there on the mall. These men and their firm—he motions toward Crowe and Pick—want to bring jobs and industry to our state and they are rightfully angry at the reception they are getting here. I guarantee you, I am going to bash some heads until I find out who's pulling their good names through the mud. The governor will not stand for it. He'll continue to push for the jobs and the tax revenue a great project like this will bring to our wonderful state."

That's exactly what Margie would expect Bast to say—kiss up to the public with lots of generalities like the jobs-jobs-jobs mantra, but nothing specific. Each of the various gentlemen, except for Mr. Pick who remains rigid as a Marine, says the same thing in a slightly different form, and then the meeting opens up to questions.

One critic, watching in Margie's office, says, "The New York cry-babies are upset. Why do they need a press conference to tell us that?"

"If they start with the bribes and payoffs, I want to know where I can show up to collect," says another.

The suits yapping on the TV remain serious. One reporter asks Crowe how he 'feels' after being accused of being a hired killer. It's a telling question, thinks Margie, and it's subtle. That reporter skillfully skirted the big question on the table: *why did you bastards murder those poor farmers?* He'd skipped over any facts and into feelings. *Crowe's* feelings. And that's exactly what Bast wants to talk about. Can it mean Bast won this first skirmish?

Crowe ensures the viewers that his employer is a sensitive entity and has feelings too, and those feelings are hurt by such an outrageous accusation. In answer to another question, Crowe says that Mr. Pick, early this morning, flew up to talk to Sheriff Gaffey to get the real story from him, so that he could give an air of authenticity to his comments at this news conference. He reports he'd been treated badly by a hayseed sheriff who, although well-intentioned, couldn't find a clue if it jumped up and bit him in the ass. Bast feels the good people of North Dakota will eventually thank the saintly folks from New York for providing more jobs for the state in one project than the ignorant local bozos might provide in a decade. And Crowe suggests that the lefty anti-capitalists parading on the mall should get jobs like the rest of the movers in the community and do some work for a change.

Leon does not do isolation well and eventually leaves his cave and stomps into the outer office to watch Margie's TV with the other legislators.

"You're a little late for the important stuff, Leon. They're about ready to shut things down."

"I think that Crowe guy is right." He says this loud enough to be heard by the group over the noise of the TV. "We should do what the gentleman suggests, and go back to our work. Let the New York thinkers solve this refinery thing for us. They'll straighten out the things that need straightening out."

"I'm glad there is no reporter in here to hear that little editorial," says Margie. "I don't think those professionals appreciate sarcasm as much as the enlightened folk in this room do."

"Sarcasm, my ass!" says one of the enlightened. "Leon's right on. If those hired guns think smarmy talk is going to win them friends and influence our decisions, they are badly disillusioned."

"First thing they gotta do is distance themselves from the murder thing. They didn't say much about it, but until that gets resolved, nobody is going to give 'em squat."

Leon senses the fun winding down. He wanders back into his office and grabs what's left of his cookie. He has serious work to do.

Chapter 15

Leon's serious work environment lasts for only an hour. He hears frivolity in the outer office, once again undermining decorum. It sounds like a bunch of third graders on a field trip have invaded his front room. Nobody respects the sanctity of his office anymore. Eventually the noise dies down. But then his office door slowly opens. Margie steps in rather formally and announces, "Steffie Cobb and a friend request an audience."

Leon looks up at her. "You mean just you two were making all that noise?"

"Hi, Leon." Steffie tries to break through Leon's shield. "I just listened to Bast's news conference-pep rally thing. I almost threw up. Not much news being conferenced in *that* room."

"And I'm not getting much office work done in *this* room."

"Cut it out, Leon," says Margie. "You've made your little point. Mind your manners."

"Unlike Mr. Bast," says Steffie, "I do have important matters to share. You might want to put that pencil down and pay attention now."

He finally looks up. "Oh, who's your friend, Steffie?" He rises from his chair, comes around to the front of his desk, and reaches down to tend to Ruby. First you kiss the babies, then pat the dogs, and only then comes the hard work. Ruby, apparently, has not received that memo. She growls at him, then recoils a few short steps.

"Ruby!" Steffie jerks on the leash. "What's that for? Be nice to Leon. He's one of the good guys."

But Ruby does not relax. She stations herself at the front of his desk and gurgles softly. Steffie pulls her away to the couch on the far side of the room, and they both sit and stare at him. "I'm sorry, Leon. I don't know what got into her."

"Maybe she smells the same thing my sister's dog does. That crazed spaniel starts yelping at me as soon as I pull into the drive."

Ruby curls up at Steffie's feet. "Leon, you know about a guy named Martin Pick? Hedge fund security from New York?"

"The ex-Marine muscle at Bast's news conference? I saw him on the tube. What's he done now?"

"That's the guy. He flew up early this morning to see Gaffey, and the sheriff called me afterwards to report on the confrontation before the vision faded."

"Before the vision faded? I can't wait, Steffie. What happened?"

"I don't think Pick made the impression on Gaffey he'd hoped for, even though he exchanged his suit for an outfit meant to strike fear into the hearts of anyone who'd seen a Rambo movie. Gaffey had fun describing his desert boots, tight jeans, leather bomber jacket, Marine Corp baseball cap keeping out whatever sun the aviator glasses missed, and the straps of his shoulder holster showing over his white tee shirt."

"Sounds like fear wasn't the sensation Gaffey experienced."

"Apparently he wanted the sheriff to rush out to the farm with him, so he, as an experienced and ruthless man who knows the kind of thoughts murderers thunk, could find the few clues the sheriff, in his haste, had missed. He could then solve the mystery for Gaffey, pin the murder on the real culprit, and ride his white horse out of town like the Lone Ranger."

"That must have established some rapport," Leon says. "Doesn't he realize we Dakotans can take care of ourselves all by ourselves, without a Lone Ranger?"

"Gaffey told him to butt out and let the law do its work. He wasn't persuaded Pick was going to take his advice and was relieved when he showed up at that news conference. It meant he'd gone straight back to Bismarck."

"Crowe can easily overplay this. Everything could boomerang right back in his face if he's not careful. But that's not the real reason Ruby and I had to see you this afternoon. We've got some additional news from the sheriff to share. He wouldn't let me tell you till now."

Margie's intercom voice interrupts Steffie and informs Leon that a Mr. Francelli from a firm called HF&G in New York is holding on line one.

"Sorry, Steffie. I gotta talk to the big gun. You want to hear what Mr. Hedge Fund Guy has to say?"

"Maybe you wanna ask him a question, Leon. Like why does a hedge fund guy need a head of security? ...a vigilante bounding through the countryside, packing heat and intimidating the local law?" Both Steffie and Ruby growl. Leon pokes the button to put the call on speaker.

***

"G'morning, Mr. Speaker. Enrico Francelli with HF&G, calling you from New York."

"Good morning, sir. What can I do for you this fine day?" He looks at Steffie as if to say, *See, I can be gracious—if I have to.*

"I just talked with J.D. Crowe. I understand he met with you this morning."

"Yes, sir, he did. If you're wanting an assessment of his work, I can state he behaved himself admirably. He's a nice young man, a real gentleman."

"Fuck you, Mr. Speaker. Don't play games with me."

"No more of that, sir. Be civil with me or I'm hanging up."

"J.D. told me you're stodgy, old school, and uncooperative. He told me I needed to have a frank discussion with you. You know the basic facts here, I'm sure."

"Yes, sir. The Prometheus folks met us here in this very building. They warned me *your* machine is headed in *my* direction."

"Machine?" Francelli paused to let the odd metaphor evaporate. "Do you know what a frank discussion is, Mr. Speaker?"

"I've been a representative here for thirty years, sonny. I've been involved in many frank discussions."

"That don't mean diddly, old man."

Ouch! Leon thinks. But it serves him right for trying to play the wise-old-man card right off the bat.

"Because here it comes. You seem to think you North Dakota folks are the only hard-working, self-reliant, salt of the earth types around. Bullshit! Everyone in the world can do that. You're no different from folks in Mississippi or Bangladesh. Hard work doesn't drive progress. It's the guys like me, guys who move the money; we make everything work. You can work all your damn life, Mr. Speaker, and not make as much money as I do in one day. Frankly, you don't matter to me, and neither does your puny little state. I can put my refinery anywhere I want.

"That being said, Mr. Speaker, I do need you to get out of my way. I can make a call and in two hours have your whole office stuffed to the transoms with hundred dollar bills. Can you do that? Your whole stupid state can't do that. And you've got to realize that the opposite is true too. Life can get awful repressive out there on the prairie if I get no cooperation. Does this make any sense to you?"

"Mr. Francelli, I cannot lie. You do frighten me, and I have no doubt that you can either fill this room with cash or make me disappear, but—"

"You don't have the luxury of a 'but' in a frank discussion. I thought you might have learned that in all your experience. I want you to forget about whatever piddling stuff is on your desk right now. It doesn't mean shit to me. From now on, I need you to push twenty-four hours a day for the approval of the Prometheus proposal. I've also had a frank discussion with the governor. He *has* seen the light, and I'm glad to report he's going to make a strong effort on our behalf. He told me that you, as speaker, will help me. It won't be so hard for you to follow your governor, will it Mr. Speaker?"

"Mr. H F and G." Leon pronounces it like H F'n G so it sounds vaguely demeaning, almost as vulgar as Francelli's word.

"It's Francelli, speaker. Enrico Francelli."

"I know that, Mr. H F'n G, but it appears that you are too big and powerful for just a single person, so understanding that corporations are people too, I am addressing your corporate personhood. We in this state, being a reasonable bunch, do not take to being played by you folks in the big city."

"I am not playing... I'm threatening you. I'm throwing you a goddamn ultimatum."

"Oh, cut it out Francelli! Ultimatum? I don't think so. But you've had a high-priced education, and I'll bet that you know enough about those Greek gods to understand that your Prometheus guy didn't have such a rosy life after he tricked Zeus into releasing the fire."

"I've no time to discuss Greek gods. I'm a businessman, for God's sake."

"Zeus got mad, chained Prometheus to a post, and let eagles eat his innards. That doesn't sound pleasant. So I am warning you, sir. Don't try to trick us, or sneak something past us in the dark. If you get careless and don't watch your step, Mr. H F'n G, your Prometheus project will also end up as roadkill. Good day, sir." He hangs up.

"Now that," he says to Steffie, "is my idea of a frank discussion. I think we cleared the air, didn't we?"

"You pretty much cleared all the air between here and New York, Mr. Speaker. I enjoyed that."

"You may have enjoyed it, but it's off the record, ya hear? You didn't officially hear a single word. You may, however, use the impressions you got of Mr. H F'n G to color the edges of this story as it moves through history. Am I clear?"

Steffie laughs. She appears to be clear.

"Now that that's out of the way, what's this news you and Ruby have for me?"

But before Steffie can get started, Margie shouts at her, "Sorry to interrupt you yet again, Steffie. His Honor has another call. It's *his buddy*, Kathleen." Margie uses the words *his buddy* to indicate the caller is not high on her list of people who should be allowed to interrupt the important state business being considered in the speaker's office, but whom she has to accommodate because the speaker has his own list of worthy people. Kathleen is on *that* list. She only talks to him when she's on the clock, lobbying for one of her firms or her clients, many of whom turn out to be her own companies.

Leon shrugs his shoulders. "I'll make this quick, Steffie. At least I'll try." He picks up the phone.

"Good afternoon, Kathleen. Haven't talked for a while. Hope you're well. What can I do for you?"

"Afternoon, Uncle Leon."

Leon notes that, as is her habit, she does not affix the modifier 'good' to the noun 'afternoon.' Her address thus becomes a statement noting the time of the conversation, rather than a wish for a pleasant day. She's called him 'uncle' ever since she could talk, but the emphasis of the word changed as she grew older. Now it means that Leon must recognize that, since she is 'family,' he is expected to give deference to her interests. The fact that this expectation has never been fulfilled has, over the years, become somewhat of an irritation to them both.

"I'm supposed to give you a heads-up about the Prometheus refinery. My firm's been retained by the developers to help them smooth some feathers, grease some skids, and help blaze a trail through the approval process at N-DOPE. You know the drill.

"We're a known quantity over at N-DOPE and so should be able to help Prometheus steer clear of the normal roadblocks. And I know I will be able to count on you to make sure there is plenty of grease on those gears grinding away over on your end of the mall. My clients want me to keep the petal to the metal here, Uncle Leon, so I expect full cooperation."

"You are exactly the person I need to talk to about this, Kathleen. I've already talked with O'Donnell over at the Development office and neither he nor I understand the requirement for speed that is pushing this thing faster than is comfortable. Can you help me here?"

"This refinery has international implications. We're competing with the Chinese and Saudis. Their money moves quickly. We, therefore, gotta move quickly as well."

"You telling me I gotta scrap my timely and reasonable review schedule? That seems strange, doesn't it?"

"Uncle Leon, you can't live in the past! It's the twenty-first century now. You gotta do things faster than they did back in the sixties. It's why we've got email, Twitter, satellites, and super computers. Speed, Uncle Leon. It's all about speed. If you wanna be a player, you gotta do *quick*. Trust me. If my client doesn't get speed, then he's off to Wyoming."

"Then your client better schedule a trip to Cheyenne. We're backward folks here, Kathleen. You're not convincing me we gotta move that fast."

"You want to force me to bring in the heavy artillery?"

"Listen, Kathleen, I'm not forcing you to do anything. I just got off the phone with a smart-ass weasel named Francelli. He's the prima donna, New York, hedge fund guy throwing money at this refinery."

"Francelli's a fuckin' idiot."

"I agree with you there! He essentially told me what you did, but was ruder, gruffer, and more disagreeable. Can you even imagine that? He didn't appreciate my enlightened viewpoint. He didn't call you, did he? Have you orchestrate the bad cop-good cop thing?"

"I'll deal with Francelli. Your job is to listen to me."

"Sorry I called you the 'good' cop, Kathleen. It was unintentional… not meant as an insult. However, your argument does not change my position. This approval will move at my speed, not the hyper-speed Francelli and you want."

"Sorry Uncle, I gotta go. Something else here needs me. You think about speed. This is twenty-first century business. Be quick or die. I'll stay on your ass. Somebody's got to push you into the future. Might as well be me."

Leon turns to Steffie. "I didn't hear any *goodbye*! Did you?"

"Who was *that*?" Steffie asks. "Sounds like she studied phone etiquette with Brian Bast and that Francelli guy. And what's with the 'Uncle Leon' thing?"

"Kathleen is Nathan's daughter. She lived mostly with her mom in New York, but during her teenage years and into college she spent summers out here with her dad. Nathan was always busy, so she followed Larry and me around a lot... fed the chickens, played with our horses and tractors. We had a good time. The dynamic changed abruptly after her sophomore year summer. Nathan never told me, but something between them snapped. She never summered with us again. Hardly even talked to us. She started running with the vultures and vampires and chose the city over the grassland. I think she moved over to the dark side."

"What does that mean?"

"It means she disappeared into the concrete canyons for twenty years. Then six or seven years ago she surfaced as a mover in the Williston oilfields. But she's changed. She doesn't quite seem human. Nathan thinks she's a vampire. We old fogies aren't her three musketeers anymore."

"Vampire? How can Nathan call his own daughter a vampire?"

"I'm not sure. I can see a lot of Nathan in her, except one has to watch out. She has a furious temper and probably does drink blood."

"If she's splat in the middle of the Williston oil boom, what are the odds she's connected to this refinery deal too?"

"Oh, I'm certain she is connected in some way. She's not your average low-level PR lady. And part of me thinks I should be worried, though she did seem quite mellow on the phone. She didn't go berserk and yell at me, which is her normal style. I wonder what that means. Hard to believe she's going soft."

"I'll have to research her, Leon. Why've I heard nothing about her? I know the oil stuff pretty well and her name's never come up."

"Vampires keep a low profile, especially in Dakota. She uses her mother's name, Carter, so only a few of us know she's connected to Nathan. She spends most all her time in Houston, but she moved a small part of her operation into North Dakota several years ago when the fracking industry moved in. I think her outfit manages leases, perhaps half the oilfield equipment, and about two thirds of the trucks ruining Williston's highways.

"She once bragged to Nathan that she owns most of the fracking sand reserves within a five state region. She probably owns other things too, but hides them all deep underground like her oil. Nathan taught her to do that. She sometimes lobbies me to put pressure on N-DOPE for her, but does not expect that pressure to work. She does frighten me, however. She's absolutely ruthless, and I sense if ever I cross her, that junkyard dog will come pouncing."

                              ***

Kathleen has been working very hard, for a very long time, but she's done her work quietly. The three musketeers know little of her activities down in Houston, and neither does Francelli, though he's tried continuously. She's hidden herself under an umbrella entity named BOLT. It, in turn, buys other oil industry related companies, like it did Petrotec a few years ago. Petrotec then purchased Oil Equipment Leasing LLC, an oilfield equipment firm which then bought a stake in an Alaskan drilling firm. BOLT also owns a rail-car leasing company, which owns a test drilling service, which now owns an environmental engineering firm. Attached to other ownership chains, she controls lobbying firms, an oilfield management software business, and a company pioneering the deep drilling technology in Dakota, Wyoming, and Colorado.

She bundled several of these firms into a package and trolled it past a couple potential buyers. As she hoped, two funds, one of them was HF&G, grabbed the baited hook and, after a brief bidding contest, HF&G bought her package and then gave it a sexier name, Prometheus Inc., thinking a sexy name would increase its value.

The package that HF&G swallowed contained a poison pill—a nicely dressed harlot, with little current value but presenting the possibility of turning an outrageous trick. This harlot firm owned a contract to develop a refinery project in North Dakota. This looked good, but once HF&G acquired Prometheus, the pill, as designed, started to dissolve. With respect to the oil refinery part, all sorts of its pieces were scheduled to go haywire: a testing firm would default; a design engineering firm would estimate development costs double the pre-HF&G estimate. And an oil supply contract tied to world oil prices would demand additional payments as the OPEC index rose—one thing after another. HF&G would quickly realize they had a leaker on their hands and schedule a fire sale to rid itself of the dripping parts fast. They'd have to dress the floozy up pretty, bring her to a flashy party, and hope some lonely, rich suitor in need of some arm candy would take her home.

***

"I have to brag about my friend Ruby," says Steffie. "When I first visited Gupchal's place, Sheriff Gaffey had me take Ruby along to sniff for clues." She pats Ruby's head. "Well, Ruby did her sniffing and dug a small hole in the gravel in front of the garage door. Deputy Turnquist took a sample, then poked around and found more evidence on the Buick's grillwork. The State Crime Lab said all those substances are the same—human vomit. And the DNA on all samples match. As a result of *Ruby's* investigation, the sheriff now has the DNA of a probable killer. All he has to do now is match it."

"Wow! That's some weird story," says Leon.

"Isn't it though? I tried to get sneaky and grab a little more. That's why Ruby is with me. I took her to Bast's news conference and thought if I got her close enough perhaps Ruby might recognize Mr. Pick if he's the one who stomped around her house and killed her owners."

Leon looks at her skeptically. "And what did Lassie tell you?"

"They wouldn't let me bring Ruby into the event. I had to keep her in the car."

"Nice try though, Steffie. If Ruby takes a bite out of Pick's leg we arrest him. Sounds like an air-tight case to me."

"You've quite a sarcastic attitude, Leon. You suppose that's why Ruby's angry with you?"

"Bah."

"It's time to go now, Ruby. Say goodbye to the nice man."

Ruby of course didn't say anything, but she did give him a look that he thought said, *If I wasn't on this leash, mister, and if I was about five years younger, you'd be dead meat.*

"Not so fast, Steffie. I've got a crazy idea why Ruby's upset with me. Brian Bast visited here this morning and he towed along Crowe. Crowe did sit in that chair Ruby growled at. And I shook hands with him too. I'm sure Crowe's smell is all over me. I'm thinking Crowe could be the guy Ruby is smelling."

"I'll work on it," says Steffie. "Why don't you leave the room so you're not a distraction? When you're out of range I'll take Ruby over to that chair and see if she's interested in it.

"Oh, and something else." Steffie's words stopped Leon halfway through the door. "Sheriff told me Pick also informed him HF&G has established a $50,000 reward for information leading to the arrest and conviction of whoever killed the Gupchals."

"That's interesting, huh, Steffie? Pretty ballsy charade if they were the ones who actually did the murder. But they have lots of money to throw around. It seems a good investment, and probably not a bad PR move for them." He closes his door, walks over, and leans against Margie's desk.

A few seconds later Ruby barks.

"What's that dog doing in your office, Leon?" Margie asks.

Steffie emerges and pats Ruby on the head. "Good girl, Ruby."

"I heard her," says Leon. "All you have to do now is see if you can trick Crowe into giving you some of his DNA. If you can, wrangle an interview and ask him if he vomited on Gupchal's car. You give him the reaction test. If he did do it, the question would scare him silly. If not, he would just think you lost your marbles, a fairly normal reaction to a reporter lady."

"I might just do that, if I see him again. And if we ever catch the guy, Sheriff Gaffey thinks Ruby should get a piece of the reward money."

Steffie pats her buddy on the top of her head, waves goodbye, then exits the office.

"Even more funny stuff going on around here," says Margie. "I don't suppose you're going to tell me what that's all about either, are you?"

Chapter 16

Friday, September 20, 2013
Bismarck, ND – 7:45 a.m.

Leon nears the halfway point on his walk to work, a crosswalk protected by the Clark Elementary School flag brigade. He notices the lack of extraneous noise.

"What's happened to the crazy people this morning, Matthew? Awful quiet around here."

"Bunch of sissies, Leon," says the young teacher overseeing the crosswalk operation. "They give up as soon as the temperature dives into the twenties."

The walk puts him in a good mood and he anticipates a productive day. But, as he walks past Margie at her desk, he senses that construct crumble. Shards of his finely crafted schedule hit the floor near his feet.

"You've got perfect timing, Mr. Speaker. Steffie Cobb's on line one. She seems excited."

"Tell her I am not doing excitement today. I'll call her back in a week or two."

"I could be a good gatekeeper and tell her exactly what you said."

"Bah! Tell her I'll hang up my coat, take a couple antacids, and be right with her."

***

"Hi, Leon," Steffie says. "There's something we gotta discuss. But it's super secret."

"Just a sec, Steffie. Not so fast. You have to hear somethin' first." Leon swivels his chair to face the window, slides the sash up, extends the cord to its extreme, and waves the phone outside for a few seconds.

"Do you hear that?"

Margie giggles.

"You're playing a game with me, aren't you, Leon? Bit of stump-the-reporter?"

"This is serious. What sound do ya hear?" He waves his phone at the open window again.

"Okay. All I get is Margie laughing in the background. So you two are sharin' a joke? How nice for you! May I get back to work now?"

"What you're hearing, Steffie, is what I've been hearing all morning. It's the sweet absence of screeching bullhorns and shouting college kids. Serenity has returned to my front yard."

"Whoopee! Can I talk now?"

"Not until you tell me why it's so quiet. I've studied the high art of public demonstration, and it strikes me as quite abnormal for those do-gooders to pack up their stuff and go home after but one or two days on the job."

"You've got a point, Leon. But yesterday, weren't you also surprised they'd come back for day two? Can't have it both ways. You're thinkin' it's strange if they're here and strange if they're not; though, everything about that protest is strange."

"Just put it in your notes, Steffie. It's a piece of useful information."

Margie shakes her head and walks toward the door.

"It's my duty to keep the media on the scent, Margie. Don't laugh at me."

Leon sits down at his desk and takes a swig of coffee. "Now, Steffie, I'm ready for your super-secret."

"I've interesting news regarding yesterday's phone call."

"What, Mr. H F'n G?"

"No, your *other* call."

"What *other* call?"

"Concentrate, Leon. I heard the Kathleen Carter call too. We know she's Harvard Law because, I find out, she, unlike her dad, broadcasts the fact at high volume to the locally educated underclass, though she does not broadcast that she is Nathan's daughter. Did you notice that although she called to lobby you, this supposed ruthless tyrant didn't pitch much of a heavy duty argument at you? Why didn't she confront you? It's why she called, right?"

"That, except for the sarcasm, is correct. I agree she didn't seem very focused. And you're right—that's not normal."

"Would Kathleen play both sides of this, working with her father on one side while lobbying for Prometheus on the other? Then she gives you the silver and a kiss. It reminds me of a Judas syndrome thing."

"Silver and a kiss? Judas Syndrome? What the hell does that mean? Did you just make that up?"

"I heard it on *Law & Order* the other night. Now, here's the bombshell part. Last evening, while poking around resumés and bios, trying to flesh out those HF&G guys, I noticed your buddy, J.D. Crowe, who I think is about the same age as our friend Kathleen, is also a Harvard Law product."

"Yeah, he told me that yesterday."

"Well, I wondered if those two knew each other at that esteemed institution."

"Crowe and Kathleen together? Wow! What a thought! And what's the answer?"

"Ta-da."

"Don't think I want to hear this, Steffie."

"Oh, yes you do. I found a photo. I just emailed it to Margie. She should be bringing it in to you about... now."

Margie walks in, just as Steffie choreographed it. "Here's a weird photo from Steffie. You two building a scrapbook?"

"Will you two girls stop picking on me! Now, where are we Steffie?"

"Okay, Leon. Look at that photo. We see several members of the *Harvard Law Review* acting silly. Note over on the left, according to the names listed under the picture, a youngish J.D. Crowe, grinning strangely with his arm rather proprietarily draped around the shoulder of your sort-of niece, Kathleen Carter."

"Son... of... a... bitch!" Leon says slowly.

"Notice the look Kathleen is giving him—like a sophomore cheerleader to the senior quarterback. I'd swear they're more than classmates. Picture's dripping with lovey-dovey."

"Lovey-dovey? I can't picture Kathleen doin' lovey-dovey with any guy... let alone a prematurely slick and smooth J.D. Crowe. And by the way, isn't lovey-dovey stuff illegal at vulture school? It doesn't fit in with vampire stuff, does it?"

"Concentrate here, Leon. I wonder about the nature of their current relationship. What are the odds Crowe's firm buys a piece of refinery land and uses Kathleen's firm to paperwork the deal, without either of those two formerly lovey-dovey sharks knowing the other one is in the same tank?"

"It's a fairly small tank, Steffie. And right in between them is a Buick holding two dead farmers. Can that be a coincidence? Son... of... a... bitch!"

"I've got to talk with her, Leon."

"Lots of luck! First you have to find her. I know she's been spending time out in Williston. Rumor says she bought a ranch somewhere north of Dickinson because the land contains a reasonable deposit of fracking sand. I heard she's refurbished the old house. Even if you can find her house, I wouldn't bet she's there. If the temperature is below fifty, I'll bet she's in Houston."

"I think I have her Houston office number. I've talked with several firms down there on stories about Williston's boom. If she's as big a player in the fracking business as you say, I'll be able to find her. I'll also bet Margie has a record of yesterday's call too. I'll talk to her."

"Good luck with that trace. I'll bet she owns a truckload of disposable phones. She makes me shiver in my boots. Better you talk to her than me. Make a copy of that photo and stow it in your safe before you talk with her. And maybe put an Uzi in your purse."

"I might give you some personal safety advice also, Leon. This little play is now only one person removed from your best friend. I'm not saying Nathan's involved in whatever game Kathleen's playing, but—"

"I don't think he and his daughter move in the same circles or breathe the same air."

"But she's his only daughter, Leon. She's probably going to benefit from his real estate speculation. So she wouldn't sabotage Nathan's work. Family is family, right. Must be something there, know what I'm sayin'?"

"I know. I know."

"A quick note before you hang up. Ruby's not going to have a chance to snag a killer just yet. Crowe's gone back to the big city. I'll let Gaffey know about her sniff test in your office. If he wants to push it further, he can do it."

"Good luck with that. Let me know what you find out."

***

Leon watches the birds and squirrels play in the elms and feels Margie enter his office behind him. The smell of coffee breaks his concentration.

"A very pensive pose, Mr. Speaker. You having trouble concentrating?"

"The more information I have, the less I know. Ever get into that situation?"

"All the time, Leon. It is called politics. What's troubling you?"

"The silence out there fascinated me, so after talking to Steffie, I got this idea to take a little survey to satisfy my curiosity."

"Surveying the birds and squirrels? Quite innovative! But they don't understand politics any more than we do."

"Sarcasm is not the road to enlightenment, Margie. I made a few calls to a few hotels to confirm if all those crazies dancing on the lawn over the last few days had really left town. None of the five big hotels in town has a vacancy for *the entire weekend*. Folks aren't dancing on my lawn, but apparently they're still in town. What are they all doing here, and being quiet at it too? Hundreds of sneaky bastards creeping around my town! Should I be concerned? Should I hide in the closet?"

Chapter 17

After talking with Leon and the other two musketeers, Steffie realizes she has to get back up to Bottineau County and see if she can find any refinery project information up there that would shed additional light on the Gupchal suicides. Her first stop is Sheriff Gaffey's office.

"Sheriff," Steffie says, "the day after the Gupchals died, I analyzed the landscape up there for you. I poked around the house, interviewed the neighbors, completed the intellectual exercise, and reported my findings to you. That report is only four weeks old. But I think you must now toss all that stuff into the trash. This ugly refinery machine dropping out of the sky makes that whole report worthless—blasts the entire catalogue of my earlier work into meaningless gibberish. The dynamics of those deaths are profoundly changed."

"Take it easy, Steffie," says Gaffey. "You've done excellent work. Your insights are still valid."

"I appreciate the positive attitude, Sheriff. But you're wrong. It's all garbage now. I'm gonna take a fresh look, and this time I'll use the physical and legal data as a base on which to build any scenario of suicide or murder, and as a base for whatever else jumps into my notes."

"You've turned on me. Done a Jekyll and Hyde. No more sweet little Steffie, huh?"

"Absolutely not, Sheriff. And I know this time I must first understand the legal and real estate landscape where Frank and Helen Gupchal lived. Then I might possibly understand the impact of those landscapes on their lives and deaths, and the impact of that big machine falling from the sky. It's all much more complicated now."

"I'm sorry. I didn't want you to get so—"

"Forget it. No longer is this a favor for you. This is my story now. And, by God, I will get to the bottom of it. The potential for a great story here is colossal… fireworks-and-Sousa-band-music-type colossal. I cut fifteen minutes off my fastest time to Bottineau to get up here to tell you that."

"You could have just called me."

She looks at her watch and then stands up. "Can't talk now. I've gotta get across the parking lot to the county courthouse by nine. That's when Norma Schaffer unlocks the door."

"Be careful, Steffie. Do I have to tell you that? Keep me in the loop, please."

***

Norma Schaffer unlocks her door at 8:57. "Wow, Steffie," she says. "You're up here early. I can tell you're on a story, aren't you?"

"You bet I am, Norma."

"This is neat. I haven't had folks camping out on my steps waiting for me to open the door for quite a while… maybe eight, nine years. It was that summer when all the oil lease hunters from Texas showed up."

"I'm probably going to have to ask you about that sometime, but right now I need to camp out in your map room. You got time to help me unravel a mystery?"

"Oh, wow! That sounds exciting. How can I help?"

***

After working for two hours, Steffie realizes they are spinning wheels and will not be illuminating any landscape today. They find lots of information that isn't very helpful. Hardly anyone buys land in their own name anymore, at least in the general oilfield area, so it is impossible to find who owns what. Prometheus' refinery, if it is a real project, is still in the dream stage. No property has changed hands, and no deeds have been recorded. Steffie does find the three properties assembled for the Prometheus project, and notes that the Gupchals still are recorded as owning their land. That probably won't change until the death certificates and the wills are distributed. That could be months. The other two parcels have been titled to a real estate trust named PRTI LLC. The accompanying paperwork shows no phone number or email address, only a Minnesota mailbox, though that address is probably a dropbox monitored by a legal firm.

"I see much more ownership-obscuring stuff now," says Norma. "Nobody wants to tell nobody about nothin' no more. People are playing *protect the land from the oil monsters* even though, best I know, there's not much retrievable oil up here in Bottineau County. There's some natural gas hiding in the crevasses, but not much oil."

"Seems lots of folks are cloaking their land even if oil is a long shot," says Steffie. "I wonder why?"

"People are just gambling and greedy."

Steffie had talked earlier with the tenant caretakers on the other two PRTI sites, but neither knew anything about ownership of the land they lived on, or about farming. They send rent checks to an address—probably another dropbox—but know no phone numbers or email addresses. They talk only to a real estate agent.

"Ya know, Norma," Steffie says, "if Prometheus is planning on developing these parcels, they'd have to own them first wouldn't they?"

"Yes, they would. Either own outright or own a right-to-purchase option."

"So how could the refinery people have found out who owns this land if we two experts can't find out?"

"I've heard of cases where an extremely motivated hunter, in order to find the recorded mineral rights owner, would stake out a

PO box and watch for someone to come in and empty it, then follow him back to his house."

"That's bizarre! I'm thinking the owner of record, PRTI LLC, is only a holding company for that parcel. All these sales deals are five and six years old. These properties were assembled several years ago, specifically for some purpose. Is there any way to find out what that purpose was? Do your records show that?"

Norma finds the first title transferee to PRTI LLC about three years ago, and the others dribble in during the years previous to that. She then goes down the hall and checks the mineral rights log. She finds the mineral rights transferred at the same time intervals to another entity living at a different address.

"Whoever this PRTI is, they started this deception a long time ago, well before Prometheus became interested. They got the land first and then they waited patiently for someone to come courting. I wonder how that could possibly work."

"Doesn't seem it would work at all," says Norma.

She then wonders if Nathan and Larry own property in their own names and finds Larry's name attached to several parcels, though Goodbrother has not one square foot registered in his own name.

"Here's another question for you, Norma. I can't find Nathan Goodbrother's name in the records. He must own some land in Bottineau County, doesn't he?"

"I know he does, Steffie. I just don't know *what* land he owns. I know him well. He's in here often, and he's a master at hiding his ownership. But that's not unusual. He, like every smart developer, uses shell corporations. It's the way real estate is done now."

Steffie then calls several real estate contacts around the state, and they tell her there are many big players moving North Dakota real estate around so nobody could know who owns what.

"It's an attempt to keep the oil drillers at bay," one realtor says. "It's hard to buy or lease land if you don't know who to make the check out to. Most of the obscuring is legitimate. There are hundreds of land trusts out there. Some are innocent family-run consortiums, and some are shady investment operations overseen by companies using frivolous and serious names to identify the various independent LLCs that technically own the land. Who knows which are which? Even legit firms like Agribus are buying up land and hiding it under fancy names so they can ensure stable harvests for their ethanol refineries. The names of the real, live investor entities are hidden several layers below the surface."

Steffie says, "I've got to find out who owns all this land, Norma. Only then can I know who has something to lose or gain with this refinery."

"Lots of luck Steffie. It's like playing hide and seek in a rain forest. Nobody never sees nothin'. Ceptin' maybe shadows."

***

Same Day
Leon's Office at the Capitol – 1:45 p.m.

After several hours of relative peace and quiet, Margie ushers Larry and Nathan into Leon's office.

"Damn it, Margie. Didn't I tell you to give me a warning before these idiots show up? That way I can hide in my closet."

"Afternoon, Leon."

"What the hell you goons doing here? And with your game faces on. Didn't I just see you yesterday?"

"We got business, Leon."

"I've been doin' business all day. I don't need more business. I need diversion. How about a game of horse?" Leon picks a tennis ball from a cup on his desk and arcs it toward a fuzzy, pink, eight-inch hoop anchored to the wall above the couch. "Swish! My shot is on! You guys are in for a battle this afternoon."

"That's not happening today," says Nathan. "This is *not* a social call. We got serious business."

"Shit! You're supposed to be friends. I know plenty of lobbyists for serious business. I seek entertainment!"

Larry laughs. "Okay, Leon, then consider this visit entertainment. I'll guarantee you'll think of nothing else for the rest of the day."

"That doesn't sound like good news. I don't suppose I can go home now? Pretend I'm sick?"

"I want you to do me a favor." Nathan fiddles in his jacket pocket, pulls out a newspaper clipping, and puts it on the table in front of Leon. "Take a minute. Read this little article. The first couple of paragraphs are the important ones."

The article, copied from a several-year-old issue of the *Bismarck Plainsman*, describes the remarkable victory of the new Prime Minister of Israel who, only six weeks before the election was outraged by the polarization of the electorate—both the Labor on the left and the Likud coalition party on the right. He resigned from Likud, formed a new centrist party, grabbed sixty percent of the vote in the election, and cruised into power. Rolfes reads it, then reads it again.

"Okay, Nathan, so what? Last time I checked, Israel's still out in the Mid-East, quite a ways from Bismarck. Isn't it?"

"One more time, Leon. You step in front of the pass. We run another fast break. Boom!"

"Boom? What does that mean? That sounds loony, even for you."

"Just consider the similarities. The dismal impoverished State of North Dakota, under ruthless attack from immoral outside forces, faces an election where the two parties, kidnapped by their fringes, are surely going to destroy the state unless a courageous visionary, sunlight glinting off his armor, steps—"

"Stop this right now, Nathan. Hold on one goddamned second." Leon stands up, thinking it gives him more authority than does slouching in his ergonomic leather chair. "You can push and cajole all you want. There's no way in hell you'll get me to run for governor. It's just not gonna' happen."

"The problem's been there for some time, Leon. And this refinery's cranked up the intensity. The right wing's going bonkers—pushing hard with massive TV ads, whipping up counter demonstrations, bashing poor North Dakota with big money from big business, big politics, even big religion."

"I know all that, you goofballs. I sense 'em crawling through this building's air vents. But I'm not going to step in front of their cannon and take one for the team. I'll quit first. Let 'em have their refinery. I'll go live on the beach... Cancun maybe."

"You can't do that, Leon! Politics is like basketball. It's a team sport. Each of us has a part to play. You're the one who makes the team work. You organize the action, feed the ball to the guy with the step. We all win because *you* do *your* job."

"Lay off the smarmy metaphor—"

"The state needs you to step up. Play tight defense, take the ball away from the out-of-state guys, feed it to in-state interests. You can do that."

"Stop it! Stop it! I can't do that. I'm not a governor type. I'm a legislator, an enabler, not a leader. Do it yourself, Nathan. Your loony basketball analogy works that way too."

"But you have name recognition. You've been in the public eye for thirty years. Everybody in the state knows you and, even more powerful for a politician, respects and trusts you."

"Stuff it, you jerk. The answer's no!"

"Bast and Conlin can't buy those attributes with a slick PR campaign no matter how much money they throw at it. You're the only person in the state who can do this."

"Republicans are playing to your strengths," says Larry. "Everyone knows Conlin won't be the *actual* governor any more than the current bozo. He's Bast's puppet and his organization's constructed with out-of-state guys and being run from Washington by zombies who can't tell Fargo from Dickinson."

"And the refinery project's the key," says Nathan. "You know that. It's all about the refinery, and about North Dakota maintaining her own image and character. It's about preventing New York vultures from grabbing the good meat and leaving the bones and skin for us."

"And don't think refinery guys from Louisiana will respect our prairie," says Larry. "They don't know a cow from an oil drum.

How are they gonna help a cattle rancher like me? Please, Leon? Save us farmers before the slimy rapist steps in—"

"Oh, God, Larry! Not rape again. I'm not listening to you idiots anymore. Drink up your booze and get out of here, or I'll have Margie bring in her shotgun. Of all the stupid things I've heard, that's the stupidest."

"It's not stupid, Leon. It'll work. Everything's set up beautifully. The filing date is Friday, next week. We got time. Think about it for one day." Nathan pulls several papers from his pocket. "I'll leave these on your desk. I've done some thinking and listed arguments, stuff you gotta know before you make up your mind. I'll be out of town tomorrow during the day. Let's say we get together for a beer tomorrow night at Scotties. About 8:30?"

"My mind's already made up, you loonies. I can't believe today started out so peacefully I worried about the quiet. Everything's quickly going down the proverbial toilet."

As Leon shoved them out the door, Nathan turned back. "Your instincts are right, Leon. Things *are* going down that proverbial toilet. Someone has to stop that! I can't think of a better guy. Time to grab your plunger. See you tomorrow night."

Leon pushes them all the way past Margie's desk to the outside office door. "Get the hell outta my office! And don't *ever* come back! This time I really mean it!" He shuts the door behind them, then locks it to ensure they can't come back.

"I'm not the plumber here," he says to Margie, then shakes a finger at her. "I don't do toilets!"

"Another quite dramatic exit. Wow! Sure is fun being your gatekeeper." Margie puts a *please tell me what just happened* look on her face.

"Bah!" Leon strides into his office and slams his own door for emphasis.

***

Same Day
Leon's Mom's House – 6:39 p.m.

"Yoo-hoo! Earth to Leon! We seem to have lost contact. Where are you?"

Leon gives his mother the kind of look only a son can give his mother. "Sorry, Mom. My mind is elsewhere. It's that Prometheus refinery. I'm having difficulty separating the good guys from the bad guys."

"Well, it's time to eat now. Come into the kitchen. You go back to your dream world on a full stomach. Spareribs are therapy. It'll be good for you."

***

As his mom predicted, after spareribs and blueberry pie the world seems a bit easier to grasp. He leaves the table, takes a mug of coffee and his yellow pad out to the porch, and turns on the outdoor lights so he might appreciate the flowers and hedges. His mother loves him, the evening air wafts flowery scents, his friends trust and depend on him, his job satisfies him, his bank account looks good, and his stomach contently purrs. He fears everything will change if he takes Nathan up on his silly idea. He realizes the big problem, of course. Once again, Nathan has given him the correct answer before he's aware there's even been a question. Nathan recognizes a complex situation way before he does, and he designs the perfect course through the quagmire. And once again Nathan's perfect course has *Leon Rolfes* written all over it. Why can't Nathan ever be the best guy to solve his own problems?

This problem, however, is not Nathan's alone—it concerns the whole of North Dakota. And Leon can't dispute the fact that as Speaker of the House, empowered with three decades of expertise and the trust such longevity represents, he can do a better job than Nathan, or anyone else, can possibly do. "Damn you Nathan!" he says. "Damn! Damn! Damn!"

"Such words coming out of your mouth so soon after my pie went in. I must have screwed up the recipe. Need a refill on the coffee?"

"It's not the pie, Mom. It's that refinery that's affecting my normally sweet disposition. I see the machine coming, and I'm standing in its path, and I don't know how to get out of the way."

He suddenly realizes he's talked himself into admitting Nathan's suggestion is something serious, and he hasn't even opened Nathan's papers yet. He stands, looking out the window. "Shit!" he says. "Sorry! Can't do this on coffee, Mom." He fills a glass with brandy from the side cabinet, then goes back to his favorite chair to work on his yellow pad. He orders his notes, studies them, and meticulously arranges them until they make some sense. He convinces himself he'll be ready with an answer for Nathan tomorrow. And when he finishes his arranging, he understands what's about to happen. Once again, he sees Nathan halfway down the court, moving counter to the flow of the action. He knows he's going to step in front of this errant pass and in one motion whip him one very risky, but perfectly accurate, outlet pass. And, of course, that action will win the game!

It's happened several times before. It may very well happen again.

Chapter 18

It's a fine evening for a walk. Leon accepts that. But several contrary and fearsome aspects regarding the reason he must take this walk are now more compelling to him. They overpower the pleasure offered by this walk, a mostly downhill one from his house toward Scottie's. He considers this might be his last chance for a pleasurable walk for a long time, so he's determined to lose his funk and enjoy it. Normally, this walk of a dozen or so blocks takes him about twenty minutes, but not tonight... not with his time so fouled up. He has this odd feeling that perhaps years have passed since he left his house. His travel through time, slowed by pleasant thoughts of the past and accelerated by a terror-laden future, act to screw up any appreciation of reality.

All of a sudden, he finds himself standing in front of Scottie's heavy wooden door. That's strange, he thinks. He has no memory of the walk down the hill—no images of crossing streets, passing other strolling folks, having his eyes blinded by flashing headlights, or being accosted by lit storefronts. It seems reasonable to conclude that such time is now lost. Perhaps he has crossed into a new time-zone. He takes a deep breath and pulls open the door.

Once inside the pub, the happy sounds, a warm humid atmosphere, and the muted, non-aggressive lighting eases him somewhat. He doesn't see Nathan sitting at their favorite table holding the ball and chain with his name on it. That allows him to relax a bit. The crowd appears normal for a Saturday evening. Half the tables are occupied, and a dozen customers at the bar are watching the Twins apparently losing another important late-season game. Leon signals to Scottie at the bar, acknowledges a few acquaintances with a disinterested wave, walks across the room, and sits down in his overstuffed chair by the fireplace. Scottie brings his beer and some peanuts over and lingers a bit discussing the refinery-murder thing.

It's possible he allows another chunk of time to pass him by, but he can't confirm that. He can't find his reflection in the big mirror above the fireplace either. Is it the angle? Or could his image be hiding in the same crevice where his time has been stuffed, somewhere he can't discern it? Eventually he hears Nathan's voice—loud, confident, and cheerful, as it engages in light banter with Scottie over at the bar. That sound returns him to the present, or at least to a time concept approaching normalcy. But Leon knows normal will not last. It might even explode once his buddy crosses the room and sits in that brown leather chair lurking a few feet to his left.

Nathan strides by and musses Leon's hair as he sweeps behind him. "Hey, buddy. Good to see you." He sits down, smiles at him with his big toothy grin, raises his eyebrows like he's done hundreds of times before, and says, "Well?"

Just a single word. Leon knows it contains three or four pages of intricate and troubling thoughts, innuendos, questions, doubts, and promises. They will figure out the details later. All that is necessary now is his answer. And a simple question deserves a simple answer.

"No," Leon says.

They sit there, these two old friends, and they say nothing for a long while. Scottie brings a beer over for Nathan and puts it on a coaster on a side table. "You two are being awfully quiet... just sitting there looking goofy. You sick or something, Nathan? You look like shit."

"We're using mental telepathy, Scottie, to keep all our secrets from your prying ears."

Scottie laughs. "You *are* full of shit. It's no wonder you look like it. You need a bacon burger, don't you?"

"I appreciate the concern, Scottie. I'm just tired. Had a long day."

Scottie leaves their table, slowly wipes down the adjacent one, and makes his way back to the bar.

"When I walked in here tonight, my answer was gonna be 'yes.' But I got cold feet waiting. I'm not sure I can do it, Nathan. I'm a point guard, not the franchise player."

Nathan digests that slowly. "I understand your reluctance, but you *cannot* make that choice."

"And why not?"

"Because if you do, North Dakota gets run over by the machine. Junk and debris will be strewn all over the prairie. Smoke and ashes will obscure the sun. Soot-encrusted hawks and vultures will swoop through the mess looking for roadkill."

"Good God! That's pathetic! Did you actually say that?"

"I've got other metaphors, some even more disgusting."

"If I say *yes* then you'll stop. Is that it?"

"Stuff it! Pretend we're in your office. I go to your shelf, grab your basketball, zap you a brisk two-handed pass, and say, 'You got the ball now, Leon. Let's run the bastards off the court.'"

"If we were there, I'd zip it right back at you, you jerk. But I get your point, thank you. We did make magic happen, didn't we? We led old Rugby High to the championship. And we have a chance to do the same thing here for the whole damn state. Not a bad analogy, Nathan. It's a bit too sweet and syrupy for this mud-encrusted political arena, but not bad."

Leon takes a sip of beer. "You know what I did today?"

"No. Does it matter?"

"I took the day off and drove up to the house in Rugby. I thought I could think clearer thoughts up there, sitting in my chair looking out the window. I thought maybe I'd get a clearer idea of the political landscape... have the prairie speak directly to me."

"And what did the prairie tell you?"

"Damn it, Nathan. It told me you had the right idea. Told me to go for it. So I came back here to tell you I'll do it. Such a strange idea would never have occurred to me."

"I was expecting a bit of a contest here. So I readied myself for heavy lifting—an argument or two, some throwing of pottery. I've got ammunition left over." He spreads his hands wide in a gesture of resignation. "I'm done here. Maybe I'll go home and get some well-needed sleep. I burned a lot of calories today. My body's yelling for sleep."

"Don't give me that, Nathan. If I have to work, so do you. And I believe you know that it's going to mean a lot of work for you. I need money! People and money! Position papers and money! Schedules and money! I need answers to about ten thousand questions, and money! You have some of that for me, right?"

"It just so happens, you're correct. I've a reasonable handle on these things, and I can go over 'em with you, if you want."

"Thanks, but later will be fine. First I want to tell you why I'm doing this. And don't be surprised if my reasons differ from yours. I know why *you* want me to do it. You don't think the refinery, as proposed, is good for our state. And you think a governor named Leon is the quickest and surest way to kill it."

"Well, I cannot tell a lie. Yes, that's my primary—"

"That's not a bad reason, Nathan. But the refinery is only a symptom of North Dakota's problem, not the problem itself. The real problem is that we people of North Dakota are in danger of becoming insignificant. Outside money, outside interests, outside values, outside everything. And these outside interests control the fringe loonies on the right and the left, which is where all the energy is going. Nobody's aiming their pitch to the common people in the middle."

"Except the *Plainsman*. Did you see their editorial this morning? Kind of surprised me."

"I did, and that editorial convinced me. If that gung-ho business crowd over at the paper thinks we should wait till after the election to take up the refinery question, I'd think it means I have a chance of bringing them over to my side. Don't you?"

"You're absolutely right, Leon." Nathan knows when he has to be the cheerleader, and he can wave a pom-pom with the best of them.

"My hesitation is that I'm but a legislator. I'm driven by the needs of my constituents, and I know almost all of 'em by name. I'm an enabler. I don't think of myself as a leader. You're always the one with the big ideas. You've got to help me here. I'm thinking of a team approach, like it's always been in the past."

"Somewhere it's written down that governors have to be leaders, Leon. Don't ya think?"

"Watching the tube last night I heard Bast screaming about the refinery, pushing it as good for jobs. He talked about jobs and money pouring into Dakota. I've done the research, Nathan. Even our own State Development Director, one of Bast's loyal goons, is skeptical of his job creation numbers. And the lefty guys… all their money and agendas are set nationally as well. Somebody has to represent the people in the middle."

"Sounds like you're ready to go, Leon. Can we set up some sort of schedule?"

"We've got to get a team together. Like basketball, politics is a team sport."

Nathan stands up. "I need another beer, how about you?"

"I'm fine. But as long as you're going over there, can you order me a bowl of chili?"

Nathan weaves his way over to the bar. Leon sees him stop and talk to patrons at a couple of tables. He's a much better schmoozer than Leon and he actually enjoys talking to strangers. That's why the team thing is going to be important.

Nathan puts two beers on the table, one in front of each of them.

"I thought I said chili."

"Scottie will bring it right over. You looked thirsty so I bought you the beer too."

"Do you see the problem, here? You think I'm thirsty even though I said no. Ya gotta be careful, Nathan. When I'm governor, you gotta stick to my rules. If I say chili, I don't mean beer."

"Yeah, yeah. Well, I can still buy you a beer whenever I want."

"I've a feeling my decision's not going to surprise many people. At least not as much as it surprised me. You've been working on this for a while, right? Been buying my beer for a while? I assume money's available?"

"You can so assume. I've been talking to local movers and shakers."

"I'll need tons of cash, and quickly. I've got to explode this thing... make some big noise up front. Let's say I don't chicken out. How quickly can the moolah start flowing?"

"The money is there. I'll talk with Margie. But remember, you're an actual flesh and blood guy. So, unlike Conlin, you'll get most of your money from in-state sources."

Leon makes a gesture indicating *hey, this is me—what you see is what you get.* They discuss plans. Leon eats his chili and drinks his beer.

"You're the one that made the thing work on the court, Leon," says Nathan. "You organize the action, feed the ball, take the best advantage. We win because you do your job. It is pretty simple, Leon—*do your job.*"

"Okay, Nathan. You've talked me into one more absolutely outrageous prank. I hope you're satisfied."

"Damn right I am. Let's get out of here… I'm beat."

They exit into the brisk air. "Want a ride home, Leon?"

"No. I need the thinkin' time the walk allows. You run home and get to bed. Looks like you need sleep. You want me to drive you?"

"Thanks, but I'll be okay."

Leon takes a few steps, then turns back to Nathan. "This is absolutely the last time, you jerk."

"Yeah, yeah! I've heard that before. Get some sleep tonight, it may be in short supply from here on out."

***

One block up the hill, as he passes the hardware store, Leon removes the cell phone from his jacket pocket and looks at it. He's

thinking this next conversation is going to require a bit more control than he'd exhibited with Nathan. It will also mean that once
he dials the number he will absolutely not be able to turn back.
He might consider this call to be his first act as the new, or at least
probable, Governor of North Dakota.

"Good evening, Steffie. You gonna be in town this weekend?"

"It's Saturday night, Leon. Weekend's about half over. You
gotta wake up."

Leon feels he *is* awake. To be honest, he thinks he's never before felt as awake as he is right now.

"Give me a break. I've an exclusive story for you. But there's a
catch."

"Imagine that, Leon—a politician's story embedded with a
hook. Whatever am I supposed to think?"

"First of all, behave yourself, and watch your tongue."

"Yes, sir, Mr. Speaker."

"That's more like it. Secondly, if you're in town tomorrow, my
mother would like to tempt you over to her house for Sunday dinner. Say about five-thirty. Will you be able to make that?"

"You want me to spend Sunday afternoon with your mother?
Nice try, Leon. I know you, you devious SOB. And I know you
want her there for a reason... as a witness to the truth for instance,
or as a silence enforcer, or some other little trick. I've a good mind
to turn you down. But I'll bet it's her meatloaf and scalloped corn,
right?"

"I think that may be a distinct possibility."

"Good! Then I'll be there, and I'll bring some beer. It goes
better with meatloaf."

Chapter 19

Steffie knows the rules. No business talk allowed until everyone's plate is filled and the gravy, rolls, and butter are distributed. So she talks to Leon about her boys, who are actually getting along since both made starter on the football team. She talks about the harvest chores that keep everyone's interest focused out at the ranch. Steffie plays it by the book. She waits until Leon sticks his first forkful of meatloaf into his mouth, and then she begins her dissertation.

"Right at the beginning here, I want to make a statement for the record, Leon. Any topic enticing enough to get me over here tonight must be one challenging not so much my investigatory and literary skill set, but my personal analysis tools as well. I figure you want my reaction to some juicy news item."

"Are you finished? Can I talk now? This is *my* party, for God's sake."

"Not yet, Leon. I've not finished my statement yet." She winks at his mom. "I reviewed last week's activity around town and stirred in that interesting meeting in your office with Larry and Nathan."

"I knew this had to do with Nathan," says Mom. "He's got you in trouble again, huh?"

"Steffie, I—"

"Hear me out. I checked a few sources, made a few calls, and…" She pulls a folded paper from a pocket, puts it on the table, and places her hand, palm down on top of it. "Here's my prediction for tonight's hot topic!" She hoists a forkful of meatloaf with her other hand. "Now you can talk."

"I thought we should celebrate," says Leon. "The Twins won their last game of the season in a blowout."

His mother swats him and Steffie laughs. "Okay, okay. I'm sorry I misbehaved. Tell us *your* story."

"You guys are making this harder than it has to be. I find myself in a strange position and need your help. But, Steffie, I worry you can't give it to me, because you are…" He makes a pair of air quotation marks by wiggling his fingers above his head, "…'technically,' not one of *us*. You're not an elected politician. You're a reporter, and a damn good one… and a reporter who is all wound up in the *amazing, mysterious, suicide or non-suicide* story, and also in the *who is really pulling the strings on both sides of the big refinery proposal* story. And both of these stories are strangely linked by some ethereal threads."

"You've put that quite poetically, for you at least."

"Hush! And it's gonna get even more poetic, just so you'll be aware and not get nauseated. I've got another story I want you to focus on. It's an even bigger story because it's one that's constructed on top of those other two stories. The solution to those stories cannot be revealed without the telling of this third story."

"It's like one of my son's video games, huh? Stories within stories, with secret keys. Wow! Am I excited Leon, or what? I can't wait. Tell me, tell me!"

"Hush again, Steffie. Show a bit of restraint."

Leon sneaks a piece of meatloaf in, thinking it might be his last chance for a while.

"And Mom, this is going to come as a surprise story to you too. Last night I made a decision. I'm going to enter the race for governor."

Neither of the girls gag or spit anything out.

Steffie takes her time, chews carefully, and swallows.

Mom gets her act together and fires first. "Sure you are, honey, and I am going to run the Boston marathon."

That sets him back a bit, but he doesn't take it as completely negative.

Steffie grins like a schoolgirl, turns her secret paper over, then waves it in front of Leon's face. "See! See! You're so transparent. It's obvious the climate out there troubled you. I think it's a brilliant strategic move and a very courageous thing to do. I understand Nathan's tape-playing demonstration the other day. We're all on the same team, huh? The opening in the opponent's game plan is obvious. So, seize the moment and charge through that opening right to the basket. Or to the governor's chair in this case. Pretty good breakdown, huh?"

"Nathan and I—"

"Aha! I knew it!" says Mom. "Nathan has to be involved in something this crazy. Okay, now I believe you're telling the truth."

Leon pretends to show little concern for his mom's reaction and he takes a gulp of beer.

Steffie jumps back in. "I see it now. Nathan played that tape for my benefit. He wanted to set the background, to explain what you'd be doing. He knew about all this way before you did, right?"

"He sure did," his mother confirms.

"But my run for governor isn't the story, Steffie. Or maybe it's only a part of it, like the Gupchal thing is a part and the refinery thing is a part."

"So, what do you think *is* the story?"

"The story is a mystery, to me at least. And it's gonna be your job to solve this mystery. You're not a political reporter. Your paper has plenty of those guys running around with nothing to do since Conlin has the election sewn up."

"Not any more, he doesn't." Mrs. R gets up. "Anyone want more coffee?"

"I'd like you to officially chronicle my campaign, not for the governorship, but for the rights and dignity of our state. I'm convinced that big story contains all three and probably a couple more of the smaller stories you're interested in. I think you alone have the introspection and the integrity to report them all without getting lost.

"And in exchange for you getting the inside edge on those stories, I'd like something in return. I require your guidance through the quagmire of stories number one and two. Without you carrying the light, I don't think I can find my way. I see a symbiotic relationship, with maybe a bit of Heisenberg uncertainty in it."

"You're thinking I can get close. I can observe these stories and predict their outcome. Maybe change how the big story unfolds?"

"Perhaps, and from my perspective I'm thinking that the big story *must* change. I'm counting on it. There's a minefield of unknowns out there and I need you to find 'em before I step on something and it goes boom. I'm certain your vision will alter my path, and I'm hoping it will allow me to get out alive on the other side."

His mother understands these references to some vague future reality. "You're worried about Nathan, aren't you?"

"Well, Mom, don't you think I should be? I pretty much decided this on my own. He suggested it, certainly. But he used little pressure. He hardly had to make an argument, though that's only my impression. I realize he could have manipulated things to make me think I did it. He's done that before. Right, Mom?"

"All the time, Son. All the time. But, to be fair to Nathan, most all the things he's pressured you into doing were good things. I recall he pushed you into running for the legislature and pushed you even harder for speaker. You'd never have jumped off that ledge without his shove. It's not so surprising he's pushing you off the governor cliff, is it?"

"I know Nathan will be better off if I'm the governor than if the present crew stays in control. But I don't know how or why he'll be better off. That refinery project frightens him. Hell, it frightens me. But I don't understand why. Nathan's connected to everything, and although he would never share details, or consider bribes or paybacks, he might push the limits. He might embarrass or compromise me. You remember the Neil Sedaka concert, Mom?"

"So," says Steffie. "Let me get this straight. You want me to let my paper's political staff cover the race for governor, like they have been doing so far without much trouble, while I work on a longer-range personal quest sort of story—*Leon Rolfes fights the evil New Yorkers for the good of North Dakota.* And just maybe that turns out to be a book. Good for me... could be my big chance to break out of this North Dakota rut. But you think that, because I'm hanging with you, I can bring the Gupchal murderers to justice and expose the anti-Dakotan agendas of the evil *state rapers*."

"What?" asks Mrs. R.

Steffie catches Leon's *how did you know that* expression, and smiles. "Margie told me about the rapers. She has to tell *somebody* juicy stuff like that."

"You've got the correct scenario, Steffie."

"Well, Mrs. R, how can a good investigative reporter like me turn down such a sweet offer? Would it be all right if I asked your boy a couple of questions? Can I do a little reporter business right in front of the meatloaf?"

"Go for it, honey."

"I'll write up a statement, put it out on the internet and the evening TV and into tomorrow's paper—"

"You can't do that! Slow down. Please. First I've got to tell Margie, and my fellow legislators, and probably the governor, and organize my thoughts. I'll do all that tomorrow, then we put the news out on the TV and internet tomorrow night and your paper hits the porches on Tuesday morning."

"Then you can set a news conference for Tuesday afternoon, maybe one or two o'clock. And maybe, since it will be a nice day, you put yourself on the steps of the Capitol with its great stone tower as a backdrop, which demonstrates that, since you've been working in that same building for the past twenty years, you're not jumping off a cliff, only taking one small step for mankind. Specifically, any mankind in North Dakota."

"Womenkind too, sweetie," says Mom. "We live here too."

"Behave yourself, Mom." Leon points a fork full of meatloaf at her, then turns to Steffie. "That sounds very nice. Just make sure it gets in Tuesday morning's paper and onto whatever information superhighways you have access to."

"How do you know Tuesday will be a nice day? You clairvoyant or something?"

"How can it not be, Mrs. R? The master of the universe has Leon's back. I can feel it."

"I doubt that, Steffie. If He was lookin' out for me, He wouldn't have allowed me entry into Scotties with Nathan last night."

"This is going to be so much fun. Would you please pass the meatloaf, Mrs. R? I need another serving of your finely crafted fuel."

***

Even without Leon yet officially in the race, election junk is clogging that information superhighway. Leon and his mom watch the ten o'clock news, and a large chunk of both the stories and the advertising concern the election, now about six weeks away. A good percentage of news time is spent on the race for governor, even though it ceased being a contest long ago. Both Conlin's election machine and the reporters covering it consider the race over, but that fact only increases the amount of mud they think they gotta throw.

However, the big news tonight is that Dennis Hickmann, the Democratic candidate who is so far behind he has nothing to lose, has managed to grab a reasonable chunk of airtime because he has just proposed one rather outrageous scheme to solve North Dakota's *getting itself raped by outside interests* problem.

"Did you hear what Hickmann just said, Mom? He wants the state to seize the oil rights for every property in the state. He thinks once the state owns all the oil, then the state will negotiate sales and distribute the profits from those oilfields back to the land owners with a yearly check that cuts out all the speculation from Wall Street and Houston. Wow! And I thought I was poking my sharp stick at the evil oil industry. Hickmann wants to castrate the whole bunch."

"He sounds a bit like a dictator from some third world country, though I guess he can afford to say anything—he's not going to lose any worse no matter what he says."

"I don't know, Mom. It almost smells like a rational idea. I think that's kind of the way Alaska works too. They have the same population we do. If it works up there, it might work here also. It would sure stop all the speculation and the running of funny projects through my legislature."

"I'm no finance expert, Son, but I think Hickmann's scheme will drive those Houston and New York speculators right up the wall. Where are they gonna make a buck? If for some reason his idea starts to gain traction, those vultures are going to crucify him."

"Watch out you don't stumble over your metaphors, Mom. It could be a lot of yelling for nothing. Who knows?"

Leon's cell dances around the top of the end table emitting gurgles.

"What ya want to bet that's Steffie, Son? She's just heard the Hickmann news bite too, and she sees a story."

"Wrong, Mom. It's President Obama." He picks it up, slides the button, and gives his mother the evil eye. "Good evening, Mr. President. Isn't it past your bedtime out there on the east coast?"

"Pathetic, Leon," says Steffie. "Shameful. You got to be serious here. I'm afraid I don't have time to play."

"Hi Steffie," yells Mom. "I'll make sure he behaves himself."

"Hickmann is right," says Steffie. "He's made a brilliant move. If you're jumping into the race, you're going to have to start paying attention."

"Nobody's going to pay any attention to him. I don't think brilliant's the word—maybe hot air."

"I think he's right. I called to warn you that both Hickmann and I read the same little news article buried in the middle of page thirteen in the New York Times today. As a heads-up, I'm emailing you a copy. Read it. There will be a test tomorrow. And mark my words, Leon—that article is going to *change your life*. Gotta go. My paper's holding a thousand-word slot for me on the front page. I've only got an hour and a half to deadline. Bye!"

Leon goes to his computer, pulls up Steffie's email, and reads the article. It says that Brazil just discovered a tub of oil several miles off their coast, and it might be twice the size of the Saudi's tub. And the stuff is not hidden in shale like Dakota, or in sand like in Alberta. Though it is deep in the ocean, the stuff will be much easier to extract than Dakota oil, and thus can be sold much cheaper than Dakota oil on the world market.

"Look at this article Steffie sent me, Mom. She thinks Hickmann's statement about state control was prompted by this article about Brazil discovering a new oilfield. I'm not making a connection. What am I missing?"

"You have to pay attention to the competition, dear. I'll give you a list of words and you tell me which words don't fit in."

"Jeeze, Mom—"

"One is Brazil, two is Saudi Arabia, three is little Nathan Goodbrother from Rugby, four is the state of Alaska."

"I didn't know you taught at the business school. Where'd you get that?"

"Think about which of those four have the best chance of controlling the market."

"You're right, Mom. It sure ain't gonna be that farmer from Rugby, is it? And that's what Steffie's story in tomorrow's *Plainsman* is gonna say?"

"Yep! And think of the potential for some new guy to hop up on the capitol steps tomorrow and make some sense of this puzzle."

"Make it the day after tomorrow, but I get your point. My timing is impeccable, huh?"

***

Back on the TV news, pro-refinery and pro-Republican adherents parade past the lens to persuade, cajole, seduce, or otherwise inveigle prospective voters to buy into their dream. One ad includes a computer-generated vision of an overly bucolic scene, with cattle grazing, tractors plowing, and farm families picnicking in the foreground, while a clean glistening jewel of a refinery, with orderly rows of candy-stick chimneys and lollypop domes, hovers in the background. It makes Leon think of Disneyland.

"Makes me want to throw up," says Mrs. R. "Neat little picket fences and villages with white churches tucked into a pretty green glen. It doesn't look much like a prairie to this hick. I'm thinking Vermont, maybe."

"Our prairie's flat and beige, Mom. Endless brown fields covered in harvesting debris won't put a viewer in the mood to open his heart and his checkbook. Idyllic Vermont? Now that makes a better sell."

"I can't be the only grandma in North Dakota feeling nauseous right now, can I?"

"I don't think so, Mom. In fact, I'm counting on the intelligence of our electorate. I'll bet you won't see that touchie-feelie ad any more. Nathan thinks as soon as I jump into the pool the rightwing poll numbers will head for the basement, and that means a new strategy. Bye-bye green fields, white churches, and yellow brick roads. Hello to mud. It will *not* be fun, Mom."

"I'm ready for 'em, honey." She strikes a Muhammad Ali pose. "Don't you worry 'bout yo' mama."

Chapter 20

Leon, thinking this is a rather important day, is wearing his best three-piece suit. He notices Margie do a double-take as he enters the office. He thinks she gets the message. Something special is in the book for this morning.

"Morning, boss. My, my, don't you look spiffy this a.m."

"Morning, Margie." Leon walks through his office door. He turns around and says, "We need to talk."

He immediately walks around his desk, sits down, folds his hands on his desktop, and waits for Margie to assume a position of anticipation on the other side of his desk. When she gets into position, he says in a rather profound voice, "I have an announcement to make."

Margie jumps to attention in front of his desk and repeats his words in a rather haughty voice. "I have an announcement to make!" She then breaks with all the formality and sits down. "Normally you would've said, 'I got somethin' for ya.' But you didn't do that. So this must be big. You gonna run for governor or something?"

Leon immediately understands he's lost this encounter. "You really know how to make me feel like a jerk, huh?"

She jumps up and claps her hands. "You are! Aren't you?" She runs around his desk and gives him a humongous hug. "I'm so proud of you. The other day you asked, 'How do those good people of my district want me to react to all this?' Remember that?"

He nodded.

"Well, I'll tell you, Leon, this is exactly what they'd want you to do. They don't want Conlin to give away the state, especially to those New York hedge fund guys."

"I still haven't told you what my announcement is."

Margie went right on by. "Wow! This is so exciting. When do we start?"

"I still haven't told—"

"Oh, stuff it! I heard you the first time."

"You realize things are gonna get hectic around here, don't you?"

"Hectic never hurt anybody, let alone me. Don't worry about me. I'll get Debbie to come over and be your gatekeeper for a couple of months. She'll love that. I'll take a leave of absence and work full time for the *next governor of the great state of North Dakota.*"

"Just take a deep breath, Margie."

"You saw Steffie's article this morning, about Brazil shaking up the oil market? What else could you do? Whoopee! Here we go!"

"For God's sake, calm down. Now, if you want to do this, your first job is to get rid of that stupid banner about killing farmers. It's driving me bats. Can you handle that?"

"Yes, sir." She gives him a kiss on the top of his head and waltzes through the door looking, to Leon's eye, about ten years younger than when she came in.

"That went well," he says. "Maybe it's an omen. If she so easily accepts it, maybe it's not such a crazy idea as I think it is."

***

By the time Nathan shows up a half hour later, Margie has shifted the personnel around, set up a temporary campaign office in Leon's small conference room, and brewed some fresh coffee. Nathan has a long conversation with her in the outer office before he enters Leon's den and seats himself.

"G'morning, Leon. I see Margie is halfway down the slope already. She's a miracle worker. I've found an office for your campaign HQ. It's just across the street from the *Prairie Pioneer* statue." He points out the window. "I can almost see it from here."

"I gotta tell you, Nathan, the more research I do, the more clairvoyant you seem."

"I'm not sure, Leon. Is that good or bad?"

"Oh, it's certainly not bad. You see Steffie's article this morning? You probably knew all that stuff already, but it does illustrate the enormous pressures being applied to our little state. Huge outside interests, completely lacking any compassion for us small folk living here, are zeroing in on us like the black stealth bombers the Air Force hides in the caves near Fargo. And reading that article makes me think that North Dakota's future as an oil producing state has just vanished overnight."

"How you gonna fix that Mr. Governor?"

"We could call out the National Guard and invade Brazil and take their oil."

"Back to earth, Leon. Steffie's article puts Prometheus in a big bind too. It makes their refinery an even bigger gamble, because if Brazil will be able to pull their stuff out of the ground for half the price we can, our stuff ain't gonna get pulled out. And a refinery will have nothing to refine. How loud can you yell turkey?"

"Yet several groups are thinking the same way as Prometheus. The State Development Office tells me they have competition, or to be absolutely proper here, have probable competition from a couple possible entities who might give their right arm to be assured that Prometheus fails. But as far as I know, Prometheus is the only firm currently talking to N-DOPE or sending goodies to the governor and us legislative leaders now. If someone else is out there stirring up a bit of dust, I'm sure you'd know about it, wouldn't you? I don't think anyone can keep *you* in the dark, can they?"

"Secrecy is necessary, Leon. Everyone's afraid of rustling the bushes and rousing any wildlife hiding there. And wildlife can only harm a project. Believe me, Leon, I've done hundreds of deals, and I'd never tell anyone what I'm doing, even, now don't take this the wrong way old buddy, an old buddy like you."

"Understood, Nathan. But the pressure here is immense. Prometheus is pushing hard for me to give them all sorts of goodies. Do we want the refinery here or do we want to send it to Wyoming? I'm assuming if we turn these guys down, we'll have to go through the whole thing again with the next applicant, probably some other hedge fund, owned by another consortium from Dubai or Texas. Oil makes good folks go crazy."

Leon walks over to the window. "Ya know, Nathan, I think I've given myself one very good reason to forget about being governor. Hell, I'll even forget about being the representative from Rugby. I'm thinkin' the Virgin Islands. It's warm down there, and I hear the women are good lookin' and the piña-coladas cheap."

"You could do that, Leon. But your mom and Margie will kill you before they let you step onto the plane. Also, winter is just getting started up here and I am sure you'll want to stick around for that, and finally, you'll start Brian Bast dancing on the ceiling, and you wouldn't want to see him *that* happy, would you?"

"Three fairly good reasons, Nathan. And on such short notice too. Do you know anything about those other proposals floating around?" Leon hopes to catch Nathan off-guard and get a truthful reaction. But a quick facial scan tells him his friend didn't even come close to letting his shield down. It's a reaction which he believes his mother would put in the *nice try but I am a professional and not so easily fooled* category.

"I don't think it's time to jump in yet, but some folks are looking. The activity does illustrate the potential for a refinery in the upper Midwest. The consensus, as I read it, maintains a refinery project up here is a couple of years away, and now is too early to take on such risk, especially with the news out of Brazil. There are three big variables. The first is proof that the Alberta shale can produce a dependable volume of the right kind of stuff… that they can alter the consistency enough to get it to flow, and at the right price to warrant the expense of all the work they have to go through to make it flow. The second is the problem Canada Oil has with pumping their gooey, peanut-buttery crude to either their refineries in Ontario, or to ours in Louisiana. Some folks think they should refine the thick stuff up here first. Then they can cheaply pump the thin stuff wherever they want.

"The third has to do with the complicated technology required to get to *our* new deposits. Currently, even using all the tricks of horizontal drilling, sand fracking, and chemical persuasion, we can only remove four to ten percent of the oil that's hidden down there. Most think the big investment needed for a big refinery can't be made until a way is found to cheaply harvest that remaining oil.

"The common wisdom is that those things are not settled enough for anyone to take a chance on the refinery part yet. But Prometheus' quick strike indicates that analysis may be wrong. Apparently it's not too early for position jockeying, though I personally don't see any folks out there being as obvious as Prometheus."

"That sounds reasonable, Nathan, but sometimes the oil supply isn't the driver. Sometimes it's greed, or intuition, or manipulation. If there are other guys out there thinking about this, those guys will cheer if Prometheus fails, won't they? So the potential exists that those other guys might derive benefit from the Gupchals' death. As one refinery project implodes, another project pops up. High stakes whack-a-mole."

"I know the potential exists for a competing project. Everyone knows that. As we speak, there's another refinery project moving through the regulators in South Dakota. It's even named after another Greek god, Hyperion."

"Just a side note from the classics guy here, Nathan. Hyperion, you realize, is or was or might have been, Prometheus' brother. Is that a coincidence? You thinking there's a story there?"

"Might be you're right, Leon. It's a story about gods being gods, or about vultures being vultures. Technically, I suppose, other gods or vultures could jump in. But we have to focus here. I'd let the sheriff concentrate on those deaths and let me concentrate on the whack-

a-mole game, and you concentrate on running Bast and Conlin out
of town. They're the immediate evil threat."

"That's putting it so simple even I can understand it. I think I
can do that."

"The people of North Dakota can, indeed they must, realize the
danger here, Leon. It is time to don your armor, grab your lance,
saddle up, and head for Jerusalem."

"Oh, cut it out. That's not the way it's gonna happen. This cause
needs a wider appeal than one guy charging into battle on a white
horse."

"But I rather do like the visual."

"I'll give you a visual—one of those John Deere combines with
the double-wide swath. That is what that Israeli guy you made me
read about actually drove into Jerusalem."

"And you think *my* metaphors are stupid?"

"His campaign succeeded because he tied it to his new party. It
gave him instant continuity. Few voters will jump to the *other party*.
Many, however, may be intrigued by a *new party* which incorporates
the best elements of the existing ones. Then they don't feel they are
deserting their principles."

"You sound like you've been working on this overtime, Leon.
Forming a new centrist party seems a great idea. Grab some conservative potatoes. Grab some liberal beef. Make a tasty stew."

"And one more thing, Nathan. With only me on my own as an
independent candidate, the race has the possibility of becoming a
referendum mainly on the refinery. It doesn't address the wider issue Hickmann is raising. With a new political party occupying the
middle of the spectrum, a much broader appeal can be made to the
entire state and to the dreams and goals of our citizens. I want to call
this new thing the *Dakota First Party*."

"Brilliant! It underscores your point that the governor must
work for the people of North Dakota and not for New York refinery
developers."

"And it allows many of my legislative friends who are not so
right-wing or left-wing, and not so beholden to national interests,

to find themselves a comfortable spot in the middle. I should talk to Hickmann. He might consent to jump on board. Wouldn't that blow Conlin out of the water?"

"I'll get the presses running pronto and have T-shirts and posters rolling out by tomorrow. And speaking of hoopla—"

"Oh, no you don't, Nathan! I'm not going to run *my* campaign *your* way. And I say this even before you tell me what your way might be. Margie is running this thing. She's ordered me to make *that* my first campaign decision. And the second is that you cannot have any official capacity in it."

Nathan smiles. "You think I don't know that? I know you are one obstinate son of a bitch and wouldn't listen to a thing I'd say anyway."

"We both know that's not true. Sorry. I had to get that out of the way. Now, you were speaking of hoopla?"

"I'll stay well away from your campaign, Leon, except for one thing which I already have a great handle on, and that's the opposite of hoopla. It's the moolah."

"Some might consider moolah a variety of hoopla, but I get your distinction."

Nathan takes an envelope from his jacket pocket, opens it, and takes out several papers to show Leon. "I'm hooked into most all the big agribusiness and bio-energy people in the state, and can assure you that almost all non-oil business will support your effort." He shook the envelope. "Only twelve hours since you said the magic word, Leon, and lookie here! I've already extracted checks for over three hundred thousand dollars. This is gonna work, Leon."

"Talk to Margie about setting up campaign accounts. Then do what she tells you. She's the boss—understand?"

"Yes, sir!" Nathan salutes and goes out front to talk to Margie.

Chapter 21

The Tuesday morning phone calls begin before 6:00 a.m., before Leon finishes his wake up ritual, before he recognizes the face looking at him from his own mirror, before he dons his cloak of reality. Eventually, he makes it down the stairs, walks through the family room to the porch, and looks through the patio doors at the blackness of the predawn. Little touches of blush in the eastern sky suggest that the sun just might show up today. He flicks on the yard lights. The tranquil scene of his mother's dying flower garden and the semi-green lawn running back to the hedge bursts into view.

"What ya do that for, dear?"

"Don't know, Mom. Thought I'd check and make sure I still have some connection to the ground, that I haven't been beamed up to the starship. I don't recognize the landscape in my head any more. Kind of hoped I'd do better with the real thing out in the yard."

"An interesting experiment, Son. Is it working?"

"I'm not sure. But I'd better make some kind of adjustment fast, huh?"

"That would be my advice, dear. Here's the paper. Steffie's got the whole thing spread out on the front page. And she's used that nice picture of you from the river carnival last summer. It makes you look ten years younger. So dashing and so confident. I hardly recognize you."

"Nice, Mom. Your opinion's always appreciated."

His mother retrieves five sticky-backed yellow messages she had attached to woodwork about the kitchen. "These people insisted you call them back as soon as you walked into my kitchen. And can you believe not all of 'em recognized they were talking to a sweet little old lady? A few turned downright mean when I told 'em you had a big day ahead and needed your sleep." She gives him the messages and goes back toward the stove.

He scans the messages quickly.

"I almost threw Mr. Bast's message in the trash. My advice to you is don't call him back. Such a rude person!"

"Bast's a machine. I don't believe he has a human mother to tell him when he's acting like an ass. Steffie's article mention anything I should know about?"

"Her paper partnered with Channel 7 to conduct a quick state-wide phone poll to gauge immediate reaction to your announcement. Results should be available for the ten o'clock news tonight. That'll be interesting."

"Interesting's an understatement. It'll be the most important piece of news since Nathan put his layup through the hoop, forty-five years ago. I'm not sure I'll last till ten o'clock, hanging around for hours waiting for a couple of numbers to determine the rest of my life."

"You just relax and do your job. Concentrate on your oatmeal and sausage."

***

HF&G's office, New York City – 9:10 a.m.

J.D. Crowe's morning starts out even more confusing. He doesn't make it past Angelina's desk in the outer office. His 'good morning' to Angelina was pretty much normal, but things quickly went south after that.

"Morning yourself, J.D.," she says. "Don't you get too comfy. You've gotta play fireman this morning."

"What?"

"Mr. Francelli's really upset. He told me to tell you to grab the rest of the team and meet in his office, pronto. Then he asked me to make sure his jet is ready. Sounds like somethin' ugly's just hit the fan."

Crowe rounds up the other junior partners and parades them into Francelli's office. Francelli is not there yet. They seat themselves around the conference table and wait.

A few minutes later, Enrico bursts into the room, clears the screen-saver, and then brings up a photo of the *Bismarck Plainsman* headline on his big screen. He skips the 'good morning group,' part.

"Look at this, J.D.! Apparently your friend, Speaker Rolfes, pulled an end-run on Bast. Faked Bast out of his shoes. Rolfes jumped into the governor's race and your boy thinks he's got a reasonable shot to win it."

"Rolfes is not 'my boy,'" says J.D. "He appears a hayseed, but he is a serious guy. What he needs is somebody big to sit on him."

Francelli slaps the huge screen. "You may be that guy. I just got off the phone with that idiot Bast. He's running scared. All upset. Cryin' like a baby."

"This Prometheus thing's been nothing but a headache ever since we bought into it," says J.D. "Seems the whole thing's falling apart."

"It'll work out," Francelli says. "All we need is a few more days, maybe a week. Then we sell Prometheus and get out. But until then the pressure must be constant. The future owner has to understand we're pushing this hard. Keep the value of this turkey elevated as we lower the price."

"I'll fly out again. It's the last time Enrico. I mean it. I think the governor and our investors would expect a vigorous reaction, and I don't want them to be disappointed."

"Take Pick along. He apparently made a good impression last time."

"Good idea. We'll only be away one day. Then, hopefully by the end of next week, I can rid us of this turkey. After that, maybe we can relax."

"I don't think that's gonna happen," says Francelli. "I sense something evil and messy going on. It's possible you may never relax again."

***

The warped, unpainted front door slowly opens, and she sees him standing there, his right hand clutching the knob. He's wearing mud-splattered jeans and his pajama top and clutching a bottle of peach brandy. The sudden sunlight startles him. Then recognition hits him. That startles him even more. His eyes go big as golf balls. But he manages to maintain some control. He doesn't drop the bottle.

"Hi, Tommy," she says. "How's our friendly neighborhood lush this morning?"

"What the hell you doin' out here at my house? How'd you find out where I live?"

"Oh, for God's sake! You think I'm an idiot? This ain't 1950, Tommy. We searchers all got computers now. Makes finding scum easy."

"What ya mean, scum? I'm your partner here, sweetcheeks. I'm the one doin' all your dirty work. Remember?"

"Look at you! You're the epitome of scumbag! Yet you're callin' my work dirty?" She pulls a paper from her pocket and waves it in his face. "Now this!" she says. "This piece of crap is what I call dirty. You're stupid as shit, Tommy. Tryin' to blackmail me. And slipping your filthy ultimatum under my email door? You stupid drunk. You think you're gonna blackmail me?"

"It wasn't meant to be blackmail. Just want my fair share. Thought we might work out a little business deal. What ya think, huh? Wanna do a bit o' business?" He reaches through the open

doorway and tries to grab at her hair. "We're equals in this. I do some dirty work for you. Maybe you do some dirty work on me." He takes a long gulp of brandy. "We have a contract. We're partners, right? I'm not workin' no more without no contract."

"You've stepped over the line, Tommy." She slaps his hand aside, then quickly puts both her hands on his chest and shoves him back into the room. "Blackmail's not gonna happen, Tommy. You're not gonna be able to blackmail me. Dead lawyers can't blackmail anybody." She gives him another shove.

He still doesn't drop the bottle. Timmins is more coordinated than he looks, and he almost regains his balance before she shoves again. He stumbles backward onto the steps going up to the second floor. He recovers, leans in close to her, breathes in her face, and puts his hand on her neck. "I think you owe me, sweetcheeks. You got debts you gotta pay. I wanna take it out in trade."

"Don't you worry, Tommy. You're gonna get paid."

She punches him hard in the soft flesh just below his belt buckle, just below his bulbous belly.

Timmins gasps. He staggers back and sags against the wall. This time he does drop his bottle. Sweet peach brandy splatters about. Glass shards dance on the bottom two steps. The remainder of the bottle rolls slowly across the floor dribbling brandy in a wide arc until it hits the mildewed baseboard. "What the hell was that for?"

"You're a piece of crap, Timmins. You understand that?"

"You come all the way out here. You pay me a visit. I'm just bein' sociable. I'm just trying to re-cip-ro-cate, sweetcheeks... trying to be sociable."

"I came out here to kill you, Tommy! Nothing much sociable about that."

"I dropped my brandy. Shit! Gotta get a refill." He's able to peek over his extended belly and find a path through the glass so that his socks, although now quite aromatic, do not acquire many glass shards. He makes brandied footprints across the dusty wood floor, opens a cabinet and grasps another bottle. "Can't discuss our *contractual relationship without some lubricant, can we? Ya want a swig?" He tries to twist the top but is not successful. He shuffles back and extends the bottle out to her. "You open it for me, sweetcheeks. Take a swig if you want, but give it back, a'right?" As she grabs for the bottle, he pulls it back and then tries to throw his other hand around her shoulder.*

She yanks the bottle away. "Ya know any prayers, Tommy?"

"Prayers? What the hell good are prayers? If I say my prayers, you gonna crawl into my bed?" He half laughs, half coughs. "Think it's worth a try?"

"Prayers grease the skids to hell, Tommy. That's all. I think you might need that… make your slide down that ramp easier."

"Whatcha mean, ramp?"

"I'll open your bottle, Tommy." She winds up and swings the thing at his head. Lots more glass and brandy splash on the dirty floor. And there's red splashing about too. She thinks it adds some color to this dismal, dreary room. And she doesn't intend to clean this mess up. She thinks it will almost pass as art. It will certainly tell a story.

Chapter 22

Most state capitol buildings are Greek Revival knockoffs... sacred-appearing structures, topped with a dome reminiscent of St. Peter's in the Vatican, and meant to hint at the high moral aspect of the work being conducted under their influence. Leon's Capitol Building is very different... a fifteen-story slab of administratively undecorated concrete and stone. It's not designed for pomp and pageantry, but rather to allow the state's workers to efficiently do the state's business. It is the ordinary people, like Speaker Rolfes, who represent the body politic and toil at their sacred work, who are being elevated in this structure. It's the tallest building in Bismarck, and probably, with the exception of a few grain silos and ethanol factory cooling towers, the tallest structure in the whole state. It exudes civic strength and power and, in Leon's opinion, is the perfect location for this morning's announcement.

Leon wants folks to understand that he considers this building his home. For many decades he's toiled here, working on behalf of the good people of North Dakota. He wants people to know that when he becomes governor he will continue toiling for them *right here*. Decisions will be made in this refined and serious-looking structure, not in a glitzy, glass monument-to-excess anchored into the concrete of New York, Washington, or Texas, where his opponent, Mr. Arthur Conlin, will certainly have his decisions made and his money banked.

Leon can't see any signs or banners yet, but Larry and Nathan insist something hangable or wavable will show up before air-time. He'd argued with Nathan about wearing a suit or a V-neck sweater like the ones he's worn often for the past twenty years... a symbol of his populist approach to government. He chose the sweater. He thinks it makes him stand out from the cookie-cutter Washington and New York suits Bast and Conlin throw onto their battlefield. He thinks of himself as his constituents' friend and neighbor, rather than their representative.

Leon wants to project the image of a solitary man speaking about the fortunes of his specific state to contrast with the party hack preaching vague and generic national values. He's committed to use the words 'we' or 'North Dakota.' Conlin, on the other hand, always says 'I' even though he knows he's only the mouthpiece for the general themes of 'Republican values' or 'conservative positions.' Leon has prepared a simple, focused, and non-nuanced message: North Dakota First.

It was this simple thought that persuaded him to take this big step. He works for the people of North Dakota and will fight, like he has for twenty years, for their interests and their welfare. Leon fears his people will suffer if Conlin, Bast, and their interest groups maintain control for another four years. That potential for suffering drives Leon's vision. Specifically, he worries about the suffering caused by the proposed refinery—not so much the issues arising from its physical construction and operation, but rather the many outside interests sucking the blood and resources of the state and piping them to New York and Texas. He knows Nathan, and to a lesser extent Larry, have dollar signs dancing in their heads, and they see the development of the refinery as an opera providing a venue for such dancing. He also knows that many operas end in piles of death and destruction. He will be more comfortable if he can exchange that metaphor for one involving a basketball court, one where he and his friends are much more comfortable, and where he can be confident the game most certainly will not end in operatic death and destruction.

Leon mounts the steps to the first landing where the microphone array is located, one-third the way up the full stair height. He is alone. He has no need for a backup band, a marked contrast to his opponent. Conlin, a newcomer to politics, travels with a full orchestra of a trophy wife, a cadre of pushers and shovers in suits, and the handlers from various national Republican and values lobbies who hover around him to visually represent the piles of money and advice available to him. Rolfes knows his constituents are not stupid. They understand the contrasts he is emphasizing between local versus national, between honest talk and election hyperbole, and between electing a single man they know well versus a committee of strangers.

Leon begins with the kind of folksy introductory drivel every campaign in every jurisdiction must include. He verbally kisses the babies and pats the dogs.

"But, enough of this, folks," he says. "I would like to spend my time patting dogs and kissing babies. But anybody can do that, and many better than I can. I have a much more serious role here. I must convince you, my friends, that the machines are indeed coming. And if they find pasture here, our prairie, and thus our lives, will vanish. Even if Prometheus' model is defeated, another one will certainly come, and then another, and another. They are being driven by remote control from a glass tower somewhere in New York, or Houston, or even Dubai.

"And soon after they come they will be abandoned... sores on the landscape, the economy, and the very fabric of our community. How are we, in the future, going to feel about these machines and the developers who forced them on us?

"The only truth is that those responsible for the carnage will not be inconvenienced. They will not be crying; they will have reinvested their winnings in the next scam; they will have erased every word and photo from their memory and will be flying with the elite;

and they will be laughing at the fools picking up the pieces in North Dakota.

"If you elect Mr. Conlin, he will lead you into that wasteland of broken machines and broken promises. But you have a choice. If you vote for me, if you vote for reason and against greed, the outcome will be much different. The grasslands will be greener, our wallets fatter, and our communities healthier. I offer you a stark difference—Rolfes versus Conlin, North Dakota versus New York and Houston, and yes, I have to make you see it… good versus evil.

"We must establish our defenses immediately if we are to ensure our future. And the first step is to make sure Mr. Conlin does not ever become governor. He will open the gate and accept the Antichrist into our midst. That cannot happen."

He hadn't planned a long rambling monologue. That would get people thinking of that windbag Conlin, who can, and does, talk until everyone either falls asleep or runs up against deadlines. Leon stands on familiar ground and breathes familiar air, while talking to familiar people. And he's confident the people of North Dakota, to whom he's aiming his words, will receive the correct message.

"That's enough my friends. It's time we all got back to work. Thank you for listening to me. Thank you."

After the formal phase of the news conference is complete, Leon descends the steps, walks out onto the grass of the great mall, and talks with his people.

***

Leon's Mom's House – 5:30 p.m.

He remembers blinking his eyes a couple of times while scenes change and the day flicks past in mostly unfocused film frames. Even before he realizes his toes are touching earth again, he finds himself sitting in his usual chair in his mom's kitchen, looking at a plate of pork chops, mashed potatoes, and peas. His mom waits until after Leon's finished the main course and is starting on his rhubarb pie. She makes sure his mouth is chock-full of the good stuff when she springs it on him.

"I had a visitor late this afternoon, dear. A nice man from New York named Pick... Martin Pick."

Leon, even knowing this woman for some sixty-odd years, does not expect her to play him like this. He commences some frantic chewing, his face reddens, and his fist pounds on the table until finally he can swallow. "You what?" He manages the crisis expertly so the words escape with hardly any ejected pie.

"We had a nice conversation about responsibility and duty." She smiles sweetly at him. "Does the pie taste all right?"

"Not any more, it doesn't. If you were not my very own sweet little mother, I would hop over there and wring your sweet little neck!"

"Don't worry, dear. Mr. Pick behaved himself. We had some pie. He only wanted to make sure I wasn't too upset with all this turmoil over that refinery thing. He said he was worried that maybe your brash action taken in front of our beautiful tower might lead to little ol' me worrying myself into a heart attack."

"I'll bet he was. You should have called me as soon as that goon showed up. He didn't threaten you, did he?"

"Oh, I think he meant to. It was fun to watch him try. But I'm born and raised on the prairie. It takes more than innuendo and a leather jacket to frighten this old lady. And he didn't have the guts to take me on in fisticuffs."

"Fisticuffs? What the hell do you mean? Fisticuffs?"

"You remember. I took tae kwon do lessons a while back at the senior center. To be honest, I don't remember much about that."

The visual picture of his eighty-six-year-old mother surprising a commando-type like Pick with a crafty martial arts move makes him smile... and settles him down. "So, did Pick tell you to talk to your wayward son, tell him to forget the governor nonsense and concentrate on rushing that refinery thingie, as Margie calls it, through his House of Representatives?"

"He didn't specifically tell me that I had to do that, but I think he meant me to get that message. I told him that he was full of shit if he expected me to convince a headstrong boy like you to do anything you didn't want to do."

"I'll bet he gagged on his pie when you told him that."

"I did have a good time. And I think Mr. Pick did too. At least he thanked me for the pie."

"Would've paid good money to see that. I'll bet his commando training didn't include taking on old ladies armed with county-fair-tested rhubarb pie."

"Just to be accurate, it was the state, not the county, prize winner. I may be old, but I wasn't born yesterday, dear. I know guys like Pick don't call on little old ladies like me, in the middle of the afternoon, just to rake in some pie."

Leon knows that also. It's another message from the glass tower, letting him know the dire potential consequence of dragging his feet regarding the approval of the Prometheus incentive package. It seems a transparent message—an abundance of theater but a dearth of reality. Somehow, it doesn't seem right. It appears HF&G is playing him unusually hard, yet unusually shallow. *What's the point of pushing the full-court-press in the last minute even though the game's already decided?* He wonders if these are more scare tactics. *Maybe they don't think it's over.*

"I think your news conference announcement kind of threw him off his stride." His mom's words slipped through his dream. "It's one thing to threaten some low-level pencil pusher, deep in the bowels of the statehouse machine, and something else again to threaten the next governor of the state of North Dakota."

"Did you just call me a low-level pencil pusher?"

"That's called irony, honey. You going to eat that pie or just stare it to death?"

Leon realizes that staring at it would never afford him the same wonderful benefits as inhaling it. He obeys his mother and goes back to work.

Until his mom mentioned the afternoon's news conference, he had pretty much forgotten about it, or blocked it out. It happened in the past, maybe years ago, in another time and place, after which his sense of reality abandoned him for some fantasy kingdom in the clouds.

His cell phone rings. It's Steffie, intruding into his fantasy.

"Just wanted to give you a heads-up about our poll results, Leon, before our political reporters start salivating over this and blast it at ten. Ready for some good news?"

"Always ready for that. What ya got?"

"Our poll shows you with forty-six percent, Conlin with forty-two percent, and poor Denny Hickmann down at twelve."

"Nathan predicted I'd get two-thirds of my support from Republicans and one-third from Democrats. Last week Conlin had seventy and Hickmann thirty. So we took twenty-eight points from the right and eighteen from the left. I'd say Nathan hit that pretty much on the old nail. Right there where I'm supposed to be, huh?"

"That he did. And I will not be surprised if, as this thing goes on, there's more soft support from both left and right."

"Wouldn't that be nice? Thanks Steffie. The info's much appreciated."

The Channel 7 part of the poll-taking consortium phones him fifteen minutes later wanting a pithy comment from the new front-runner. He must have told them something appropriate but does not remember what he'd said. He'll have to wait until the ten o'clock news to find out.

He gets up, walks to the back wall and turns on the yard lights again to confirm everything still exists as he remembers.

"Things haven't moved much since this morning, have they, dear?"

"No. But don't you think they should have?"

***

The sound of the doorbell pulls him back into real time. He hears his mom tromping through the living room complaining that she should have expected visitors, and should have taken the brownies out of the freezer, and should have put coffee on. By the time he reacts and enters the living room, his mom has the door open and is welcoming intimidator number two. John David Crowe enters the foyer.

"Would you like a coffee? I can put a pot on."

"No, Mrs. Rolfes," says the proper and respectful young intimidator. "Thanks, but I'll only be a minute."

Leon thinks his mother, lingering in the next room, might protect him from serious harm. He read somewhere that hitmen didn't usually do their deed in front of the target's mother.

"Good evening, Mr. Crowe. What do you want with me at this hour? I'm assuming that the word congratulations isn't going to jump off your lips, is it?"

"I need a few minutes in private, Mr. Rolfes."

At the risk of encouraging him, Leon leads him back to the screened porch with the tranquil view of the garden. His mom's white mums sparkle under the floodlights.

"I'm delivering a message from my boss, Mr. Francelli."

"I had the pleasure of participating in a frank discussion with Mr. Francelli the other day," says Leon. "It ended rather abruptly, as I remember."

"Many things can end abruptly, Mr. Rolfes. And Mr. Francelli strongly suggests this power grab, this pursuit of the governor's chair, should be one of the things doing so. And quickly too. Our firm's put sweat, time, and one hell of a lot of money into Prometheus and we expect a return on our investment. Your maneuver has the potential to screw things up dramatically, thus jeopardizing the fruits of our labor. We do not think such action is moral, and it may be illegal, and I must warn you, Mr. Rolfes—"

"I told you before, Mr. Crowe... first you answer a few easy questions—"

"It's way beyond that now. You stood in front of the Capitol this morning and, supported by the grandeur of all that white building in the background, referred to us as the Antichrist, and promised you would stop the carnage we would cause. That sounds seriously anti-refinery to me. Seems you're deliberately sabotaging our project. And I must warn you, we've powerful lawyers who know how to protect our investment, and they also know where you live."

"I admit, I used those graphic words. But you understand politician-speak as well as I do, and you know no politician makes his point by being bland. You never heard of hyperbole? Calm down. I had to put some spice—"

"Bullshit, Mr. Rolfes."

"Do you need a brandy? Seems you are hyperventilating just a bit. I have nothing against the refinery, Mr. Crowe. That may even be a great idea, though I do have some serious problems with your firm."

"Rolfes, I will make this simple... so simple even you can grasp it."

A nice bit of condescension, thinks Leon. *I may have to start calling him Mr. H F'n G as well.*

"Stop this foolish quest for governor right now. It's easy to do before all the machinery starts grinding away and creating inertia. Stop it now! Help your *real* governor get our project approved... or there are other things that might abruptly stop."

"Mr. H F'n G, your boss told me the other day that he's able to fill my office with hundred dollar bills up to the transom. I think you're suggesting that might not happen if I stay in the race? Or was that just a bit of hyperbole also?"

"You are a piece of work, Rolfes, but you are not a stupid man. Cut out the bravado. No matter what happens out here, HF&G will not lose any money on our investment. We'll only make less than what we originally projected, and we have ways of mitigating even that. But I cannot say the same for you, or your state. If you continue your plan and our refinery project dies, you forfeit the jobs and industry your sorry state needs to join the twenty-first century, and it will make your job as governor much more difficult. You will incur a huge debt to HF&G, Mr. Rolfes, and since you don't have that room full of money Mr. Francelli talked about, it's going to be difficult to pay us back, or even pay your lawyers. But you will pay it back, and on our terms, and on our timetable, and with appropriate interest. The burden on you and your state will be immense, Mr. Rolfes. I'm hoping you come to your senses and make the right decision."

"You can leave, now, Mr. Crowe. And you can tell your boss I've *already* made the right decision. He's going to have to live with it. You guys made a nice try with the *old jump in, make a bundle, and jump out* gambit. But it's not going to work this time. That's just the way it is, Mr. Crowe. Better luck trying your scheme in Wyoming. I hear they also would like to join the current century."

After Crowe leaves, Leon has the same feeling he did before after Pick's rather gentle confrontation with his mother. It seems Pick and Crowe have switched their game from playing *to win* to playing *not to lose*. One only played like that when he thought he had the game won. But the game had just started. Why would HF&G be using their prevent defense? It didn't make sense.

Leon walks into the kitchen. "I think we two did well today, Mom. Two to nothing against New York hedge fund hitmen."

"We've earned a rest. If you turn out the back yard lights, I'll pour us each a coffee. We can sit in the living room and discuss where the path leads from here."

At a few minutes before ten, Nathan bursts into the kitchen through the side door carrying a bottle of Leon's favorite, Jack Daniels, and two gallons of rocky-road ice cream. He puts his packages on the table and gives Leon a crushing bear hug. "You did it, Leon. You pulled it off. Remarkable!" He relaxes his grip on Leon, then gives his mother a hug too. "Your boy done good today, Mrs. R. He done very good."

"I'm not sure if I should hug you or slap you, Nathan, but I'll agree it's a great day," says Mom. "Leon, you take care of the drinks. I'll dish up the ice cream and then we'll all watch what the news guys have to say about your day. Let's see if they agree with the snake-oil salesman who just now brought that ice cream into my house."

The news guys confirmed what Steffie had told Leon earlier— that Leon's bold move had pushed him ahead of the Republican candidate Conlin by four points, forty-six to forty-two.

"That's not bad, is it Leon? In fact, I'd say it's better than I expected." Nathan raises his glass to Leon with one hand and exchanges high fives with his mother with the other.

"I'm glad you two are having such a good time. You're both

whooping it up while I'm peeking over the edge of this cliff. It's a long way to the bottom. I'm about to jump and I'm scared out of my wits."

"Oh, you'll do fine, honey. Would you rather have coffee than bourbon?" She asks this sweetly, as if changing the lubrication would lessen the friction.

"This really is a great first step, Leon," says Nathan. "And you can be comforted by the fact that you are now the only politician in North Dakota who knows where the ball is and where the path to the basket is hidden. You're the only one with a game plan. Hell, you're the only one who even knows what game is being played. If you feel lost, think about them poor suckers." Nathan knows his friend feels the weight of the sudden responsibility and seeks to lighten the load. He knows this because he's been illuminating a goodly percentage of Leon's pathways since they both played in their sandbox.

"You'll make a great governor," his mom says. And yet she acknowledges her son will need Nathan right beside him to relieve the pressure, to illuminate the opportunities, and to make the runs that determine the tempo of the game.

Leon has other thoughts. He's voluntarily stepped off the edge of this cliff now and, with no parachute that he's aware of, finds himself diving straight down to the rocks. His cheerleader buddy, Nathan, the one who urged him to jump, apparently is contriving a safe landing procedure for him while he's on the way down. And there's his mom, standing up on the cliff edge, cheering his descent, seeming confident that Nathan will find a way to break his fall. He sees no way this is going to work at all. And the rocks are getting bigger fast.

Chapter 23

Leon and Nathan both know the status quo is a powerful impediment, especially with respect to politics, and seldom does it make changing direction easier or less messy. Most successful attempts to drastically alter the existing political landscape must rely on a time-tested menu of rather crude methods of persuasion. The entrenched players, burdened with a paucity of enlightened forethought and an elevated sense of self-importance, usually oppose any step forward not of their own devising. For Leon to successfully sell his unorthodox scheme he must either enlighten these important players or marginalize them.

Enlightenment is the preferred path. In the two days after Leon's sudden announcement, Nathan and Larry managed to organize a special meeting of the Bismarck Business Roundtable, a long-established, though loosely organized, group of movers and shakers from North Dakota's professional and business community.

By 10:30, the invitees have settled into the comfortable chairs in the Mandan Room, a meeting venue located on the top floor of Heartland Bank's downtown headquarters. This room, though only

eight stories above the ground, effectively elevates the attendees, separating them from the quasi-urban clutter scattered about at ground
level. The unobstructed view through the massive windows rolls right
over the mess of unorganized urban sprawl below them and focuses
on the magnificent prairie landscape spreading north to the horizon.

Leon, confident his words will also be able to soar above the
messy slum of the existing political landscape, will focus on the
varied futures of the people in this room... the rich and fulfilling
futures promised by that very prairie, glittering in the harsh morning
sun just outside their window. He looks forward to this challenging
opportunity to sell his abrupt changing of the political landscape, to
convince these longtime acquaintances of why they need a change,
and to show them how it will work for them. If he cannot, with the
confidence of a certain winner, project this change as a sure and positive thing, then the static thinkers in this room will not buy it. These
conservative minds only choose winners. That's rule number one to
any investor or gambler. Most believe a candidate's ability to win
is a stronger quality than his politics. The newspaper's quick poll
results have been confirmed by others conducted by academic and
political outfits, and such evidence of possible success has elevated
him to a strong position... strong enough, he is sure, to convince his
friends in this room. Most know him well and have lobbied him for
decades. But his independent quest for governor might be considered an untraditional and maybe even reckless move. Certainly it's
not a conservative one. He must be careful. He must stay positive.
He must appeal to their baser instincts, like greed, for example.

He will get to the greed part in a few minutes, but his first task
is to establish the political rationale for this change. He then must
show these business leaders the reason immediate and directed action is necessary to preserve the high quality of life in North Dakota.
Leon's job here is to convince these leaders that they don't have
a choice. The machines are coming and must be confronted. They
must take immediate steps to avoid being run over. He must expose
Prometheus' refinery project as an attack on North Dakota instigated
by forces from New York and Houston. Time to begin.

***

"My dear friends, thank you for coming here this morning and giv-ing me the opportunity to lobby *you* for a change. I realize my an-nouncement the other day caught many of you by surprise, and I'm hoping skepticism hasn't had a chance to creep in and cloud your views. North Dakota has a chance here to play a greater role than our small population has traditionally been granted.

"International energy politics, financing attitudes, and scientific advances have dramatically changed the landscape within the past year or so. I believe that, if we can transition ourselves properly, North Dakota can take advantage of these developments to the ben-efit of *our* people and *our* state. To avoid being taken advantage of by big government and big international business, I am proposing that we take our own path... that we position ourselves so that the good of our state is our prime concern. And by *good* I mean a broad, all-encompassing good that includes economic, environmental, and even social factors.

"So much for the hors d'oeuvres, folks. Here comes the meat and potatoes." He pauses for a sip of water.

"Frankly, all this proposed 'good' has special meaning for you, my friends. As the business leaders of this state, you will be the prime beneficiaries of that good, just as you will be the prime losers if our state is savaged. My dream is for a state that is willing to take the necessary steps to leverage our unique position in order to secure our future.

"And I use the word 'our' in both the community and individual sense."

Leon tells them about the Prometheus project and explains that most of its jobs and revenue benefit New York and Texas, yet neither will suffer the ecological damage. He describes how the Republican candidate for governor would give away most of the tax revenue, thus essentially paying these outside interests to—and here he uses Larry's word because of its caustic and immoral overtones—'rape' the good state of North Dakota.

He tells them of the probable long–term threat to their economy that's hidden in Steffie's article about the cheap Brazilian oil that may be flooding the market in the next decades. Leon feels the atmosphere in the room change and with that comes the realization that he's done his job. He cuts short his prepared words and dives straight into answering their questions.

***

Ben MacGregor, an influential lawyer-lobbyist rises to ask the first question.

"We all know you to be a straight shooter Leon, but we all believe your understanding of the viability of alternative energy sources is plain wrong." MacGregor uses the third person so as to include the entire audience in the question, an insinuation that he represents many constituents less well-placed than those in this room. "Oil is what's driving North Dakota now, and we cannot just throw that away and go chasing solar, and then just ask the Saudis and the Russians for oil."

"I am glad you made that statement, Ben," Leon said, "and for three reasons. First, it's not true, and second, if we in North Dakota accept it as true, we'll pay a very high price for that choice. I don't want North Dakota to be taken advantage of by big oil and big money. In this modern, flexible world, each of the several energy sources has its own dynamic… its own set of questions and answers. Third, market factors, over which we in North Dakota have absolutely no control, are driving energy dynamics, and we must respect those factors and base our plans on those dynamics.

"We all know things are booming in Williston. Drilling technology will soon allow us to reach new, previously unreachable or unharvestable reserves. Those New York boys would not be pushing that refinery if that technology was still in the dream stage.

"Our current deep oil, like the Canadian sand oil, is very expensive to extract. Its sustainability *requires* oil prices to remain high, and for the deeper stuff we need still higher prices. However, we are not able to determine the price of our oil. Oil is a worldwide com-modity and, like it or not, its price is controlled by the OPEC cartel led by Saudi Arabia. And the Saudis are telling us that our expensive deep oil is good only for the future, not the present.

"The dynamic requires us to wait, use up the world's cheap oil first, and only then will our more expensive oil become viable. Our now-inaccessible oil is our insurance policy. It's our *future*... but not so much our *present*. This situation therefore demands we must di-versify our energy production now, in the present, in order to control our current costs."

The very impatient Brian Bast jumps in. "You're talking crazy, Leon. This refinery's a big deal. But you've said nothing about the issues which are more important to us than oil."

"What issues are you talking about, Brian?"

"You know exactly what I mean—bloated government spend-ing, immigration, gay rights, abortion, your war on religion, the global warming nonsense. You gonna let the liberal agenda ruin our American culture?"

"Cool down, Brian. Breathe in some fresh air. First, we gotta worry about North Dakota. We've got to keep it from being ravaged by out of state oil monsters. That's the culture I'm worried about. And that is an immediate problem... as in right now immediate!"

"Pardon my French, Leon, but you're taking a chicken-shit position on these fundamental moral issues. We've worked hard to bring value is-sues into the heart of the Republican platform over the last few years and I'll be damned if I'll support your attempt to trivialize our core beliefs."

"I can understand that Brian, but I don't think your agenda is a legislative problem. Those are personal value issues or even reli-gious issues, and I don't think the government should get into the position of confirming one person's religion over—"

"These are not *personal* issues, Leon. They are universal moral considerations... your basic rights and wrongs. I'm going to fight you every damn step of the way."

"Brian, you have just made my point for me. You pound the idea of moral issues relentlessly but don't notice our state is under economic attack. We have to prioritize our efforts and pick our battles. Do the first things first."

Leon is thankful Nathan excluded the press from this meeting. If Bast's exchange had been recorded, any reporter would use those fireworks in order to grab space on the front page. Leon cannot allow extraneous issues to overpower the big issue, to obscure his purpose and weaken his message. He has to keep all these constituencies on message.

Chapter 24

Several days ago, in one of their first planning sessions, Leon had asked Margie, "If I run for governor, what's going to happen to my district? I've represented the good people living near Rugby for twenty years. How can I tell them they're now on their own?"

"The first thing you gotta realize, Leon, is there's no *if* anymore. You *are* indeed running for governor. The second thing is you've already got a solution in place. Vernon Benner is up there. He's been running your Rugby office for the last eight years and knows your constituents and their problems as well as you do... maybe even better. He's smart, dedicated, and having a wife and two small daughters makes him, if I might be blunt, a bit more of a photogenic package than you are."

"You think he'd be willing to take over?"

"You've groomed him well. He can step right into your shoes. Don't worry too much about it. In fact, I've already talked with him, given him a heads up, told him you'd follow up and confirm as soon as you've caught your breath. I've already emailed his application to Beverly up on the tenth floor. And I'll have yours ready to submit by this afternoon."

Leon realizes he owes an explanatory statement to his constituency. He must address his district… explain what he's doing and
why he'll not run for reelection as their representative. He'll tell
them that they might consider themselves to be blessed with something even better. They will, in effect, be getting two representatives.

This duty to his constituency is why, on this Friday afternoon,
one day after his meeting in Bismarck, Leon finds himself standing
between Nathan and Larry in a packed high school gymnasium, in
his hometown of Rugby.

Spotlights illuminate the banner proclaiming the <u>1968 BOY'S
BASKETBALL STATE CHAMPION</u> that hangs on the wall high
above the eastern basket. Forty-five years ago Leon, Nathan, Larry,
and the rest of the team brought the state trophy home to a reception
in this very gymnasium. The high school pep band is blasting out
what, to Leon, sounds like the same Sousa march the band played for
their triumphal entry back then. But now the conversational din is so
loud it almost overpowers the band noise. Leon walks to the center of
the court accompanied by the high school cheerleaders who line up
and, as soon as the band finishes with Sousa, will start a hastily put
together routine for the inauguration of his *Dakota First* party.

"Gimmie a D! Gimmie an A! Gimmie a K!"

After the final 'T' of the cheer, Rolfes steps through the line of
pom-pom-waving cheerleaders, spreads his hands out in front of the
crowd, and like Moses at the Red Sea, stills the frenzy. It's so quiet
he could hear the proverbial pin, should it drop.

"Dear friends," he states seriously, "we North Dakotans are a
special people, raised and tempered by the prairie. We Dakotans
are different from the people who live out on the urban and urbane
east coast and the glitzy, decadent west one. We cannot afford to
bounce along in the back of their pickup trucks, going wherever
they are driving the rest of the country. We are North Dakotans first,
and so I refuse to have national Republican and Democratic party consultants informing our local candidates how to run our local
campaigns, or crowbarring our local messages so they fit into their
national agendas."

The crowd roars their approval of this raw meat.

"We don't need talk-show personalities assailing us from Los Angeles or New York with their quasi-political values messages. We are North Dakotans, and we can think for ourselves, thank you very much, and can find the solutions to our problems without outside meddling. We have the experience, the knowledge, and the faith to do what is best for our own people. We will not let North Dakota be usurped by outside forces. We are Dakotans! First!"

The crowd stands up. Folks stomp their feet and clap their hands.

"I've come back to Rugby this evening to formally announce two campaigns that will result in this district having, in effect, two representatives in Bismarck." He pulls Vernon Benner forward from those standing behind him and puts his arm around him. "I'm back here in Rugby to formally kick off my campaign for governor and Vernon's campaign for the house seat I will be vacating when I become your next governor."

The crowd cheers and the cheerleaders can't help themselves— they bounce and pom-pom.

Steffie, swept along in this emotional tsunami, metaphorically slaps herself in an attempt to maintain a semblance of the dispassionate reporter the paper pays her to be. She feels something powerful at work here. Her boss, Meg Kirchmaier, had been right. There is a sense of history being made. Steffie had talked Meg into letting her do background on the historical nature of Leon's third-party run, and to allow the political reporters to do the political reporting. She will record Leon's run as history, but she worries about her lack of experience on the political beat. She worries she'll get caught up in the emotion and miss the hard news. She worries she'll lose the objective eye, and that her act of recording might possibly end up as part of the story. Even worse, if she gets herself caught up in the frenzy, instead of acting professionally, she might act as a lubricant for Dakota First. On the other hand, she might cause some embarrassment to Leon that might backfire and fuel the Republican cause.

Musing on her own troubles, she loses track of Rolfes' speech. She has to force herself to pay attention. She sees a better idea of how to make this work, presses her way to the door, and exits into the lobby. The diminished pressure out here allows her to hear Rolfes' voice clearly from a ceiling speaker and watch him through the glazed double-doors. She can breathe now and concentrate on what is going on without getting caught up in the emotional frenzy.

She knows Rolfes speaks correctly about being shanghaied by national interests. North Dakota is unique, with its own culture and dynamics, and quite different from New York or Texas. It's basically rural, spread over a large area and containing few people—even its big cities are small towns compared to cities in most states. But, like every other place on the planet, the larger towns are slowly sucking people and resources from the less populated areas. This sucking creates a vacuum in the outer regions, like up here along the border in Leon's Rugby district where family farms are disappearing and large, land-holding trusts are taking over.

Agribus Corp. is building new ethanol refineries, and a Dutch wind-power company is making a large investment in this, one of the windiest areas in the US. These investments help mediate the damage sustained by the loss of the sugar beet market caused by the NAFTA trade negotiations. As a farmer, Steffie knows the political pressure must be maintained on Washington or these investments will go away as quickly as they came. She knows Leon is concentrating on these things, as his Republican opponent's backers worry themselves into a dither about secondary issues like gun control, budget balancing, immigration, and gay marriage.

She finds a few other people quietly standing in the lobby with a need to decompress. She sees Leon's buddies Larry and Nathan, and Charlie Neubauer, from Agribus Corporation, accompanied by a few other guys she doesn't know. They're listening intently to Rolfes' words. The volume of the sound is diminished by the intervening walls, but the power comes through, and she sees these men overwhelmed by it.

She watches Nathan listen to his childhood buddy talk about North Dakota as if it is Shangri-La. He most likely knows these words by heart. She assumes that it is he, rather than Rolfes, who has been preparing this speech for the last several years. And now, finally, his personal harvest time has arrived. As he turns, Steffie notices his eyes actually tearing. He suddenly clamps a bear hug on his buddy Larry, the third member of the Rugby troika.

Since these two encouraged, pressured, or at least sweet-talked Rolfes into trying this third-party craziness, she walks over to them hoping to solicit a printable comment or two.

"Steffie! So, you came back to your roots for this big event?" Nathan, in a hugging mood, gives her one too. "I gotta congratulate you on that article about the Brazilians. It woke a lotta folks up. Made them pay attention. I think it means that we as a state have got to start taking more responsibility for controlling our resources. Leon's right! We have to start pushing the broad agenda ourselves. It's a great theme for a gubernatorial candidate, don't ya think?"

"It seems from the early polls that Leon's got a good chance to pull this off. Is that your read, Nathan?"

"Steffie, don't you get it? Once those early numbers hit the street this thing was over. No way in hell Leon is going backward. He protects a lead better than any point guard I've ever known. No way. You can print that too, Steffie." Larry laughs. A thunderous outpouring of applause means Leon is finished, so everyone in the hallway now pushes themselves back into the gym to bask in reflected glory.

***

The building is empty fifteen minutes after the band stops playing. Inside the humid gym, only a couple of janitors remain on trash detail. All *North Dakota First* partygoers have been shooed outside and the doors locked. A dozen cars still litter the school's parking lot. Leon, Nathan, Larry, and a few of their high school buddies stand under the yard light outside the gym's rear exit and decompress, unable to step away from the magic of this evening quite yet.

The setting sun throws red paint around the western sky, and long, eggplant-purple tree shadows spread across the asphalt parking lot. Steffie is walking on the sidewalk alongside the building and talking with Vernon Benner. They approach the group collected around Leon.

"Have a nice evening, guys." Steffie walks past the group. "I've got a story to write."

"I'll walk with you Steffie," Leon says. "We have issues to discuss. I'll be right back guys."

They start the walk across the asphalt toward Steffie's Honda.

"Got some great news, Steffie. Something to put on your calendar. North Dakota Public Television just invited me to join Hickmann and Conlin at their candidate debate scheduled for next Thursday."

"That's great, Leon. Instant credibility! How'd you do that so fast?"

"It was Margie's work. Told me it was the first thing on her to-do list. She hand-carried the request over to George Packer as soon as those first poll results came in showing me in the lead. She told me she wouldn't leave Packer's office until he agreed."

"Margie knows how the game is played, Leon. You'd better just do what she tells you, and everything will work out okay."

They're still fifty feet from Steffie's Honda in the almost empty lot when Ruby barks a greeting.

"Patience, Ruby. I'm coming." She turns toward Leon. "I completely forgot I left Ruby out here. I'll bet she's ready for a break. Oh, and where are you gonna be tomorrow? I've really gotta know your schedule. Is it okay if I get Margie to email your itinerary update every day?"

"I'm going to Minot tonight. Staying two nights, then off toward Williston. Why?"

"I got refinery stuff we gotta talk about. Any possibility we can meet tomorrow, maybe in the afternoon? I need a half hour."

"Okay, sure. There's an Irish bar, Leonardo's I think, or something like that. It's just south of the railroad tracks, maybe on Third. Low lights, leather booths, and dark wood so we won't be bothered. And the food's reasonable."

"Sounds good, Leon. How about 12:30? Then I can do some work in Bottineau in the morning. That's where I'm staying tonight."

They approach her car. Steffie turns back to look at the gym. "Wow, Leon, look at that sky. Isn't that color beautiful!" Steffie sees a dark sedan slide in from the highway and very quietly, with a careful hesitant pace, come down the drive and across the blacktop. Halfway through the lot, the driver turns on its bright, blue head-lamps. Then the thing turns and aims right at them.

"What the hell?" says Leon. He pushes Steffie out of the way up against her car. Ruby barks again as the car shakes.

It's a big car, Steffie thinks maybe a Lincoln, and it pulls up quickly and jerks to a stop. The driver has corralled Leon and Steffie between her Honda and his Lincoln. The rear passenger side door opens and Arthur Conlin steps out.

"Oh for God's sake Arthur!" says Leon. "What's your problem? You want to talk you could call me ya know. Don't have to run me over in a deserted parking lot."

"Tell your girlfriend to get lost. We've got to talk… in private!"

Leon immediately sees that Conlin has misread the situation and sees a chance to embarrass the buffoon. "Hey, girlfriend," he says to Steffie. "Take your dog for a walk while I talk to my boyfriend."

Steffie acts fast. An agile reporter, she's already activated the voice recorder on her phone and, as she opens the rear door to get Ruby, she carefully places the phone on the roof of the Honda up against the roof rack support. Only then does she snap the leash on Ruby's collar. "Come on Ruby, let's go for a walk." They walk around the far side of her car and into the grass.

"Why all the cloak and dagger, Arthur? You could have called. I have my own little smartphone in my pocket all the time." He pats his pocket to make sure it's still there. "So I'm always available to answer my constituent's questions."

"Don't be such a wise ass, Leon. North Dakota's a small place. People run into each other all the time. I just happened to be in the neighborhood, as if you didn't know. I thought I'd better do this face-to-face, just you and me. Nice and private like."

A list of Conlin's scheduled campaign events materializes in Steffie's memory, and she knows he's scheduled a pancake breakfast for tomorrow—Saturday morning—right here in Rugby. Could that be a coincidence? Could Leon have quickly scheduled the first stop of his campaign in his hometown, without knowing Conlin's movements, and unwittingly stolen his thunder up here? Or did Margie schedule this conflict on purpose? She can understand why Conlin is ticked. The local paper, and all the lunch-counter talk, will push their favorite son, Rolfes, to the front and no one will even care if Conlin's in town. *This should be juicy*, she thinks, and knowing her phone is doing the hard work for her, gives some attention to Ruby.

She watches the two men argue from a distance so hears very little, but one thing she does hear are Conlin's punctuation marks.

"…bullshit!"

"…*not* Brian's puppet!"

"…so, fuck you, Leon!"

The pyrotechnics die down and after only a few minutes she sees Conlin suddenly move to get back into his car. The door slams. The engine growls. She watches the car back out and spin itself back to the highway at a considerably quicker pace than it had entered. "Wow, Ruby. What do we have here? What a story! And just plopped on my doorstep." She heads back toward Leon.

"You gonna tell me what that was all about?"

"It appears my friend, Mr. Conlin, is disappointed that I entered the race, and he found a few choice words to emphasize the point."

"I hope you're not too upset, Leon. I need you alert and refreshed for our discussion tomorrow."

"Conlin's the one upset. And I understand his frustration. All of a sudden he's toast. Not an easy thing to accept. We'll talk about it tomorrow. I've got to get going, Steffie. Things to do. People to see. See you tomorrow." He walks back toward Nathan and Larry.

"You be careful!" she shouts after him. After Leon leaves, Steffie retrieves her phone from under the roof rack. She turns off the recorder, saves the conversation, and then opens the door for Ruby to hop in. Later tonight, after she sends off the story of Leon's historic rally, she'll plug the phone into her computer, upload the audio, then convert it into a word document and drop it in her Leon folder.

Neither Leon nor Conlin are aware a copy of that spicy conversation exists. She may also have to run the legal and moral aspects of clandestine recording past the *Plainsman's* legal staff before she even thinks about whether she will have to tell Leon. She remembers he said he would tell her tomorrow, and if he does it may all be a moot point. Only after she listens to the audio, and reads the text, will she think about how she will use the conversation.

After the ten o'clock news, the rest of her sister's house goes up to bed. She sits on the couch with her computer on her lap, moves the cursor over the icon labeled *[9/27, Leon/Conlin]*, and clicks.

"Leon! We need to talk."

"And good evening to you too, Arthur. Why all the cloak and dagger? You could have called, I have my own little smartphone in my pocket all the time... so I'm always available to answer my constituent's questions."

"Don't be such a wise ass, Leon. North Dakota's a small place, people run into each other all the time. I just happened to be in the neighborhood, as if you didn't know. I thought I'd better do this face-to-face, just you and me. Nice and private like!

"Your little stunt pulled the rug right out from under me, Leon. I had a good lead at fifty-eight percent. I paid my dues and waited my time and now you've destroyed everything."

"I know it's hard for you to understand, Arthur, but this election isn't about you. It's about North Dakota. We politicians need to start paying attention to the needs of our people, not the needs of the money-toting, big-city lobbyists. That sounds trite, doesn't it? But it's true. And it's time to give our state and its problems some local attention."

"*Bullshit! We both know this is only about getting to the Mansion. You're not playing fair, Leon. If you continue your misguided campaign you're going to pay a heavy price.*"

"*Don't even try to threaten me. You don't care about the health of this state. Your focus is on keeping Bast and his zealots happy. You have apparently made some kind of devil's pact with him and I find that disgraceful. I won't allow him to own the next governor for four more years, like he does his current puppet.*"

"*I am not Brian's puppet! I'm going to ask you nicely to stop this little charade, return from that liberal la la land where you seem to be living now, and come back to your Republican roots. If you don't come to your senses, we will show no mercy. We'll pound you into the ground and leave you a broken and bleeding wreck.*"

"*However, if you do cooperate, Leon, I'm prepared to make it worth your while. I'll make you a deal. When I'm governor, I'll let you run the Development Office. Make it a cabinet position if you want, so you can work on your alternative energy nonsense. Together we can get everything we both want. How about it?*"

"*You're pathetic. The Plainsman's new survey puts your support four points behind mine. And ten percent of that is very soft... made up of those family values folks that Bast's national lobbies are, for the time being, keeping in line with threats of hell itself swallowing up this godless prairie if you should lose. But those people are decent folks, and I think I have a good shot at them as well. Once they see you care more for the national agenda than you do for North Dakota, they'll jump your ship. I'm guessing that'll pull you down under forty percent. In my book, Mr. Conlin, that is not a position of strength. I will not back off.*"

"*Fuck you, Leon. We'll not let you get away with this. Either you give up this stupid Dakota First shit or, so help me God, we will stop you. One way or another you'll be dead meat.*"

"*Oh, cut the histrionics, Arthur. You've already been outmaneuvered and are powerless to stop my campaign because it reflects the feelings and ideals of the great majority of our citizens. It's time to get real. Time to admit your Republican Party is but a tool of Washington's special interest loonies and cares nothing about local issues."*

"You're not going to get away with this Leon. We will not allow you to—"

"Forget it Arthur. I've already gotten away with it. Just keep focused on my forty-six percent, and watch it rise. And I've only just given my first speech. Just wait till the reviews come in on that. It'll bump me another five percent easy. It's over Arthur. Live with it."

"Fuck you, Leon. You'll never get it done. Do you hear me, Rolfes? You're dead meat. We'll stop you any way we can."

Chapter 25

Steffie gets to Minot earlier than she had expected. She finds Leonardo's Pub and plops herself into a dark corner booth with a view of the entry door. She has hopes of getting some work done before Leon joins her. She's hiding because her clothes are grubby after stomping through the Gupchal farmland this morning looking for clues. Her jeans are dirty and her frazzled hair is in a rough ponytail. She's changed her sweat-stained shirt, washed her face in the restroom, and hid her hair with a ball cap. But several hours of fruitless, inconclusive work have taken a toll; she looks like something the cat dragged in. There are times, she thinks, when investigative reporting sucks. After working for a while, she glances up and sees Leon enter the front door. She sees him look around for her and, acting like he's arrived first, take a stool at the bar and order a beer. She watches the bartender set the glass in front of him and then point in her direction. Leon swivels on a stool.

She waves meekly at him.

"What are you wearing a cowgirl costume for? Just because you're in the wild west, you—"

"Oh, stuff it and sit down. I've had a rough day already. And why are you talking? You're wearing *your* local costume also. Neither of us wants a camera following us."

"I have an excuse. I don't want us to be interrupted by folks running to shake the hand of the next governor."

"Nice try, Leon. I'll get straight to the point of my problem. I've come here to talk to Mr. Rolfes and warn him he will be receiving information on something he must keep confidential if he wants to avoid getting sucked into the other story, the delicately put *Two Dead Bodies in the Buick* one."

"I'm not sure how I fit in with that story, Steffie. But you're making me nervous. Help me out here."

"Well, you've just hit on the problem. Deep in my soul, I absolutely know that you have no connection to those murders. But they undoubtedly have a connection to my story about the gubernatorial candidate. Those deaths sparked the reaction to the refinery that generated the support for an alternative direction for state policy, which Mr. Rolfes glommed onto as the cornerstone issue for his campaign. And if I'm not extremely careful, said Mr. Rolfes will be sucked into my story number one."

"But Steffie, I had no—"

"I know Leon, that's what I am trying to get across to you. I trust you. I know you're a decent guy, and I don't want you to be hurt by the adverse story Bast and his buddies are already spinning. Most importantly, I need you to keep me informed about the official goings on behind the scenes in the statehouse regarding story number two."

"And I need information you dig up on story number one. That might keep me from stepping in the piles of bull-puckey hidden like land mines out there in the political landscape."

"Exactly! And I haven't a clue how we can both do that and still remain friends, and still keep our jobs, while letting each of us reach the goal we have set. For me, that's getting my stories, and for you, it's winning the governorship."

"So what do you want me to do, Steffie?"

"I know I've said this before, but I need you to trust me. Trust that when I tell you something, I may be keeping other connected things from you. But I will do absolutely nothing to hurt or embarrass you, even if it means compromising my other stories, and one day I will let the world know what a courageous, unselfish, wonderful governor you turned out to be."

"You seem to have lost your objectivity on that last one. Other than that, you can be confident that, as you suspect, I do trust you."

"I ran out here to see you because I need you to go over a legal document very carefully and see if we agree on what it means to both the white Buick story and the New York vulture story."

"That seems like a task undertaken only after I have another beer, Steffie. Where did this document come from?"

"Oh, it's legit. It's public domain stuff. Any bozo could've found it... if they knew where to look. It's just that an investigator like me knows how to investigate. I know which dark corners to poke into and how to spot camouflage. This is a letter putting NDOEP on notice that someone is watching them and they had better pay strict attention to the law, or else that certain someone will sue their pants off."

"I'm assuming you're talking about our favorite refinery."

"You can so assume. And would you be surprised if I told you that NDOEP has not sent the applicant of that refinery project any notice either accepting or denying its package for review... even though such notice is normally sent within a week or so of receiving the packet?"

"You've done it, Steffie... sucked me right in."

"And some more bizarre sucking sounds. The lawyer who sent this letter is saying, or I think he is saying, that the someone who is threatening the suit, and that would be his client, I think, *does not physically exist.*"

"My brain cannot process that, Steffie. Let's see the damn document."

This letter serves as notice to NDOEP that the undersigned, a person with standing on this matter, has reviewed the Application for Project Review #A47-2012-10-107 and has determined that it is not a complete application as per the requirements listed under Section III, Paragraph 4, Subparagraph b, item #5;

and, that fact being established, NDOEP is mandated under Section III of the NDOEP Charter, Paragraph 7, Subparagraph c, item #3, to respond in a specified manner;

and, that fact being established, that since the application is not complete, then NDOEP must, as instructed in the above-mentioned paragraph, immediately return said application and all associated materials to the Applicant for the insertion of the item(s) that is(are) missing before it can be resubmitted by the Applicant to the board;

and, until such re-submittal is accepted, NDOEP, including any employees, or consultants, or department, by regulation, must not commence review of any other part of the application;

and therefore this letter alerts NDOEP to this condition, and asserts that if notice of such rejection and return is not made public within seven (7) days from the date of this letter (noted above), NDOEP will be served with suit to force it to take such action as is required by law and stated in the Charter.

encl: #1,   proof of Standing

encl: #2,   copies of appropriate statute pages (for reference)

encl: #3,   copies of appropriate documents reviewed for proof of Non-completeness

encl: #4,   appropriate maps and plats reviewed for proof of Non-completeness

encl: #5,   proof of Non-completeness with Section III, Paragraph 4, Subparagraph b, item #5;

"That looks tame enough, Steffie. It's nicely legal. You could probably print that on the front page of the *Plainsman* and not get a single response."

"Exactly! And that's why it's so interesting, why it's so important, and why you have to know about it. It explains so much that has been confusing me, up to now."

"Okay. Although I am completely lost, I am waiting for you, O' Swami, to explain it to me in goddamn English."

"First you have to understand that there are only a few wonky types in the bowels of NDOEP who can tell you what Section III, Paragraph 4, Subparagraph b, item #5 of the State charter is about. It's about control of the land. Essentially, if you don't either own the land, or have a legal option to buy it, you cannot apply to develop anything on it. And so, what this thing is all about is that the writer is telling NDOEP, in his own convoluted way, that he has proof the developer of that project doesn't have control of the land.

"And the second thing is a number. A47-2012-10-107 is completely devoid of any controversial element, until it is noted that the number refers to Prometheus' refinery project. The contention of this letter is that Prometheus doesn't control the land its proposed project is supposed to be developed on!"

"It doesn't seem credible that a sophisticated operation like Prometheus would forget such a reasonably sized detail, does it?"

"No, it doesn't. And I'll bet 'forget' is not the operative word here. Since NDOEP records of Prometheus' application do not include any notification of the acceptance or rejection of the application, there is a good chance that, without that paper trail, your friend, Mr. H F'n G, is not yet aware that Prometheus, the firm he now owns, does not control the land."

"Unless the lawyer writing that letter copied them," Rolfes said. "Isn't that the way reasonable people do reasonable business?"

"It doesn't say he did that, and he wouldn't do that if, as one scenario goes, this is all a stalling tactic, and as another goes, it is true. But HF&G, by design, is not *supposed* to be aware of it. And this is where weird twist number two comes in. Would you like to know which *person of standing* sent that letter to NDOEP?"

"I am thinking by the way you phrased that question, that it is a name I would recognize. It's not our buddy, the real estate wizard and NDOEP insider Kathleen Carter, is it?"

"No, but you may be close."

"You can't mean close as in her father and my friend Nathan! Did he do it?"

"No. At least I don't know, and cannot possibly imagine that he did. The lawyer signing that thing, Tom Timmins, operates from a little hole in the wall office in Rugby. That practice, called *The Pierce County Legal Office* was started thirty years ago in collaboration with Nathan Goodbrother, although I think he severed connections with that office after only a few years. And it's gone through several lawyers since, including Timmins stepping in about four years ago. I highly doubt the place has any current connection to Goodbrother's consortium. Seems this Timmins is the lawyer for the ethereal preservation organization that supposedly owns the land."

"What the hell does 'ethereal organization' mean? What's Timmins' reaction to this?"

"I would like to answer your questions, Leon. But he doesn't answer his phone or return my calls. I stopped by his office on the way over here this morning, but found a typed sign Scotch-taped to the glass indicating the office is closed. The coincidences popping up here make me nervous."

"Maybe that means Mr. H F'n G got to him. Don't suppose their Mr. Pick, while he was up there last week, did some commando style business on him, do you?"

"I don't even want to think about that, although Sheriff Gaffey had the same question when I talked with him this morning."

"This makes me dizzy, Steffie. Let's go back to the document. What's that first thing mean? Proof of standing?"

"That's lawyer-speak meaning Timmins can confirm a legal interest in this case. And, according to that innocent looking enclosure one, his *proof of standing* is based on the supposed fact that Timmins is the attorney of record for PRTI, the entity that is noted as owning the very land in question. Then, in enclosure three, he baldly states that the reason Prometheus cannot claim ownership is because the supposed owner, PRTI, does not physically exist, and therefore it cannot own the land in question. Since the project cannot be *accepted* for review, Timmins says, technically there is no project yet existing *to* review, even though it has an official project number granted by NDOEP. I don't think I can even *say* that without tying my tongue in knots."

"Doesn't exist? How can a lawyer go on record saying his client doesn't exist? So, HF&G doesn't know about Timmins' conundrum or PRTI's vaporization, and they cruised right ahead and got the Gupchals' signatures on their option, something which would be quite normal. That can only mean that HF&G did not know about this suit, and so, because they already had the Gupchals' signatures on the option, they had no reason to kill them. And it would also seem that Timmins is removed as a suspect. Since he already knew the project was bogus and going nowhere he had no reason to kill them either. So who had reason to kill them? Does it bring the suicide thing back in?"

"See what I mean, Leon? It's super confusing. I think we have to keep this information to ourselves, at least until I get a chance to talk to Timmins, Sheriff Gaffey, and eventually, I'm thinking, to HF&G."

"Well, even if you find Timmins, he'll only tell you one thing— that he can't answer any questions because he is party to the lawsuit. And you can't talk to HF&G because, if they apparently don't know their project isn't accepted yet, you can't be the one to alert them to that rather important detail, can you? Especially if Pick took care of Timmins. I'll tell you one thing, Steffie. It means I have to talk with George Bronson at NDOEP and get the real story. All these sneaky dealings make me think a murder or two would almost be necessary to keep a mouth or two closed. You talk to Sheriff Gaffey and tell him I will personally report anything I find out to him, or at least to you."

"You'd better talk to me. I'm the one who owns this story."

"And you be careful, Steffie. With this much intrigue, this thing has to be a dangerous story, doesn't it?"

"Yes, it does, Leon. It certainly does."

Chapter 26

Leon and Margie walk into the lobby of North Dakota Public Television and immediately feel the pressure and animosity bouncing off the walls. It's Brian Bast. He bounces off some wall and lands awkwardly in front of them. The abruptness of his appearance startles Margie.

"Evening, Brian," says Leon. "You're moving quickly tonight. Pretty agile for a desk jockey."

"You don't belong here, Leon. You can't just walk in off the street and start swinging at my candidate. You gotta establish yourself as a contender first. You have to turn around and go back out those doors. Let us two established party candidates duke it out."

"Your feet may be moving quickly, Brian, but your brain's in the slow lane. Don't you read the paper? Listen to the radio? I'm the first place guy! We can't have a debate if the head dog don't show up. Can we?"

"I'm not letting you into this building, Leon. You can't just barge in and jump to the front of the line. We've been working nonstop on this campaign for a year, while you've only been here a week. It's not fair!"

"Thank you, Brian. I want you to make that same argument in front of the camera. I'll even agree to let you go first, right out of the chute. You can tell the audience that Leon can do more in a week than your guy Conlin can do in a year. That's such a great line I might stick it on my campaign poster. I can see a billboard—Vote Conlin, he does as much in a year as—"

"Screw you, Rolfes." He simply stomps away without bouncing off any walls on the way out.

"This may turn out to be more fun than I anticipated, Margie. I can't wait till the start buzzer."

Leon hopes this candidate debate, the only forum being broadcast this election cycle, and being broadcast from the Public Radio Television studio at the University of North Dakota-Bismarck, will give him the chance to show the many sides of the complex actor who is hoping to become North Dakota's next governor. The three candidates draw straws to determine who gives their opening statement first and Leon wins the first slot.

"It is my responsibility," he begins, "now as the current Speaker of your House of Representatives, and tomorrow as your governor, to represent every one of you. I must make sure that every resident of this state is being treated fairly and with respect, that common interests are satisfied, and that threats to this state are effectively dealt with.

"I've become quite uncomfortable with the modern notion that I am allowed to present only those views the Republican or Democrat party leaders in Washington allow me to push. That effectively halves the weapons I have at my disposal even before I start. I cannot in good faith do that. And I won't do that. I must use every weapon I can find, and choose the one most effective for confronting the present task here in North Dakota. That's why I have formed the Dakota First Party. I intend to be the governor for every citizen of this great state, and I will govern with equal respect for every one of you."

"Thank you, Speaker Rolfes. Our next opening statement is from Mr. Conlin."

"I'm going to yell foul here right at the start, Mr. Zack. You cannot elevate Mr. Rolfe's position by calling him speaker. You cannot give him more stature than you give me."

"I could address you differently if you had held elective office before, Mr. Conlin," says the moderator. "Which public position have you held?"

"The point is not that I've never held office. My point is that you are elevating my opponent at my expense. And that's not fair to me or Mr. Hickmann."

Dennis Hickmann jumps in. "Just for the record, Mr. Zack, you did address me as *Representative Hickmann.* And I'm with Leon on this one. It's only fair, and absolutely no insult, to establish that Mr. Conlin has no legislative experience, and to do so by respectfully calling him mister."

"Please, gentlemen, it's Mr. Conlin's turn, let him talk."

"And I've got an even bigger complaint with PBS," says Conlin. "You allowed Mr. Rolfes a spot in this debate at the last minute. He doesn't belong here. I've been running for the whole year. Letting him sneak in at the end is not fair. I demand that he be removed from the stage."

"Mr. Conlin," says the moderator, "Speaker Rolfes did not sneak in. He turned in his papers before the deadline. That's all that counts. He's an official candidate, and one, I might remind you, who is in first place in our, and every other, poll. It would be foolish to leave him out, so we won't."

When Arthur Conlin finally begins, he exaggerates some employment numbers and then draws an inference that must be refuted. But Leon does not get drawn into the *he said-she said* trap. Instead, he uses his two-minute rebuttal time to ridicule Conlin's exaggeration. "A friend of mine, he's a minister, is partial to the term 'bull-puckey.' He likes the word because it kind of means whatever one thinks it should mean. It certainly doesn't suggest a positive feeling about the thing or person thus described. He figures if someone with a gutter mind defines the word to his baser instincts, that's his own business. He really doesn't care because he knows, since he almost made the word up, that there's nothing inherently tasteless in such a neutral term. And unlike its close relative bull…" he lets this hang a bit for emphasis, "... feathers, it contains no sense of whimsy and so indicates a serious reaction with perhaps a dash of contempt that the word 'feathers' lacks."

Leon turns to the moderator. "That's my rebuttal Mr. Zack. I'll take my next question now."

Leon's subtle counter-attacks confuse and dishearten the one-dimensional Conlin who comes off as under-armed for the conflict. Conlin stumbles around until, mercifully, the ending horn sounds.

***

Two days later, at a joint appearance sponsored by the League of Women Voters, a cowardly Conlin feigns illness and lets Brian Bast stand in for him. Bast assumes the low road with a vengeance and tries to get the audience to picture Leon as a degenerate old windbag, while the Prometheus folks shine with a pureness only a God-fearing entrepreneur can corral.

Leon easily parries the attack. "Our friend, Mr. Bast over here, is broadcasting an attack ad on me that insinuates my depravity by noting my two divorces and the fact that I still live with my mother and play with flowers, and implying perhaps I'm hanging out with Lucifer himself. He doesn't tell you that unlike Messieurs H, F, and G, I'm not the one instigating my divorces. But, all three of those gentlemen... that's such a nice word isn't it—*gentlemen*? It's kind of like *feathers,* I think."

Leon continues with these little side explanations in the middle of hot discussions, and it drives Conlin's crew nuts. He can say any contrary thing he wants, but since the stinger is encased in a metaphor, or a parable, or a definition, it defies easy rebuttal. When he's good and ready, and when his opponent has forgotten what the topic is, Leon then continues with the main track of his original thought.

"Those three gentlemen, none of whom are over fifty years old, have been married a total of eight times and were the instigating party on all five of their divorces. But, *unlike* my friend Mr. Bast, I do not mean to accuse *any* of them of *any* immoral activity, or *any* deceit, or lying, or cheating, or promise breaking. I really doubt that they did any of those awful things. And I am sure Mr. Bast, the next time he sees me off-camera, will indicate that he does not actually believe I did those kind of things either."

Leon could take such a personal tack because Mr. J.D. Crowe, speaking for his boss, had unwittingly opened the door to the morality vault. Dismissing charges that the murders up north had anything to do with him personally, or HF&G collectively, he'd told a talk-show anchor: "Prometheus is not some backyard loan sharking operation with a psycho enforcer like you might see on TV. We don't kill people. We base our arguments on reason, not criminal behavior." And then prompted by the fact that his talk was given for a mostly religious crowd cobbled together for that episode of *Today's Focus on the Truth,* and later used in a 'we are holier than thou' attack ad, he had let slip that his firm was so righteous it based its business practices on, of all things, the *Ten Commandments.*

Rolfes, asked by a reporter for a comment on HF&G's remarks, had said that he actually knew those *Ten Commandments* well, and was trying to find something in there that governs hedge fund operations but was having a difficult time. "Those stone slabs said nothing about walking into a factory and firing every other person to crash personnel costs… or about shipping the whole operation to India and forcing hundreds onto the street, jobless… or taking away health insurance, family, or bereavement leave… or of making these decisions from their multi-million-dollar yachts, while their employees struggle with payments on their Chevys." He did however acknowledge that: "…those *Commandments* did have strictures against lying, stealing, and perhaps cheating and deceiving and breaking promises." And then he turned and headed up the steps. But Leon couldn't help himself. He turned back and, when some reporter obliged him by sticking the microphone in his face, he added, "And if I am not mistaken, the *good book* does say something about murdering aged farmers in their Buicks."

Leon had thought *that should stir the pot up a bit.* He couldn't wait to hear Bast's response.

Chapter 27

Leon's favorite restaurant in all of North Dakota, a place called The Whole Enchilada, shares a parking lot with the Hampton Inn, just off the Interstate 94 exit in Dickinson. If Leon has to suffer a night away from his mom's cooking, this might be the most bearable place to do it. He's used the thought of their enchiladas with salsa verde to energize him during the long afternoon as he slogged from small town to small town, giving little pep talks and shaking hands. He normally enjoys these meet and greet sessions away from the bombast that accompanies him in Bismarck. These are his people, North Dakota farmfolk like himself, whom he knows share his opinion of the mean-spirited politics being imported into the state by Conlin, Bast, and *Today's Focus on the Truth*. He tells folks that such garbage reveals the morality of the outsiders who produce it.

In the middle of this warm October afternoon, in a small community appropriately called Burnt Mesa, Leon stands on the sidewalk at the main intersection and talks politics with a few locals. He notices his buddy, Nathan, walk across the background accompanied by a tall, gangly blob of a man, dressed in typical rancher clothes... a denim jacket, Stetson hat, and dusty, western boots. Nathan signals to him, but doesn't pressure him like he usually does. Nathan would never make a politician. He doesn't have the patience or the ability to see value in the opinions of the common folk. But Leon can read Nathan pretty well, and it seems obvious to him that Nathan doesn't consider this guy as common folk. Not a deference, as Nathan defers to absolutely no one, but a respectful, comfortable attitude that exhibits the signs of a shared history or shared philosophy. Leon finishes a conversation with three local farmers, then saunters toward Nathan.

"Leon, here's someone you know, but haven't yet met." That's Nathan-speak, meaning the stranger standing in front of him has contributed big bucks to his campaign. "Russell Cordoba, meet the next governor of North Dakota, Leon Rolfes."

Leon treats him with the respect Nathan expects. He recalls the name from the computerized printouts of major campaign donors, and realizes this hayseed has more invested in him than most any other resident of the state, excepting Nathan and Larry. He realizes right away that the Whole Enchilada meal just vanished, that instead he and Nathan will be eating barbecue and talking business at this guy's ranch.

But that doesn't happen. After only a few minutes of introductory small talk, Nathan says, "I've taken the initiative to invite Russell to dinner with us at the Whole Enchilada. Turns out, it's his favorite place too. Nice to know you two share the same values."

They all laugh at Nathan's little joke.

"Make it seven-fifteen, Russell. We'll meet you there."

Russell grabs the brim of his hat and nods to Leon. "A pleasure to meet you, Mr. Rolfes. See you guys later." Then he walks across the street to a dusty, black Ram pickup.

"I expected big money like Cordoba to be a suit rather than a cowboy, Nathan. Kind of threw me for a second."

"That's what I like about Russell. He's neither. If you consider him as anything but one sharp cookie, tending first to his own interests, and not caring who he might upset with his aggressive stance, you will lose."

"Okay, so tell me who this guy is, why he's helping me, and why I shouldn't be wary of both him and his money."

Nathan slaps him on the back. "He and I have an understanding, Leon. You will not have to worry about him. He's firmly on our side. He's fiercely independent and doesn't cotton to Washington or New York telling him what to do. That's the connection."

But, as Leon knew well, that may not be the *only* connection, or even the most important connection. The story must be more complicated. He knows Nathan's using Cordoba, and to some extent, Cordoba's using Nathan. And they are both probably using good old Leon. That might be uncomfortable with the election drawing near and Bast looking under every rock for more mud. From his rear pocket, he extracts the folded piece of lined yellow paper he carries with him to record notes, and reminds himself to ask Margie and Steffie to fill him in on this guy.

***

Saturday, October 5
Leon's Mom's House – 9:33 p.m.

The next evening Leon gets a phone call from Steffie. "I have a bit of a follow-up to the question you asked me the other day," she says.

"I've got a truckload of questions dumped on my desk, Steffie. Which one's bothering you now?"

"It's that Timmins' lawsuit threat again. Got me running in circles."

"Maybe," says Leon, "your circle running has nothing to do with the suit itself, but the thing Timmins' suit is attacking… the transfer of title to the land."

"Talk about circles, Leon. What do you mean?"

"You said Gaffey petitioned the probate court to release the Gupchal documents, right?"

"Yes, so?"

"So why is this thing even *in* probate? Why would Timmins seal the Gupchals' estate in probate court? The only possible answer is to make sure the title situation will be in limbo for months. Looked at that way, the purpose of this suit has nothing to do with land ownership. It's only a message to N-DOPE alerting them to the fact that they will have to wait for the probate decision before they can start their review process. Why else even go to probate? Billionaires with assets scattered all over the globe and dozens of squabbling kids and ex-wives do that. In this case, the only thing of consequence is that one interesting piece of land."

"I don't think you're helping me here, Leon."

"Sure I am. Don't you see? Think of probate as one huge boulder plunked down in front of Prometheus' machine. Plunk! Probate stops that machine in its tracks, right?"

"That's a rather high-octane professional obfuscation for a low-grade, country lawyer to manipulate. Don't you think?"

"Seems so, Steffie. And I'm thinking he must have received a truckload of high-quality legal assistance. And who do you think might be driving *that* truck?"

"Who knows? I think I need a vacation. I'm tired and confused. I can't stand any more of this now."

"Yes, you can. Remember the other day I was wondering why all of a sudden Prometheus didn't seem to care about their time schedule from hell anymore?"

"Right, and I was wondering why Timmins closed his office and took his sabbatical in the middle of this swirling firestorm. Seems everyone's needing a vacation."

"And you poked around, thinking it's a small town and somebody must know something?"

"Yup, that's what we reporters do. And I can report, I got nada. Except folks at the coffee shop next door tell me the note didn't appear on the inside of the glass door until a couple of days after Timmins vanished. That might mean someone else has keys to his office. Maybe if I find out who has the key, I solve the *Dead Folks in the Buick* thing too."

"This gets stranger every time you open your mouth, Steffie."

"I told Gaffey we could break into Timmins' office, officially like, as part of the Gupchal investigation. He told me he does his investigations 'by the book,' whatever that means. Then he smiled and, in his wise old lawman voice, said he was way ahead of me. He'd already applied for a search warrant."

"So did you open his office?"

"Not till tomorrow. So I'm going to stay one more night with my sister up here in Rugby, then accompany Gaffey and the Pierce County Sheriff when he cracks open Timmins' office tomorrow morning. Depending on what we find, I might go out and poke around the Gupchal place again before I come back to Bismarck tomorrow."

"Okay, Steffie. Hope you find something useful."

"Oh, and one other thing. Sheriff had the Gupchal bodies dug up and autopsied. Told me he'd just gotten the results in."

"And?"

"He wouldn't tell me. Said he had to keep it secret until he could be sure he knows what's going on. Means the plot's thickening though, huh, Leon?"

"It's already too thick for me. I've gotta get my sleep. Say g'night, Steffie."

"G'night, Leon."

***

Leon leans back in the recliner and closes his eyes. His mom is ironing his shirts. She watches the evening news lumber by on Channel 7. He listens with most of his machinery turned off. Some strange words sneak under his defenses and prick his attention: ". . .that the *Prairie Preservation* folks are responsible for the Gupchal murders."

"That's a very strong accusation, Mr. Bast," says the young reporter interviewing him. "Do you have any evidence to back that up?"

"It's no secret," says Bast. "Mr. Rolfes has access to the same evidence I do. And because that evidence would clear HF&G, and therefore hurt his chances for governor, he has a motive to use his influence to have the state crime lab sit on that evidence... perhaps until after the election."

"That is an outrageous accusation."

"And you media folks are so chummy with Rolfes, you won't report it."

"Mr. Bast, this station does not favor any side. We report every piece of appropriate news."

"Well, *pardon me,* Mr. Ethical Reporter, but you just proved my point. You don't respect views opposing your liberal agenda. You want to tie the refinery developers to those deaths. And I am sick of your bias."

Leon is fully awake now. He's chasing Bast's words around the fringes of his brain and connecting them to his conversation with Steffie concerning whose interest is advanced by the Gupchals' deaths. Bast usually tells technical lies; he doesn't baldly make stuff up. But this salvo seems close. Leon needs guidance from his political guru.

"Mom, were you listening to Bast the Beast just now?"

"What a sleaze-bag!" she says.

"I take that as a yes. Did he just charge Jane Whats-Her-Name's environmentalists with killing those farmers? Did he say I knew that, but am withholding evidence so I can blame the New York hedge fund? Think I should I call my lawyer?"

"You have to be full awake to understand him, Son. He's very slippery. You can't turn your brain off for a second."

"But that's hard for me to do after ten o'clock. The fog rolls in and—"

"Well, *I* understood what he said, and *I* was concentrating on ironing! You should have been able to pick it up, if you'd been paying attention. I thought he threw a nicely crafted piece of mud. Still only wet dirt, but a nicely crafted wad of it. He said he had access to the information regarding the *Prairie Preservation Foundation.*"

"Okay, so?"

"So most likely you, me, and the rest of North Dakota have access too, if only we idiots knew where to look. Like I said, I thought he did a wonderful job on you."

"I'll get that son of a bitch's autograph for you next time I see him. You can tape it on the refrigerator to inspire you every day."

"You're getting pretty snippy. It's past your bedtime, Sonny. And it's making you ornery."

"Not ornery, Mom—I'm mad! And, damn it, I'm so mad I'm not tired anymore. I'm going out on the porch and do some work."

Chapter 28

Steffie sits on a concrete abutment supporting state road 397 as it crosses over two tubes of corrugated metal culvert. Her feet dangle over the edge, so when she bends over and looks down between her boots she sees a thin stream of dirty water exiting each tube. The two trickles quickly join, resulting in a small streamlet, which then snakes itself east through the naked cornfield in front of her. She's investigated several of these streamlets over the past week and now thinks she's done enough. She's taken enough punishment. The only fun she's having is watching Ruby bark at gophers. She's fallen numerous times and several big, black, winged things have taken bites out of her. Mud covers her boots and decorates another pair of her jeans.

Once again, it's been a waste of her time. She's been hiking for hours over these naked fields and has found nothing. She's been trespassing, looking for evidence of the testing equipment required for a project submittal to NDOEP. That preliminary proposal, by law, must include a humongous pile of physical information concerning this site—soil loading potential, stream and surface water flow, wildlife habitat studies, pipeline and electrical easement locations, and wind conditions.

Although some surface information can, using current technology, be mapped by drones or satellites, other tests require physical soil investigations conducted in and on the dirt and water. Soil bearing capacity and sub-surface water table conditions require drilling rigs and backhoes. Historical conditions must be compared with post-construction conditions to confirm compliance. Therefore, testing points must be well marked because the N-DOPE inspection teams will have to use the same equipment and the same locations to verify both pre- and post-construction conditions and confirm test results.

Evidence of this investigation should be obvious to even a casual observer. Most monitoring equipment is painted day-glow orange so the state inspectors can't miss it. But she's slogged through these fields for a dozen hours over three days and has not found any evidence of such an investigation. She's tired, sweaty, and frustrated. Thinking Leon should have to share in her discomfort, she takes out her phone.

"You ready to help me solve another problem, Leon?"

"Solving problems is your job, Steffie. I don't want to know anything about it. I got my own work here in my own office."

"What would you say if I told you that the fast-moving Prometheus machine plowing into your prairie from the east is a mirage? Or maybe it's a hologram. I can see gobs of tinfoil, smoke and mirrors, but no metal gears grinding away under the flimsy shell."

"Why can't you ask me questions I can understand? Are my flowers dead yet? Do my socks match? Is it raining? Easy stuff like that."

"Focus, Leon. This is important. I don't have the slightest idea what I've found here, but whatever it is, it's shouting to me that Prometheus' refinery project is a mirage."

"How the hell can you use mirage and refinery in the same sentence?"

"It's almost impossible to imagine, but the environmental paperwork Prometheus delivered to N-DOPE with the preliminary application has got to be bogus, and only constructed to look like real data. I've spent a lot of time stomping around in the mud out here, and I cannot find a single piece of evidence that *any* on-site investigations have actually been done. It's bizarre. I'm thinking that they must've made up the whole preliminary report."

"Developers can't make up stuff like that. Those sharp engineers at N-DOPE would pick up on that as soon as they opened the envelope. No developer in their right mind would do that."

"Exactly! But since I cannot verify N-DOPE has even opened Prometheus' envelope, they may not have had the opportunity to acquaint themselves with Prometheus' shoddy engineering. As I'm talking with you, I'm watching a rather typical field stream as it leaves Gupchal's site, and I note several critter tracks, including a few deer, coming down for drinks, but no evidence of even one human boot. If I remember my EPA manual, this stream, at the point of leaving the property, would be an ideal place to set up a station to monitor water quality and impact on wildlife. That station would normally be a small mobile building, like a trailer, and usually painted orange so even a blind guy could find it. But even that's not here! I'd think any competent sham artist would have parked an orange trailer out there in the mud, just to keep up appearances. Just to try to fool a busybody like me."

"Okay. So what the hell do you want me to do with this? You want me to call up Crowe and ask him why he faked the preliminary report?"

"I think the report's been faked because Prometheus never intended for N-DOPE to open the submittal. I think this goofy opera will be over by then. HF&G will have their money and who cares if the package is real or not. Say some guy in Bahrain wolfs it up for a hedge against his oil profits. He doesn't care if the thing's bogus because it's only a hedge. All he needs is the piece of paper. He doesn't need the site data. Ya think he'd ever pop over here to our prairie and actually look at it? I don't think so."

"I can't imagine even a bunch of money-mad MBAs like HF&G would make jokes like this, Steffie. Some other drama is going on here. Ask Sheriff Gaffey. He's the one who thinks this thing is theater. Maybe such performance art fits into his tableau puzzle."

"I'm seeing him this afternoon. I'll let you know what impact my astute observations have on him."

"That sounds nice. I'm going back to work now."

***

Steffie feels she must reinsert herself into the Gupchals' death scene and experience it anew. She's not satisfied she's found the hidden key yet. She must reinvestigate based on the fact that this is not only a farm, and not just a refinery site, but is now the pivotal piece of drama in a huge scam operation of some sort. She must stand quietly and look for the small things, the little things that escaped her search before, or weren't yet relevant.

And there's another thing that affects her observations. It's October now, only seven weeks since the dog days of August when the deaths occurred. But the sun is substantially weaker, the temperature is sixty degrees cooler, and low, iron-gray overcast replaces the white, wispy summer gauze. The fields lay barren.

A different kind of lonesome confronts her now, and it transforms the landscape. The horizon stays farther away in this clear, cold, dry air. This is a darker, bleaker prairie, one suggesting little promise, and no future. Steffie thinks this landscape more compatible with suicidal intentions than any scene an August artist might produce. This atmosphere, reinforced by the specter of winter creeping over that horizon, more easily embraces the negative attitudes leading lonesome and depressed folk to think about ending their lives. She recognizes the bleak signals from her research last year—the dead vegetation, the birds gone, the sun weak and powerless even on a clear day.

She knows this discouraging aspect was not present in the equation that governed her August inquiries. So why did the Gupchals do the deed when they did? Why wouldn't they have waited until now, when Mother Nature might scream at them, rather than accept her whispered invitation way back in August?

The answer is sitting there like a pink elephant as she walks across the yard after Ruby and looks up at the Gupchals' porch.

"It's the refinery, stupid," she says. "Their deaths occurred when they did, not because of *ideal suicide conditions*, but because of *ideal refinery submittal to NDOEP conditions*." She thinks that's such a strange thought she's not comfortable even telling it to Gaffey.

She reaches the porch and looks through the window into the living room. The seasonal difference is immediately apparent. In August, with the brightness of the sun bouncing obliquely off the glass, she couldn't see inside, and remembers seeing nothing but her own reflection. Now, with the sun lower in the sky and with its power diminished, she *can* see through those windows to the inside. She takes this as a good sign. Clarity may now be possible. Confident that she'll find a clue, she starts a systematic inspection of the buildings and yard and leaves Ruby to sniff whatever Ruby wants to sniff.

She stands in front of the garage door again, and again tries to imagine why someone would throw up on the ground in front of it. *No,* she thinks, *that's not quite right. Gaffey told her the deed was done with the overhead door open, because some of the vomit reached the Buick's grill.* She walks to the side door and presses the opener but nothing happens. The electricity has been shut off. She returns to stare at the closed overhead door. "Imagine..." she says out loud to ensure her reasoning string is accurate, "...someone has to be shocked in order to throw up. Why would someone who just went through all this ritualistic murder be shocked while reviewing his handiwork? He'd be the opposite of shocked, maybe satisfied he'd done a great job. So, assume the murderer did not do the throwing up. But the villain certainly would have closed the door before he left." She stands there looking at the closed garage door. "If I had just murdered two people in their garage, wouldn't I keep the door down, especially if I went through all the trouble to erase everything else? Damn right I would. I would make it look neat and tidy."

She continues to imagine the action that may have taken place. *Okay, let's say I'm the throw-up guy. In order for me to see the car with the dead bodies and thus shock me into chucking up, the door would have had to be open. But the door needed to be closed for the asphyxiation to happen. So maybe the guy who threw up had no idea there were dead people in the garage. He went over and, like I just did, pushed the button to open the door, then went around the front and watched the thing go up. Stood right here. Now that makes sense. Gaffey insists that the neighbor who discovered the body didn't contribute the vomit. So maybe now we do have a second person on the scene... a post-murderer.*

The whole thing changes for Steffie now. She thinks *maybe the post-murderer didn't want anyone to know he had been there, so he would clean up the vomit. Who would want to broadcast he'd stepped into something like this? But would the post-murderer spit-polish the rest of the goddamned house as well? That seems kind of extreme. But then, why would a post-murder visitor need to clean anything up? Wouldn't his first thought be to call 911? And why didn't he do that?*

Steffie suddenly feels exhausted. Nothing is making sense. She gets a water bottle from her car and sits on the back steps facing the closed garage door.

She continues her examination and thoughts. *So who put Ruby in the basement? And when? And why? She's an old dog, and prone to curling up in a corner. And what else doesn't seem real? What else am I not seeing?*

She suddenly jumps. "Suitcases!" *If, as the neighbors told her, the Gupchals were readying themselves for a trip to Dickinson, wouldn't they have been preparing suitcases? They were supposed to be leaving that afternoon, but no suitcases were in the car, or on the beds, or anywhere in the house, or even in Gaffey's report. Did the mysterious cleaner take them away also?*

And how many people back their cars into their garage? She knows of only a few. *Does it mean someone other than Mr. Gupchal backed that car into the garage to increase the fright meter when some post-murderer happened on the scene? Was the murderer expecting a post-murderer to visit the place? Was that another bit of set design?*

She calls the neighbor, John Blakely, but he has no idea whether Gupchal parked his car head or tail first. She can think of no one else who would know the answer to that little question, except maybe that ghost Timmins. And he's now left the reservation.

Steffie can take no more of this today. She stows her stuff in her Honda, coaxes Ruby into the back seat, and heads for home. On exiting the farm, she stops at the end of the drive. She notices the leaning mailbox with a silly looking crow perched on top. The scene seems absurd. The crow bends down as if pecking at his toes. Then he does it again, and again. "You stupid bird," she shouts at him. "It's sheet-metal! You'll chip your beak!" She laughs and turns onto the county road. Then she stops. *Might that crow be trying to tell me something? Is some clue to solving this mystery hidden in that mailbox?* She sometimes thinks the fantasy world drops little hints, for her eyes only. She needs to pay attention, stay alert for nuance.

She walks back to the mailbox. The crow flutters away, apparently satisfied he's done his duty. But the box is empty. Steffie feels a bit silly. She closes the lid and takes notice of its condition. It's overdue for replacement, or at least some major attention. The thing leans to the east, and a couple of vowels are missing but their souls remain, outlining a U and an A. The flag arm, rusted in place now, cannot be lifted to indicate letters to be picked up are inside, though with the Gupchals gone it will never need to perform again. Affixed under the address numbers 2774, she notes an official-looking seal, maybe a Farm Bureau decal. It looks like it's been there awhile, but it's not as faded as the name and numbers and, surprisingly, it is still readable. The words *Prairie Reclamation Trust Inc.* and *Demonstration Project 2B* circle a faded picture of a clump of wheat, or maybe prairie weeds.

Steffie's been poking into the corners of North Dakota all her life and has never heard of Prairie Reclamation Trust. She thinks that odd. It's also odd that two old fogies isolated up here along the border would have been aware of such an environmental organization, let alone have its membership decal on their mailbox. She takes a picture of the seal to show Leon, then heads east toward Bottineau for a bit of lunch before her meeting with Sheriff Gaffey.

Chapter 29

After lunch at the Bottineau Diner, Steffie walks down the street to Gaffey's office.

"Afternoon, Sheriff. Here I am, ready to run down to Rugby with you and toss the office of Mr. Tommy Timmins, Attorney at Law."

"I'm sorry, Steffie. The judge hasn't faxed me the search order yet. Appears he's not available today. Probably hunting. Duck season's open."

"But Sheriff, I can't wait. How much would it take to persuade you to do a bit of a search even though—"

"No, Steffie. I can't just go over and break down doors. Why would I want to do that?"

Steffie told him about her current analysis of the vomit story. Told him someone visited the site after the murder, and that if Timmins was involved in both the deed for the ranch and the Prometheus proposal submittal, maybe Timmins did the murders or did the after-murder cleanup, especially as it looks like the N-DOPE proposal may be bogus. Or, it could be Timmins took the suitcases back with him for some reason and stashed them in his office.

"These things are connected, Sheriff. I know Timmins is woven into this story."

"Even so, Steffie, I can't go barging into his office without a warrant. And warrants don't happen like magic up here. None of that *presto, and it's done* stuff like on TV."

"I am thinking, Sheriff, that perhaps you could look at it in a different—"

"No you don't Steffie. I can't be flexible with the law."

Steffie didn't even slow down, "...a different way. Let's say Mr. Timmins is my friend. I am concerned about him. I hear rumors he's running with a pretty rough crowd and got into something a bit over his head. I haven't been able to find him for a couple of weeks now, and I am worried that he may be, well... dead or bleeding all over the floor of his office."

"Cut it out, Steffie. Don't even go there."

"Wouldn't it be prudent for us to go over there and just make sure my poor friend is okay? You wouldn't need a warrant for that would you?"

"Well... no. Since you put it into an emergency humanitarian type situation, I think I might even be *required* to go over there and have a peek. You are one sneaky reporter, lady. I'm glad you're on my side."

"And maybe you just might have some evidence bags with you when we go in, just because you are always prepared since you're such a wonderful lawman."

"And if I did happen to have some with me, what might I want to put into them?"

"I was maybe thinking of a DNA sample you could compare with the vomit to see if Mr. Timmins was the guy who tidied up the scene to protect one of his rough clients who may have done in the Gupchals."

Sheriff Gaffey opens a cabinet and removes a small black suitcase. "As the wonderful lawman you think I am, I just happen to have my kit with me whenever there's a chance some evidence might pop up. But remember, Steffie, Rugby's in Pierce County. I gotta give Sheriff Joe Stacy down there a heads-up call first. I'll make sure it's okay with him and then we can head out."

***

Gaffey takes Deputy Turnquist with him and stuffs Steffie into the back seat. A half hour later they are joined by Pierce County Sheriff Stacy and they all break into Timmins' office. It's a small hole-in-the-wall place with a private office, conference room, toilet, storage room, and reception area. All the furniture, books, and files are casually arranged around the place as if business was suddenly interrupted. But they find nothing. Three experienced lawmen and one reporter sifting through the place, and they don't find one fingerprint, or one piece of paper with either Gupchal or Prometheus or NDOEP's name on it; no hair in the sink; no dandruff or dust on the floor under the desk. Nothing!

"This remind you of anything, Sheriff?" asks Steffie.

"Déjà vu, Steffie. Damned déjà vu. I suppose I gotta call the state lab in to ensure, like with Gupchal, there's nothing here. Somebody's pulling our chain, Steffie. Building us a little puzzle."

"So, Sheriff," says Steffie, "I guess next we gotta check his house. See if any bodies show up there."

"I would if I could, but I haven't any idea where he's living. Do you?"

"Well, sort of. According to folks at the diner, he lives on a farm out west of town."

"West of town? Oregon is west of town. Doesn't narrow down my search much, does it?"

"I think I can get you closer than that," says Sheriff Stacy. "Timmins has a huge drinking problem. I'm thinking he's in my computer several times for driving under the influence. Let's look him up. Maybe he acted the drunk rather than the lawyer and gave us his actual address." He goes out to his car and works on the computer for a bit.

"Yes, here he is. Ah, it says here I ain't got to worry about him, Gaffey. He's your problem. He lives just across the line in Bottineau County, near a dump called Willow City, which consists of a few shacks and a grain silo on the Ox River."

"I know it," says Gaffey. "Maybe a dozen houses just off Highway 60. We went close to it coming down here. It's only about twenty miles."

"But since I can probably see his place from Pierce County," says Sheriff Stacy, "and since ya got me interested in your problem now, I think I'd better go out there with you."

***

Timmins' house, hidden in its copse of windbreak elms at the end of a long drive, looks uninhabitable and in the process of falling down. It is, however, the only structure still standing. A couple piles of weathered beams and planks are all that's left of the barn. A rust-eaten, brown pickup slouches in the dirt, blocking direct access to the front door. The crows are active, however, and scream at Steffie and the lawmen as they step out of their cars. They peek into the pickup and head for the house, but the smell hits them even before they step up onto the small, wood-framed porch.

"Stay out here Steffie. I'll feel better if just us officers go in there. We'll secure the scene first. Darryl, will you run back and get the kit? And the camera? And grab us four masks from the glove box."

The door is locked, but Gaffey puts his shoulder to it and it falls apart easily. He pushes what remains of the door aside, takes only one step, and says, "Oh, for God's sake. I ain't seen anything this disgusting even when I worked narcotics thirty years ago in Minneapolis."

Timmins' body is arranged on the wood floor of the living room, naked and with his arms and legs extended, looking like that da Vinci drawing of a naked guy strapped to a wheel. Except this naked guy is lying in a pool of dried blood. The blood came from a single deep gash sliced just above the genitals, marking the geometric center of da Vinci's body. The knife, one of those foot-long serrated kitchen swords is still upright in the dead center of the open wound. And, judging from the wildlife crawling through and buzzing around it, this message has been waiting for them for a long time.

"What ya think, Sheriff?" asks Deputy Turnquist. "Two, three weeks?"

"At least."

"And nobody cares he's not showing up for work or anything else? Must have led one hell of a lonely life, huh?"

"Somebody was passionate about him, it seems. A guy doesn't get himself killed in such a complicated ritual unless he's had some strong personal connection to somebody, right?"

"Yeah," says Gaffey. "This passionate message was intended for someone, but apparently that someone has not happened by to receive the message. Ya think that's strange?"

"Could be," Steffie yells at them from the other side of the open front door, "the someone that message is intended for is you, Sheriff."

The lawmen all escape to the fresher air outside.

"What ya mean, me, Steffie?" asks Gaffey. "What am I supposed to do with a message like that? I've never even met the guy."

"I'm thinking it might be best if we torch the house," Sheriff Stacy says. "We all stand here, watch it burn to the ground, then go back to my office for a drink. We don't ever think about this thing again."

"Don't think that's gonna happen," says Steffie. "Remember, *we've* got a reporter standing right here listening to your every word. Plus, if you do that then I'm thinking you have indeed received the killer's message."

"You're talking riddles, Steffie. What message you think Timmins' corpse is sending me?"

"You just said it. The killer is telling you to do what you just said, *never think about this thing again.*"

"Wow! That's bizarre. So I better get the ME out here pronto and have him autopsy Timmins quickly. Shall we see what other clues I'm not supposed to find?"

"Yup! I'm thinking that'd be the thing to do, Sheriff. And just so you don't get disappointed, I wouldn't count on finding any clues left lying around the house. You're gonna find absolutely nothing in there."

***

Sheriff Gaffey's Office in Bottineau, ND – 5:33 p.m.

A couple of hours later, after they've returned to Sheriff Gaffey's office and swallowed the first sips from their coffee, Steffie says, "I have an idea that'll add a bit of drama to your day, Sheriff."

"Oh, God! I don't like the sound of that," says Gaffey. "I'm not looking for any more drama. I've already had enough for one afternoon."

"But you need more! Listen! It's a fail-safe way to solve the Gupchal case. I've been thinking about the vomit thing again."

"Fail-safe sounds a bit optimistic, judging from the smirk on your face."

"Okay, here's the thing. Ruby found the vomit, right? And she seemed to get an adverse reaction to Crowe's scent in Leon's office, right? Wouldn't it be a great idea if you, acting on *official business* were to call this Crowe guy, secure in his steel and glass cage in the Big Apple. You ask him a single question, right out of the blue. I'll bet his reaction would give a sense of direction to your investigation."

"And what question do you have in mind, Sherlock?"

"Well, I thought something like, 'Mr. Crowe, can you confirm that when you were out at the Gupchal place and threw up on the front of their Buick, Mr. and Mrs. Gupchal were already dead?'"

Sheriff Gaffey chokes on his coffee. He spatters a bit on his desk and grabs a Kleenex.

"Don't you see? If Crowe knows the true answer is *Yes, I threw up on the Buick,* he wouldn't admit to that, of course, but he would be taken completely by surprise. He'd stutter and gulp like you just did, and probably say something stupid like 'What on earth makes you think I was ever out there?'"

"I don't want to hear anything more, Steffie. Stop it."

"On the other hand, if he knows he didn't do it, his answer would be simple and unemotional, like 'No, you hillbilly lawman. You're crazy! I'm going back to work, goodbye!'"

"You've got this all worked out, huh? Tell you the truth, Steffie, I've changed my mind. I rather like the idea. It has a degree of bravado to it that's a bit out of the ordinary. They don't teach that at sheriff school. Let's give it a try."

***

Arming themselves with cups of fresh-brewed coffee, and a hastily written script, and the business card that Martin Pick gave him a couple of weeks ago, Sheriff Gaffey dials up HF&G in New York, hits the record button, and puts the instrument on speaker. A secretary, after getting his name, forwards his call to Crowe.

"This is J.D. Crowe."

"Good evening, sir. This is Sheriff Gaffey out here on the North Dakota prairie. I have met your compatriot, Mr. Pick, before but I've never spoken with you. I know it's late there but this is kind of important. I have a question I thought you, rather than Mr. Pick, could answer for me."

"Wow, this is a surprise, Sheriff. What information could I possibly have that'd be of interest to you?"

"Mr. Crowe, I would like you to confirm something for me. When you were out at the Gupchal place and threw up all over the front of their Buick, were Mr. and Mrs. Gupchal already dead?"

After several seconds without a response, Gaffey says, "Mr. Crowe? Are you still there?"

"Sheriff, that's the most bizarre question I have ever been asked. What kind of game are you playing with me?"

"No game I'm afraid, Mr. Crowe. I'm dead serious. I'm having a bit of a problem constructing the timeline for the Gupchals' deaths. But since you were there and know who was where, and when everyone did what they did, I thought you'd be able to help me out. I'd like you to answer my question."

"I'm amazed you had the temerity to interrupt my busy schedule with such nonsense, Sheriff. I'm a serious guy with huge responsibilities. I don't play frivolous games."

"It's an unusual question, Mr. Crowe. But I'm dead serious. I need to hear your answer."

"The answer is that I cannot possibly answer such an obviously hypothetical question. As a skilled and well-trained lawyer, I understand your pathetic question as an attempt to catch me off guard. Guys try that all the time. It's an amateurish attempt to shock or confuse. I'm above such tactics and I simply refuse to answer your speculative question."

Sheriff Gaffey hangs up the phone. "That went rather well, Steffie. Have any other brilliant ideas?"

"No, Sheriff, my first thought is that now's a good time for me to crawl out to my car and head for the comfort of my bedroom for a good cry. My second thought, however, is... I think it worked! You noticed, didn't you, that Crowe got snippety and turned on the high-powered force field. And he refused to answer your carefully crafted question. That *is* worth something, isn't it?"

"First, and just for the record, it was not *my* question. It was *your* question."

"Put this episode down in your little book, Sheriff. It will come up again... I can feel it."

"And second, don't slam the door on your way out."

***

Leon's Mom's House – 8:10 p.m.

Leon's mother walks out to the porch. She reaches out and hands him his mug. "Okay, dear, what's bothering you?"

"Mom, I'm starting to get an awful feeling. Something's very wrong."

"You want I should give Dr. Dornboss a call?"

"No, no, Mom. Not that kind of wrong. Got a minute? I need to talk this out."

She sits in the wicker rocker and sips her coffee. "You can talk now, dear. I'm ready."

"When I was just getting started with this campaign, Nathan and I discussed financing it."

"I remember. You told me he'd be in charge of that. I thought, here's trouble."

"Shush! He's already lined up several corporate donors. He told me I needn't worry 'cause the Supreme Court ruled that, in effect, corporations are people too, and so can donate big bucks to campaigns, just like you can."

"I cannot! I don't have those big bucks. But you do realize, if you get deep into financing stuff, you're going to lose me."

"You'll be fine, Mom. This is about philosophy, not numbers. Here's a list Nathan gave me of large donors to my campaign. He thinks I could be asked about these foreign or odd sounding names. He wanted me to know they're only local folk doing local business here in North Dakota, even though their exotic names make 'em sound like formidable global corporations."

"I know the concept, Son. Gotta strut like a player. Makes folks think you are one. Didn't I teach you that?"

"I'm tryin' to be serious here, Mom." He hands her the list and reads it with her.

Donor name - Kazakh-American Exporting LLC. This may sound Russianish, but it's the business Larry set up to export cattle to the central Asian republic of Kazakhstan. He's set up a separate company like this for each of the several countries he flies his cows into.

Donor name - BSAG Political Fund-ND. As everyone knows, Agribus is an old Winnipeg and Minneapolis firm, bought out by the Swiss agri-giant, Burnbohm Schneider, A.G. a couple of years ago. These funds are set aside from money earned in North Dakota to be used in North Dakota. The fund is managed by my good friend, Charlie Neubauer.

Donor name - Goodbye California Fund. This is a personal foundation, not a corporate fund even though it sounds like it. The donor, Russell Cordoba, a large land owner in the state, was born and currently lives over near Burnt Mesa, but still maintains a business base in California. And, as his fund's name implies, he wishes he could follow his money and move back here as well.

Donor name - Marchant International. This is a Dickinson-based trucking company, with terminals in Winnipeg, Calgary, Edmonton, and Regina.

Donor name - AKO Skandia Political Fund. A Grand Forks manufacturer of wind-turbine blades, partially owned by a Dutch company.

Donor name - Prairie Reclamation, PAC. Neubauer solicited this one from a Canadian firm, now partnering with Agribus and UND to develop alternative biomass options for ethanol. It's essentially one of those anything but crude oil outfits that'd naturally put their money against any oil development.

"These people are Nathan's friends," says Mom. "Doesn't seem strange they'd support you. This list seems okay. What am I missing?"

"See that last one? The other day Steffie showed me a photo of a medallion stuck onto Gupchal's mailbox. It had the same words— *Prairie Reclamation.* I called Neubauer and questioned him. He never heard of mailbox medallions… says they're not connected with his organization. Isn't that strange?"

"You may have to learn to live with the idea that *strange* is the new normal."

"What?"

"It's the twenty-first century, Son. When you get as old as you and me, everything is strange."

"I'm not as old as you, for whatever that's worth. It's a physical impossibility."

Leon's cell phone rings. It means his mom's off the hook and doesn't have to answer the question.

"Hi, Steffie, what's up?"

"Waa-hoo! Did *we* strike gold or what?"

"Such strange words, especially for a twenty-first century person." Leon winks at his mom.

"What?"

"And who, precisely, do you mean by *we*?"

"You feelin' okay, Leon? Did I wake you up? Pay attention! I got big news."

"Okay, spill it."

"Sheriff Gaffey and I made that vomit call."

"The *vomit* call? What the hell is that?"

The response grabs his mom's attention. She almost gags on her coffee and spills a few drops on her napkin.

"You remember, Leon. I am sure you're the one who suggested I mention the word 'vomit' to your friend, Mr. Crowe."

"I don't remember that, Steffie. We talked about trying to get his DNA, though. Is that what you mean? And he isn't my friend."

She tells him about Sheriff Gaffey's vomit discussion with J.D. Crowe. "Gaffey could not tell from his reaction whether or not Crowe is the source of the vomit. But I am sure he's our man. He danced quite beautifully and that means *something*. It's not hard evidence yet, but I know it's there, and I think I can force Crowe into admitting that the vomit was his. His act of vomiting clears him of the act of murdering. And murder's the thing hanging over him now."

"You're saying murderers are too sophisticated to vomit? Don't get ahead of yourself, Steffie. And no murder charge is hanging over anybody yet."

"Technically you're correct. But somethin's gonna be hanging over somebody's head soon. I just know it."

"I doubt it. As repugnant as it sounds, vomiting is not yet a crime in North Dakota."

"I wish I'd been a fly on Crowe's wall, Leon, just to see his reaction. It would have been priceless. Don't forget, I can use all this in a 'what if' type story because I do not need to have actual proof like Gaffey does. It's beautiful."

"It's not either, Steffie. It's ugly. Stop it! I'm now going to talk about something else. I've some *actual, true, non-fantasy* info for you."

"You do realize reality's not all it's cracked up to be, don't you?"

"Pay attention! I'm looking at a list of donors that Nathan gave me and I notice a contribution from an organization called *Prairie Reclamation, PAC.* That's the same name as is on that mailbox medallion you faxed me. Right?"

"Yeah. So?"

"So listen to this. Charlie Neubauer's firm, Agribus, is working with another firm, *Prairie Reclamation Trust Inc.,* to develop a prairie grass alternative to corn-based ethanol. The interesting part is, he's heavy into the PR for the group and he hasn't heard of any mailbox medallions. That's an interesting anomaly. Thought you would want to investigate it."

"That's great, Leon. I'll put it on my list of four thousand things to do."

"Oh, and one more thing for that list. More fishy business out here on the prairie. I went upstairs to N-DOPE to get Tony Webber's reaction to the stalled refinery. All he'd say was that, despite all the hoopla, no formal refinery proposal has yet been submitted to N-DOPE for review."

"That's weird. Certainly he's been talking with Prometheus, hasn't he?"

"He artfully danced around that question. However, he was quite surprised I knew the official log number for this non-submitted project. Remember that number was on Timmins' letter. As soon as he realized I knew that, his shield wall went up and his fog machine kicked in."

"Gotta go, Leon. Important call incoming. Talk to you later."

"Am I on the right planet, Son? Weren't we talking about campaign donors? Then Steffie calls, and suddenly the topic changes to vomit, DNA, and prairie grass. Time for me to play grandmother. I'm getting my knitting."

Leon's mom gets up and heads toward the kitchen. "Shield walls? Fog machines? I'm done. I gotta get back to the good ol' twentieth century."

Chapter 30

Leon stands on the warm side of Larry's huge picture window and watches the setting sun dance along the western horizon, then slowly slip below it. As the glare and energy drain from the tableau, it allows him to recognize several thousand cattle, standing motionless in the distant field, silhouetted in front of the swirling pink and purple sky. Leon is exhausted. He's got no more energy than those lazy cows. Only three weeks into this election madness, and already his watchers forcefully requested that he stop for a few days and rest. Margie told him he'd become grumpy, dour, and humorless. His mother, with less need to muffle the blow, told him his demeanor had become 'Bastian.' Since Margie's job is to get him through October alive, she ordered him to Larry's guest house for a couple of days with no distractions other than his mom and perhaps Steffie.

Leon wonders again how he could have let Nathan talk him into such a goofball scheme. "Mom, you remember just after I got my driver's license, when Nathan talked me into driving him and his girlfriend, Peggy Nilband, to that concert in Minot?"

"No way I could forget that, Son." She puts a hand on his shoulder, and squeezes it gently.

"Neither one of those idiots had their license yet, so Nathan talk-ed his mom into letting me drive her car over to Minot. He'd figured since I was *not* going to the concert, and *not* borrowing my own mother's car, and *not* spending any money, and *not* doing anything illegal, then there was no reason that I needed to tell my mother. I'd just be helping a friend solve a technical transportation problem. There was no way I could get into trouble.

"And it would have worked, except I forgot that North Dakota's a small place. While he and Peggy were at the theater, I went to Bob's Bigboy for a snack. I had his mom's new Belair. It was a neat car… made me feel like a big shot. I didn't notice Tom Douglass, from two farms down, was there too. He saw me, and when he got back to Rugby he saw you mowing the front yard, stopped, and asked you what I was doin' in a shiny red car, trolling for girls in Minot."

"I had my scouts out." She laughed. "I think you learned a les-son there."

"You're laughing now, but I don't remember any laughter when I got home. Boy, was I ticked with Nathan. Though I'd pushed the enve-lope farther than I should have, I was not specifically breaking any of your rules. Still, I did let him talk me into it, and that made me angry."

Leon walks away from the window and collapses into one of the overstuffed chairs in front of the fire.

"And Nathan's going to be angry with me too, for taking these days off, especially if I end up losing this thing by one or two votes. He's putting in longer hours than I am, and he'll be crushed if I don't pull this off for him."

"Maybe, but he'll feel worse if you run yourself into a heart at-tack. He should also take a break. But I can't make *him* do that. I'm not *his* mother. Thank God for that!"

Behind them a brusk voice throws itself into the room. "It's not about him, Leon. It's about you. It's your election. If Nathan wants to run himself into a heart attack, it's his business."

Leon didn't turn around, didn't even flinch. "I don't hear you, Steffie. I'm in the act of decompressing. I'm chilling out, concen-trating on scenery. I'm not talking business with you."

"I mean it, Leon. You're not feeding him passes anymore. He's the one throwing the assist to you this time." She gives his mom a big hug from behind. "Hi, Mrs. R. How ya doing?"

"One doesn't 'throw an assist' Steffie. Ask your sons. It's 'throw a pass' or 'make an assist.'"

"Evening Stephanie," says Mrs. Rolfes, paying no attention to Leon. "We're talking about the absence of mothers in politics. Neither Bast, nor his stooge, Conlin, have their mothers around to tone things down and keep Conlin's campaign human. Can I get you some tea?" They giggle and head into the kitchen to plan dinner.

Leon thinks about what Steffie said. He isn't so sure. Nathan's almost his brother. He pushes Leon to do things. That's a good thing. Leon looks at the stained pine-board wall, fading darker in the dusk. Tacked to those pine boards, over near where they collide with the fieldstone of the fireplace, Larry's hung his copy of the team picture—the official, *Winning Team holding the State Tournament Trophy* photo. He sees himself kneeling in the middle of the first row hugging the trophy. Larry and Nathan are standing behind him, each with a hand on his shoulder. That's the way it's always been. They're together in this thing like they were in that tournament and a hundred other experiences. And he just knows, just as he knew then, that he must be the one to do what has to be done. He will make this assist. He knows in his soul it will happen. And, just like at state tournament, they're gonna win.

***

After the meal, Leon's mom shoos him and Steffie out of the kitchen.

"So, Mr. Speaker..."

Leon immediately dons his lawmaker coat, noting she addressed him as a professional man, and not the kind of father figure she'd bantered lightly with over lasagna.

"Mr. Speaker is not in this room, Miss Reporter-Lady. I think he's taking a few days off."

"I want to talk with him about a couple of other things gone missing."

"Oh god, Steffie. This doesn't sound like a talk I want to have."

"You're right about that. But we gotta do it."

"Just remember, you have me at a disadvantage. I'm recharging, only semi-conscious, and so not every response is going to be top quality."

"Stuff it. Let's talk about your Mr. Timmins."

"Did you find out where he is hiding?"

"The correct verb, is *was*. Timmins is now past tense. Sheriff just cleared me to tell you the news. We found his body three days ago."

"Where? And who do you mean by *we*."

"At the house he rented in western Bottineau County just across the county line. Somebody really did a job on him. Gaffey and I found him on his back on the living room floor with a kitchen knife stuck in his gut."

"What's happening to my North Dakota, Steffie? That's big city gang stuff. It does not happen up here. And at least Gaffey can't think *that's* suicide."

"No, but same as at the Gupchal house, both Timmins' office and house were wiped clean of prints. Gaffey actually used the word *déjà vu*."

Leon's mother exits the kitchen with her brandy glass and gracefully spreads herself on the couch. "What are you two whispering about?"

Not wanting to tell her about the murder, Leon says, "We're discussing why urgency has disappeared, with respect to the refinery."

"Seems obvious to me," she says. "The reason those New York bozos eased off is that they don't have a purpose to push anymore."

"Brilliant, Mom!" Leon reassesses the tone of his response. "Sorry, didn't mean to jump on you. But it's sort of obvious, isn't it? They must've had a reason for easing off. It's just that nobody knows what that reason is."

"That's not exactly true, dear. *I know!* Though I'm not an international finance expert like you two, I do know why all of a sudden

HF&G seems to lack a purpose." She sips demurely at her brandy, waiting for one of them to bite.

Steffie caves first. "Okay, Mrs. R. I'm not too proud to ask. What's the answer?"

"Hedge funds only do three things, dearie." She deliberately excludes Leon from her response, as if hedge fund analysis is a subject fit only for refined ladies. "Buy! Savage! Sell! What is obvious is that HF&G sold Prometheus. They see it diving into the ditch, realize it's never gonna be the instant gold mine they thought it would, and axed the thing. They sold it before they lost any more money on it. Let some other fool play chicken with that idiot Rolfes."

"Mother!"

"Sorry, Son. I'm saying those might be HF&G's words. They certainly aren't mine."

"When did you become a hedge fund expert?"

"I had some time while the lasagna pan was soaking."

Leon thinks about throwing something at her. He wonders at times whether his mother uses him as a shill. How could they all not have sensed the obvious answer staring right at them. He watches his mom and Steffie laugh and carry on like two little kids in a sandbox. She's probably right, though it seems too simple.

However, two big red lights start flashing somewhere in his head. Number one: Who did HF&G sell Prometheus to? Who might be so magnanimous as to quietly take the turkey off their platter on such quick notice? And why wouldn't that buyer also push to keep the approval process moving along quickly? And, number two: Why did Nathan not tell him this before his own mother did? He's the sharp Harvard lawyer who made his fortune buying and selling property. He aims an evil stare at his mother.

"What ya lookin' at Leon?"

"My mind's still paralyzed by the lasagna. Seems it's lost somewhere between buying and selling."

"Time to pay attention, *Governor*!" says Steffie.

That wakes him up.

Steffie continues. "The concept your mom's pushing is universal—acquire, use, and discard. Universals are not news. I get a quart of milk at the grocery. I drink the goodness stored inside, and I throw away the empty container. No story in that. The story comes in only if I look carefully at the details and they don't fit the universal. Maybe I steal the milk rather than buy it, or I buy the milk at a dry-cleaners not a grocery, or I didn't drink it but poured it onto the street. Now those kinds of things *could be* stories. My job is to study the phenomena and figure out what particulars don't fit the universals."

"Sounds clinical, Steffie, but it doesn't throw a whole lot of light on our problem, does it?"

"Funny, you talkin' 'bout light. That brings me to the second thing I found missing today, and it's a doozie."

"Excuse me, Steffie! Aren't I supposed to be up here so's to ease my tension? I feel sleepy. I'm gonna go out on the porch and listen to the coyotes and let you and Mom work this puzzle."

"Here's more tension, Leon. I think Mom's wrong about HF&G buying, savaging, and selling."

"But it's such a great metaphor," Mom says.

"Oh, it is that, Mrs. R. But I think, though they did the buy and savage parts, they didn't sell it. Though they did *discard* it. As in… toss the thing in the dumpster. I tried to reach Prometheus today and discuss their predicament, but they're gone."

Leon is suddenly fully awake. "What the hell does *gone* mean?"

"It means when I called their number, the mechanical voice said that number is not in service. When I Googled it, nothing but Greek gods showed up. N-DOPE hadn't talked to them recently. I called HF&G to find out if they knew and they wouldn't let me talk to anyone. Let me die three times on hold. As of noon today, the firm we all know as Prometheus appears not to exist."

"Damn! I should have gone out to the porch when I had a chance. How can that possibly be so?" Leon gets up and walks over as far as the window.

"Be patient, Leon. This is complicated. I've got to deftly assemble several pieces of my argument here. If the sheriff thinks he's being used, it might mean he's worried he'll end up *discard-ed*. Does the fact that the Gupchals, Timmins, and now apparently Prometheus, all have been *discarded* mean they'd been *bought* and or *used* prior to the discarding?"

"At the risk of encouraging you two goofballs," Leon says, "this line of thought suggests another question. The Gupchals, Timmins, Sheriff Gaffey, and now Prometheus all being used suggests that I should be interested in the entity that is doing the using. Hell, should I be worried about little ol' me being used? Weren't we just talking about that? Whoever's inserting these characters into this North Dakota setting is behaving like a playwright, setting a scene and *using* his characters."

"And that," says Steffie, "brings to mind the second word Sheriff Gaffey mentioned—*tableau*. There *is* a certain stage-set quality about these connected stories, Leon. And I hesitate to mention this, but Nathan Goodbrother is the one character in all the various stories I am chasing whose creative mind develops a situation in ways a playwright would envy, and *uses* people to play parts in these *tableaus*. The thought scares me. First, we all know that in some sense Nathan is using you, Leon. Both you two guys admit that. Perhaps the thought that you knew you're being used will protect you, will tend to make your relationship with Nathan transparent, and that will allow you to develop your own character and story-line.

"But there's a big hole in this conspiracy blanket we have just thrown over Nathan," Steffie says. "So far we've put together a playwright, several actors, lots of scenes, and plenty of atmosphere and passion, but we have no idea who is playing the starring role. Who is the evil, dastardly dude here?"

"There's one dastardly dude you haven't talked much about, Son. Could it be a dudette?"

"A dudette?" asks Leon. "What's... oh, for Christ sake, Mom. Kathleen can't possibly be the villain in this play, can she?"

Steffie walks over to the window and stands next to Leon. "I shouldn't have let myself get this sucked into these various stories without establishing a platform high up in the theater where I can observe all this action. I feel I've lost my standing as a reporter. I also feel used."

"I can fix that," says Mom. "I can tell by the aroma that the apple pie's done. A bit of pie and ice cream has been known to provide magical relief for feelings of anxiety and frustration. And, consumed with a bit of brandy, it will ensure a good night's sleep, and even a wonderful day for fishing tomorrow."

"Wow, Mom. That's some powerful pastry. You need a special license to dispense it?"

"Be a good host, and pour us all some brandy while I do the hard work, would you?"

"Yes, ma'am," says Leon.

***

Just as they're finishing with the pie, Steffie says, "I've one more bit of interesting news to impart before our work is done this evening." She tips up her brandy glass and drains it.

"It's the dudette story. It needs to be updated before you two head to bed."

"I knew it," says Mom. "It's the dudette? I'm right, aren't I?"

Leon gives his mom a look, then turns his attention to Steffie.

"She's been quiet, Mrs. R. But there's a reason for her silence and if we tell you, you cannot divulge it to any of your friends. It's an absolute secret."

"Oh," Mom says. "So you two Sherlocks think she's the one who offed the two farmers in the Buick?"

"Offed? Since when does a nice grandmother-type use a word like offed?"

"She's just trying to fit in, Leon. I'll counsel her." Steffie and Mrs. R exchange high-fives.

"Now, Mom, we're a long way from that," Steffie says. "Just slow down a bit. I tried to talk with Kathleen using the phone number she used when calling your office the other day, Leon. But it just rang and rang... and no message. So, I did the next best thing. I was able to track down two other classmates of hers from that Law Review photo. They were neither shy nor secretive. They filled me in on the *lovie-dovieness* of the photo. And something else. After graduation, both Crowe *and* Kathleen went to work for... drum roll please... HF&G in New York."

"I didn't know that," says Leon. "But you'd think Nathan must have known, right?"

"And it seems that once at HF&G, she threw Crowe away and glommed onto one of the partners... Mr. Boss Man with the wonderful phone etiquette, one Enrico Francelli. Then, after several years of blowing up deals and marriages at HF&G, the partners couldn't take it anymore and axed her, though she apparently did take several of HF&G's clients with her when she left. These guys enjoyed talking about Kathleen, but it's all secondhand hearsay stuff. So, other than telling me to be careful, they couldn't tell me anything specific, like where I might look for her now."

"So, sweetie, you're saying Kathleen kept this Crowe character as her chief squeeze in law school, then once at HF&G, she dumps him, jumps into Francelli's bed, and plunges her fangs into his neck?"

"Mom, that's awful! That—"

"As usual, Mrs. R, you hit the nail on the head. My theory is that HF&G's rejection still smolders deep inside her. Since Francelli refused to make her either a partner or a wife, she turned to revenge."

"Wow, so she sabotaged Prometheus' refinery to bankrupt them?"

"You girls have ingested too much brandy. That's plain bizarre!"

"It's called feminine intuition, Leon. And it's *never* wrong. I think there are some cases where it is admissible as evidence. We girls just know these things. After talking with her classmates, I would bet my farm she'd give her right arm to sabotage any Francelli project in any way she can. I am not saying she killed those farmers, or Timmins, but I'll bet you a hundred dollars she'd do anything, and that includes a timely murder if needed, in order to stick it to her former lover. Makes me think I've uncovered the motive for some large part of this mystery."

"You two girls are hallucinating. You're saying all this non-sense... what's been giving me all this indigestion... is all about lovey-dovey, as you call it? It has nada to do with the refinery?"

"No, no, no! It has everything to do with the refinery, but not for economic, development, or ecological reasons. It's only because Francelli and Crowe *wanted* the refinery project. They'd be drooling over the money the deal would make. And Kathleen would know that. And she, by god, would make a pact with the devil to sabotage the thing."

"That's bizarre! Too stupid to be true," says Leon. "Like a TV reality show. All this money, all this work, all this political tur-moil—hell, even my becoming governor happens just because some hot-headed girl gets herself dumped. I don't think so. I dumped my share of girls, but—"

His mom and Steffie hoot with laughter.

"Laugh all you want, but your concept is way off the charts, Steffie. It's supermarket checkout-magazine stuff. Low-rent, reali-ty-show stuff. Maybe even science fiction—du du, du du, du du, du du. I'm going to bed. And no more brandy for you two idiots."

Chapter 31

The few days at Larry's guest house did clear out some cobwebs and increase Leon's efficiency. He and Margie are working on his schedule when Steffie barges into the room.

"I am wondering," she says, "if Google hasn't heard of something, can it still exist?"

"Morning, Steffie. That's the dumbest question I've been asked in some time."

"It's the Gupchals again. They just won't go away, but I can't get closer to resolving it either." Steffie taps on her phone to bring up the picture she'd taken a week ago of the metallic seal on the Gupchal mailbox. "Remember this thing? It says 'Member-Prairie Reclamation Trust.' I've asked several folks who should know, even Googled this organization and get nada. Normally, the first thing a fuzzy, save-the-planet type organization does is get their websites up and going. So I'm thinking that this is a private joke, or some scam operation, or an under-the-radar group that doesn't *want* publicity."

"It sounds a bit like that group that Jane what's-her-name heads up that organized the demonstration that started all this nonsense."

"It is similar, but that one was about *Prairie Preservation*. This Gupchal thing is about *Prairie Reclamation*. But that bit's the appetizer. Here comes the more interesting stuff. A judge just allowed Sheriff Gaffey's appeal to unseal the Gupchal probate. It will probably take a few days for everything to be worked out and a few more for review by the judge, but soon the mess may be less confusing."

"Well, we certainly need help now," says Leon. "As it stands, the Gupchals gave an option directly to Prometheus. But Timmins' suit tells us that the Gupchals gave him power of attorney regarding the land. And lastly, that preservation organization PRTI claims to own it. And right now none of those three entities seem to be existing—even the entity who supposedly gained title… Prometheus. I'm thinking no probate judge in the state will want to look at this case."

"Even with probate released, it is going to take several months to straighten all this out," says Steffie.

"If the Gupchals belonged to some save-the-prairie organization, that might mean they'd be willing to *donate* their place to ensure prairie flowers and buffalo with little or no remuneration, in deference to selling it for some really big bucks for a filthy oil refinery. Isn't that right?"

"You're on the right track, Leon. If the Gupchals were so unimpressed with money that they were going to donate their place to Save-the-Prairie that would leave HF&G no leverage. Wagonloads of their money would mean nothing to them. Maybe HF&G did have to kill them to get their signature."

"Maybe that's why they committed suicide. It might be the only way to keep the land from going to the refinery. They die, the title gets buried in probate, and Prometheus never gets title to their land."

"And, if that is true," says Steffie, "then the only other person I can think of who benefits from this is you!"

"Steffie?"

"I didn't say you did it, but you did benefit from it—big time. If the Gupchals don't die, there's no party on the mall, no super-clash of governing philosophies, no Governor Rolfes. You are, at this moment, the only winner I see around here."

"I know that Steffie, and it troubles me greatly. But there's one other person it has benefitted, and not so directly as me I don't think, and that troubles me even more."

"Nathan, right?"

"Yeah. My good friend. But other than getting his buddy Leon into the mansion, I don't see how he is helped. I know he's got something going on. He always does. But right now, I don't know what."

"That's why I'm here Leon. I wanted to alert you that I'm going to have to dig harder into his stuff, and so am warning you about what I'm doing. Your friends may get hurt. If there's anything there, and I find it, I'll let you know before I use it. Okay?"

She gets up and puts her coat on.

"That's fair Steffie, and I'll prod him a bit myself. Not so's I alert him to what you're looking at, but I've got questions too, and I need answers even more than you do."

"Okay. I gotta go, but *one last thing*. You gotta ask a couple questions for me. Ask your buddy at N-DOPE if he knows the data on the environmental impact statement was faked. See if that shakes him up. Also, ask him who's pushing the refinery proposal now that Prometheus has apparently stepped off the cliff. Oh, and last thing. While I was running Kathleen down, I found several references to a lobbying firm called BigOilLobbyingTeam LLC. It condenses into a neat moniker—BOLT. The group seems tied tightly to her business empire, with many contracts between the two. I'm thinking if Kathleen needed a fake environmental report, perhaps a shady lobbying outfit like BOLT could get it done for her. Could you see if any of your buddies at N-DOPE have heard about them? I gotta go. See you later, Mr. Governor!"

"Don't rush it Steffie. I'm not the governor yet. And if this keeps up, I may quit this foolish quest and..."

He finds himself talking to the wall. Steffie's left his room.

Chapter 32

Nathan Goodbrother stands on the top of a small rock outcropping poking out of the sparse tufts of prairie grass on the top of a low, rough hill. He leans over, hands on his knees, and breathes heavily as his body recovers from the half-hour climb up from the trailhead where he'd parked the truck. He'd pushed himself hard over the uneven terrain while he followed the faint unmarked trail through the loose rocks and clumps of grass. It took him longer than he thought it would. It hadn't looked that high, or that difficult, when he looked up from the bottom. But now his knees and calves ache, and his lungs scream for air. The work certainly is purging sweat and salt from his body and extraneous thoughts and rubble from his mind.

A purification rite of sorts. The thought seems poetic, but damn, his chest hurts. His body badly needs oxygen. He sits down on a smooth hunk of rock outcropping and, though minimally relieved, he continues to pant. The wind swirls tons of chilled air around him but not much of it slips into his lungs. But then he looks up and the panorama grabs him.

"What a view!" he shouts. The view to the west presents no sign of human intervention. Nothing is moving. There is only the gray sky slamming into the beige ground, probably over in Montana somewhere. And now most all that beige stuff belongs to him. "Spectacular," he shouts to the wind.

"At least," he whispers to whatever spirits may be out there listening, "all the goodies *buried beneath* that scrub brush and alfalfa belong to me." At this precise moment, he neither owns nor has a right to use the surface of that land. Yet he must, and certainly does, think of it as his. He almost has the liberty to use it. He's secured one verbal commitment allowing him to use it, and another commitment from a consortium of Canadian interests promising pre-construction financing to develop the plan for its use. And he can hear that first verbal commitment behind him now, grunting and wheezing his way up the hill. The raspy sounds of labored breathing interrupt his silent ceremony of landscape communing.

"You son of a bitch, Goodbrother. You didn't tell me I'd have to do a goddamned marathon."

Nathan turns and watches his pathetic companion struggle with the last steps of the incline and finally come to a stop in front of him. "It's nowhere close to a marathon, Russell. More of a nature walk. This exercise will do you good."

"Nature walk, my ass! I've a mind to tear up that lease and ram the pieces down your throat. You son of a bitch!" Russell Cordoba uses brusque, unsophisticated language, but then he always does that. His words seem harsh, but his tone is not. The effects of the climb color his vocabulary, as they torture his body. Russell, in fact, actually expected such discomfort because he doesn't exercise. He seldom even watches others do it. So he knew his body would have to pay. And his beer and cheeseburger isn't helping, either. But the trek still required more effort than he'd envisioned when a half hour ago he'd stepped out of Nathan's truck, looked up the slope from the bottom, then stupidly agreed to climb it.

"I should never have allowed you to bully me into climbing this hunk of rock."

"Stuff it, Russell. The trail is sand and dirt... hardly see any rock. And the exercise is good for you."

"Yeah, yeah! That's what all you friggin' outdoor freaks say. I don't buy it. Exercise kills lots more people than fat does." He watches Nathan pant, gulping great breaths of the muggy air while his own breathing recovers to almost normal.

"You sound awful, Nathan. Goin' to be okay?"

"Yeah. I'll be fine. Just give me a goddamned minute. Gotta catch my breath."

"You didn't have to race to the friggin' top, you know. You could have stayed back and walked *with* me and listened to me wheeze and complain all the way up. Would've humbled you."

Goodbrother hands him a bottle of cold water from his insulated backpack. "I'm plenty humble enough, thank you. Here, suck this down and relax. Enjoy the view. It's this landscape that's humbling to me. This land of yours contains *the magic power*. Or it soon will, with a bit of a nudge from you." He pokes Russell playfully and points to the barren landscape in the west. "With your help, Russell, North Dakota can move to the next phase of her dream to realize the potential and extract some of the power of this sacred land."

"You don't fool me Nathan. You say you see sacred. Bullshit! We both see oil. I hope we're on the same track here."

"We are. But understand the wonder of what you see. Millions of years of wind and water have been working on those rocks. I see an ocean out there, and we are sitting on an island dabbling our toes in the surf."

"You *are* feeling sick, aren't you?"

"And ten million years before that, I'll bet a thick forest covered this entire panorama."

"I can't get much interested in the history and geography stuff. All I know is, if some expert tells me there's oil down there, then next thing I do, I pull the oil out. End of history lesson. You're not going to go all weepy-eyed on me about holy groundhogs or sacred scrub brush, are ya?"

"No, no, no! We're together here. I'll argue that sacred means these sand hills protect my oil deposits. Protect them from extraction… that is until all that shallower stuff south of here is harvested."

"I've had my fill of your charts and graphs. I'd like to actually feel some of that crude running over my hands and through these fingers." He wiggles them in front of Nathan's face. "When do you think we can start an exploratory well?"

"First things first, Russell. Don't be greedy. We're talking a long-term investment here. The oil is down there, but remember two things. First, any oil waiting way down there belongs to me, and I decide when to pull it out. And second, the ability to extract it *at a profit* is not yet a reality."

"I know, I know. That's your long-term scenario theory. First you build your goddamned refinery, then the drilling comes later, sometime in the distant future… maybe. But I learned my business lessons in Silicon Valley. We don't do long-term out there. You start thinking long-term in the Valley, you die quick!"

Cordoba takes a long swig of water. "And talking about things dying… you look awful."

"Don't worry about me, Russell. I ain't never gonna die."

"Yeah, I've got that dream too. We're all thinkin' we can sweet talk St. Peter into letting us sneak in the side gate without needin' the dying part."

"Speak for yourself, Russell. But I understand what you're sayin'. Sweet talking is the only way I'm going to sneak into *that* real estate."

But then, a second thought forces itself in. He still isn't feeling so well, and his breathing hasn't fully come back. Might that be his buddy St. Peter throwing him a warning signal? Nudging him toward that side door?

"I'll be fine, Russell. Look over there, just behind that tree-covered hill. That's the reason I brought you up here."

"What do you mean, look *behind* that hill? Neither one of us can see anything *behind* that hill."

"Exactly! So that's where our refinery goes. It will, for all purposes, be invisible. And just beyond that is a bit of a valley which you also can't see, but which will funnel the wind to supply our wind farm with a steady supply of operational power. No coal. No oil. A stealth refinery no one can see, causing little pollution for any-one to breathe. Is that beautiful, or what?"

"It does sound good, Nathan. Gotta admit that."

"But remember… by no means is it a sure thing. It's long term, but neither of us have any real money in it yet, so we can afford to be patient. We will be beautifully positioned, with the land and perhaps the wind farm at the ready. Should global warming be the fraud the right wingers believe it is, or the Saudi and Brazilian oilfields ex-plode or something, then we have the answer to the world's low-cost oil problem."

"That's a big if, Nathan."

"Of course it is, but who cares? Like I said, neither one of us has spent a penny on this dream so far. If good things happen, our estates will rake in billions. If it doesn't work, there is great hunting and fishing down there. We can enjoy that right now. We win by doin' nothin' that way too. You do realize I also own the fish. They're just another treasure hanging below the surface. I own everything below the surface."

"Nobody owns the fish, you jerk."

He swung at that curve ball and fouled it off, Nathan thinks. *Now, for the fastball.*

"Even if the technology and the price both work for us, there's a good chance that by 2050 or so my oil will be worth absolutely nothing. By then the Brazilians can stick a simple straw into their huge cheap reserves and suck it up and sell it to the Chinese at half the break-even cost of my hidden, hard to reach stuff. The world will probably outlaw carbon-based fuel by then, so our oil rights will be as worthless as the rights to the prairie dust I see blowing across the landscape down there."

Nathan grabs a handful of dust and tosses it into the air to make a lame visual aid.

"Things are much too fluid now, Russell. Nobody's making any big investments. You've got to be patient. Refineries are huge in-vestments, amortized over long time spans. Even if everything looks rosy in the near term, by the time the mortgage runs out and the big operational bucks are scheduled to start rolling in, there may be no market for the expensive oil it processes. At that point, somewhere between now and say 2050, somebody is going to be stuck with the deed to a very big and very expensive dinosaur, and a dead dinosaur at that. So for the next thirty years or so, we North Dakotans are playing a high stakes game of Musical Dinosaurs. Who gets caught holding the leash when the bottom falls out?"

"That is the most mangled metaphor I've ever heard, Nathan."

"It's all I can think of right now. I've got one terrific headache making me say stupid things."

"And you still look pale as a ghost. You gonna be okay?"

"Yeah, I'll be fine. You ready to go?"

Russell Cordoba laughs. "I'm ready to get down from here, Nathan. I've seen the light. You've made your goddamned point with your usual goddamned flair. Made me climb all the way up here so you could hook me with the visual effects. I appreciate the way you did that."

Nathan picks up his backpack and struggles to get it arranged on his back.

They start back down the slope. Nathan insists Russell take the lead. So Russell does his duty and stops every so often to let Nathan catch his breath. Thus interrupted, the trip down takes twice as long as the trip up.

"You okay with stopping for lunch? Or ya want to go straight back to my house for a nap?"

"I'll be okay, though I am beginning to think it was a stupid idea to climb that thing rather than heading straight for the burgers. I could've told you the same stuff from a comfortable chair while sippin' a cold beer, couldn't I?"

"The twinkle's back in your eye, Nathan. That's a start. I'm thinkin' you're gonna be okay."

***

The little battery-powered drone emits but a whisper of sound, like a hawk's wing cutting a mist, or a sagebrush recoiling from a bounce off the sand. Travis expertly swings the thing in a wide arc from east to south from about four hundred yards out while always keeping Nathan and Cordoba in the center of the picture which it is transmitting, in real time, to the monitor in front of him. He zooms in closer. Hell, he can almost get close enough to knock Cordoba's hat off his head. He finds many chances to use his Special Forces training, and he needs practice like this to keep his skills honed. He sees Nathan pointing to the northwest, so he lines up the drone's camera with the angle of his pointing arm and easily understands its target—that reddish-colored mesa a mile northwest. He zips his mechanical hawk over to that small, brush-covered mesa for a look-see. On the back side of it, out of sight of the two gentlemen doing the pointing, Travis brings his bird down to within ten feet of the ground and looks for tire tracks, footprints, or any remnant of human activity. They did this kind of study all the time in Iraq looking for IEDs—you watch 'em point, follow that vector, find the IED. That dry desert gave up its secrets quickly, especially since the live shots were scanned through a visual analysis program in real time.

Though there are more weeds and brush obscuring the sand here, his software easily finds the several regular, non-natural patterns embossed into the soil. These patterns indicate many vehicles had recently rolled through the area. The equipment left all sorts of indicators of their presence indented into the crust below the sand and scrub brush on the surface, indicators undetectable by human eyes. Someone moved a lot of trucks and machinery through the area recently.

Kathleen had instructed him to document this meeting and Travis was doing a thorough job. Sitting in front of her screen, she watches her father sit on his rock gasping for air, and takes pleasure in that she's been able to sneak her nose in under her own father's rather exotic security blanket. The egotistic fool thinks he's king of the subterfuge, when actually he doesn't have a clue.

And he'll be pissed if he ever finds out she's the one who helped finance that environmental testing that made those tracks in the soil. She owns a minor stake in the Canadian cartel that financed the se-

cret investigations to confirm the capability of the soil to support a refinery. Those tests proved the viability of this site, which now will be ready to go immediately, once Prometheus' own refinery project crumbles and dies. And Kathleen knows for certain that Prometheus' project will crumble and die. She's got it all under control. She loves this game.

Chapter 33

Leon approaches Scottie's Pub. Bits of fluffy snow, fluttering around in a light breeze, tease him all the way from his house. That flirtation with the coming winter soothes him... takes the edge off his anguish. He enters the dark, quiet place to find not much happening. That's the normal condition for midweek. He hangs his parka on the rack and walks over to his regular chair in front of the fireplace. He slaps Nathan gently on the shoulder, eases himself into the big leather chair, and takes a long draught from the pale ale already delivered to the table.

"G'd evening, Nathan, thanks for seeing me. Nice job with the fire."

The place is about half full. Several nearby tables are occupied by couples or foursomes finishing their meals and intent on their own conversations.

"Thanks, Leon. Somebody has to do it. Scottie doesn't have a knack for setting a good fire." Nathan usually arrives before Leon so he can build up the fire, order the drinks, and set the scene for his buddy. They both understand Nathan's heavy-handed attempt to control the situation. But by now they both also know that it has no effect on whatever premise Nathan will be trying to push into Leon's head. These old friends know exactly what is playing out, and both discount it.

"We have to have a little chat, Leon." Nathan starts the conversation even though Leon called this meeting. Another Nathan trait—always push the offense; concentrating on defense is for losers. "Some things have started moving faster than they are supposed to, and unfortunately, I don't think I can slow them down this time. Some proverbial shit may be hitting the proverbial fan here pretty quick, and you'd better be prepared."

"Two proverbials in the same sentence? And what do you mean by *this time?* I seem to remember soiled fans being the default condition of your pranks."

"First, we're not doin' pranks here. I'm trying to be serious. And second, the problem's not about anything *I* did. The problem's about how other people, folks I have no control over, are moving quicker than I imagined they might move."

"I don't remember your buddy Shakespeare having that problem with *his* actors."

"Jesus, Leon, gimme a break. I've one hell of a headache and I'm tired as hell. Take it easy on me, will ya? Then there's this third thing. The problem I'm concerned about has to do with oil."

"That Prometheus thing, again? Is there a bomb about to explode here? Cover us all with oily shrapnel? I'm thinking somebody might want to cover up a murder with oily shrapnel too."

"Those Gupchal deaths are an entirely separate deal, Leon. I have no idea who did it, or even why. It might still turn out that they're suicides. I only took advantage of the situation. I had to do that Leon. It was a gift, dumped on my doorstep with a 'use me' sign stuck on it. What else could I do? I just took advantage of the deed to slow down Prometheus and frustrate HF&G and their New York money men."

A couple about Leon's age walks past the table on the way to the exit. "Hey, Leon, Nathan... you guys are being quiet. Didn't see you from over there." The man pats Leon on the shoulder and his wife musses Nathan's hair.

"What are you two fine gentlemen doing out so late?"

"Hi, Charlie… Claire," says Leon. "You'd better bundle up. It's snowing out there."

They discuss the campaign with Charlie Neubauer and his wife for a few minutes and then get back to their discussion.

"Quit patting yourself on the back, Nathan. You put me in an impossible situation. Whether your gambit worked or not, is *not* the question."

"Beg your pardon, Leon, but that is the *only* question. Force those guys in the flashy suits out of our back yard. That's all that counts."

"So who did the killing up there, Nathan? Don't you think it would be good to find out who did it before you go accusing HF&G of murder?"

"Leon! I did not accuse HF&G of murder! And you know that. All I did was point out the coincidence and demand HF&G prove their hands are clean. Same line you took! I made sure I never mentioned the word murder. I craftily hooked the evil of the one act to the potential evil of the other. Hell, Leon, you made that same argument yourself."

"I was using *your* information, Nathan. If the thing I said was a lie, it means the thing you told me was a lie."

"You're looking at this all wrong, Leon. Neither you nor I ever told a lie. There's a difference between telling a lie and telling the truth, but with emphasis. Novels and movies are lies. They are not true. But their purpose might be to expose a truth. Consider Greek tragedies—lies designed to expose the truth. Twain's *Huck Finn*, or *To Kill a Mockingbird* are both lies, but exquisitely fabricated ones that changed people's perception of the truth."

"I'm not talking about a goddamned movie, Nathan. I'm talking about my personal integrity, and that of our state's government."

"But I don't think I did anything wrong, Leon. I may have just saved our state from a financial disaster. Let's not forget that."

Nathan gets up and pokes at the fire a bit. He puts another log on the pile and jabs at it a few times.

"Isn't that my job?" Scottie passes by with a coffee decanter to service a nearby table. "Hey, you guys want some coffee on this chilly night, or are ya gonna stick with the beer?"

"Think we're all set for a while. But we'll probably need a beer refill in a bit."

After getting the flames dancing again, Nathan returns to his chair.

"It's this thing about saving our state that I want to talk with you about tonight, Nathan. We need to outline the next step in averting financial disaster. You may have, in a certain preliminary way, saved our state. And thank you for that. But the machines keep coming. You've more saving to do. Your next trick, Mr. Clark Kent, is you gotta save me. If your stupid story gets out, my credibility goes into the toilet. However, good ol' Leon is looking out for you. I see the way to repentance opening up."

"Repent? What the hell are you talking about?"

"Have you been listening to the news? My competitor? That Democrat, Hickmann? I think he's onto something, Nathan."

"Or maybe he's *on* something! He's starting to sound like Castro, for God's sake. State takeover of the oilfields? The guy's hallucinating!"

"Nathan, you've taught me everything I know about the ins and outs of oilfield leasing. You are the primary expert. And based on what I know you've told me, I'm betting that it's time to short your position, right? Sell your damn leases as fast as you can?"

"Well, okay. I have been thinking about that. It's the Brazil thing, right?"

"Exactly! And how many takers are you finding out there, wanting to take those oil rights off your hands?"

"Not many. But I've not tried too hard yet. May I ask where this is going? I thought I was the expert on oil rights."

"My mom asked me a question the other day, and I wrote it down so I could ask you about it. I want to test it for truth." He takes a paper from his pocket and smooths it out on the table. "Look at this list. Tell me which of the four doesn't belong on it."

1. *Saudi Arabia, a country*

2. *Alaska, a large state*

3. *Nathan Goodbrother, a hick land speculator from Rugby*

4. *Brazil, another, even larger, country*

"Anything stand out, Nathan? They all have something in common."

"You've been drinking something. What? Let's see. They all... Sorry Leon, but it's something to do with oil, right?"

"You must be as tired as you look. Concentrate here, Nathan. All four of these entities own every drop of the oil under the land they control."

"Okay, I'll buy that. So?"

"So, which of the four has absolutely no chance of selling his oil on the open international market for a price that will cover his expenses?"

"That's obvious."

"Of course it is! Now do a bit of time traveling with me. Thirty or fifty years go by. The international community is phasing out fossil fuel. Because of that, the price of oil is hovering around twenty dollars a barrel. That seem right?"

"Probably... it certainly isn't unexpected."

"And so, here's the big question. What happens to Nathan Goodbrother's oil investment?"

"I'm thinking that Goodbrother guy is pretty well screwed, right?"

"You got it! As soon as either the Brazil fields can be verified, or the climate change folks outlaw fossil fuel, the pumps from every place except Saudi Arabia must shut down because the Saudis must work to exhaust their humongous supplies at bargain basement prices, hoping to sell it all before the deadline. And that means the rest of us are screwed, especially Mr. Goodbrother who needs at least sixty-dollars-a-barrel oil to break even."

"That's a very dim scenario."

"But very possible? Right?"

"Okay," says Nathan. "I'll give you that. All of Dakota is worried sick oil prices will crash."

"You see where I'm going here, Nathan? The path out is obvious. And Hickmann suggested it first, so it's a freebie for me. Every halfway intelligent investor in the state knows Hickmann has the obvious answer. He's found the only way to protect the natives of North Dakota. But no politician will touch it because the common people and the right wingers like Bast will be shouting 'the communists are coming, the communists are coming.'"

"You're right, Leon. Alaskans are as far from communists as it's possible to get, yet they control their own oil."

"And you know, Nathan, the big players like HF&G know all this too, and so I am wondering why they're still sticking around. Shouldn't they be sprinting back to the big city? Why are they still hanging around here?"

"Simple. They intend to get in and back out in record time and make their money before the international market goes down the drain. There are lots of stupid investors out there. They'll find some idiot to take the big loss."

"Right. Someone like that third guy on the list, correct?"

"There are plenty of stupid rubes out there to do the required buying, Leon. I realize that, and that is expressly why I jumped at that demonstration on our mall. And the truth is that since I helped orchestrate the little drama out there on the mall, both the status of the refinery and the status of the state government is much improved. And you can't deny that, Leon."

"I don't know what to deny. What is good? What is evil? I don't understand state government as a morality play. All these events are orchestrated from some far mountaintop, and we folks down here just react the best we can, with the purest of intentions, not understanding the meanings or the import of the things moving around at higher levels."

"Well, Leon, there is some truth in that. HF&G was on that mountaintop pulling some strings, and I think you and the good state of North Dakota should be thankful that I hang out up in that rarified air once in a while too. I know how they operate, and I know how to stop them from causing destruction down here in the valley."

"Whoop de do. I'm having a beer with my hero, Saint Nathan."

"I need another beer. You ready for one too?"

"Sure, Nathan, but this is my meeting. I'm buying." Nevertheless, it's Nathan who waves to Scottie to take care of the refills.

Nathan pays no attention to Leon's sarcasm. "I'll concede we've got some educating to do. We have to explain how world oil markets work, how refineries are supposed to work, and how hedge funds work. And the first thing I gotta do is explain to you the three ways to play the game called *I Want To Build An Oil Refinery*."

"Good grief, Nathan. I don't need games."

"Oh yes you do. Listen up. If you're a big oil company, like Shell or Mobil, with refining as part of the business, you can build one by yourself. This works in unsophisticated environments like Nigeria or Louisiana where potential social and environmental obstructions are obvious, and the requisite bribery payments are legal. A second way relies on a separate developer who designs and builds the refinery. This is used in areas populated by more enlightened, or might I say, *refined* citizens."

"You might say that, but then I might slap you."

"He jukes and fakes and draws the fouls on his money and when the deal's complete and ready for production, he makes a quick pass… leases, or most often sells it to the big oil company for their use. That way the guys who are good at developing do the developing, and the guys who are good at refining do the refining. Prometheus is that type of developer. Fewer people get hurt or lose money that way."

"Except rubes like me and the rest of North Dakota, huh?"

"That's the whole point, Leon. Prometheus might find the land, get the approvals from about a thousand different authorities, build the thing, then sell it to Mobil or Exxon and go on to look for the next project."

Scottie brings their beers and another bowl of popcorn. "Kitchen is closing shortly. You guys need any solid food before that door shuts?"

"We're fine, Scottie. Thanks."

"However, what we have going on here in our back yard is the third kind of *Let's Build A Refinery* game. The end purpose of this particular North Dakota drama we find ourselves involved with is *not* about building a facility to refine oil. HF&G's *only* purpose is to make money. Let's imagine that a Wall Street hedge fund, hell, let's call it HF&G, buys a refinery development company called Petrotek. These hard economic times are bad for refinery developers, and Petrotek is in a bit of a financial pickle. So HF&G takes it for a song. Petrotek, however, does have one valuable subsidiary, a well-respected planning and design outfit called Petroleum Site Design Inc.

"There are lots of grungy oil images connected to these old oily names, and they're dragging down the value, so the first thing HF&G does is rename the company something fancy and not so contaminated with oil. Let's call them Prometheus. There! Doesn't that sound better? The name change alone adds several hundred million to the company's value. Then they find themselves a project to develop... even a sham project will do. Then after they've sold a bit of extraneous real estate, replaced many of the design and engineering jobs with cheaper labor from India, and leveraged the thing to the hilt, they can sell off this newly lean Prometheus company with the nifty new refinery project, make a pile of money, and then spend a month on their yacht celebrating."

"Prometheus didn't tell us *that* at the governor's secret meeting!"

"No, and they wouldn't have. Their lawyers wouldn't let them. For the first two kinds of projects to succeed financially, the economics of the oil business have to work. For the third kind it doesn't matter, and that means that the risk of North Dakota having a vacant turkey in its backyard is much greater, since no one, except some Middle East sheik, or Russian billionaire looking to hedge some other investment, has a stake in it. Follow me so far?"

"I see where Larry gets his rape analogy. Can HF&G really make money working like that?"

"HF&G wouldn't touch it if there wasn't a bundle of cash in it for them. They don't work for chicken feed. And they only harvest the motherlodes their computers tell them to harvest."

Nathan took a little stroll over to the fireplace to inspect his handiwork, to stretch his muscles, and to give Leon's stare a moving target.

"And I must admit, Leon, HF&G surprised me. I knew several players were in the early stages of a refinery project, juking this way and that, looking for land, investigating the supply potential, and doing the long-range planning. It's the kind of fantasy game-theory stuff I can get interested in. Everybody is playing the same game with the same risks, strategies, and pitfalls. Everything's well known to all involved. I didn't even consider a hedge fund would jump into this. Refineries are normally too risky for their algorithms."

"Too risky for their algorithms? If I knew what that meant, would I still be sitting here talking to you? Nice fake, Nathan, but I know where you're going. You had your fingers in one of those second-tier projects, didn't you? And HF&G struck first and that made you angry, and you did something stupid, huh?"

"No! First, you should know by now that I do not do anything that might ever be classified as stupid. It's more complicated than that and, I admit, I was overconfident and got blindsided by the speed and the purpose of HF&G's proposal."

"I think I can tell you why Prometheus was able to get this thing going faster than normal."

"You can? Aren't I supposed to be the development expert here, Leon?"

"You can't know everything, Nathan. The villain is Prometheus. They faked the major parts of the preliminary environmental studies they sent to N-DOPE. Doesn't take nearly as long, or cost nearly as much, as invading the prairie with real machines doing real work."

"What? How can you know that? That's not the way these things happen. You can't fake stuff like that. No way!"

"I'll get to that after I throw my second bombshell—Prometheus Inc. has just vanished, like Houdini threw a cape over it and said *Shazam*!"

"Who's telling you this stuff? That can't be right either," Nathan said. He got up and poked at the fire again.

"Oh, but it is. And the whole refinery project is now, technically, dead in the water. When the developer vanished, the project vanished too. You can relax. Your buddies with the second proposal in the pipeline are safe."

"That's just bizarre, Leon. It's too bizarre to be true. All I was trying to do was slow down HF&G's fake money-making project. Such a defensive tack will enable some real developers to surface, ones who will actually benefit North Dakota rather than those rapists Larry is talking about."

"That is quite magnanimous of you, Nathan. Are you going to present North Dakota with a bill for your services? Shall I build you a statue on the mall next to the *Prairie Pioneers*?"

"You're still on the wrong track, Leon. Let loose of that prejudice. Here comes another intriguing morsel. The other day I talked with your buddy, Steffie Cobb. She threw several questions at me. Made me think she's getting close to figuring out how that demonstration outside your window got organized so fast. And I get the inclination that she thinks that I had something to do with it."

"Well, didn't you just tell me you did?" Leon watched his friend nonchalantly poking at the fire logs.

"I didn't do much, Leon. I noted the Gupchal suicides and realized I could use that bit of horrible news to stall HF&G's forward progress until after the election. That would allow the *real* refinery projects to line up their ducks in nice yellow rows. Yes, I saw an opportunity to politically cut the legs out from under the Prometheus proposal. I headed for the basket, knowing that my good buddy Leon would see me breaking open and pass me the ball for the game-winning bucket. And it all worked perfectly."

"I want to know exactly what your role was, Nathan. If this comes back to bite me, after I jump off the cliff chasing your stupid dream, I'll slap you silly. What did you do?"

"All I did was make a couple of phone calls. I got a heads-up that the sheriff was going to change his diagnosis away from suicide, and I saw a way to stop those vultures from New York from, as Larry said, raping the good state of North Dakota. I think it worked very nicely, didn't it?"

"You wouldn't have acquired that heads-up from a sleaze-ball lobbying firm name of BOLT, would you? Know anything about them?"

Leon was not prepared for Nathan's reaction. In an instant, all the energy left his body such that Leon imagined a puddle of it on the floor beneath his chair. His face turned white and his head slumped to his chest.

"Nathan! What's going on?" Leon leapt to comfort, perhaps even to save, his friend. "Nathan? Talk to me. What's wrong?"

A customer in a hooded sweatshirt at a neighboring table, looking barely out of high school, jumped into action. "I'm a doctor," he said. "Lie down on the floor and let me take a look." Nathan seemed to respond quickly.

After a few minutes it seemed the crisis might be over. "I feel better now," said Nathan. He looked at the young man. "I'm okay. Thank you, doctor. What the hell just happened here?"

"I don't know for sure. One's body has a wide range of defense mechanisms that kick in at times of real or perceived crisis. What I think happened is that something stimulated one of those defense mechanisms to kick in and protect you. Often the reaction can be more dramatic than the initial stimulus. I didn't see you dancing on the tabletop or hear any mad shouting, so the trigger may not have been an external thing. I am thinking a mild stroke or heart timing malfunction. Perhaps a mild attack. Do you have a history of any of those things?"

"Several years ago I had a stent implanted, and I monitor my cholesterol carefully, but I am a pretty healthy guy, I think."

"Who's your doctor? I'm going to give him a call to see if he wants you hospitalized for observation, or thinks you need an MRI."

"I don't think I need that. I'm pretty much good to go."

"Not till your doctor says so," says the stubborn Good Samaritan. "You just stay relaxed here on the floor till I talk to your cardiologist."

His cardiologist demands that Nathan get to Methodist Hospital pronto. So Leon drives Nathan and the young doctor, Danton Dalton, over to Methodist Hospital where Nathan's cardiologist joins them and takes over the analysis work. Nathan is ordered to spend the night under supervision, have an MRI in the morning, and if all goes well he'll be released after the test results come back.

Dr. Dalton's wife stops by to pick up her husband, Nathan is placed in a secure watch ward somewhere in a far wing of the place, and Leon gets back into his truck and drives home.

***

One hour later, Leon is alone on his porch, watching his mother's flower garden react to the yard lights. He's sipping his coffee, thinking about Nathan, and worrying about the affect the word BOLT had on him. He needs help, so he calls his guru.

"Hi, Steffie. I know it's late, but I gotta problem. I need your help."

"You okay?"

"It's not me. It's Nathan. He may be in big trouble. I just don't know." He tells her of the problem at Scottie's and how Nathan's in the hospital and would be MRIed in the morning. "Here's where you come in. The thing that seemed to trigger Nathan's reaction was that I'd just asked him if he'd ever run across an organization called BOLT. He reacted like I swatted him with a concrete block. And since you're the one who gave me that word, I'm gonna have to ask you why it had such a strong negative effect on my good friend, Nathan."

"Wow. I bet I know why. After I got back to the office yesterday, I poked around to see if I could get any information on BOLT and I got myself tangled up in a strange web."

"I have no idea what you mean, Steffie. But strange web? That doesn't have a nice sound."

"I found there are half a dozen entities with BOLT in their titles and most have a number attached as in BOLT1 or BOLT4. And just as weird, a BGLT1, which seems to be related. Could be dozens of entities all promoting, or lobbying, or hiding money for businesses in the energy sector."

"What do all these BOLTs do?"

"BOLT1, as we assumed, is a lobbying group, and a fairly high profile one, involved in oilfield real estate. But BOLT has many fingers in different pies. I think BOLT6 is advertising, BOLT7 has some sort of consulting role in Alberta's oil-sand operation, and BOLT10 might be a truck leasing operation. Several BOLT entities are active in our Williston oilfields. They are cover names for the convoluted LLCs that actually own pieces of the operation. Very stealthy, intricate business structures.

"The economics and business expert at my paper thinks such shenanigans might be an attempt to avoid a takeover. If a vulture cannot find all the legal pieces of the corporate puzzle, then the vulture cannot plan an effective attack. Oil exploration and extraction companies apparently need to hide assets, responsibilities, and subcontractors from their fellow raptors, and from the various tax men."

"So why would Nathan be shaken by my mention of BOLT?"

"One guess. He might be one of the few people savvy enough to know who is hiding behind BOLT, or who is throwing cloaks over these companies so that nobody sees them. And maybe he can even guess why."

"Oh, oh! I think I know where you're going here. It's Kathleen, right?"

"She has the education, the credentials, the personality and the passion, and even the required tutor. And she does a lot of business in Williston. I'm saying that is the first place I'd look."

"So with that background, and I'm going out on a limb here, I'm thinking Nathan did not connect Kathleen with the Gupchal deaths until I mentioned that BOLT thing. I'll tell you Steffie, that really surprised him. He didn't fake that heart attack, or whatever it was."

"Even so, Leon, we had better tiptoe carefully through this swamp. Go to bed. We'll talk tomorrow."

Leon's mother brings him a cup of hot cocoa. "I was hoping you'd take this upstairs, get ready for bed, get a good book, and slip into a good night's sleep."

"Thanks, Mom. But I doubt that's gonna happen. I'm just too wound up."

"You've had a rough night. Not as rough as Nathan's, but I can tell you're exhausted."

"I know, Mom. I'll go right up and take my medicine. But I've got one more call to make."

"Larry?"

"Yeah, Mom. He's got to know. Maybe he can come down tomorrow and stay with him for a few days... make sure he's doin' okay. This will only take a second, then I'll hit the sack. Good night, Mom."

***

Thursday, October 17, 2013
Bottineau County, ND – 10:30 a.m.

After doing a bit of hunting, Steffie finds five properties in the area with a mail box, or a post near the driveway entry, marked with the medallion from *Prairie Restoration Inc*. Three of those properties, including the Gupchals' land, are included in Prometheus' submittal to NDOEP for the oil refinery. It has taken her longer than it should have, but it finally clicks that the owner of the land in the county records, the cryptic PRTI LLC, must stand for *Prairie Reclamation Trust Inc.*, and that name was on the medallion she'd photographed on the Gupchals' mailbox. And that name is only one word removed from the research outfit *Prairie Reclamation Inc.* whose PAC gave Leon's campaign a big donation.

Someone, it appears, is running a scam. They've attached these parcels to what seems like a bogus conservation entity, which has turned them over to a refinery developer. It's quite unlike anything an environmental cover organization should be doing.

Since she is thinking investigative reporter thoughts, a connected thought sneaks in. *If someone is manipulating the land ownerships to keep something a very big secret, would that someone hes-*

itate to murder if it was necessary to preserve those secrets? She understands the need for secrecy with respect to land transactions in the path of a refinery project, but this degree of subterfuge is unusual and hints at something more sinister than pieces of land changing hands. A profound, deep-rooted, highly emotional force must be driving such subterfuge. Black anger, greed, money, or blood-red revenge would power this type of fraud. Or it might supply the motive for cold blooded murder, as in Mr. Timmins' demise. She recognizes a similar deep-seated emotion she's run across while investigating this drama—Kathleen's. And she's the one who had the flaming relationship with the very firm financing this refinery—HF&G. Something sinister must be hidden in there.

Last night, Leon added fuel to the fire Steffie was building under Kathleen. She had no solid physical evidence to link Kathleen with BOLT, or its actions with Nathan's medical problem, or the nonexistent conservation scam, or the Gupchal farm murders, or even Prometheus' vanishing act. Yet, at every turn, Steffie seems to find a flashing yellow arrow pointing in the general direction of Kathleen Carter.

***

Bottineau County Sheriff's Office, ND – 6:30 p.m.

Since Steffie is already in Bottineau County, she decides it is time to shake the tree and see what falls out. She enters the Bottineau County Sheriff's office, removes her muddy boots, and stashes them on the mat.

Sheriff Gaffey comes out of his office. "Hey Steffie, what are you doing up here again?"

"We need to have a little talk, Sheriff. Wouldn't happen to have a hot cup of coffee hanging around here someplace, would you?"

"Okay, Steffie. What we gonna talk about?" Gaffey makes a little play of pouring them each a cup of coffee from his thermos.

"You remember that interesting phone call we made to J.D. Crowe last week?"

"Oh, god, Steffie! Please don't go there. That was embarrassing."

"I'm thinking it's time we call him again. I think Crowe's the key. He's the only one who can substantiate the reason for the Gupchal murders. I am absolutely positive neither he nor his firm had anything to do with killing them. However, only he can help us nail whoever did."

"So, you've got it all solved now? And who's the bastard we're nailing?"

She told him how Kathleen's law school classmates responded to her questions about her relationship with Crowe at Harvard and HF&G and about the ties between the Gupchals' farm and the faux conservation entity, *Prairie Reclamation Trust*; about the fact that the three properties tied to *Prairie Reclamation Trust* are all involved in the refinery project; and lastly, she revealed the possibility that Kathleen controlled the site development firm using all this secret information. "I think it is Kathleen's boiling, festering revenge that powers this whole story. And for good measure we might, potentially, add her possible role in Timmins' bloody exit tableau."

"So you're telling this stupid old man that I have a serial killer running around up here, somehow avoiding my capture? And presto, you've now figured it out? What a bumbling idiot that sheriff is, huh?"

"Cut it out, Sheriff. I'm trying to help here."

"Your theory's kind of far-fetched. I'm going to have to think about this."

"It all points directly at Kathleen. I'm confident she's out to sabotage this refinery thing to get back at HF&G. And the only way we can confirm that base assumption is to get Crowe to admit to you that's the way it happened."

"First, I don't like the *we* part, Steffie. Second, I'm not about to make a fool of myself again. Third, you want me to tell Crowe that I'm sorry 'bout that last joke, but this time I'm serious?"

"I've got the whole thing scripted for you, Sheriff. Once you are comfortable, we'll give him a call."

She puts her tablet on the desk so he can read it. After going over the text a few times, Gaffey says, "I'm gonna have Deputy Turnquist sit here and monitor this conversation for my own protection. That gives me a witness so I can sue you for illegally pressuring a police officer, if I have to. If any investigation is to be done, I want it done legal like… nice and tidy."

"I can live with that, Sheriff." Steffie punches a few buttons on her phone, then puts it on the table for Gaffey. "That's Crowe's personal cell number on my phone. I can dial it for you if you want."

"How did you get his cell number?"

"I'm an *investigative reporter*, Sheriff. That's my job!"

"I'll use my phone, Steffie. I'll put it on speaker so all three of us can hear everybody, okay?"

Crowe answers on the third ring.

"Good evening, Mr. Crowe. This is Sheriff Gaffey out in North Dakota, again. First, let me apologize for that conversation we had a week or so ago. I had you in my sights as a murder suspect back then. But things have changed dramatically. Right away I want you to know that I am totally persuaded you had nothing to do with those deaths. Do you understand that, Mr. Crowe?"

"Yes, I do, Sheriff."

"Good. Thank you. But I am still running that same murder investigation and have recently come onto some information that, I believe, only you can substantiate for me. I want to first tell you what I think happened, and then I am going to ask you several questions about my thinking, okay?"

"I'm ready, Sheriff… I think."

"First I'm going to tell you this whole story concerns Kathleen Carter, a woman you know personally. Am I right?"

"Oh shit!" Crowe says.

Sheriff Gaffey looks at Steffie, smiles, and gives her a thumbs-up. He then tells Crowe the whole story—the Harvard affair part, the wronged woman part, the revenge plot part, the vomit on the Buick part. And he fits all the parts together for Crowe.

"That bitch is crazy, Sheriff. She's a goddamned genius, though she's crazy as a loon. She helped me get through more than a few classes—almost wrote my thesis. I probably would not have made

Law Review without her. She was driven and a whiz, but she was crazy, jealous, demanding, overbearing, power hungry, and way too much of a package for me. I told her I'd had enough. But you got it wrong. I didn't jilt her. She quickly threw me aside and stuck her fangs into the bigger fish, Francelli, and several others. She left a trail of blood through HF&G and the partners finally fired her ass.

"Even after she seduced Francelli, she used to stalk me! Showed up at places right out of the blue to stare at me. She told me that she'd kill me if she got the chance. But she told the other guys that too, so I wasn't too worried she'd physically kill me. There are plenty of other ways she can hurt me though, and I don't doubt she'd do it."

"When was the last time you saw Kathleen?"

"It's been fifteen, sixteen years since she walked out of HF&G's office the last time. It was a big deal. Several of the guys, me included, stood and applauded her exit from the firm. She turned back and gave us all the finger. She tried suing HF&G for gender discrimination. That didn't work. She's ticked at HF&G, no question about it. You should talk to my boss, Enrico Francelli. Can he tell you stories! The fireworks those two set off scorched several city blocks."

"Do you know where she is now? Ever wonder what she might be up to?"

"Houston, I think. Francelli knows. He actually pursued that megalomaniac. He used to spend weekends in Houston with her… to satisfy a death wish I should think. But even he gave up five, six years ago after she pushed him down a flight of marble steps and then threw a vase at him. He broke a couple of ribs and punctured a lung. It was pretty messy. She's a passionate lover and runs a primo hedge fund, but she's vicious, jealous, and volatile. She's just not human."

"But she'd know exactly how HF&G's business works, wouldn't she?" Gaffey read the question off Steffie's notepad.

"Oh, shit."

"Her name ever come up with respect to the refinery project out here?"

"Oh shit!" said Crowe again, twice as loud.

"What is it, Mr. Crowe?"

"Please don't tell me what I think you are going to tell me."

"What would that be, Mr. Crowe?"

"Damn! You know that little nagging gremlin that whispers stuff into your ear when you're drunk, Sheriff? I should have listened. You are right. Her name was attached to that project, but only very, very marginally. There was nothing specific, but when we were going over the corporate documents just after we grabbed that firm, one of our techie guys made a crack like, 'Wow, I haven't seen such an innovative debt restructuring maze since the Dragon Lady left.' We all laughed, and nobody really thought much about it. When we initially bought Petrotek, they owned a sub-company, Oil Facilities Design Inc. What a stupid name! How're we supposed to market that? We quickly changed its name to Prometheus. The firm had already started some preliminary design work on the North Dakota project. They'd analyzed potential supply volumes, set site design parameters, and developed preliminary budget calculations. That project was the single biggest reason Petrotek was a valuable entity. It was a huge project… a potential money machine.

"But Petrotek would have been doing their land studies and site analysis work on the project way *before* we even got involved. No way even Kathleen could know enough to tie either HF&G or me to the shady financial firm that purchased the holding company that owned the design firm whose subsidiary hired her. That's way too convoluted, isn't it? Plus, when we do get involved, we know how to cloak our participation very well in the early stages, so we don't get the phone calls from irate employees, and local economic development directors and such, when we pull the kind of plugs we have to pull on these deals. Understand, Sheriff?"

"Could she have figured it out by herself?"

"She couldn't have known we were involved. We cloaked everything professionally."

Steffie shoved a list of several questions over to Gaffey, then tapped one with her fingertip.

"Okay, Mr. Crowe. I'm now going to change course and play a game of 'Let's Pretend.' Let's pretend she *did* find out HF&G was connected to the refinery project. From what you know of her, do you think that she could have purposely sabotaged your project, just to get back at Francelli or HF&G for jilting her?"

"In a heartbeat, Sheriff. In a goddamned heartbeat. And she would know how. She was in the joint *Business and Law Program* at Harvard, and wrote her thesis on *real-estate confiscation strategies*. It raised a few eyebrows I tell you, even for that bunch of bloodthirsty capitalists at the Business School."

Gaffey read another question Steffie handed him on a page torn from her notebook. "Okay, Mr. Crowe, I'm changing the topic a bit. You guys finally sold Prometheus, didn't you? Can you tell me who bought it?"

"It was a private sale, off the books. Almost *gave* the damn thing to an oil services investor from Dubai who used the loss as a tax write off. I reviewed the closing paperwork myself."

"This may be a critical question, Mr. Crowe. Who bought it?"

"What difference does that make? Oh shit! Don't tell me she…" Crowe managed to wrestle some control back into his brain. "Yeah, we sold it off, or we thought we did. There's some glitch in the final paperwork, but we're working it out. Pretty soon—"

"Are you sure?" Gaffey read from Steffie's prompt. "Did you personally talk to this investor? Your glitch wouldn't be that you can't find Prometheus in order to sell it, would it?"

Gaffey could feel the doubt creeping into Crowe's voice. He paused for a few seconds to build the suspense.

"What would you say, Mr Crowe, if I told you that we believe that the parent, or rather grandparent, company of the entity that promised to buy Prometheus from you, though technically licensed in Dubai, is actually located in Houston, and we are thinking it is, in some way, controlled by Kathleen Carter?"

"If that's true, Sheriff, you will have a real murder on your hands. I'll personally fly down there and kill that bitch myself."

"You do realize who you're talking to, Mr. Crowe?"

"Okay, Sheriff, I wouldn't do that, but my boss, Francelli, certainly would. He has more fang punctures on him than I do. But you catch her and we'll both be dancing at her hanging."

"This may be the wild west, Mr. Crowe, but we don't do hangings anymore. I want you to call me if, or when, you eventually find Prometheus. And one last question, Mr. Crowe. How did HF&G become aware of Petrotek? What made you first interested in the firm? Who red flagged them as potential takeover material?"

"I have no idea. That would have occurred many months ago. The zombies downstairs in the number crunching and analysis part of the business might know."

"Could you find out for me? I want to know if, like a good card shark, someone 'forced' HF&G to choose the Petrotek card." That was Steffie's question word for word. Gaffey had no idea what it meant.

"I don't think that would be possible, Sheriff. We do all our own research and we identify susceptible takeover prospects based on raw numbers generated by data crunching programs we developed ourselves. It is all numbers... brutal, crystal-clear numbers."

Once again Gaffey read from Steffie's notes. "Would it be possible for someone with knowledge of HF&G machines to either pirate your algorithm, or use a similar one in order to understand your machine's appetite with the purpose of catching your computer's attention?"

"That's pretty far-fetched Sheriff." He paused. "Pardon me sir, but I am afraid I have to put a question to you, and it's a strange question. I am wondering how a hick sheriff in a rural area of a backwater state knows enough about the intricacies of hedge fund operations and computer algorithms to even ask me that question. All of a sudden things aren't sounding right. I see red lights flashing. I think I'll have to stop answering your questions, at least until the ground stops shaking under my chair."

"I can appreciate that, Mr. Crowe," says Gaffey. "Maybe we're not as *hick* as you think. I need information. I want you to look into something for me. Use Mr. Francelli and perhaps include my friend,

Mr. Pick. Find me an answer to that algorithm question. I'm pretty sure I know what happened, but I'll give you one day to confirm it before I start making some arrests around here. I can't wait forever, Mr. Crowe, because I'm sure several federal agencies will be getting involved in this very quickly. You know what that means. Means your quick cooperation is essential and will pay dividends, if you get my meaning. Am I clear?"

"Yes, Sheriff, crystal clear. I cooperate now and the necessity to dig through my files evaporates. I appreciate the heads-up."

Steffie shoves Gaffey a paper with a penciled note. He shoots her a strange look.

"Just ask him," she mouths.

"One last thing, Mr. Crowe. When you are talking to your boss, I want the two of you to find me an answer to my latest quandary. As far as I can tell, Prometheus no longer exists. How is that possible? Where did they go? Did their vanishing have anything to do with the fact that they faked the Preliminary Environmental Report to our NDOEP? You and Francelli figure it out and get me an answer by tomorrow. This thing's been crawling along for a month, but it's speeded up now. It's moving fast and I can't hold the feds off much longer. Call me as soon as you have anything. Is that clear?"

Sheriff Gaffey hangs up his phone. "Much more productive than our last discussion, huh?"

"You realize, Sheriff, every investigative reporter in the country would die to have been able to help you do what you just did?"

"I do, Steffie. But also, you have to realize that every sheriff in the state would die to have a sharp investigator like you helping an old man like me put words he doesn't even know the meaning of into his own mouth. If you didn't make me practice saying that stuff about algorithms, I could never have pulled it off. I still don't know what that means, but thank you, Steffie. We will get this solved. It may take a while, but we will get her."

The sheriff starts putting papers into files. "Then that brings us to the next problem, Steffie. I must speak to her father, and very carefully."

"You can't think Nathan is involved with Gupchal's death, can you?"

"I don't have the luxury of just thinking he's involved, Steffie. I have to be sure of his innocence or guilt—just do my due process. Either clear him or arrest him."

"I'm going back to Bismarck now. Can I tell Leon about this conversation?"

"No, Steffie, we can't do that. This thing's jumped to the next level, and that means at least two things. The first is about what's involved now—big money, big corporations, big government, big area! It's a big problem now. I can't even begin to sort it out, especially on my budget. I gotta call my friend, Brett VanderLoo. He's with the State Criminal Investigation Unit, down in Bismarck. And the CIU will probably bring in the FBI to help them trace the international money movement part of the story—Houston, New York, hell even Dubai. They're all part of this story now."

"I can understand that Sheriff. And what's number two?"

"It's a bit of a conflict with number one, I'm afraid. The very next thing I gotta do is talk to your good buddies, and also my friends, Leon and Nathan. I need to know exactly how close those two are to this explosion. I can't have 'em catch fire as the feds start poking around, can I?"

"You can't believe—"

"I don't have the luxury of believing. I gotta know things. I gotta know about business and finance where, as you just witnessed with Crowe, I am absolutely beyond my comfort range. But you gotta help me out one more time before the feds show up."

"Sure, Sheriff, whatever ya need."

"I need to talk to Leon and Nathan before the big guys come stomping in. I want them up here. No, I've a better idea. I'll go down to Bismarck where we all can have a discussion. Let's do it tomorrow morning. We have one last chance to figure this out before VanderLoo shows up. Once he gets the case, I lose control and that means we'll all be in the dark for the next couple of months."

"Where do you want to meet 'em? Leon's office?"

"Hell no! That's like grand central station. Might as well put it out on TV."

"We could meet at my farm. Won't be another microphone for miles. That way I keep ownership of my story. Gotta look out for number one, don't I?"

"That's not a bad idea. We'll call Leon and have him get Nathan to your place at eleven tomorrow morning. We make the call first thing. I don't want them studying their answers overnight."

***

HF&G's Office, New York City – 6:47 p.m.

Immediately after J.D. Crowe finishes his session with Sheriff Gaffey, he summons Martin Pick, then calls Francelli at his favorite Italian restaurant, several blocks away. "I got bad news, Enrico. Nuclear stuff! You just listen. Don't say anything back to me. Don't give anything away to the guys around you. Not even facial expressions. I mean it! Sober up, quick. Here's the story. Your whole Prometheus thing has just fuckin' gone up in smoke. We gotta talk—right now. Immediately! You gotta get back here to the office. Now!"

"Can you give me an hour? I've got Angelina—"

"No! Enrico. Didn't you hear me? I said now. Get her out of there, quick. Put her in a cab and you get back here now! I know why the money hasn't arrived in our Dubai account. And get this Enrico. It's never going to get in there! Ever!"

"What the hell you mean, ever? We had a deal. I'll sue their fuckin' ass."

"We're way past that, Enrico. Lawsuits are for people, not holograms and dragons. We're talking AK-47s and rocket launchers now. All-out metaphysical war. You get back here, pronto."

"Okay, But Angelina is not going to be happy—"

"She's going to be even unhappier when she finds out you're broke, or in jail, or dead. We're going to be talking about your crazy, radioactive Kathleen. Angelina's not going to want to hear *that* bitch's name bouncing off your lips. And I guarantee this'll get bloody, and you don't want any blood to splash onto her, do you?"

"Alright, alright. I'm there in ten minutes. Don't kill anybody till I get there."

"I can't guarantee that, boss. I'm so fricken steamed I could kill my own mother!"

Crowe then makes a second call to the research guys in the dungeon. "Jason, I need a favor and it is absolutely for my ears only, and I can give you only half an hour to crack this. I got two familiar names—a firm named Prometheus Inc. and a hedge fund player based in Houston named Kathleen Carter. Both entities seem to have disappeared and I need to make them reappear immediately. Any information is gonna be severely cloaked, so put all the manpower you got on it. It's a major emergency, code red or some such fuckin' thing. Find these two entities now. I'll need an update in a half hour. Then I got more work for you. You're gonna be up all night, Jason. Maybe all week. You may never sleep again. I'll be on my cell."

Chapter 34

It's another overcast day. But this time it's cold, with the wind chill hovering around zero and a few snowflakes swirling in the wind. Winter's snuck up on Leon while his mind is concentrating on Kathleen, the refinery, and the election. And it's still October. Leon thinks this is a bad omen. The weather also attacked his mom's sister. Gave her a cold bad enough to require his mom to stay overnight and be the nursemaid. He has to make his own breakfast. He messes up the microwave doing the bacon, breaks the spatula handle, and probably screws up the automatic part of the coffee machine. His shower is cold and the newspaper, blown off the porch into the bushes, requires his forest ranger skills to liberate it. He traipses bits of mud and snow across the front hall and anticipates a scolding when his mom returns.

But he does manage to get himself to the Capitol Building, and by 8:05. He opens his front office door, stomps right past Debbie, who is occupying Margie's desk, and heads toward his office. Margie is working behind Debbie in the file room.

"I need coffee," he grunts, seeking pity, or sympathy. The ploy doesn't work.

"I beg your pardon, you grumpy old man," Debbie says to his back. "That's the speaker's office. You can't go in there. If Margie comes back and finds a stranger in there, I'm going to be in big trouble."

"Jeese, Debbie, it's a rotten morning and I feel awful. Can't I throw a tantrum in my own office? And may I have some coffee, please?"

Margie hurries out of the file room. "Leon, you cannot go into your office. You gotta snap out of this funk, and quick. We got work to do... a full schedule. Plus, Steffie desperately needs to talk to you."

"What the hell does she want?"

"She wants *me* to call *her* as soon as *you* walk through that door." She points to his office door. "I told her you may be with Nathan at the hospital, but that didn't seem to take her edge off. I'm supposed to call her the instant you cross that threshold." She points again at the threshold.

"I don't suppose I can hide in the closet and you tell her I flew to Minneapolis for the day?"

"Pay attention to what I am saying, Leon. Once *you* cross *that* threshold, *I* must call Steffie. Any talking we do on this side of that threshold is okay, but as soon as you cross into your own office, I have to call her. Is that clear?"

Leon understands something is not right and also that his morning schedule is garbage.

Margie asks, "How's Nathan doing?"

"I haven't seen him. Larry came down last night. He seems fine and ready to go. Larry is with him for tests this morning. He should be finished by mid-morning. I've still got his truck here, so he's supposed to stop over to pick it up."

"That's a relief. Anything else you want to discuss before I have to call Steffie?"

"You've done your job, Margie. I'm well frightened."

Leon steps into his room, takes the basketball down from the shelf and bounces it a few times on the floor, as if that will help get him back in the game. He stands, looking out his window at the mall—a bleak, dark and overcast day, with nothing vaguely human doing any frolicking. A white snow dusts the grass and a few tentative snowflakes swirl around the naked trees. A car headlight flashes at him as it passes the openings between the elms lining the street, but not much else moves. Did he miss an entire month? Could this be December already? The phone on his desk buzzes.

"Hi, Steffie. You've got Margie all upset this morning. What's going on?"

"I don't have time for chitchat, Leon. We've got serious problems. Is Nathan with you?"

"No, he's at the hospital with Larry. Doc wanted to do another test. I expect Larry to bring him over, maybe 10:00 or 10:30. Why? What's wrong?"

"Sheriff Gaffey is here. He needs to talk to you. He's on speaker with me."

"Morning, Leon. John Gaffey here."

"Morning, John. What do you need? Should I be concerned about the way this conversation is tending?"

"Yes, you should, Leon. This is very serious. I need to talk to you and Nathan. After Nathan finishes with the hospital, I want the two of you to drive up to Steffie's farm. We're here now. I must talk to both of you. Get here as soon as you can. I repeat—this is extremely serious. I'm assuming you won't need a lawyer with you as Nathan will be with you, but keep in mind that this will be a very serious discussion."

"You're scaring me, John. What's this all about?"

"I need to talk to you guys. It's critical to a criminal investigation. That's all you need to know for now. And speed is of the essence. And if Larry's there, then bring him along too. All three of you try and get to Steffie's place by eleven. You check in with me if Nathan's delayed. And don't tell anyone about this meeting—not Margie, or even your mother. Can you do that?"

"Yes, John. I'll do that. I'm suitably frightened."

"Good! You should be. Means you understand *serious*."

"Can I talk with Steffie?"

"No! The only thing you think about is getting to Steffie's place as quickly as you can. Keep me updated."

***

Steffie Cobb's House,
Ten Miles North of Bismarck, ND – 11:10 a.m.

At ten minutes after eleven, Steffie leads Leon, Larry, and Nathan through the front hall to the kitchen at the back of the house. The big bay window half surrounds the kitchen table. Low black clouds hang over the farm and dense swirls of dust rush by outside the window. The landscape looks bleak, even for North Dakota.

Sheriff Gaffey stands up. "Good morning, Nathan, how's your ticker doin' this morning? I hate to put more pressure on that thing, but I got serious questions."

"That's all right, John. My doctor says I'm solid as a school kid."

"You don't fool me one bit, Nathan. If you feel any discomfort at all, you tell me. You understand that?"

"I'll let you know if he's troubled," says Leon. "I know that jerk, and he'll never tell you himself if something's wrong."

"Okay, let's sit down and get to work. Here's my problem. The deaths at the Gupchal farm have gotten way more complex than you can possibly imagine. It's gone international. Way out of my league and my resource capability. I've called Brett Vanderloo from the State Criminal Investigation Unit, and he might want to bring the FBI in as well. I am going to lose control of this thing. I expect Inspector VanderLoo to show up here this afternoon and, before he gets here, I need to know what the hell I find myself in the middle of. I need your help badly.

"Steffie's been helping me, and we have a working theory, but we need you guys to confirm that theory and show us how it all fits together. And Nathan, right up front, I'm gonna state that our primary problem is your daughter, Kathleen. She's woven a piece of this mystery around her, though I can't yet begin to understand even what that means."

"Theory? Kathleen? About what?"

"Well, Nathan, it would be good if I could talk to Kathleen before the feds show up, but finding her is impossible. You wouldn't know where she is or how to contact her, would you?"

"I've got a phone number. It's only a message drop, but I can try it. Where she actually is, I have no clue. I would guess she's in Houston, now that it's cold up here. I know folks have seen her shadow haunting the oilfields near Williston, but all of what I hear is second hand. I've got ears out there, and people tell me things. I'm sorry, John. I haven't talked to her face-to-face in years."

"You know where she stays when she's up here?"

"I know she has a farmhouse out northwest of Dickinson. I've never been there, but I can probably Google you to the general area."

"Give that info to Deputy Turnquist. Then we'll get started here. I know you haven't had much contact with Kathleen, Nathan. Nevertheless, I'm going to treat you as if you are her lawyer. So if the answer to some question has to be carefully crafted, I'm expecting you to do the appropriate crafting. Is that clear?"

"Yes, Sheriff, I understand."

"First, I am going to ask you some background questions. Then I'll have all of you listen to a tape of a telephone conversation, and then we will get down to the real business of trying to find out what the hell is going on up in Bottineau County. Okay?"

"You've got me frightened, Sheriff," says Leon. "But we're ready."

"We understand the rules, Sheriff," Nathan says. "Thanks for being patient with us."

"Okay. Nathan, question number one. I'd like to know if the letters HF&G mean anything to you."

"That's the name of the hedge fund, a New York group, that either owns or is using Prometheus Inc., the firm proposing the oil refinery project."

"When did you first hear of that firm?"

"A week or so before that demonstration on the mall. I know guys, some who work at N-DOPE, who told me the money in the project is coming from HF&G."

"Leon, how about you? When did you hear about HF&G?"

"The governor, or maybe it was Brian Bast, let it slip on the day of the first demonstration. Then Nathan, Larry, and I discussed HF&G bringing truckloads of goodies to the various state officers."

"How about you, Steffie?"

"I think I first heard that name from Jane Blackburn of the Prairie Preservation group, on the first morning of the big demonstration. I was talking to her on the mall."

"Any of you guys remember HF&G from ten or fifteen years ago?"

Leon and Nathan looked strangely at each other. "Why should we know that?" asks Nathan.

"Do either of you know if Kathleen has any connection to HF&G?"

"Kathleen's based in Houston, not NewYork," says Nathan. "Been down there for fifteen or so years."

"Nathan doesn't know this, Sheriff," says Leon, "but Steffie and I are aware that Kathleen knows HF&G intimately. Isn't that right Steffie?"

Nathan jumps in to defend his daughter, as a good lawyer should. "Kathleen could not possibly have anything to do with—"

"I've had several talks with members of that hedge fund," Leon says. "And I know that a Mr. J.D. Crowe, of that group in New York, is part of the story that involves the Gupchal murders."

Gaffey continues Leon's thought. "Nathan, you must be patient. Listen to everything we tell you about what we know and then react to the complete story. The tricky part is that so much is hidden, purposely confused and distorted, so it tends to muddle everything. Frankly, I get lost. I'm just not able to handle it.

"I am expecting that after the feds take over I will be out of the loop and you will be dealing directly with the State Crime Unit or the FBI. Okay, let's get things started. I am now going to play you the tape of a conversation that I, with Steffie's assistance, had late yesterday with J.D. Crowe of HF&G in New York. I know Leon has talked with Crowe before, but I am assuming that you, Nathan, do not know him. Is that correct?"

"That's correct, Sheriff. I've seen his picture in the paper but never talked to the man."

"I would like to play the thing straight through, then we can go back and tear it apart sentence by sentence. Understood?"

***

Near the Theodore Roosevelt National Forest, Western ND – 11:45 a.m.

At the same time Leon and Nathan are listening to a tape of the J.D. Crowe phone call at Steffie's farmhouse, and about a hundred and fifty or so miles west of that farmhouse, J.D. Crowe is driving another rented black Escalade. It is carrying his boss, Enrico Francelli, Martin Pick, and two of his commando buddies north on US 24, and is aiming toward wherever Pick's sophisticated electronics are telling them to go. They are ready for a fight, well-armed and well-protected, just like they'd never left Afghanistan. In the far back seat, handcuffed to the seatbelt strap, Kathleen's security captain, Trevor McManus, sits quietly and listens to his cell phone vibrate on the seat next to him. It's just out of his reach, or would be if his hands were capable of reaching anything.

Martin Pick turns around, laughs at Trevor, picks up the phone, and notes the caller ID displayed on its black glass. "Another call from BAT PHONE #1. Isn't that cute, Trevor? BAT PHONE #1. I wonder who that might be."

"If I don't answer that phone, she's gonna know something's wrong, and she disappears. You'll never find her."

"Let me worry about that. In the meantime, that phone is telling us her exact location, and so fairly quickly our location and her location will match. And then you can watch the carnage as we tear her apart and stick sharp objects into her eyes. And then you realize who we're goin' to deal with next, don't you?"

"You'll never get close enough. She's able to sense trouble approaching. She'll be gone before it gets there. Hell, she's probably gone already. You're only chasin' her phone, you stupid jackass. You're not chasing her. She could be in Houston."

"Shut up, Trevor."

"And don't think she'll hang around and worry about me. I'm a disposable piece of garbage. If I cease to function she'll throw me out with the other garbage and find another newer model—one that will make me look like a wimp."

"If it makes you feel any better, Trevor, I agree with your boss. I also see you as that disposable piece of garbage."

"Fuck you, Pick."

"And, I am thinking that sooner or later I'll also be required to implement my garbage disposal function."

Through her cell phone use, Pick uses a tracking program he'd pilfered during his time in Afghanistan, which has set Kathleen's location in a sparsely settled area northwest of Dickinson near the Theodore Roosevelt National Forest.

Francelli's ETA to that location is now nine minutes. The bat phone rings for the third time, resulting in the repetition of a similar conversation with Trevor. Francelli feels the tension build, and it feels good. He envisions fire and smoke and a bloody heap, splat on the floor, and sees the misshapen pile of fiery garbage that used to be Kathleen. He imagines thrusting his sword into that pile. At least that's the plan.

***

Steffie Cobb's House,
10 miles North of Bismarck, ND – 12:30 p.m.

After the excitement of the recorded interview dies down, Sheriff Gaffey addresses the group.

"I've got an update which adds a bit more confusion to this already supremely confusing story. I received a call from Enrico Francelli of HF&G this morning. He was complying with my request for information as discussed on the recording. In essence, he confirmed the assumptions I threw at Crowe yesterday afternoon. Yes, it's possible, and maybe even probable, that Kathleen is somehow messing with HF&G's operations. It's possible, and maybe even probable, that their computer operations have been hacked, though it must have been done very professionally and, until now, no evidence of the act has been detected. But Francelli thinks he is going to have to completely rebuild HF&G's computer network to eliminate anything Kathleen may have stuck into them to ensure the kind of security they require. Steffie will elaborate on this. I'm in way over my head."

Steffie continues for him. "HF&G cannot be assured that any information inside their system is not now known by someone outside their system. And that someone we are talking about might very well, either now or in the future, be the regulatory agencies of the US and several other governments. HF&G cannot know if every bit of quasi-illegal, or quasi-fraudulent, or quasi-unethical behavior might be broadcast on the evening news at any time. All their offshore accounts, and all their passwords, are potentially compromised. That situation makes it kind of impossible to run a successful hedge fund operation."

This level of confusion astonishes Nathan. "I would have thought HF&G was better protected. How could an uber-professional bunch like that be hacked? I'm certain they'd have better protection."

"Sheriff Gaffey and I talked about that this morning. Let's say it's possible Kathleen did entice the HF&G computers to recognize what I will call the *takeover-ripeness coefficient* of the firm she put together, now named Prometheus Inc. HF&G would then have to do their due diligence and vacuum and digest all the financial information on the company they'd just purchased. It is possible that HF&G's act of vacuuming that information also sucked up one or more viruses that Kathleen may have planted in Prometheus' records. Once HF&G's computers digested Prometheus' files, viruses implanted in those business files could act to make every piece of HF&G information transparent to Kathleen's computers."

"We're not saying this is what happened," says the sheriff, "only that it is quite possible it could have happened."

And Nathan is quick to see the problem. "Oh my God, Gaffey! Do you know what this means?" He stands up to give himself more room to maneuver his arms. He twirls around, places his hands on the sides of his head, and rubs hard.

"What do you see, Nathan?" asks Leon.

"This means Kathleen's motive is *not* to feed HF&G a company, say Prometheus, whose refinery is destined to fail, thus causing HF&G to take a serious loss. That's but the peanuts. Don't you see? She could be going for their jugular."

"What do you mean?"

"It's what you just said, Steffie. If every piece of HF&G information is transparent to Kathleen's computers, that means all that information can also be made available to the IRS, the SEC, and the EURO and Saudi banking officials. All of their offshore vaults, their sneaky deals, their lack of ethics… everything is exposable. Kathleen, if she in fact engineered this convoluted piece of takeover theater, may have effectively killed, and certainly bankrupted, Francelli's entire firm—every memo from every computer in the entire HF&G LLC vault. His finely tuned machine is now, or could be at the touch of a button, a hunk of toast. And his high-flying investors are also toast! They'll be running for the exits, running to the feds, running to their lawyers, strapping on their guns."

"And," said Sheriff Gaffey. "It's also possible that by now she may have cleaned out his offshore accounts. Wouldn't you, if you had his passwords? I think we have to now assume that the next sounds we hear are the explosions of HF&G's retaliation. And the only way they can possibly retaliate, since their entire electronic operation is now toast, is with acts of physical violence."

"They have to prevent Kathleen from pushing that big red button," says Steffie, "the one shoving all those compromising files over to the feds."

"Or all the money into her accounts."

"Francelli's got no choice, does he?" Nathan slams the table with a fist. "I see no way out! He has to kill her, right? My Kathleen's as good as dead, isn't she?"

"And even if they don't kill her," adds Leon, "she'll end up following Francelli into whatever executive prison he will undoubtedly be heading toward."

Nathan sits down clumsily and hits the chair unevenly and a bit off center. He rests there for a few seconds, then slowly continues the slide down to the floor.

Steffie screams, "Nathan! Nathan!"

Chapter 35

As directed by the animation on his computer screen, Crowe spins the Escalade off the gravel county road, onto a long gravel driveway and then stops the car. "Here we are guys. See that windbreak, 'bout a mile down this drive? According to the computer, this should be Kathleen's place. What's the plan?"

"There's only one simple plan. We go down there and shoot her." Francelli says. "That's all there is. What's the story here, Trevor? What's she got for defense? Where are the machine guns, the mine-fields, or her IEDs?"

"What makes you think I know? Whatever I tell you, we both know there'll be something else. Also, I've been known to lie. If I were you, I'd already be worrying about being sucked in too far. I'm thinking that, right now, everyone in this car is toast. I'll bet we all have already eaten our last meals. So I guess I'll see you losers on the other side." He laughs.

"What are you jerks waiting for?" asks Francelli. "We have to get out to that house. So we hit a fuckin' mine? Well then, we all go boom. But we gotta go. We can't stay here shivering like sissies.

Draw your guns, check your radios, and turn on the cameras. We go in guns a blazin', just like in a video game."

The windbreak trees are so thick the house itself is not apparent until they are almost on top of it. Crowe breaks into the clearing and slides the car to a stop about a hundred feet in front of the house, throwing gravel around like Escalades do on TV ads.

Pick says, "Mr. Francelli, you and Crowe stay here. Tim, Reggie, and I, we trained for this in Fallujah and Bagdad. We'll go in and check it out. That way, if it all explodes, you don't go up with it." He and his two commando sidekicks get out. They test radios and helmet-cams, adjust backpacks and goggles, go down their lists, then start toward the front door, jumping from one tree to the next. But there are only a few trees close in around the house. Unlike in video games, they're pretty spruce things, like Christmas trees. The branches sweep down to the ground leaving plenty of room for stray bullets to slip through the foliage. They're not much good for re-straining a bullet, like the heavy trunks of the elms in the windbreak.

The house is not old, probably built in the nineteen-fifties or sixties. It's a fairly simple, aluminum-sided ranch with a double-car garage. A little jog in the front wall allows the roof to cover an entry area with a white door and a vertical piece of glass next to it. A short wainscot of red brick is along the front with the rest colored non-descript beige. It doesn't look anything near to being the fortified headquarters of a raging megalomaniac. But they all also know it still might be heavily defended or booby trapped.

"The front door's unlocked," says Pick over the radio to Francelli in the Escalade. "We're goin' in." Francelli and Crowe watch via Pick's head-cam that sees pretty much nothing other than what they'd see in their own grandmother's house. They look into the dining room. On the middle of the table is a black box about the size of a cake box from a bakery, with a white card taped to its top. On it, written in magic marker, is a message: "Hi, Guys. For instructions, please open the box."

"I see no wires here." Pick takes out a pen. "I don't think it's a bomb."

He sticks an end of the pen under the cardboard flap.

"No," cautions one of his teammates. "That's either a bomb or it's a joke. Why take the chance? Let's all go out on the porch and you put one round through it. If it blows, fine, 'cause we're outside. And if it doesn't blow we put the pieces of the box back together and see what the surprise is."

They all agree and retreat to the porch. Pick fires one round at it. The cardboard box pretty much disintegrates, debris flying everywhere. The bullet buries itself into a piece of wainscot molding on the wall. There is no explosion. The two things stored inside the box react to the bullet's quick passage in quite different ways. The iPhone suffers an almost direct hit and disintegrates into little dust-sized pieces of debris which fill the room like a gas. The manila envelope on which the phone was placed has hardly moved at all. It, along with the bottom of the cardboard box on which it rested, is physically attached to the table top with a single, six-penny, galvanized steel nail. Pick opens the flap on the envelope and pulls out a piece of paper, folded four times so as to allow it to be inserted into the envelope after it had been nailed to the table. He takes the paper out, opens it, and reads aloud: "Enrico, you can thank your god, you're also going home."

Pick has not a clue as to what that means, but thinking the note is meant for his boss, repeats the words into his microphone so Francelli can appreciate them. He stuffs the note into a pocket and waves at Tim and Reggie. They split up and start a careful search through the house to make sure it's empty. But then, about two or three seconds later, he hears Francelli yell into his earpiece: "Get out now, Pick. It's a trap!" Pick sees it too. Two words from the message—going home—suddenly resonate, and they trigger a well-developed response mechanism. "Get out of here, guys! Now!" he yells into the back room. "This place could be booby trapped. Get out, now!" Pick sprints toward the front door. His two buddies are a couple seconds slower to react and several yards deeper into the house, and so they do not follow him through the front door before the whole structure erupts in a ball of fire. The noise is unbelievable. Pick just makes it out the door and is on the entry porch when he's lifted into the air and thrown a couple dozen feet to where his body skids to a stop up against a small bush.

Francelli and Crowe, nervously pacing and arguing near the black Escalade parked a hundred feet from the house, feel the compressive force of the blast a split second before the fireball erupts. They see Pick somersault off the entryway slab and into the shrubbery, then watch the house behind him explode. The concussion wave knocks them to the ground. Bits and pieces of the former house rain down, and smoke and flames quickly consume the remaining structure. Crowe and Enrico run over to where the lower half of Pick's crumbled form sticks out of the bush.

Pick yells at them. "I think I'm okay but I don't see Tim or Reggie." He looks at the inferno blazing behind him. "No way they're getting out alive now."

He tries to untangle his two bloodied arms. "Quick, guys, pull me back to the car." J.D. and Francelli each grab a leg and pull him clear, then drag him toward the Escalade. They reach the car before a secondary explosion throws even more flaming debris around.

"That would be the propane tank," Pick says. "The place will be cinders in no time."

Pick works his way to sitting up and tries, unsuccessfully, to make his fingers work.

"She left a note for you, Mr. Francelli," he says.

"I know, you read it to me. Remember?"

"I don't remember nothin'. Fish it out of my pocket for me. My fingers can't figure out how to do that yet." Francelli does as he's told and extracts the folded note. He reads the thing to Crowe. "Enrico, you can thank your god, you're also going home."

"It's the same words as on Gupchal's suicide note, right, J.D.? This confirms this whole Prometheus fiasco, right from the start. It's all her work."

"Just as that hick sheriff told me," says Crowe. "I'm gonna kill the bitch with my own bare hands."

Pick struggles to sit up and leans lopsided against the front tire. "My arm's not working good yet. I can't draw my damn pistol. Crowe! Pull it out for me. Then bring Travis out here so I can shoot him. I'm gonna make him pay for Tim and Reggie. Right now, Crowe! Do it!"

Crowe hurries to the rear of the Escalade and opens the door. "Goddamn, Pick! He's not here!"

Francelli's right behind him and pokes around inside. "The seat-belt strap we cuffed him to has been cut clean off! Where'd he get a knife? Didn't you search him, Pick? How'd you miss a fuckin' knife?"

Crowe runs down the drive and looks out through the windbreak trees and over the vacant fields. "Where'd he go?" he yells back at them. "Ain't nothin' out there for miles. Where the hell did he disappear to?" They both have the same idea and look up into the trees. But it is October and the trees are naked and quickly reveal that no one is up there.

"Don't you worry, Mr. Francelli," Pick says. "I'll find 'em. I'll kill them both. That's my only job from now on. I'll track them down, both Kathleen and Travis. I'll make them pay for this. Blood oath, Mr. Francelli. Blood oath!"

Chapter 36

Friday, October 18, 2013
Methodist Hospital, Bismarck, ND – 6:10 p.m.

After three hours of hectic work in the ER, a nurse wheels Nathan into recovery. "It doesn't look good," the cardiologist tells Leon. "My opinion is that he'll not make it. He might have a few hours left, but the damage is massive and he's going to die, and fairly soon. I'm sorry, Leon, but there's nothing more I can do."

"Can I sit with him, Doctor?"

"You three stay here with him," says the sheriff. "I'll go out to the waiting room and get a couple chairs."

Leon, Larry, and Steffie sit in their various chairs, waiting in silence and listening to the mesmerizing sound of the monitor beeping. They anticipate the change in cadence that might signify the beginning of the end. On the other hand, they believe that the beeping will, even must, continue forever.

But the doctors were correct, and Nathan's monitor becomes suddenly silent at two minutes after seven. After that, there is nothing left to do. They cry and hug each other and realize that is all they can do. Even that doesn't change the fact that Nathan isn't with them anymore.

Sheriff Gaffey, who waited for them in the lounge, rejoins them in Nathan's room. "I think it's best we all go home now," he says.

"There's nothing more to do here. Since Steffie rode down here with me, I'll take her home. If you two want, I'll give you a lift as well."

"Thank you," Leon says. "But I think we're okay. Larry's got his truck, so he can follow me home. I want him to stay with me tonight. I don't think we two can be separated yet. I'm feeling perhaps that part of Nathan is still around if Larry and I can stay close."

"Leon's right," says Larry. He embraces Gaffey. "Thank you for staying here with us. We'll get home by ourselves. We'll be fine." He hugs Steffie too, cries a bit, and releases her. "Good night Steffie. We'll talk with you in the morning."

Leon and Larry walk across the well-lit parking lot to where they parked their trucks. No words are needed, and none are spoken. They climb into their trucks and maneuver them through the payment station, eventually finding themselves back on the streets of the real world.

***

An hour later, Leon sits at his computer and composes a message noting the details of Nathan's death. He then emails it to several of his close associates and to an address he believes is Kathleen's. Neither Leon nor his mom know of other family. Steffie had said she would take care of the public announcements. There isn't much else to do. He and Larry go out to the porch. Leon turns on the yard lights and pours each of them a tumbler of the good bourbon Nathan had brought him to celebrate those first Channel 7 gubernatorial poll numbers.

"I never saw this coming, Leon. I assumed he'd never die. I thought if anyone could beat the system, Nathan could."

"Sudden death is always a jolt, though thinking back, we really should've expected it. His father, remember, died in his fifties. Even his younger brother was taken by a heart attack, what, three, maybe four, years ago?"

"But he was generally healthy, I think. Everything was still running nicely, 'cept the ticker, I guess."

"Could be. But then, Nathan would never have told us even if he knew he was sick, would he? He'd be needing to project his invincibility."

His mother comes into the room, kisses Larry softly on the head, and hugs him. "I made everything ready in the guest room, Larry. You look beat. Go get some rest. Then tomorrow morning we'll talk about whatever we've got to do for Nathan."

"Thank you Mrs. R. I am absolutely bushed. I know it's only 9:30, but you're right, I gotta turn in. I'll be lucky to make it up the stairs." He gets up, pats Leon on the shoulder and then hugs his mom.

"What are we going to do now?" asks Leon. "How'm I gonna be doin' governor stuff without Nathan making runs? How am I gonna do *anything* without Nathan making runs?"

"I hear you, Leon," Larry says. "What the hell good are only two musketeers? See you in the morning, Mrs. R. G'night, Leon." Then he disappears up the stairs.

Chapter 37

The frigid air rushing across the open field of Calvary Cemetery is a gift to Nathan from his friends in the Canadian oilfields. The fierce wind, an Alberta Clipper, drives the wind chill down to five degrees above zero. That is exactly one hundred degrees colder than it was about two months ago, on that August day when John David Crowe threw up on the grill of the white, 2009 Buick Century. J.D. is back in North Dakota, and he doesn't like this reception any better than that first one. The vast quiet still overpowers the endless white landscape that seems unaffected by the roaring wind.

He does see several dozen people, however, even though the unusual cold has driven almost every human in the state inside. And those remaining out here on this hill seem unable or unwilling to generate any noise. The stupid sun is also mocking him. It is boiling away much lower in Rugby's almost-winter sky, but without any of the warming one expects from the sun. It certainly is feeble, and maybe vindictive. J.D. looks right at the evil ball. He challenges it to turn up the heat. He dares it to blind him.

"You puny jerk!" That makes him feel better. Staring down the major body in the heavens is a good way to start any day. It's hard to believe it's the same fireball that browned his body and burned his eyeballs on his last trip up to this god-forsaken landscape.

"Okay, Mr. Crowe, time to go." Sheriff Gaffey interrupts J.D.'s fantasy and gives him a slight push in order to get his freezing bones moving.

Crowe turns around. His eyes record the landscape in slow motion. Ten thousand acres of barren, white nothing glisten silently in the great void. He focuses on the only thing he sees not colored white or black—the greenish-beige tent erected over Nathan's grave, fifty yards away on the top point of this slight hill. Accompanied by Gaffey on one side and State Criminal Investigation Agent Brett VanderLoo on the other, J.D. begins the long walk along the path stomped into the thin snow crust by dozens of mourners. They walk up from the roadside to the gravesite.

Sheriff Gaffey cannot be sure Kathleen will show up for her father's funeral, although both Larry and Leon were positive she would. "She'll find a way," Leon had said. But Gaffey's problem is that he doesn't think a single person in the entire crowd, with the possible exception of Crowe, who hasn't seen her in a dozen years, knows even the general measures of her height and weight. She may be short and fat, or tall and skinny, blond or black hair, in a wheelchair, or with one arm amputated. Kathleen could be standing in the front row and no one would recognize her. However, the sheriff thinks Crowe will be able to recognize her or, more probably, she would certainly recognize him. And that act of recognition will be noticed by the expert people-watchers he and VanderLoo have placed throughout the crowd to register that unexpected reaction. Her act of recognizing Crowe might give away her presence, which will certainly be disguised. And also, Sheriff Gaffey is quite positive Ruby will remember her. It has only been two months since Kathleen locked her in the basement.

***

But then the opposite is also true. Kathleen knows none of these assembled mourners either, except for Larry and Leon standing up at the graveside. She'd last seen those two the summer she turned sixteen, and though they hadn't aged enough to confuse her, she knows her own appearance has indeed changed dramatically since that time. Plus, the disguise would further confuse them. Few people standing on this frozen hill know she even exists, let alone what she looks like. And except for Larry and Leon, probably none will have any confidence she'll show up. She therefore feels quite safe hiding amongst the several hundred people honoring her father. She considers herself fairly invisible.

She looks back down the hill to the parking area, where several dozen mourners grieve from their warm cars. Nothing is moving down there—not even the policeman and his dog, frozen in place on the far side of the blacktop. And up here on the hilltop, perhaps fifty or so black-clad mourners cluster around Nathan's grave, braving the cold and wind. She stands on the lee side of an ancient, wind-twisted maple tree skeleton, and just behind the main group of mourners. She has a good field of view and starts a scan of the crowd to look at these unknown people one at a time, to see what information she might harvest.

***

The graveside ritual ends and then portions of the mass of black-clad mourners begin to stir. A few individuals break away and, desperate for warmth, hurry down toward the cars on the road below. Under the tent, big Larry Oosterhaus supports Steffie Cobb with one arm and Leon's mother with the other. Margie hugs Mrs. Rolfes. Leon sits frozen like a stone monument. Many of Nathan's and Leon's colleagues from various business and governmental organizations made the two-hour drive up to Rugby for this occasion, and many offer a few comforting words to Leon and Larry before leaving the gravesite. It takes a while. Both of Nathan's parents are dead, so Mrs. Rolfes considers herself to be the parent figure here, having, in a way, mothered him ever since he spent weekday afternoons in her house as a two-year old.

J.D. Crowe and his guards walk toward the gravesite, their arrival timed to coincide with the end of the ceremony. They station themselves two-thirds of the way up the hill, facing the mourners as they descend toward their cars. The three stand quietly, intently surveying the somber, black clad, mostly gray-haired folks parading slowly past them.

Gaffey does not want to push it. He wants to let the emotion of Nathan's burial evaporate at its own pace. He wants the tension to develop slowly. He wants the mourners, many who know him, to be comfortable with his presence. He believes none of them will recognize Agent VanderLoo, and only a few of the women present have seen Crowe before. But he also is betting that only one of those women, Kathleen Carter, if she shows up for her father's burial, may be visually shocked to see Crowe standing silently beside the grave. Gaffey is hoping to use Kathleen's shock to his advantage. The crowd stirs, slowly gaining the energy to move. It thins, eventually leaving only the close family and friends within the tent structure.

***

"Fuck," she says quietly. The word slips out inadvertently, though a bit louder than she'd expected. The lady in front of her turns around, scolds her with a flaming eye and then turns back. She quickly regains her composure, but her mind is now racing. That looks like John Crowe! What the hell would he be doing out here in the middle of nowhere in the middle of winter? She studies his face to confirm her suspicion. That is Crowe! Why is he here? What can this possibly mean?

And she immediately understands the answer. They have to assume I will be here at Dad's funeral. They need someone to recognize me. Well, they blew that. Fuckin' J.D. won't recognize me. I'm invisible to him, especially dressed like this. Also, he's never paid any attention to any woman over twenty-five years old in his entire life, and he won't look at me now, either.

***

Kathleen is right. There is no way J.D. will recognize her. But she's also wrong. She is not invisible, especially to an experienced watcher like Sheriff Gaffey. He now is watching the face of a woman of indeterminate age, dressed in a black coat and shawl and standing near the back on the opposite side. He notes she's a loner, not a huddler. At any normal funeral, the mourners, especially in such cold, tend to cling to each other. Very few stand alone. They are the suspicious ones. He watches the lone woman start down the hill, then Gaffey sees her look right at him, and at Crowe, and he sees the full force of the power of recognition hit her—sees her stop short and sees her face contort with pain.

"Darryl," The sheriff says softly into his small microphone. "I think I've got her. About six paces north of tree number four. Looks like she's alone. I don't see bodyguards, but you guys act as if she has protection." Gaffey watches Deputy Turnquist move around the crowd and stand immediately behind the target.

"I'm sure that's her, Darryl," Gaffey says. "Wait twenty seconds so Mark and Steve can reach a support position behind you, then move in and check her ID. Be careful. She's unpredictable and, I believe, very dangerous."

"Good morning, ma'am. My name is Deputy Sheriff Darryl Turnquist." He shows her his ID. "We've been notified of a possible threat and are checking people we don't know. May I see an ID please?"

She spins around and glares at him. *Even though I have an ID, I'm not showing it to a pig like you* is her first thought. She checks herself and takes the saner route. "I'm sorry? What did you say?"

"Sorry ma'am, we're checking all the people up here we don't recognize as family and friends. Please show me an ID."

"I'm sorry. It's so cold out here. I didn't bring my purse. I left it at home. I'm Marylou Hanson. I went to high school with Nathan. I'll be walking home now. It's awfully cold. Thank you." She turns and walks away. She approaches the point where the walk enters the car park and passes a line of hedging, behind which the deputy holding Ruby guards the path. Ruby barks softly and lurches toward her, pulling against the leash.

She stumbles, though remains in character, and yells in her old lady voice. "Get away, you stupid dog! Officer, curb your dog!"

Deputy Turnquist is following her down the path. He grasps her shoulders from behind and says, "Will you identify yourself please, ma'am?"

"I told you before, sir, I left my purse back at the house."

"Then you'll have to come with me, please. We need to talk with you. Please come quietly with me now or I will have to cuff you and walk you shackled in front of all these people."

Sheriff Gaffey walks slowly toward her, J.D. Crowe by his side. They stop fifteen feet away from her.

Kathleen lurches against Turnquist's tight hold. "What the fuck are *you* doing here, John?"

"Watch your language, Kathleen," says Crowe. "Respect for your father and all."

"What do you know about respect? If my father's funeral is so sacred, what are you doing here, you disgusting piece of garbage? Now that's what I'd call disrespect!"

"He is here, Ms. Carter, because I asked him to be here," says Sheriff Gaffey. He steps forward and shows her his badge. "I'm Sheriff Gaffey, Kathleen, and I wanted to show Agent Vanderloo of the State Crime Investigation Unit the vehemence of your reaction to Crowe, so we might confirm your motive—"

"Motive? Motive for what, you jackass?"

"And to allow another witness an opportunity to confirm your identity."

"Witness for what? There are no witnesses. You guys are way off the track here. I gotta call my lawyer."

"But Ruby does recognize you." Vanderloo removes the official Police Dept. dog coat allowing Kathleen to recognize her. Ruby limps over to Kathleen, rubs against her leg, and looks up for a treat. "This lady a friend of yours, Ruby?" he asks the dog. "She's just proved to me and to Mr. Crowe here that she knows you. You've been to her farmhouse, haven't you? That means you had the opportunity, doesn't it?"

"The opportunity? For what?"

"For murdering Frank and Helen Gupchal, back in August."

"You are insane, Sheriff! Do you know who I am? I've got high-placed friends here, Sheriff. I'll have your ass for this screwup. You just kissed your cushy sheriff's job goodbye."

Kathleen lurches mightily trying to break the grip of the two agents holding her arms. "Let go of me, you bastards!"

"Ms. Carter, I am arresting you for the murders of Frank and Helen Gupchal," says VanderLoo. "And if you don't stop squirming, I can add resisting arrest to the murder charge."

"You imbeciles are out of your minds." She shakes her head toward Crowe. "Did he set me up? You'll pay for this, John, you son-of-a-bitch." She lurches at Gaffey and Crowe.

VanderLoo jerks her around and expertly snaps the handcuffs into place. Then he turns to the officer holding her left arm. "Agent Gordon, take Ms. Carter down to the cruiser and get her out of here."

The two officers start down toward the road with the still-writhing Kathleen stumbling between them.

The officer with Ruby walks toward Steffie who, with Mrs. Rolfes holding her arm, approaches from the gravesite. "Ruby did her job well, Ms. Cobb. She's a great dog."

Ruby keeps her eyes on Crowe and growls at him as he and Gaffey approach.

"Ruby just confirmed that both J.D. here and Kathleen were at the Gupchal farm, where neither acted to release her from her basement prison. Nice work, Ruby!"

"I am sorry about this disruption, Mrs. Rolfes," says the sheriff. "But I had to prove, in front of witnesses so the State Crime Investigation Unit would appreciate it, that Kathleen has a couple decades' worth of pent-up anger aimed at Mr. Crowe here."

"I knew you looked familiar, Mr. Crowe," she says. "But I just could not remember where I'd seen that face before. You're the fella from the big city that stopped by my house to give Leon some career advice, aren't you?"

"Yes, he is," says Steffie. "I think our little play worked well, didn't it? You all saw Kathleen's anger is still potent. That's one angry woman."

"Ruby's reaction just now helps me to establish opportunity regarding Kathleen," says Sheriff Gaffey. "Like they say, nothing's more powerful than a woman scorned."

"What woman do you mean?" asks Steffie. "Kathleen or Ruby?"

"And I believe that Kathleen's scorn, boiling deep inside her, drove this entire Prometheus episode. And I believe it will lead us to finally close that Gupchal case. It was Steffie's idea to bring Crowe out here to confront both Ruby and Kathleen, Mrs. R. She thinks some very sneaky thoughts."

Steffie and Margie stabilize Mrs. Rolfes between them as they turn to cross a piece of the snow-covered lawn and head toward the cars. Steffie suddenly stops. "Where are Larry and Leon?"

They look back at the several stragglers still lingering at the gravesite and see Larry up in the tent, sitting next to Leon. Both men sit collapsed on folding-chairs, both staring into their friend's open grave, and both looking as if frozen solid by the cold.

"We can get to the car by ourselves, honey," Leon's mother says. "Go back there and get my boys to come down. This thing has crushed them both." She squeezes Steffie's hand, then gives her a little push up the hill.

***

A half mile away, hidden behind a slight rise and protected from the wind by a double row of huge, circular, plastic-wrapped bales of corn stalk debris and alfalfa, Martin Pick assumes the position, and the countenance, and the responsibility for the kill. He's stabilized the front of the barrel with a triangular bracket spiked into the hard earth. He's silenced the rifle to secure his sonic invisibility. He centers his target, clamps his finger taut against the trigger, and unnaturally measures and smooths his breathing. He is working under a small handicap as his right trigger finger is so swollen and bandaged that it won't fit through the trigger guard. He is using his left one and, though he has practiced with it, it is not as comfortable as his normal trigger finger and will require more concentration. The several other bruises and swellings are distracting him as well. Normally he would expect to drop one shot into a three-inch target area, even from this distance and in this awful wind. He's done it before, and practiced it often. He even practiced with his off hand. But he's badly hurting from that explosion at Kathleen's farm several days ago. Both arms are scraped and several muscles are still not working. Three ribs are cracked, an elbow is hyper-extended, an ankle is twisted, and he has bumps and bruises all over. But he can still shoot. That part hasn't changed one damned bit.

"You sure that's her, Enrico? I don't know her from Adam. But you say it's her, that's good enough for me. I pull the trigger—blam, she's dead."

"Those are heavy duty cops, escorting her down that hill. Who else could it be? So pull the damn trigger, Pick! What are you waiting for?"

"Can you get a look at her face? I would like you to give me a positive ID."

"I don't need a face. It's her. Pull the trigger."

"Relax, boss. Let me do my job. I need a clear shot. I am not going to risk hitting an FBI agent, or miss or only wound the target. And second, I have to understand the tempo of the wind, both here and there. It's brutal, and I can't risk a sudden gust pushing the projectile off the target. I can't afford to miss. If I do, I give our location away, and immediately we're in the crosshairs of several rifle scopes. Remember, I can't make my body run yet. The kill's gotta be clean. It will ensure that once she goes down, all the attention stays focused on the target. Even a trained lawman will watch the target fall and, for a second or two, not look up for a shooter. That small bit of panic will allow us to slip out of here unnoticed."

Francelli watches through his binoculars. Kathleen is turned around by the officer and prepared for entering the car. "I can see her face. That's her, Pick. I'm sure of it. Damn it! Shoot her, will ya? Right there, standing next to the sheriff's car. Bang! I could have done it then. What the hell are you waiting for?"

"You're making me fucking nervous, Enrico. Just shut up and let me work."

"I'm making *you* nervous? You don't pull that trigger in the next thirty seconds, I'll grab that rifle and do it myself. Can't be so fuckin' difficult. Line her up. Pull the trigger. Boom!"

"Will you be quiet? Stop jumping around. Shit!"

"What's the matter now?"

"Big guy, probably FBI or something, just moved in between me and the target. Move, you jerk, or I'll shoot right through you."

"Could you do that?"

"With this rifle, sure. I did it once in Afghanistan. Only bad thing was, it made it easier to establish an exact angle to my position. I had to move out of there faster than I wanted to. Plus, there's the possibility the thing hits a bone and ricochets off course. And the guy's probably a fed. Whatever I do, I don't want to shoot any FBI. That's asking for trouble."

"You want trouble? I'll give you trouble. You don't shoot her right now, I'm gonna shoot *you*."

"Stop it, Francelli! Let me concentrate. My heart rate's got to be calm. I can't get excited."

"Damn it, Pick. You've blown it. They're putting her into the car. Can't see a damn thing through that black glass. Why don't you put two or three rounds through that side window? Take out the glass so you can get a shot at her."

"I'm getting out of here. We gotta find out where they're taking her. Maybe get her at the other end of her ride. Don't worry Enrico, I *will* get her. You say she dies, she dies. End of story."

"The end of this story is gonna happen now, Pick. If she don't die right now, then you do."

"Ya gotta be patient, Mr. Franc—"

There is no sound, but Francelli sees Pick's whole body shudder, lift itself off the ground, and then collapse. Blood and tissue spray around as Pick's rifle skitters across the frozen ground.

**

Steffie enters the tent and stands next to Larry and Leon. They are sitting on their cold metal folding chairs silently staring into Nathan's open grave. Both are frozen in place and oblivious to anything outside their gaze. "Come on, guys," she says. "It's time to get you out of this cold."

"This is not happening, is it Steffie?" says Larry. "I'm all alone now, and I'm afraid. I just can't understand."

"Come on, guys," she repeats. She's a reporter. She has several thousands of words to choose from. But these are the only ones she can manage.

"I just can't understand!" Larry has the same language problem she does.

Slowly, Larry and Leon lift themselves out of their chairs. Steffie nudges them out of the tent and starts them down the grade.

"I heard people shouting down there," Leon says. "What was that about?"

"Sheriff Gaffey arrested Kathleen."

Larry and Leon both stop, as if hitting a glass wall.

"Kathleen showed up?" asks Leon. "Here? Why didn't I see her?"

"No. No." Larry looks around at the last few mourners walking down the hill. Despite the sadness, everything he sees is sparkling under the brilliant clear sky. Everything is dark, but it's all so bright. Things aren't making sense. "What's going on, Steffie?"

"Sheriff Gaffey, and I as well, both think Kathleen orchestrated the whole Prometheus refinery project, including its collapse, as a way to financially ruin that hedge fund guy, Francelli."

They start walking down the hill.

"That is beyond bizarre. All that trouble and disruption? Why would Kathleen do that?"

"It's the oldest story in the book, Larry," says Leon. "The 'anger of the woman scorned' story."

"Kathleen and that guy, Francelli?"

"Apparently."

"That doesn't sound right, Steffie. She could not possibly have done that."

"Why?"

"Because, oh my god! She couldn't have... oh no!"

"What's going on, Larry? You have to tell me. Please!"

"Nathan had a secret. I'm positive he kept it from Kathleen. He told her nothing. But it's possible she figured it out. She's one smart and ruthless tyrant."

"Figured what out?"

"Nathan had this long-term dream of building a refinery on some land northwest of Bottineau near Montana—twenty thousand acres within the Bakken Formation area. He's owned the oil rights there for twenty years or so, though the prospect of actually pumping anything out is minuscule. But he always thought the site ideally situated for a refinery. It's nothing but scrub grass, close to existing pipelines and railroads. He secured financing for the preliminary development with some Canadian oil interests, and then made a deal with Russell Cordoba to lease him the surface rights, in return for the oil rights. You know Cordoba, don't you Steffie?"

Steffie grabs Larry by the shoulders and confronts him. "What? Nathan was planning a competing refinery project? Really?"

"He's been working on it for years, ever since the Canadians figured how to extract their oil. He had it well cloaked of course. Only a few of us knew. And yes, I had some money in it too. He was working with Canadian oilfield guys—they're the ones throwing money at him. At first Nathan was upset. He thought Prometheus' project was competition. But he soon realized it was only a paper project, one designed to fail, and designed only to illuminate the eventual path. It's the kind of gambit hedge funds pull. They'd rev the thing up, then dump it. And Nathan was positioning himself to be first in line for a real project when the fake one went kaput."

"Why didn't I know about that? I'm the reporter! Aren't I supposed to be on top of this story?"

"You were focused on Leon, Steffie. And Leon didn't know anything about it either. Nathan thought it best if Leon didn't know. He needed Leon's attention focused on Prometheus."

"But I did know," said Leon. "Nathan told me a few days ago. I talked to Mr. Cordoba the very morning Nathan died," Leon said. "He confirmed they were working on a refinery project. He didn't specifically say Nathan was financially involved in building the refinery, but he knew Nathan had control of the land. He, in fact, is the one who gave Nathan control of that land."

"But he was using you, and your Dakota First Party, to help drive his competition into the gutter?"

"It was business, Steffie," says Leon. "Nathan needed to protect his business. And he needed to protect me. He would never tell me, even if he suspected I knew."

Larry throws his arms around Leon and hugs him tight. "Don't be angry with Nathan, Leon. He didn't want you to get hurt."

"I know that, Larry."

"And," asks Steffie, "how did Nathan know Prometheus was, as you just said, headed for the gutter? How could he know that?"

"I don't know, Steffie. Nathan just *knew* stuff."

"But Kathleen knew it was 'headed toward the gutter' didn't she? She was in fact the one steering it into that gutter. And if she knew, then it seems reasonable that Nathan may have found out." Steffie turns to Leon. "She could have seen to it that he did know! Or maybe she even acted secretly to further her father's interests. That clears up a whole batch of my questions about this crazy project. It's possible this is just another one of Nathan's theatrical productions. We all just played our parts."

"I don't think it happened like that," says Larry. "I'm positive Kathleen had nothing to do with Nathan's refinery. He would never ever let her touch it. He didn't trust her. She's the reason he so heavily cloaked all his real estate deals. She'd take advantage of every crumb he let fall from his portfolio. You make Nathan sound,

I don't know, kind of oily and dirty. I kind of thought his concept of changing the political atmosphere to his advantage inventive, even artistic. And it was all good.

"Kathleen, on the other hand! She's the evil one, a real piece of work. Nathan, however, left most of his estate to her. I'm his executor, and I am pretty sure she must know or suspect that. He didn't agree with her methods, but he was proud of her accomplishments. Family is family. Know what I mean?"

"But," Steffie says, "he was using his old friend. He was deceiving Leon."

"Maybe a little bit, Steffie. But he was also elevating him to be the governor of the great state of North Dakota. That's probably worth a little deception, don't you think? Leon would never have gone after that governorship on his own. He needed Nathan to push him. Don't get me wrong. Leon is the hardest-working, most dedicated public servant I know. He makes all the team work harder. He cajoles, and pushes, and finds the weak spots and shores them up. But he never instigates anything on his own. He doesn't have a creative bone in his body. He always needs to be pushed."

He hugs Leon again. "Don't be mad at him, Leon. His motives were pure. He was a good man."

"I know that, Larry. I didn't know exactly what he was doing, but we both knew he was doing something other than what he told me. He always did that. That's exactly what Nathan did."

"Maybe so," Steffie says, "but it sounds wrong to me for Nathan to use you guys like that."

"Nathan didn't use me in the bad sense of the word," says Leon. "He knew he could count on me to assist him. He knew I could figure out where the pressure came from and counter it. And I think, in some way, he may have been trying to protect his Kathleen. She learned everything from Nathan, except perhaps where the limits were. She has a habit of running right through the barricades."

"Nathan wasn't *using* Leon, Steffie," says Larry. "Leon is our assist wizard. His touch allows the whole team to work efficiently—to win."

"As long as we are talking about 'using' people, might it be possible that Kathleen set up this elaborate ruse? Could she have just used her father to do what he normally does, and then run full bore with the thing without him knowing she'd set the whole thing up to fail?"

"I'm thinking Nathan must, at some level, have known Kathleen was mixed up with Prometheus. He knew everything," says Larry.

Larry stops and turns to look up the hill toward Nathan's now vacant gravesite. Tears flow down his cheeks as he clearly sees, once again, that Nathan is not standing up there waiting for him.

"I don't know, Steffie," he says. "If he masterminded this thing, wouldn't he make sure he was around to enjoy it? He'd do that, wouldn't he?"

"One would think so," Steffie says.

"Nathan and I talked about building that refinery on Cordoba's land. I knew Cordoba was involved somehow, but I was pretty sure Nathan was driving the venture. I could believe whatever I wanted to, or not believe it. It was the way Nathan worked."

Steffie gave Larry a hug. "Thank you for telling me that, Larry. But we'll never know for sure, guys." Steffie tugs on Larry's arm. "Come on, let's get in the car and be on our way. Come out of the cold, please."

"Steffie, this is absolutely the saddest day possible," Larry says.

"It's the saddest day in a million years," says Leon. "I haven't a clue as to how to be governor without Nathan making his runs. How we gonna make this work, Steffie? How the hell we gonna do that?"

***

Travis braces the barrel of his favorite weapon, the CheyTac Intervention .408 LRRS he'd acquired while in Iraq, on the rotted stump of a fence post. Quietly he says, "I'm thinkin' there's gotta be no better place for dead people than this close to a cemetery." He squeezes the trigger. Through his scope he watches Martin Pick explode.

His next shot throws Francelli's body a couple feet over, toward Pick's remains.

He swivels a few degrees and puts his third shot into the side of the state crime investigation cruiser about eight inches behind the rear door opening. It would cause little damage to the car, but would alert the sheriff that he had opened a bigger can of worms than he thought he had. Although the angle would be a little off, his bullet was placed close to Kathleen, but farther than any shot that an expert like Pick would place it. Kathleen would know instantly that it is a message from him and that he had done his job—that he had her back and that she is safe for the time being.

Travis is also confident that it is close enough to aim the sheriff's search in the general direction of Francelli's location over by the hay bales. Then only later will the puzzle be exposed—that a separate CheyTac .408 rifle than the one found with Francelli and Pick killed both of them and also put the bullet in the cruiser.

And the shooter could not be Kathleen since she was in the custody of the sheriff when these two shots, committed as an act of her own self-defense, were fired.